Incubus

Succubus

Awakening

To
Andrew
The show
Rocks
Stephen
Namir

Cover art by Elizabeth Mahoney, a Detroit artist

This novel is dedicated to my grandmother, who did not live to see it published, but was my whole reason for working so hard to get it done.

I miss you grandma...

I would like to thank the following people for all the work and help in making this novel a reality.

Corrine Weibine, -my oldest friend, your input and support has from the 'beginning', been paramount to making this story come to 'life'. And I still say you went willingly.

Cori Taylor- beta reader and bodyguard, her feet kept many unwanted over the shoulder interruptions at bay, and her feed back was priceless.

Nicholas Grabowski- his review of my novel really helped me better understand what I was doing and how to get there.

Tom Schoenberg, Sue Hadley (my aunt) – your editing skills and advice were golden; I would not have gotten the book finished without your input and guidance... Tom, write a book on how to edit for the beginner, seriously.

Chris Hogan, Bruce and Jessica Brandenburg, Bill Tebo, Rebecca Felzak, and Garret Holcomb, if not for the support and faith in me from you guys, this would have failed a long time ago. Thank you, thank you all very much.

Thatdeadguy - L.a.Nantz – Vodalok the nightkiller

CHAPTER ONE - FEVERED DREAMS   7

CHAPTER TWO - MARIAN   17

CHAPTER THREE -VIVA LA FRANCE   26

CHAPTER FOUR - BUMPS IN THE NIGHT   45

CHAPTER FIVE - STOLEN LIVES   65

CHAPTER SIX – HELL IN THE BIG EASY   79

CHAPTER SEVEN – WELCOME TO THE VIPER PIT   106

CHAPTER EIGHT – STRUNG OUT IN MEMPHIS   132

CHAPTER NINE - FUNERAL PYRE   150

Part I, "are you dead yet"   150

Part II,-"The end is near"   162

Part III, -"the Trial"   175

Part IV -"Never say die"   180

CHAPTER TEN – UNDEAD HIGH JINX   184

CHAPTER ELEVEN – SEND IN THE MARTYRS!   202

CHAPTER TWELVE – THE PERFECT PRISON   217

CHAPTER THIRTEEN - BLACK OPS AT THE PARISH   222

forward

Writing this novel has been a labor of love that few can understand. Much of what is to follow is fiction, some of it however is not. Some of the material contained within this text, and those to follow, is based on my life, direct memories of things past, both good and bad. Some of those memories have been altered a little here and there. I do have artistic license you know.

Any names that appear in this novel were created, and do not reflect in anyway real people. this is after all a work of fiction, right?

You decide.

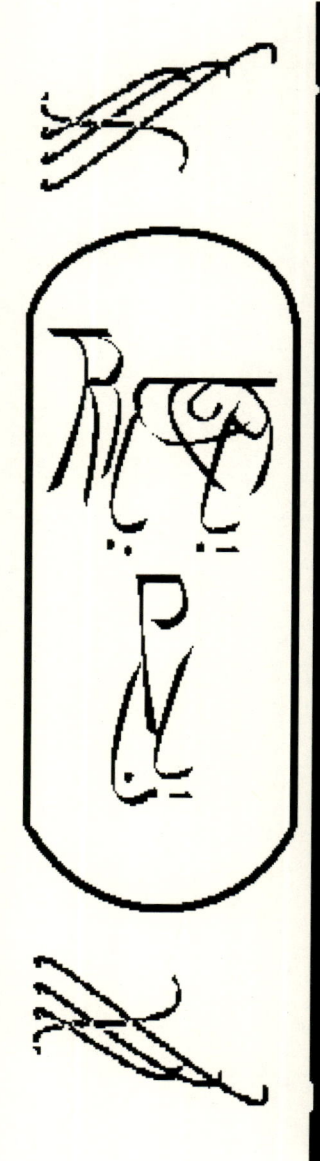
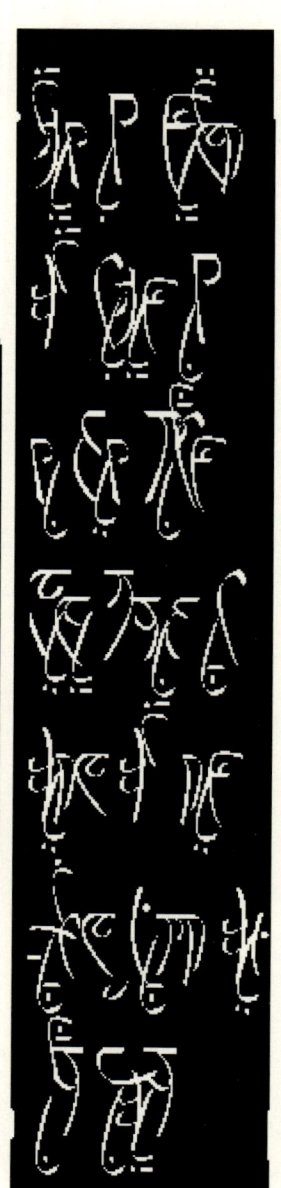
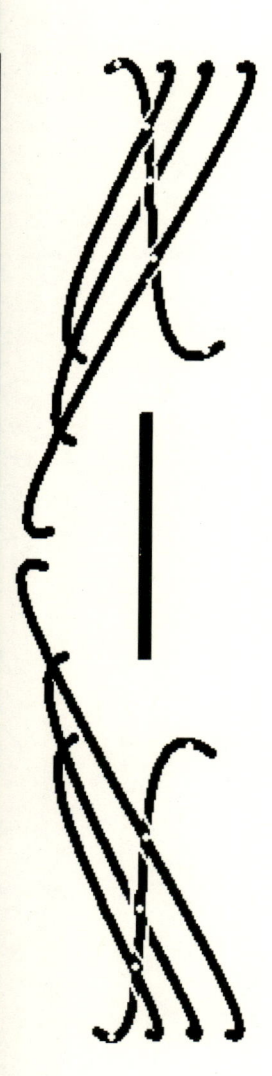

Chapter One - **Fevered dreams**

"This is the beginning of all I know

Where in I shall tell nothing to you

As in your mind you shall perceive

A light as threw my words glow

Knowledge held in hands once you knew."

-Vodalok-

I stand on the brink of all I am, and know not where to go from this point of doom, a place that has in the past been unavailable to me. How many times had I come so close, and still found I could not bring myself to this very point? I look back and see all the good and bad things I have done, all the things that have been done to me, to others by me. I marvel that I have not come here sooner, here to the edge of all I am. Then I remember the three times before that I have questioned whether or not I should remain alive, should I be allowed the privilege of life. And only once did I almost make it, to the land beyond life, to freedom.

The wind blows hard at my back as the sun sets over the edge of the world, slim light breaking the clouds into dark reds and oranges, shades of yellow and purple dancing across my face, and in my eyes. The world shows no reflection, only revulsion for what I am. Here, the rain of life has stopped pouring; the moister on my face is a salty mixture of tears, rain, and fear.

I look back at the car parked behind me, and see the face of her that has so completely given herself to me. I wonder how I can do this, how can I give to her this pain that has for so long been a part of my life. Where do I go should she in time hate me for it, resent me for it, this damnation I am so soon to place on her. Had I had the chance, would I still be standing here? Loving her? Then I realize it is only my mind wandering again, and I shake it off, as best I can.

This is the last day of my lonely life, a life spent searching for a reason to go on, searching for some way to fill the void that is the torment of my existence. Were I mortal, this sort of messianic devotion to a life that never should have been allowed would have destroyed me long ago. So this is the first day of my end, here I am born again; here I begin my story...

...I knew as a child growing up in Mississippi that I was very different from those around me. I had a gift for making others uncomfortable, just by sitting quietly in the same room with them. Watching as they breathed, feeling every breath as if it where my own, and counting the beats of their hearts. I did this just loud enough for them to hear me, to feel the pressure of my eyes upon them, in them.

I remember staring at my teacher in class one day. She was my second grade teacher. I can't remember if it was the dove white skin of her hands, or the round classic features of her face, or her eyes. (I smile and sigh as I remember...) Her eyes looked very much like those of some angel out of any painting by any of the masters of the renaissance.

Was it her hair, a very dark auburn, in and of itself not very remarkable, simple and proper? Was it the way it framed her face that caused the shine of hair to be special. Was it the fullness of her breast, firmly held in place beneath her lose angora sweater?

Whatever it was I began to stare, and she began to shake. Slowly at first, then as she watched me watching her, seeing my lips move as I began counting her heartbeats. That's when she realized that it was her beating heart I was counting, she almost screamed, (it still makes me laugh to this day.)

She tried hard not to let it show, but I was done with what I needed to do. A picture I think we were to draw, a picture of a fond memory or place that made us happy. I sat there staring at her breathing each breath, watching how her breast rose and fell. Noticing that her hair didn't move, that her clothes clung to her, showing off every inch of her frame as though she were cut from stone by Michelangelo himself. Looking at how her neck was smooth and white never touched by the sun. Till finally she practically screamed my name, Hummmp... everyone but me jumped. I merely inclined my head a little to the left, better to see her and replied. "Yes Mrs. Moore."

"Did you finish your drawing," she asked "do you need anything more to do?"

This came out of her with a quiver, almost squeaking the words out past her lips. On these, her lips, I remember focusing. The red color painted on them for the man she was having an affair with, was wet like sticky fresh life. She knew I was looking at them and quickly pursed her lips to dull the color.

Standing to move and steady her hands, she went to the board and began erasing the words from the earlier lesson.

"Yes Mrs. Moore," I replied "I am done."

Standing up, I take my project in hand and begin moving towards her. She sees me approaching, and did her best to remain in control of her will, to keep from having an anxiety attack. I offered my drawing to her, she stepped around her desk, wiping her hands on her skirt, a skirt that was brown in color, leaving chalk on her hips in the form of her hands.

The picture I held out to her. She took it but with a moment's hesitation, noticing what it was, she gasped and dropped it. She stepped back from me, from the paper, slowly but with the look of someone in slow motion moving at high speed. "Why did you...draw that?!" came her voice, "Where did you... how did you know about this!!?"

Slowly I tilt my head again and began considering what she was asking me. Then I smiled softly, and with the care of someone comforting the damned I replied. "You didn't like the riverfront, or the cool wine that was given you? You liked the way we kissed last night."

A silent hush falls after a round of ooh's and ahh's from the kids in the class. Now frightened, clutching at her chest, trying to pull the cross that hung there closer to her by pressing it into her heart. Silently begging for this moment to pass, she spoke these words to me that I only heard. "Outside, now… please get out of this class."

And to her command I go to the hallway. She follows carrying the picture I had drawn in crayon and paint, clutching it in her hand like an eagle clutches a fish or rabbit about to be eaten. Once in the hall she turns to me and kneels down to better see me clearly, then ask. "How did you know about, this, this dream of mine?" She points to the image, growing more crumpled in her shaken grasp

"HOW?"

This last was more of a statement than a request, and it erupted out of her with the force of the dying, screaming to live. The teacher passing in the hall a few doors down, stops to look and she sees only a teacher with a child, one that most know is constantly in trouble for one thing or another, and moves on.

With my soft eyes staring up into hers, my head laying back and to the left, my face forward looking into her eyes from under my brow. Once more I smile, this time letting something of the sinister nature of my soul show through, just enough to make her back away, with total involuntary motion, almost falling over. You could see the darkness settling in over me, highlighting the evil inside me, blurring the world around us.

To this I step in closer, answering her bodies need to flee with my own bodies need to be next to hers, my lips pursed to say, yet remaining silent. "Shhh… be still in your heart and mind, come closer to my words and lips, KNEEL!"

All said in a smile and in my eyes, words from my mind to hers, and as a puppet on the string dances, so then did she kneel. The horror in her eyes was now very clear, glassing over, becoming more vacant. She seemed more a deer struck in headlights before it dies than a teacher.

She sobs lightly knowing she is not in control. Again she asked, lightly and threw poorly hidden tears, these tears of hers', seemed more the mark of a soul breaking to the will of the torturer, giving in to every demand and whim. "How…"

I answer her by leaning in closer still, I were telling her a secret that no one in the entire world could ever know. Our bodies less than half an inch from touching, my nine year old body became excited over the touch of her shirt, the warmth of her breath on my ear, I whispered to her.

With every word that comes out of my mouth her world crumbles a little more, every ounce of reality melting away. Falling further from her mind as the truth of what I am saying becomes monstrously clear.

"I was there," I began," in your dream by the river. I came to your… summons. I came to you last night as I have every night for the last week. Letting you touch me, hold me, kiss me. Allowing you to guide my hands, letting you teach me the ways of a man, the way you do Mr. Hokum."

Weakly she braces herself against the wall and floor, all around her swimming as though her world had been shaken to peaces. She moves to slap me and tell me to stop, to free her from the nightmare she was slowly sinking into. All she could do was whisper,

"Please…"

…I am moved to tears now as the sun sinks just a little more. The sound of an eagle somewhere in the distance breaks the memory into billions of shards, it echoes in my mind, each color and sound of the memory, of this reality, echoes as if I were waking from the delirium of doing Freon gas. I lose the memory as quickly and softly as I have so many times before, I know a fever is building in me; I don't care and move on.

I have prayed for many years to know why I was born so different. To understand what it is that I am, to know if I am alone and if I am can I bring others over to be like me. But every time something would come and distract me completely from what I was doing. Keeping me from understanding myself, till in the end I didn't even know who I was, let alone what I am; This love affair with death, always wanting to die…my car radio playing 'Nine while Nine' by 'The sisters of Mercy' reminds me that I am always living with vampires from books and movies, the community gothic, and how they immortalize what I am.

Then when the few that do find out finally understand the truth, they become horrified and leave me for fear of me. I am left with the hollow memories of them and their music. Mostly the music, it drives in me a feeling of paradox, part solace and peace, the rest depression and despair that I shall ever be alone.

Even now the sounds of the clubs reach me, the CD player in my car blaring out 'Musette And Drums' by the band 'Cocteau Twins'. And I am thrown into yet another spin, my mind reeling from the on-slot of my past fueled by the growing fever. The fever building in me becomes a warm summer night…

…Light clouds and a half moon set the stage for a game of 'Ghost in the graveyard', a game I think that is unique to the south. We all gathered in my families' yard to play and drew straw to see who would be "IT". I chose the shortest straw and was chosen. I demanded that I should be a vampire for the night. I insisted that I would hunt them all till each of them was like me, and if I caught them all before even just one got to the base, I would have won.

Thus the game began. Everyone ran and hid so I would not see them at first. I had hoped to find Kimmy first; I was getting old enough to be interested in girls. I wanted nothing more than to feel her skin next to mine. Our yard was large and had many places to hide. Then there were the woods behind the trailer park we called home.

Ah, those woods, a wood of the sort found in back of most trailer parks of the time, with tall trees and big bush forts through out. One in particular I was fond of was directly behind our trailer. A small drainage ditch ran there as a boarder between our yards and the tree line where that one had grown. That is where I started my search; at least I had wanted to.

It was easy for me to hide in the shadows and move so no one could hear me, and the Big Guy that whispered into my ear all the time, lets just say having two sets of eyes was more like cheating than anything else. So when I came upon my older brother making out with the neighbor Mickey, they didn't even see me move past them till I had touched them and said, "You're mine, now go to base." This they did this without question.

You see, base was a storage barn built for our step fathers (everyone called him the Earl) auto parts and tools so he could work on cars or play poker without having to ask or worry who was watching. The number of nights we would hang out close to the door, waiting to be asked to come in or go grab more beer from the fridge. The amount of money we would pick up off the floor, or sometimes even directly off the table was staggering to a child of any age.

Next I caught Jim and Jeff, both of whom thought they were smart hiding under the back of the trailer that we called home. Stuck like fat little pigs I caught them easily. Again the Big Guy whispering into my ear what they were doing and where they were, again I went unseen till it was too late. I watched them playing show and tell, touching where the parents said no one should.

After a few moments I let them know I was there. They screamed and were sent to base begging me to keep quite, to not tell anyone what I had seen. They didn't want people to think they were fags. They said they were just looking, that it was Ok.

Now on to the woods and the remainder of the group, one after the other I caught them hiding and running for base. Scaring more than I ought to have, more completely than I should have, it's just when you can move so quietly, and so completely and utterly out of sight of those that are watching for you, scaring them is fun.

My favorite way to catch them would be to get right up behind them, breathe out the beginning of a breath low and quite, then end in a rasping hiss. Then my hand on their shoulders or arms as I end the hiss, they would scream so loud and jump so high, a few times I almost got hit in the face, but I was able to move out of the way, they loved me.

In the end, there were none left but Kimmy. I realized I never went to my favorite bush fort. So I approached from the east, and there she was, waiting for me, a smile on her face. I walked up to her and she playfully tried to run, but instead tripped and cut her hand. Not too deeply you understand, but this cut was one that would require stitches. It was at this time that I found myself, overwhelmed. A feeling I had never known until then came over me and I moved closer to her. "Stop" she said.

"I just want to make sure you're ok," was my reply. I was now close enough to understand what had come over me. I knelt beside her, took her hand, and told her to let me have a good look at the cut. I leaned in and looked at the wound in the dark; the smell of her blood was for the first time in my mind completely. The big Guy started talking, almost as excited as I was, "smell the blood, oh how it must taste, you must taste it, quickly before she leaves," and I knew I had to taste it. Pressing my mouth against the wound she tried to resist just a little, but swiftly relented and I tasted her.

Oh gods in all the heavens, what was this that was happening to me! So struck with euphoria was I, that I never realized that I had been drinking from her, until I was stunned by my brother hitting me. Kim screaming faintly, the Big Guy screaming in my head at my brother.

It was then that I realized she was close to passing out, my face and hands red with her blood. The odd thing was, when the parents came out to see what was amiss, she told them I was trying to stop the bleeding, and as such kept me from trouble. I was in a state of mind I had never known till that moment, and I knew for certain that I was not like anyone else there or anywhere.

What I was, I could not say, nor would I guess. The Big Guy kept going on about reclaiming my birthright, raving almost insanely about how old I was and that all I needed to remember everything was to go take her again. It frightened me so deeply that for weeks I refused to see anyone. Hiding in my room, the curtains pulled so none could look in, the door closed and the lights out. I slept in the closet for fear of being seen. My only companion was his voice taunting and teasing me, accusing me of being weak, unworthy of all he/we had been…

When I did come out, I was avoided by as many as would come near me, those that did come close only wanted to know if I had cut her on purpose, if I had taken things to far.

Our parents suggest we play this other game, red light, green light, to avoid any other moments that could leave us shaken or hurt in similar ways. The game, red light green light, we played it at night and it would, in time, become more than the parents would want. Everyone caught moving on the red light had to tell a secret, this time I was running and there was a…"

…red light, where am I now?"

I look around and realize I have driven into a small town, not much of one for being on a major road; it was however out here in the desert. I feel tired and begin looking for a place to get a room. A dinner, closed, gas station, closed, general store closed, all of them closed. The rain that had fallen most of the day had begun again. The desert road running through the town was like a mirror, slick with rain and oil. The one street lamp blaring its weak gross light on the paving, showed to me a person walking fast to get out of the rain.

I don't know how long I sat there watching this person, dazed by the movements of her body, the shape of her, so much like someone I once loved. Her hair all wet as though she had just gone swimming or stepped out of the shower, brought Brenda's memory full to the front of my mind and the pain of how we parted...

...I had just turned 18 and was living on my own, having been thrown out of my parent's house at 16. Brenda had been with me the whole time, even convinced her parents to let me live in the guest house out back of hers so I could keep going to school. I was a good Christian then, at least as good of one as I could be at my age.

For the two and a half years I lived there, she and I were inseparable, and lived a life that was perfection. Every one of our friends thought we would die in each others arms, at the ripe old age of a hundred and ten. We would laugh at such thoughts and hold each other and smile that smile only people truly in love can have.

So perfect was that life, that we truly believed it would never end. It began to crumble three weeks before my 17th birthday in August. We had gone to a party at a friend's house in northern Texas, for drinking and movies. The movie of the night was just released to video, it cost us $5 bucks to get it. The store had just converted all its beta tapes to VHS and was passing the cost down to the customer. The 'Lost Boys' was a great hit everywhere, and we had just rented it. And we were going to watch it till we knew every line in it.

At around 2:00am, everyone was breaking up into little groups for conversation, some smoking weed, and a few for sex. I found myself in a group with the girls there. Brenda was off sleeping, she had had a bit too much of the ol' Tequila.

The conversation had swung full circle back to the movie and to vampires in general, being a closet Goth at the time and having forsaken much of my true nature, I had forgotten what I was, if that is possible. Beth, the shortest among us, started talking about how when she graduates from high school, she will go to Europe, and look for a real vampire, because she wants to be one.

Everyone laughs at her silliness, and because of the drinks that we have had. Lots of ever-clear, alcohol so strong you can use it as gas in older cars. After a while, she and I are the only ones left on the back porch. I tell her the story about Kimmy, and how everyone thought I had gone to far, (for a moment I thought I heard that old voice, the one that had been silent since then, but I shook it off) the only thing she can think to ask was, "What was it like, to drink someone else's blood?"

I wanted to say "I don't remember", but just thinking about it for a brief moment, when so weakened by drink, brought it all back. The smell of the blood, the smoothness of it on my tongue, the flavor of fear... it leaves me with a very visible shiver, one that leaves my whole body covered in goose bumps.

"Have you ever wanted to do that again?" she asked me, "I mean if someone was to offer you their blood, would you take it?"

Again I want to leave, to tell her a lie, but find I can't. The sound of her voice asking me these questions, the look in her eyes, so large and dark, framed in by her long blonde hair, brings back a flood of repressed hungers and emotions, and all I can say is. "Yes..."

She takes me by the hand, and then leads me off the porch and into the night. A few minutes later she lights us both a cigarette, a clove. She has been smoking these for a while and I have never smoked up until this point. After a few minutes of just standing there smoking she asked me if I am one.

What do I say to her? I say the worst thing ever. You see, I think if I had said no at that point, and not done what came next, I would not be in the pain I am in now. I could have left it all behind and lived a normal life, but I said, "Yes, I think I am one."

She almost squeaked with glee, I laughed at her for this and kept smoking. She however dropped her smoke and pulled out a box cutter, pulled up her sleeve and showed me the many cuts on her arm, saying that each one was for a hurt done to her by "our friends". I didn't understand her, and she began to cut her arm again, saying that they had hurt her again by laughing at her.

I watched in awe of her willpower as she pressed the blade of the cutter deep into her arm, then pulled it from the back of her hand all the way up to her elbow. A thin red line formed there, and began to leak blood. The smell of it was overwhelming. She must have been watching my face because she asked if I wanted to keep it from hitting the ground, but with a little fear in her eyes.

I never answered. Instead I moved with a speed I didn't know I had, I was on her. The taste of her was so incredible, and so overpowering that I could not pull away from her. I felt her other hand touching my sex and pulling at my pants. I heard her panting as if she too were being aroused by what was happening, and I simply didn't care.   All the world fell away in the flow of her blood into me, so much more than the ever-clear could ever do.

This new drug filled me till all I knew was the wound of her arm, and the beating of my heart in my head and chest. The world began to spin, and all over my body I began to feel as though it were raining... I fell to the ground and could not move. So full of drunkenness, all I could do was lie there. When I finally realized that Brenda was kneeling over me, begging me to wake up, tears and rain in her eyes, slapping at my face the rain cold and distant, Beth nowhere to be seen, the Big Guys voice in my head again this time only laughing at me, saying "one day we will be one again". I thought to myself, "Who's trying to wake me up?" each slap on my face sounding like...

...Someone knocking on glass...

The sound of that knocking on my window stuns me. The sound is louder than the thunder in the distant dark. The person is asking if I am alright. I sat through two rounds of the traffic light it seems, not even noticing that I had done so. The young lady I was watching had noticed me... How she walked up to me without me seeing her, I can only attribute to my mind wandering again, where?

"Sir," came her voice through the glass, "are you ok?" I look at her blankly. I could smell the dirt in her hair from the dust that must consume this place, mixed with the rain and dime store perfume, something that was meant to smell like 'Obsession'. All this held me long enough to scare her.

"Sir," came her voice again, "come on, you don't look so good, "my door opened as she pushed me over to the passenger seat and climbed in, "move over and let me drive ya to the doctor's."

All this she said with the gravest of tones in her voice... her voice, like honey poured over jagged glass, pure and hardened mean from her short life in this brown dusty hell. Slowly I begin to see the face of the woman that was now in my car. Short cropped dark sandy blonde hair. Hair so thick and coarse one would think she had Spanish blood in her. One of her hands was now resting on my head, as she feels for a temperature.

"My gawd, you're burning up!" she started, "you need to be in a bed rest'n. Not out drive'n about. What's yer' name?"

I look at her and then at my reflection in the steamed window glass, "I don't remember..." is all I can manage to say.

I look into her face and see the eyes, big cow eyes, brown as the Desert Sea, and deep soft pouty lips, the kind one dreams of kissing forever and ever. Her head seemed too small for the eyes and mouth under all that hair, no matter how short, her hair seemed to want to engulf her face.

How can I refuse, with me as weak as I am now? I see the one light of the town fade into the darkness. The only sounds are of her breathing, the tires on the wet road, and 'Curtain call' by the 'Damned'. The ride seems to take an eternity, me passing in and out of waking dreams, the sweat pouring out of my skin, threatens to drown me where I have slumped in the seat. Why the carmakers ever got rid of bench seating I will never know.

Every now and then I feel her hand like ice on my face, words... what was it she was telling me? And why does she look so scared?

Somewhere, I am not sure where, I heard the engine of a big car roaring. It screamed at me with the sound of some forgotten voice... someone I had fed on only three months, or was it years ago? In... somewhere in Michigan, his voice, the man named Rob, began to thunder in my head, his story over and over...

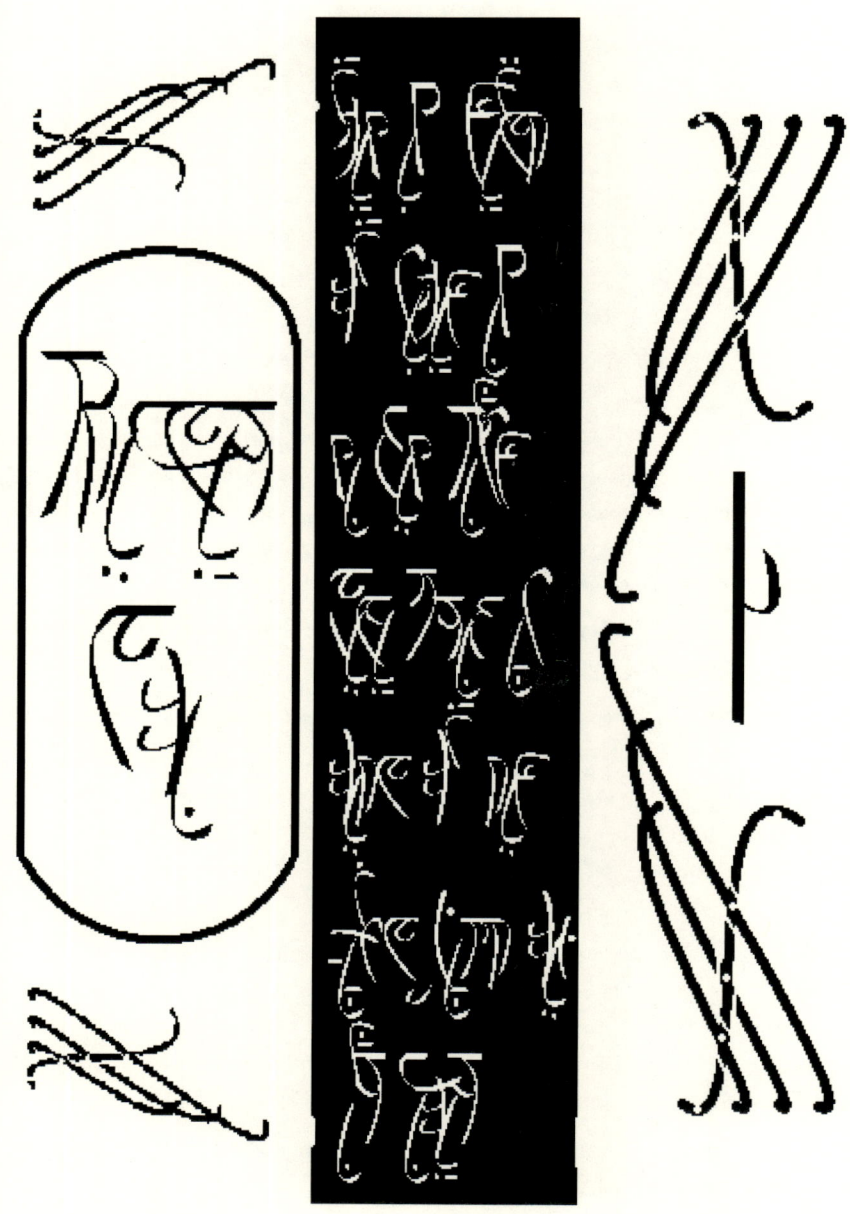

Chapter Two - **Marian**

From birth I struggled to find

In my soul darker still shines

Not that I cared but knew of difference

That which you see in eyes bl nd

A truth of souls all mine.

-Vodalok-

It's 7:30am, and the road becomes packed with morning commuters. He knew he had to get home soon. The sun was rising over the freeway. Brightly threatening to expose him to the world, it was looming under the clouds that foretold the storm to come later in the day. The sky was a gleaming red that made this one think of the night before. He thought of the pleasure, the fear, and his reason for running.

The sound from his radio came at him loudly, vibrating the rear view mirror, the dark gothic sounds droning into his head. Why did she have to be so damned insistent that he bit? Then bit harder… "Gods," he thinks to himself, will he ever get all the blood out of his clothes?

The off ramp to I-75 north was getting closer, the traffic was backing up, and he was close to home, but not close enough… a wreck. The sun light was starting to reflect in the mirror, the glare burning his eyes, as he continues to think about the night before. Where did it all begin?

"Why is the cop flagging me over to the side of the road" he thought, even more nervous now than before. The blood was still thick on his face. His eyes were wild like a rabid animal's. He knew one thing; he could not stop and let the cop see him. Slowly he followed the cop's directions, tensely he prepared to run.

It seemed that running was not needed in the end. He was being directed to drive on the curb to get around the accident. Four cars, two upside-down and one burning a little, and two bodies lay on the ground with sheets drawn over them. More blood everywhere…

The dark music continued to ring in his head 'blood' by 'Velvet Acid Christ'… he began to drift back to the club…

…It was packed with bodies as far as the eye could see. His friends said this was the place to find a girl. "If ya can't get laid here Rob, you can't get laid anywhere!" his friend Tomas had yelled this over the music to him. Tomas was a very typical man of the 90's, Dockers, slacks, and a matching tee shirt and ball cap, his shoes where way to nice for this club, some

kind of loafers. Tomas had short hair that was dyed blond and blue eyes. He considered himself man of the year, god to all women. He was here to get drunk, laid, and maybe a fight.

His friend Richard on the other hand had been coming to this club for a few years, and walked up behind Tomas smiling. He was glad to see both himself and Tom had finally made it out. He, Richard was dressed in a solid black kilt, knee high Doc Martin boots covered in buckles, and a black velvet poet's shirt. He smiled big as he approached, his long black hair and pale white skin, blue eyes and a voice that some said could melt butter, looked very much at home here in this crowd, especially with a pitcher of long island ice tea in hand.

Rob looked at himself and wondered why he was here. Yes, he loved the music and was into the whole Goth thing, but this place made him feel, well out of place. His blue jeans and denim jacket, the un-tucked button up shirt all seemed very out of place.

Everywhere he looked was a sea of black and lace, velvet and vinyl, dark make up and the music…

…As he pulled up he watched as his front porch came closer, this was a welcome site. As he climbed out of the car he frantically looked about to see if anyone was looking and ran to the door and tried to unlock it. He dropped the keys twice and barely got in before Mrs. Conner saw him and said hello. He waved a hand behind him and slammed the door.

His roommates were still out… maybe for the day, but they left the stereo on, 'Marianne' by 'Sisters of Mercy' low but strong, that name… that was her name…

…Holding a glass of Jaeger she came up to him looking for all her worth like she had stepped out of a Hentay cartoon. She had ponytails that reached her ass, and then, her breast were barely covered by a fishnet shirt, the nipples covered by electrical tape, were full and standing up like she worked out daily to maintain their firmness.

Her belly was bare and the navel was pierced. The skirt she wore was barley a skirt at all. It was more like, a thin drape around her waist that was made of vinyl. It was so tight and showed her shapely hips like she was wearing nothing at all. The vinyl thigh high boots and shoulder length gloves were just as tight and revealed more about her than they concealed.

As she approached, Rob knew he was going to have a good night if he could get her attention. His feelings of being out of place faded. He stepped into her path and introduced himself, telling her he was scouting for models for this book of his art he was preparing. Totally interested, she told him her name and they started to talk.

Talking turned to kissing; kissing led to her room upstairs in the hotel. In less than an hour they were striped of their clothes and his hands were all over her, mostly on her breast. His tongue tracing circles around her nipples, her hands on his hard member. As the passion grew so did her demands for more bizarre acts…

"Spank me" she cried, "no, grab me here and squeeze. No like this…no silly,' it's' for you, turn around. Ok now start biting my neck, don't be a wuss, and bite as hard as you can!"

It went on like this all night, till he finally gave in and began to bite her neck, she screamed. Fearing he had hurt her, he stopped and pulled away to make sure she was fine, asking her as much. This brought on a fit of hitting from her, screaming at him, telling him he was about to loose her interest if he didn't start performing as she wanted. She demanded he not stop, that she was so close to Cuming... Not soon after they were in the shower and she demanded he bite again, and to stop being such a pussy about it. So he bit in again and she demanded harder...

...The shower was cold, and the blood was on his face, he stood there alone, over her, the silence was deafening. He left her slumped on the floor, dead. He had tried to stop the bleeding and could not. The room was clean of his prints due to her insistence that he wear rubber gloves from the start, before he even entered the room... so he ran...

...His mother had called before he got into the shower to remind him of his cousin that was coming into town. That he should be there to meet her, to help her feel comfortable here in Detroit. He arrived at his parent's house where the local family had gathered to meet this long forgotten cousin from the west coast.

Everyone was standing in the living room and all was quite as Rob walked in. He wondered what was going on, as he got closer to his mother he heard her talking on the phone. Everyone there was quite and watching her. Then she hung up the phone and turned to address them all.

"It seems" his mother started, " she had a 'friend' up to her room last night, but no one saw him leave or what he looked like. The police said there were no prints or any other clues left behind...so far. But the forensics team is going over the place very slowly and carefully, he is confident they will turn something up." What the hell was she talking about?

"Ma," Rob asked, "what's going on?"

She turned to him and began to cry. "It's your cousin" came her voice through the tears, "she was found dead in her room... The police said that she was killed by a brutal attack. Her throat was torn open, she bled to death. They said it looked like she was either being intimate or she was raped, but that there was nothing to really go on..."

His heart began to race and the sweat breaking out on his brow made him feel sick. His face flushed red then white with the fear, and he almost fell to the floor right there, but he gathered his composure and steps up and stops her from saying more, then he asked two simple questions.

"Mom, what was her name, do you have a picture of her?"

She points to a frame on the table next to a cake that said welcome to Detroit. The name on the cake was Marianne. The room began to spin, the picture on the table held her face, the face of the angel that died in his arms the night before. He had killed her trying to please her. The room spun with the sound of 'Marianne' in his head, everyone in the room seemed to have blood all over them. The night of her death and the days that followed began to play itself out one more time in his head, closing in on him, threatening to destroy what was left of his mind. The walls of the cell, cold and hard, unyielding... echo the song,

'Marianne'...

..."I love this song," came the stranger's voice, "wish I had the CD."

She's still driving... still out here in the desert, the wipers of the car hammering out a beat of their own. My head now in her lap, the smell of salt tears on her clothes.

"I was afraid I lost you there for a moment. This song seems to have woken you up, your going to be Ok... I... I think the fever is breaking, please stay awake..."

Just how bad is this fever? I try to sit up but can't seem to move. With a little effort she put her hand on me and say. "No stay there, where I can make sure your still Ok. You stopped breathing for a while I ... I thought you were dead, but you started to say Marian and then woke up... please stay awake, I mean if you can't that's Ok but... *sniff* the doctors' place is too far, so I am taking you to my place. It's kinda out a ways but you should be Ok there 'til the doctor can get to you... it's not much...

"It's not much," who is this, Victor...? *"But that is all I will tell you for now."*

"Look I didn't risk being late to role call for this," Am I saying this... yeah... but when? *"You have to tell me more, come on..."*

..."Stay awake, *PLEASSSE*...."Her tears are hitting my face and she wipes them away, but there is another voice in my head, Victors. That dammed fool from Nashville...

...I met him during my short time as a member of the U.S. Army. We would go down to dragon-park and party on the weekends, lots of punks, ska-babies and Goths all drinking late into the night.

Friday's were the best, we would get dismissed and break for showers, street clothes, and run out the gate at 60+mph heading for Nashville. It wasn't far from base and we had a house we would crash in over the weekend.

First stop was the liquor store, several pints of ever-clear and Freon and we were off and running. The Freon would be done in the parking lot. Hours would go by before we would head out again. No one would say shit to us because we were government property.

20

It was funny, the cops would come up and tap on the window and tell us to move on. We were setting a bad example for the locals, showing them that the 'best' were just junkies, it made them nervous. Don't get me wrong we were just three out of forty or so in our little group. The rest were just alcoholics, we were the wild boys!

It was on one of those nights that I met Victor. He was off by himself watching the lot of us. I saw him and knew him all at once to be just like me. The 'me', I tried to deny, tried not to accept and pushed away.

He motioned for me to come closer. He was sitting on the swings next to the massive ceramic dragon that was the center of this public park. No one noticed when I walked away, that was cool. I was not much into drinking that night anyway. I approached and he stood up, beside him was a girl I had not noticed right away. She offered me a glass of what looked like wine. What the heck, I drank from it and at once felt the old rush.

It was blood, hers... I looked down at her and the darkness was pushing back. I could see a little more clearly. There was an I.V. in her arm and she was filling another wine glass for him!

I didn't drop the glass or hand it back, but found myself finishing it. Whether I wanted to or not. And now I can't remember what I wanted at that time, the swoon that was overcoming me was starting to dim my senses.

"I am Victor" he said," I have been watching you for some time now. Thank you for accepting my hospitality this night, now shall we take a little walk?"

He began to move away, the girl following, making sure her I.V. was clean and closed but never removing it. Keeping her arm strait and covered with her free hand, she looked back at me and smiled some knowing smile that was so innocent and evil all at once. I knew I had to have her that night, that I must find some way to win her to myself at all cost.

So I got up and walked with them a small pace, we were now inside some kind of large domed play thing, and they both sat down on a blanket that was waiting for them. There were three others there waiting. Victor sat next to this red head and they kissed, the other couple didn't even look when we came in, they just kept making out. I did however notice that Victors' girl had an I.V. and the man of the other couple likewise had an I.V.

I sat down and the blond whose blood I drank sat next to me, so close that she was almost on my lap. I wouldn't of minded one bit if she had; it's what I wanted right then anyways. The little blonde looked to Victor; his eyes opened a little more and nodded his head as if in approval of some silent question. She opened her vein for me again, just enough to fill the little glass still held close to my chest.

I sat there, for I don't know how long, enjoying the company of these strangers in silence. Watching the others make out, hearing Victor read poetry to his girl, Veronica. I laughed a little when I heard him call her name.

"What amuses you friend?" Victor said. To which I replied. "Your names, Victor and Veronica... that's all, it struck me as amusing."

"Well prepare to laugh some more Stephen," came Victor," and be welcomed also by Robert and Roberta and your companions name is Stephanie."

I looked at the other couple, and they inclined their heads each when their name was called and smiled at me. I felt warmness from them, as if they were thinking at me. "You are most welcome here, relax and be one with your family"

It was comfort unlike any I had known before. I looked to the little minx that had now crawled into my lap and was kissing me all over, and smiled. For a little while I did enjoy the ambiance of the moment, indulging in all the pleasures being given to me. Then I started to think. How did they know me, or my name, let alone 'This' part of my being that I have been fighting to deny for the last few years. I thought of that night in the rain with Brenda kneeling over me. Crying trying to wake me up...

The sound of the rain was so real...

..."Please don't die,' she pleaded with me, 'please, you have to stay awake... We are so close now. It's just a little further." From out of the haze that had become my world I could barley see her face, so much hair? Like a thing alive consuming her little head, her enormous eyes glazed over with tears. Her tears were so soft on my face. I watch them fall so very slowly, each one seeming to take a life time to go from the end of her cheeks to free fall.

The rotation of each one as it spiraled down to land on my face, the sting of the salt as it splashed into my eyes. The salt of those tears could be tasted easily on my face, without trying, as they were absorbed into my flesh. The wipers still pounding out their time, the sound of the rain on the roof of my old car mixed with the noise of the tires on wet pavement sounding more and more like laughter...

...*"Don't be silly Stephen, we knew you from the first we saw you... two months ago? But we needed to have you see us and have you want to come to us on your own without interfering.' Victor said, 'We simply could not come to you without causing problems."*

"So you've been watching me all this time. When, if ever would you have given up on me?" I asked him, 'Say, if I didn't come to you, and had not seen you. Would you have stopped watching? Would you have just left me alone?"

"In short, yes.' Victor replied, 'We had planed that if after tonight you had not seen us we were going to move on and leave this town. You're the whole reason we are here. Stephanie is the one that marked you, and wanted you."

Hearing those last words made me look at her. My expression must have been either rather dire or comical. Her reaction to it was not expected. She both laughed at me and pulled away with a hint of fear in her eyes and voice.

I watched her compose herself and offer me more of her life. I struggled with this but finally was able to say no before she opened her vein again. The others, I now saw, were in complete observation of me. Their every gesture showed me they were looking for something, watching for some sign... of what.

So I asked them.

"What do you want from me?"

This was hissed and half screamed. I was becoming somewhat afraid, Stephanie tried to comfort me, but it only made things worse.

"Get off me!"

I scream as I push Stephanie off and move back as far as I could; looking to them now like a caged animal I am sure. I go to stand but have to sit back down, the blood had worked its spell on me, and I can't do much other than sit there and look at them. Victor moves in close and whispers to me they must be going, that they know where to find me now, but Stephanie would stay to watch over me 'til I was recovered.

His parting words were simple and terrifying.

"Be careful never to share your blood with those that are not like us. Its effects are terrible and cruel, you do not want to be responsible for what becomes of them should you not be able to guide them. More than this and you will need to find me again in a week. It will be daylight soon and we can not be out. For now, enjoy this revelation, do not close your eyes on yourself any longer, do not forsake yourself or your kin, you ARE needed."

In a flash the four of them are gone. Stephanie is still there watching me. She comes closer and tells me I have nothing to fear from her. She lies down next to me and kisses me, I figure at this point everything is wrong already, why resist anymore.

I let her undress me down to my bare flesh and lay there as she takes full advantage of me. The light of the moon looking way to much like the light of a bulb with no covering, the sounds in the chamber, sound to much like a small room rather than some place outside.

I hear her talking to me, but there are two voices talking at the same time saying the same things. "Don't worry my darling/ Mr., I will care for you, you'll never have to worry about being hurt/ your fever any more, I will clean you up,/ love you forever..."

...Stephanie's voice fades as an echo receding into the fog of my mind. For a moment, I can see the woman whose head is too small for all the hair on it. With the great large eyes hovering over me, tucking me in, talking but I can't hear her... The fading echo of 'love you forever' is drowning out everything and I fall forever into my dreams.

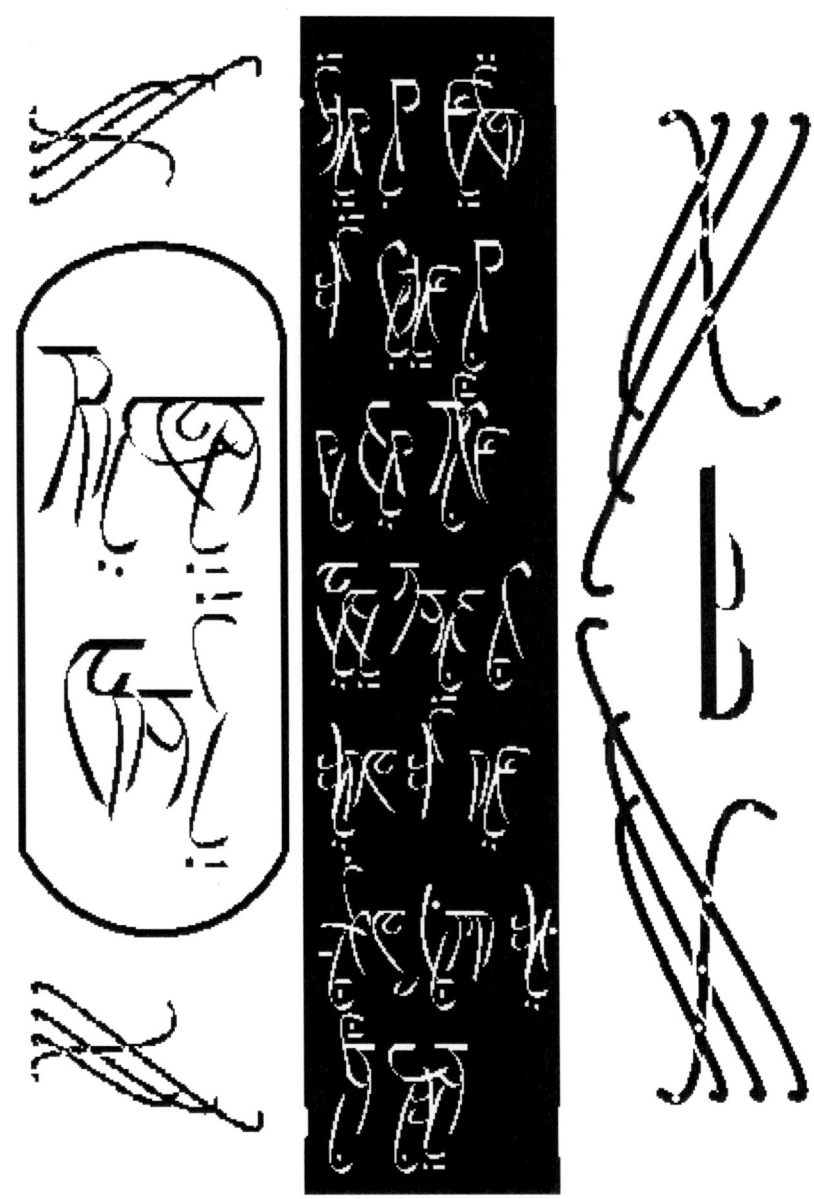

Chapter Three -Viva La France

From age's yet born

I was cast aside in hopes of losing

To eyes of others scorn

What was seen as tattered and worn

A life of my own choosing

-Vodalok-

I know that as I lay enfolded in the warmth of arms not my own, the sun shining through the window, onto myself and this angel asleep next to me. I know that I have not harmed her in my fever. A fever that I also know leads me to speak openly of things I would normally keep to myself.

I can only guess at the things I have spoken of with enough clarity that would give away who and what I believe I am. I think, as I feel the warmth of the sun coming through the window; that one time I gave it all away. That I told someone everything I knew, and they tried to kill me. I hope that will not be the case here. But I feel the fever begin to consume me once more as I slip away into that time...

...It was shortly after I was released from the army. The encounters with Victor became more than I could stand, but, I could not stay away. So seven nights we gathered there, and every time Stephanie would be there and ready to open herself up to me. I wanted to go farther but Victor told me.

"Bonding with a donor, your food is a mistake. Though we appear to be the same species, we are not. You're not ready to just take yours... as anything but food and pleasure right now. I can see in you, a desire to make her your companion. Though many do this, I advise against it while you are in my territory. It will save us all a lot of un-needed pressure from the outside world"

All night we talked like this as I fed from Stephanie. I learned everything I could from Victor. When I learned that his donor was also vampire, it confused me. I asked, was she always this way? It was then that he told me of the 'great secret' as he called it.

This was the last night I saw them, they were always on the move these four. Stephanie it turned out was still living at home there in Nashville and had found them and come to them for guidance. She herself believing she was one of them.

Victor used her as an example of the great secret and he spoke unto me these words that still haunt me. Words that I gave to a mortal once while in fever.

"We are born a normal birth' Victor began, 'to mortal men and woman. They raise us as if we were theirs, but the truth is we are not. We were never theirs. Where we came from I do not know. I doubt anyone has ever known. What is known is that we never move past this realm of existence. We are bound to this world in a way that they, the mortals of this world, will never understand.

"You see they get to move on after their soul has completed its quest, learned all it can. From there it is judged and either allowed to go to the next plain, or is consumed and its energy given up to the void... Where, it in time comes back as a new soul, fresh from oblivion.

"For us we do not get this opportunity to either move on, or be free of the burden of our former lives, as those that are consumed do. We in time remember all our lives. We never get to leave, and we never get to move on. This secret was once told to Bram, but, you see, he misunderstood and made us all immortal in that book of his. He made it so that we do not die.

"It's funny really, that's the one thing we would rather have, over the life we live, and it's something we can never have."

He paused there, to let what he had said sink in, watching my face and knowing I had understood. His eyes moved over my face as Veronica sat next to him, her head on his shoulder, musing to herself. It was some rhyme that was lost on me at the time. It comes back now more clearly than ever before...

"What is the thought that drives us, as we seek the answers to questions? Whether of wind or stone, the voice of soul sings that which we see in minds blind search for completeness.

To find this answer, rather than search with force of will the power of mind to turn the universe to ash in quest, the soft hand of open palms, this quest laid slow and bare for the wind to blow as answers are shared in the will of souls open to questions yet asked.

See in you the need, to let free your own hunting's of things yet seen through forced open doors of dreams that are not ours. The answers of questions passed, and left for others as those that came before are in truth our own memories, of dreams yet had.

Passed all this is the spring of your soul singing the songs that are the truth of your hearts seeking, which in this quiet contemplation, is the end of all you seek in a single note of time."

"Where did you hear that?" I asked her.

"From you silly, you wrote it several life times ago. Back when we were lovers. Would you like the book you wrote that time around? It's very lovely." I thought Veronica was teasing me. That she at Victor's behest was playing some foul game on me, trying to convince me that I was a writer. That I had written that very, very powerful bit of thought. Then she called me by that name, the one used in that life, the name on the book.

"Vodalok..."

...For a brief moment I was him, sitting at a desk, and writing. Veronica was in the bed beside me, moving under the blankets like an animal in pain as she asked me. "Will you please come to bed?"

"I must finish this last line,' Vodalok/I reply, 'else I fear my mind will consume me utterly until I am no more and forced to birth again from the very ashes of my own grave, so that I might this last line finish, and then die again."

"Its things like this,' Veronica said like a child upset, 'that make me love you and hate you the most. Please come to bed... it will be there in the morning..."

Veronica leans forward and touches my hand as she speaks and I am forced back into the present.

"You're not known really all that well by the mortal world, but for our kind, it is a work of wonder that is held in the highest regard. You see it's not just that piece but others in here, which hit the key of all we are in one simple thought. The other works here in were among the finest love poems ever written in this world, of all time I think. I can get another copy, so I would like for you to take this one.

'Here let it inspire you. Maybe you can add to your work this time, and increase the size of its volume."

She handed the book over, Stephanie taking it for me. All I could see was the name – Vodalok – The page open to that bit of verse, 'A Single Note of Time.' I trembled and repeated the name in my mind and quietly out loud, "Vodalok." The sound of it, the name, frightened me.

There is knowledge in that name that is beyond me or Victor. His knowing eyes feel as if they are burning into me, watching me plummet deeper into a world that has long passed and died with the end of the age of innocence, the dawn of the age of Industry.

I began to see that life in my minds eye, spiraling out and downward until I was lost in it. The carriage rides along the Rhine, the game played from town to town, being chased out by the locals who wanted nothing more than our blood. Stephanie pulled me out before I could be eaten by it. The slap of her hand on my face burned like millions of little needs setting my flesh on fire...

...Slowly I open my eyes and realize the pain I am feeling is not from the hand of Stephanie, nor is it even my muscles being deprived of blood, rather it is the billions of needles driving to the core of my being, as I am burned by the sun...

I lye as still as I can, hoping not to wake her, the woman with all that hair, but my cry's escape my lips as though they belonged to someone other than myself. Her eyes part, and widen as she sees me turning into burnt parchment. Bits of my exposed flesh cracking and separating from my body, only to drift up and off like paper in a flame turned to ash. Jumping up she screams, understanding immediately the peril she has put me in, but not how it could be happening.

With great courage she pulls me from the sun. Burning her own hands from the heat of the unseen fire consuming my body, and covers me in a blanket to keep me from further harm, begging me between sobs of grief to forgive her. To give her some sign that I am not dead, that I am still with her. In the end all I can do is pass out.

..."Monsieur, you must wake, the guard will be here soon. Please Monsieur you must wake..."

It is my servant Julien. The last night had been spent playing with Margaux. Her fixation on the occult set her in good stead as the target of 'The game'. One played out in ever town and hamlet we pass through. How many times now have myself and that bastard German, Bastian, played this game with the lives of woman so young?

I sat up; finding Julien looking like the devil himself had come to claim his soul. Franticly he moved to dress me. His rushed state didn't lead to that dressing being any to comfortable.

"Monsieur this appetite you have for young ladies must stop, leave that monstre Bastian to the Autorités, and we can still find a way to entertain your needs safely and with caution. I beg you Monsieur let us this thing do!"

Julien has been my servant for almost as long as I have been old enough to travel on my own. For long years now, he has been my confident and confesseur. Himself having been a priest who found his calling in serving me, in an effort to save my soul. Years have been spent at my side, most of them troubled and fearful. Many have been the times he decided to leave me and my sin to la Diable only to return.

When we encountered two just like me, poets, the Englishman Stewart, and his sister, Jasmine, felt he could at last save me. If either of us had understood just how much like me they where, we may have not parted company, I loved her, Jasmine Stewart, the fun that was had that year, was magical. At the end of the year however my writings were published and the Stewarts parted our company.

Then came the taking up with my now ever present traveling companions, Bastian and Élisabeth, this was almost the breaking point for Julien, mainly because I stopped writing. That was five years past; it was an encounter that confirmed for me that I was not cursed, and that if I were a monstre, at least I was not alone in the world.

The three of us have traveled most of Europe together now, quietly extorting funds from the land lords, barons and Ducs of Germany and La France. These activities are the ones that brought us here to this place we are in now. It is very small, but with a wonderful reputation, one we felt the greatest of needs to exploit.

As word spread from the little tavern's that we found ourselves frequenting until our funds began to run low. It came to our ears of this land lord, a minor Duc, whose daughter had taken into her confidence, a witch.

Much was the to-do over this among the peasantry and gentry outside of the larger cities. But as these are modern times, such things are heard of again, without the old misgivings or the call for death that had once gripped this, and many other countries.

We made our way there the four of us, every bit as grand as any of the lords or ladies that we shared company with, to this Duc for sport and gain. Our great secret being that, we ourselves had in fact; all three of us come from very humble beginnings. For myself I was born the son of a soldier, who never returned from war, a bastard orphan of fate.

Bastian was the son of a German burgomaster to all we met, but in truth was the only living son of a wood cutter whose family all died of the plague, or so he has maintained. His charms with the ladies at times proceeds us and we are force to ride as fast as we may in the other direction rather than venture too close to a town he has... seduced.

Last of our little famille was Élisabeth. To those we would gain favor with, she was born the daughter of a wealthy dealer in rare gems. Herself adorned with diamonds and rubies, the likes of which most would never see in all their lives. Even among nobles her wares are the envy of all those that perceive their value. The truth of her birth however, she would never share with us. All we have discerned is that she was born north of Paris, in a town that does not exist... anymore.

With her in our company it is much easier to move from town to town without the fear of being... held in comfort for the better of our personages, at the great cost of the local Autorités.

Tonight, however, is a different matter all together. I had won the game this time round, by wooing the pleasures of young Margaux, the acclaimed witch to my chambers here in the guest wing of Seigneur Léon's home. We spoke late into the night, her feeding me fruits dipped in soft Belgian chocolate, drinking sherry filched from the cellar of this very chateau.

As the candles dwindled, and the night creatures grew silent in the passing of the moon, I had taken her to the stables where I felt we could enjoy the pleasures, of this tryst more completely.

We had looked about the place and found a thick blanket. Once again I set out to relieve her of her garments, an act that took little effort and was a little disappointing. I would not tell this to Bastian.

As the time passed she coaxed out of me my true nature, one I was more than willing to let her experience for herself, I was 'Full of lust' and clearly not thinking things through, and in my hunger drained her of all her life...

When I recovered, I knew we would have to leave first thing come morning. I, in an attempt to cover my actions, gathered the poor dear up into the rough blanket. Her breath still coming out short and broken, her eyes almost void of life staring at me. I carried her to her chambers. There I laid her out in her bed, throwing the blanket into the waiting fire that warmed her room. It was my hope, should they come calling on her, that they would think her ill, or even obstinate in her resolve to sleep through the morning, as was normal for her and her lady Anaïs.

I returned to my own room and thought to pack. I thought to let the others know how badly things had gone for me, but in the end decided not to tell them. In this I hoped that at least they would not be lying should they be questioned about poor, poor Margaux.

Thus I returned to my room and advised Julien that I was not to be disturbed for any reason. This brings us to this moment now; It being not even an hours passing from when I made it back to my chambers, and gave my instructions. Now I find him thus, if he were not a priest I would be tempted to beat him for this.

"Monsieur if we do not hurry, they will get here before we can escape long enough for me to take your confession, then I will have failed in my oath to god to save your dammed soul! Now hurry!!!!"

Then, as if on cue, at my door came a rapping, as if someone, *tap, tap, taping*

"Étienne open up. It is me, Élisabeth!"

Julien opens the door and she storms in, fully dressed with her bags ready to go, and right behind her is Bastian.

"Fine time for the two of you to play your games, and get us run out of yet another town! So close was I to bedding the Duc and forcing him to keep our silence. Then you go and do this! This one will cost us dearly. Mark my words, if we get out of here alive... I shall take great pleasure in cutting both of you so you never have another desire for any woman ever again!"

The pure vehemence of her statement is all at once frightening, and comical. So much like some comedy by one of those Greeks of old, that I and Bastian simply can not help but giggle at her while exchanging knowing looks, each with our own mental image of just how she would "cut" us. Images she caught in her mind, then sneered at us and spat on Bastian.

"Pigs, the both of you. Julien, why do I travel with this scum? Why do you stay so loyal to an animal that cares nothing for those he bleeds, destroys!! And tonight he has pleasured himself upon this poor woman unto her death!"

Both Julien and Bastian look at me, the face of Julien stricken with pure and utter horror that I had done such a thing, and with great carelessness come back to my bed as if nothing had happened.

Bastian's expression was harder to read. At first I thought it to be shock, for we all swore never to kill those we fed upon, no matter what the reason. Then his eyes began to shine with a light that I had only seen when he was overwhelmed with wonder or happiness. An emotion rarely seen in him, though the stare I got from him, remained utterly blank as he spoke to me. "Étienne... did she die after you vere done vith her, or... or before you vere done vith her?"

His simple question stopped us all. Julien and Élisabeth, from gathering our things and packing them as fast as they could. Bastian however merely stood there waiting for the answer. I myself had to stop and look back into my minds eye to see the moment again. As I reflected on the events that brought us here, I could tell all breaths were being held in anticipation of my answer. Would they turn on me if spoke the truth?

All but Julien would know the lie for what it was as the words fell from my lips. I knew all this, and also this, that if I did speak the lie they would not turn on me, not now at least, but in time knowing I could lie to them they would leave me, a fate I didn't wish to incur.

Taking this risk I turned round to face them all. Julien was holding his coat at the ready to pull on as if frozen in time. Élisabeth was up right, with some blankets draped in her hands half stuffed into a bag, her arm slowly lowering 'til it was completely at her side. the thing held in her hand draped across the bed and her hand touching the floor. And Bastian, arms crossed and eyes full of furry and hunger for the truth.

"I say this to you Bastian, so great was my regret upon realization she no longer breathed beneath me, that I retched for more than my body could expel, and for long moments I lay there looking at her. I say to you, she would have it no other way! SHE demanded it of me! That I cross her over... but I was not able to. I did what I could to comfort her in la mort, but she slipped away quietly, smiling softly.

"I saw no other recourse but to place her in her bed and leave her as though she had passed in the night by herself. I had hoped this would

give us until morning to talk, and then make our way quietly out of this place."

Élisabeth's next statement was more than I wanted to hear. I knew she would leave, and in the end I would like wise lose Bastian, if I didn't lose him now with the passing of Élisabeth.

As she spoke the words, my world began to collapse a little more with each word. "Well Monsieur Étienne, you have killed us all this night, I fear we will have no peace in Europe from this day forward, in my dealings with this Duc... I have found that he has many friends in court, not just here in la France, but in all the other noble houses in every country on the continent!

"You are a fool to think you can cross anyone over to this life we share, how many times have I told you it is not possible! That we are what we are by fate of birth only!

"We need to flee now, and I am not fleeing with you Monsieur Étienne, you are on your own! Julien you are more than welcome to go with me as I leave, as for you Bastian, I am not certain I want you going whether I go or no, decide now for I leave at the count of dix"

Her voice became the thunder that is only felt as its power moves in the distance, each number being counted off one by one in utter painful silence. "Un, deux, trois, quatre, cinq, six, sept, huit, neuf, dix..."

She looked at Bastian, her eyes pleading to him and heaven above that he would choice her over me. All this was done knowing that I was who they, the locals wanted, knowing that she could plead her case against me, if Julien would stand by her as well.

His faith in God was in short supply these days. But this allowed that he could be persuaded to tell a little lie in order to survive.

We all jumped as Bastian spoke into the silence. My heart and mind stopped beating, I stopped breathing, and I was crushed.

"I vill go vith you, le petit. I can not go vith this one anymore. I thought to help him to become the vriter that he vas once. I see now his life in this body is more vaist than fulfillment."

They turn to go and Julien moves with them, pausing but a breath, his head turned to me, eyes down cast with a tear slowly moving down his rough fever pocked face. Pursing his lips, words begin, and then failed to emerge from them. Slowly at the behest of Élisabeth, whose hand is around his arm pulling at him with soft encouragements, he finally turns and leaves the room.

All is silent for a little while after the sound of their feet on the boards' fad. 1, 2, 3 minutes pass before I stir, my body stiff, from standing in disbelief, that I am now alone. I begin to gather my things and make for the door when it opens.

Standing there is Constable Benoît, to his left and right are armed guards with rifles levied at my chest, grinning for all their worth, hungry for the chance to fire their toys.

"Going somewhere Monsieur? It is a fine morning for a walk no? I personally like to wait for the sun to rise just a bit... before I go out, but for you I think it is different no? What with your medical condition, this aversion to the sun. I am certain now is a better time for you to go walking about the chateau than later. Here, let us four go for a walk Monsieur and see what is about this morning shall we!"

He takes my arm forcing me to drop my travel bag, and pulls me out into the hall where I am chained and led out to the servants' quarters. There is a large crowd gathered there, mostly the staff, and some of the house guest that we have spoken with from time to time in the last few weeks that we have been guest here.

As I am dragged forth, they all turn and start shouting to Constable Benoît, that I am the one, that I am the monster that killed her. I plead with Benoit, that I am being framed, that they simply are mistaken. I had been in bed all night, then the crowd grows silent, and parts to reveal one of the younger serving girls, whose affections I had turned away earlier in the week. Such easy prey has never been a fancy of mine. She stood there next to the stable boy, Robert. Both shying away from me, fear in their eyes, and then she spoke.

"That's him constable, that's the one what was with her, with Margaux, we heard them talking in the stable for what seemed hours, of dark things like the devil and vampires, then he said to her .... He told her he was one, a VAMPIRE!"

The little girl almost screamed that last part out, her arm out stretched, the hand rigid and pointing at me! The force of the moment, it left me feeling thunder struck, and then everyone began to mumble amongst themselves, the tone was not good, rather it was very damming.

"So monsieur, your... a vampire? Is this not a little bit of a monstrous claim to be making, especially out here so fare away form the cities and their 'godless' ways?"

Constable Benoit made a point of the word godless; to reference a conversation we had had only a few days past. The disdain in his voice clearly marked his intentions, but I had hoped still to win out and get away.

"Constable, you know what it is like, a man is wont to say anything to win the affections of a woman. We are willing to tell her anything to bed her, no?"

He regards me and my words with grave silence, the pressure of this moment clearly visible on his face, in his eyes.

He turns to the young couple standing as my accusers and asks of them another question. "What else did you over hear, did you see anything that would lead you to believe he had murdered Margaux?"

"Wee Monsieur, he told her after she asked if he could, that he could... cross her over, meaning Monsieur that he could make her like him, a vampire. She started to laugh at the delight of such a thing... and said that she would be immortal now. Then they started to make love in the hay, there was a sound like someone choking, then everything was quite.

"We peered over the loft we were sleeping in and there he was over her body, she was not moving and he began to retch, there was so much blood everywhere... then he wrapped her body in the blanket they were on, and carried her here back to her quarters."

Constable Benoit looked at me and asked. "Monsieur, do you have anything to say to that?"

"Wee, Wee I do. Ask my servant Julien, he will tell you that I was in bed all night! That I was not roused 'til just before you came"

He smiled and raised his hand, waving at someone to come closer. That's when I saw the three of them, each in chains themselves, and Julien was brought forward. The Constable did ask him where I was, if I had been telling the truth. I looked him square in the eyes, doing my best to let him know everything would be ok if he would just lie for me.

I was not ready for his confession; it seems he is more willing to save himself now than anyone else. Or was it simply he was done lying for me? Whatever the reason, he told what was mostly the truth, the most damming part of it. "Constable Benoît, I was alone in our chambers all night, he had told me he was going to bed this witch no matter what it took.

My master can be a cruel beast of a man at times, and fancies himself to be just that, a monster.

"When he came to me I let him go to sleep and gathered up Grande Dame Élisabeth and Monsieur Bastian so that we might free ourselves of him once and for all."

What could I say? I had been seen, worse over heard, and now this great betrayal, by those I called family. All I could do was hang my head... and as I did the crowd knew my guilt, and began to shout and yell for me to be destroyed.

The constable urged them all to be silent as he pronounced my judgment. "Monsieur, I Constable Benoit in the name of King Louis XVI, condemn you to death by fire. You shall be burned at the stake at sun rise. Carry him away and prepare the fire!"

All my pleading and struggling availed me to no end. As the time passed I began to see just how miserable my position was, and wanted nothing more than to be absolved of my sins. I begged to see a priest so that I could confess my sins, but no one would listen.

They just went about the task at hand, and before me grew the stake I was to be tied to. The faggots of wood that were laid about it, were soaked in lamp oil from top to bottom to make sure every tinder caught fire as fast as could be. I sat there chained to the wheel of a wagon waiting and watching.

It was about an hour I sat there watching, before they came for me. I was then led up and secured to it, the stake that would my last chance for freedom. However, the chains forced to fit tighter to my wrist, were pulled behind me as they dragged me backwards up the little stone stair to my fate. My hands were secured around the stake with my back pulled tight to it, to ensure I could not escape this fate. Then I too was soaked in oil.

The entire crowd stood around me in complete silence for what seemed an eternity, waiting for what I could not tell. Then as the first rays of the sun breached the horizon, as the cock crowed, they began to come forward with their touches.

Within seconds, the whole of this thing I was now part of was burning, I search the crowd for any signs that I might yet be saved. Then I saw my family. Behind everyone, there I could see the three of them being released from their bonds, and lead away at musket point to a carriage that *waited for them. From its window they watched as the fire grew brighter and then I began to burn...*

The pain of the fire faded away as the lids of my eyes burned away. I watched the world become foggy then everything flipped upside down, until all I could see were the flames and then the added pain of those very same eyes bursting in the flames....

...When next I come to, I hear two people talking in soft voices. I struggle to understand what is being said, and after a time the two echoes become clearer and I understand bits and pieces of what is taking place...

"But doctor I told you, he got burnt up like that from lying in the sun two days ago... I had ... (light sob) fallen asleep and when morning came, he was smoking and his skin just started turning black and flakein' away like paper in a fire..."

The next voice must be the doctor she mentioned when she got in my car, two, three days ago? How long have I been lying here?

"Look Selena, you could not have known that this, this person had a problem with sunlight. He is not wearing any kind of identifying markers, no bracelets. It's not your fault, Ok?

"As for the fever you mentioned on the phone, it seems that it has not yet gone down, the... burning would only have aggravated it, the fact that he is in the shape he is in, and is still alive, is a miracle, but we can't move him. Moving him to the clinic let alone the hospital, could kill him at this point. I know you were just trying to help the man... that it's gotten out of control here, I must insist that he stay here.

"It's a 2-hour drive back into town and, I really don't think he would survive another long ride, whether it was night or day. Ok"?

"Yea... I guess so. Look, can you at least bring us some supplies, and not let Justin know were I am. Please? You know how he is, and he still thinks we're married. It's been 3 years, every time I think he is out of town, moved on and let me alone he turns up again and starts his shit all over. I just hope he don't come lookin' for me here, why can't he let it go"?!

"Sure, I can do that for you at the very least. I'll be back by latter tonight Ok? Just keep as much cool water as ya can on those rags. Right now that's the best I can do. I'll be sure to bring what's needed to tend to him right and proper when I come back. Just get some rest, and stop worrying so much, ok. Oh, and talk to him, I don't care what ya talk about, just... if he can still hear let him know it's going to be all right."

"Yea, I can do that...." Is the last thing I hear before I fall back into the darkness that has become my world. And in all this I heard her voice, still grating like sandpaper. But it was bliss, golden. The more she talked, the more I loved her. I didn't want to, I fought it, and I fought it like any man fights a thing he fears. Looking inside yourself, for any reason not to love, looking for anything to hold on too to make the thing you fear go away. A thing or object of your hate, at the very least something to keep it in place as a thing feared.

But you can only fight so much when you're starving and out cold, so in the end, it happened. And the more I listened, the more I hated the one she called Justin. I want to kill him when I become strong enough. It seems to me that he has been doing everything he can to keep her here, in this little hell of a town, broken and sad.

Her words began to sing of death, a kind that only mortals can know, a death by their own hands, that ends the pain of living and knowing. One from which they can start over, and never have to deal with the memories of their past lives.

She talks of pills and how her mother found her at Justin's party 2 years ago... striped to the bare and white as a sheet. Of how she had gotten a little too drunk, and when she and Justin were alone, of what he did to her. Her tone is one of lose and loneliness, a broken child of no more than 25, and already she is dead inside.

I love her, not for her pain, or her suffering, but rather, I love how she seems to now carry the weight of the death of her soul on her shoulders with pride, and stands taller than those that don't even know that they are alive... those like Justin. Yea, this one, he will die.

How long had I laid there listening to her, Hours, days, I can't tell. However long it had been I learned to see him, this animal of a man in my mind. Tall and lanky like a rail, well over 6'3" a big lanky loser with long scraggly hair cropped tight to his shoulders, a mullet. He has Burnt leather for skin and long thick dimples that go from nose to chin like a fleshy moustache. And his eyes are beady, little brown pinpricks of hell, full of hate and sin.

I have seen eyes and a face like this before... her words fade into the darkness again carrying me to that man... Again I am forced to remember a past that I can not escape from, to remember forever the suffering and pain I have endured in this life, which has brought me here...

...It's late, and ma is crying again, Earl is not home yet. We all know why, but keep quit for fear somehow he will hear us and come home early. It's payday, and in his mind it's time to go drinking with the boys. He always comes home drunk. He is a woman hatter, and needs to be drunk to do what makes him feel most like a man.

It's dark out... here in the country when the moon is not out, it's very dark. Clouds overhead threaten storms or even a tornado. We listen for not only the storms to come but for him as well. We hope, every night that he will not come home 'til he is good and sober, even if that means days go by before he does. But, he knows the way, the cops, and they always let him go, no matter how drunk he is.

Why? He keeps their cars running, and some- times they come home with him drunk. God only knows what else he does for them. The next day when they leave ma won't come out of the bedroom for days. She just lies in there on the floor, crying and won't let anyone touch her. But she gets better and comes out, but never talks. I know now what was going on, and if I ever found them or him...

Tonight we are not lucky... as the storm breaks he comes home... the car hits the tree out front with a light crunch, but not too bad. He gets out, and in the light of the lightning, backed by a thunder clap so loud it made your ears hurt. We knew the strike was on top of us and that the devil had come home.

We see him, bottle in hand as he slumps forward and looks in at us. His eyes glowing with hell, he almost looks like the devil in the light of the strike. His eyes little dots of pure white fire burning their way into the dark, showing him everything that moves, we scream.

"He's got a gun!!!"

He starts for the house laughing, he'd heard us, and stumbles on the porch, almost falling face first into the steps... he screams and finally falls as he steps on a nail. A nail in those steps he said he would fix weeks ago. From the window we can see him pull his foot up and it's dripping...with rain and blood. The texture of it I can see even in the dim light of the storm, it's a darker color made even more visible by the storms flashes.

The gun hit the porch but didn't go off. I thought I heard someone yell duck. He pulls his boot off and throws it into the night, then starts slurring out vulgarity's that would make Satan cringe. He has that charm in an Elvis sort of way about him when drunk.

40

He takes a drink of the bottle and picks up the gun again, and starts for the door. Blue, his dog comes up to greet him from inside of the house. It's locked, the door, but blue has his own door, and out he goes through that little door, jumping up to lick Earls face.

Earl curses the lives of all rats and whores alike and levels the gun at blue and shoots... Screaming curses all the while, blue hits the porch with a thud, not even a whimper or twitch.

We're going to die.

He's at the door kicking at it as hard as he can, did he forget he has a key? Does he care? *BANG, BANG, BANG....* Earl kicks the door in, breaking the locks and hinges as he steps into the house, he calls for his mother to come serve him dinner.

"GODDAMIT YOU OLD WHORE, I AM HUNGRY! DIDN'T DAD TEACH YOU TO FEED ME WHEN I AM HUNGERY, WERE THE FUCK ARE YOU!!!! I WANT MY DINNER!!!"

We are hiding under the bed in the room adjacent to the kitchen, a room that has a door into the kitchen and the living room, it's wide enough that its windows open on the back yard and front yard, me and big brother, he's 8 and I am 7, we're both scared... But know enough to stay out of the way and quite. From were we are, we see him enter the house and move to the kitchen through the living room, trailing blood the entire way.

Half of what he says is hard to understand. We can smell the whiskey on him from the other room, it's like he was bathing in it...he's forgotten that his mother no longer lives in this house, he's far too drunk.

There is a crash, the kitchen comes to life with light and me and my brother get down lower so he don't see us. Ma is sitting there at the table, she never went to bed. She gets up as he comes towards her, and starts taking his dinner out of the stove, he grabs her hair and yells again...

"WERE THE FUCK IS MY DINNER"

He throws her to the floor and kicks her several times. She crawls to the stove and opens the oven, and puts his dinner on the table. 18 oz.'s of steak, peas, cornbread, and mashed potatoes.

Looking at this he moves to the table to eat and kicks her again in the face, he adds slut to the names and insults he's shouting at her.

She has been taking this forever it seems, and all I wanted to do is go in there and kill him. But the gun is still in his hand as he eats. Ma's face is a wreck of flesh and blood, but she sits there on the floor, curled up hiding from him under the table where he can find her with his feet.

Tears flood her face and mix in the blood from her scalp and nose and torn cheek. Her eyes glazed over with madness, not anger, rather... the loss of all reason, and she is smiling. Her mind is completely gone.

The bastard kicks her every now and then, and orders her to please him while he is eating. And she does. Like a beaten dog she does what he orders, scared of not doing it, she gives him what he wants. I turn away and cannot watch, then the scream from her...

if I never hear that sound again it will be too soon. The pain he caused her that night was more than anyone should have had to bear, ever. I turned to look, and the table is pushed away... he is holding her head down close to his lap, he is laughing and screaming at the same time, holding the remains of his steak in his free hand.

"YOU CALL THIS MEAT BITCH, WHERE THE FUCK DID YOU GET THIS, GARBAGE CAN? HOW DARE YOU FEED ME THIS SHIT"

He throws the steak at the dead dog on the pouch and does not realize blue is dead, rather he blames his dog not moving on my mother having her way with blue to much.

He pulls her head back and he is exposed but that is not what matters. He pours whiskey down her throat even though she can't breathe, and then he snaps her head forward, back on to himself. The horror of this is he turns her head just enough to force his member through the cut in her face and then down further through the cheek into her mouth and throat. She gages and begs for it to stop. He kicks her away and grabs for the gun.

"Earl, she an't no good to us ifin' she is dead.

Let me and little red have a turn at er'."

We were so focused on Earl we didn't see his brothers, they had come with him. They were as drunk as he was and already half naked in the living room. They were ready for a night with a woman, regardless of whose woman she was, and they pulled her into the living room while Earl just watched and ate what was left of his food.

All night it went like that... them kicking and slapping and punching and raping her. After a long time had gone by, Trent my older brother got up and ran into the kitchen where they were again, and tried to stop them...

Earl grabbed him from behind and spun him round and shook him so fiercely I thought his head would come off, all the while Earl was asking him what he thought he was going to do. He made him watch as his brothers' beat and raped our mother at the same time, laughing all the while. Then he did the one thing we never expected him to do, even ma in her derangement fell silent as Earl put the gun in Trent's hands.

Trent, my older brother, he just stood there with the thing in his hands, and stared at our uncles, then back at Earl. You see Earl is not our real father, but a bastard that took us in when our father ran us off, or so my mother says... I hate both of them, Earl and my real father, I don't even know his name... I jumped... Then the sound...

The gun had gone off in Trent's' hands and shot Little Red in the hand... taking his first and second fingers right off.

Earl just laughed and took the gun back, He must have been sobering up because he just hit Trent with the gun knocking him out. Earl gathered his brothers up, and took them off to the hospital to get his hand fixed. The sounds of them leaving, the voices fading, then the engine starting and fading away in the distance, the storm seeming to follow after them 'til all was quite, was like the end of a nightmare.

Trent tried to go to ma and help her but she just hissed at him like a rabid animal. He tried again and she exposed herself to him grunting like Earl or one of his brothers was on her, Trent just stood there. I looked away as I saw her grab him... His voice going no, please...

When Earl came back, around noon that following morning, he was all nice and charming. I hated him, he pretended nothing had happened, and so did ma... I hated her. Trent was still out, his face swollen. Not broken but he was unable to eat normal corn or anything solid for days...

..."I remember it was always like that night, when ever he was drunk... Whenever he was drunk I used to hide from him, and he would scream and hunt for me. All he wanted was to fuck,"

Selena's voice was coming back; I was coming back, the memories fading... The night was full with the smell of fresh desert flowers, and I was hungry. And she is one of two people I can smell. Is the other the doctor?

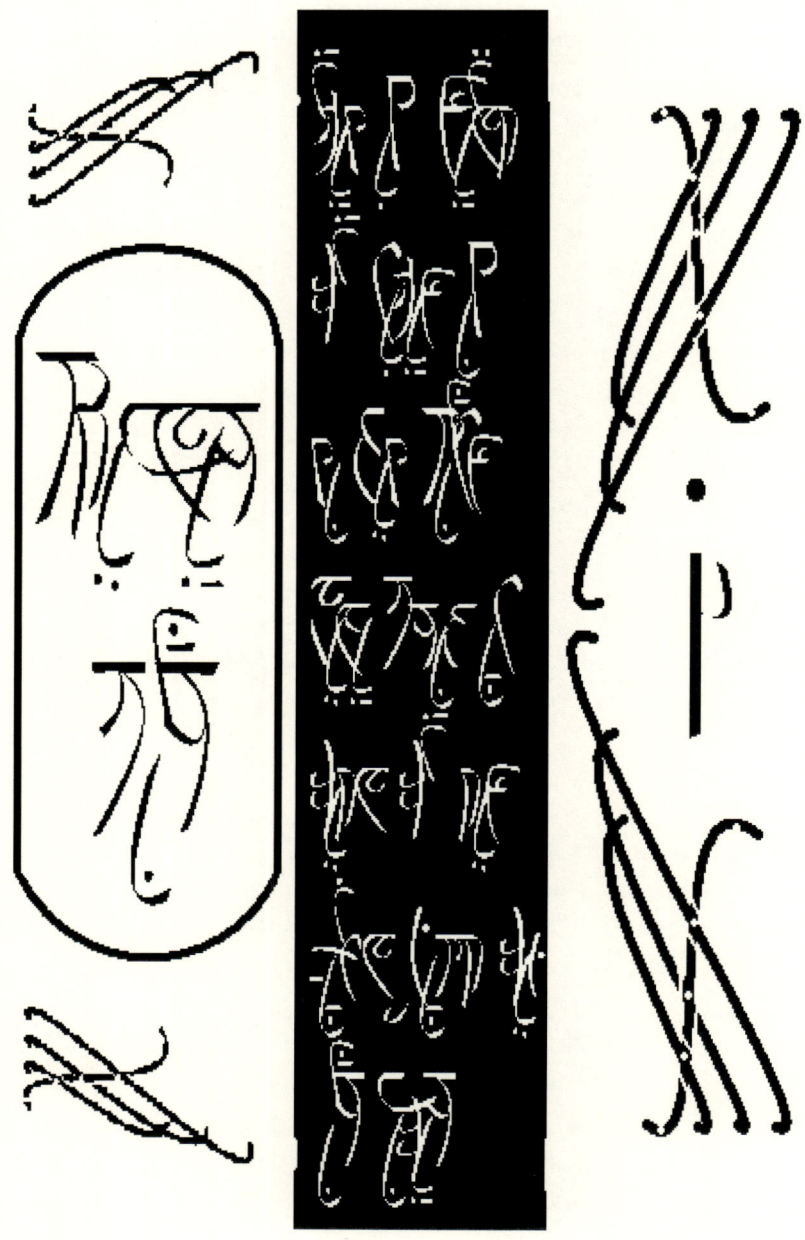

Chapter Four - Bumps in the night

'Searching in all I saw

For something akin to my lie

Alone and cold in the world of normal

Ever aware by others words my flaw

Begging to heaven above to die'

-Vodalok-

The yelling is coming from the other room, and darkness has come. The moon through the window is only half full, no clouds to mar its face, a good clean night. The man's voice is growing louder and stronger as it seems to get closer, is it the doctor, has he returned with some news of my condition, no it's not the doctor.

I here my angels voice as though it's shaken badly, fear is in her. Her tears I can hear streaming down her face, chocked it seems on one thought, "Please, he's very sick. The Dr. asked me to keep him here, He can't travel, please Justin, Don't go in there!"

So this is Justin. He is coming into the room. Good I shall get a look at him, see him for who he is body and soul. Yea I am still very week, and not moving very fast, but I am still more than a match for a dog like him, should he come too close.

!!!CRACK!!!!

I try to sit up, that sounded way too much like someone being hit very hard. Now a loud crashing of a body on furniture, breaking under weight, her sobs seem to fill the whole of this small desert shack she calls home. Then the door opens, and Justin has come in. The light in this room is out so he leaves the door open just enough to see by.

I am lying very still in bed, like a corpse on a table waiting for the embalmer. But through my eyelids I see him; he is exactly like I pictured him, very tall and lanky. Thin as a rail, but for a living man very strong. Even stronger is the smell of whiskey on him, the light of his soul is fouled, darkened by years of hatred of his fellow man. Feelings of superiority like Earl?

Sound of thunder, NO!!... The dream creeping back into my mind, I am sweating. I still have this dammed fever, I can't move! He moves closer and looks down on me.

"Damn this things dead, smells like it anyway. Was he in ah fire? How come he's all burnt up like this? "He leans in and pokes me with the bottle in his hand.

I don't move, but the smell of blood on him is strong. He's got cuts on his face. She must have fought with him. Yes lean in close! My eyes! Look at them you fuck! That's all I need.

From my mind to his I reach out and take hold of his will and probe his mind, rooting out every little piece of cruelty he has visited on this angel that now nurse's me back to health. I see the beatings when they were married, the rape of her daughter, and her daughters' death at the shame of what had happened to her.

He's no better than the pieces of shit that stood in as father for me. All I can see in his mind is the little girls' body swinging in the trees, the transition from his memory to mine is simple, then the body I see swinging in the tree is mine...

...There I am again 8 years old and hating life, one of the men in the family has discovered I am a heavy sleeper and has taken to sodomizing me in my sleep, only I wake up half way through and he learned the first night to gage me before he started.   Latter he took to tying my hands to the headboard so I could not resist and my feet one to each side of the bedpost. I would wake and he would be on me moaning.

I hated him so much and thought of how I would tell and he would be punished, but every morning I would try and no one would listen.

So I took to not sleeping at night, that didn't help. Still he would come, and inside me he would leave a mess, one that stank of cruelty and sin. I carried so much shame in me because of him.

Then it started happening in the day time. The first time he came to me and pulled me inside the barn that the Earl and grandfather had built, and in there he said to me.

"Do you know what this is?" as he pulled a condom out of his pocket.

"No" I said, trying to pull away. But his hands were so big and he never let go. He said. "It's a rubber, and you're going to like them."

Then he closed the door and I was so afraid. Then he slapped me because I must have been lost somewhere, or made a noise he didn't like. He had the thing on and was coming closer to me... I said" I can't," and he said don't worry this is not for your ass, and took my head...

For weeks he would find me and force me to do this and no one cared. My mother even caught him doing it, and just turned and walked away. Her eyes as vacant at seeing me being raped as her eyes were when she was, I hated her. No one was listening to me, no one cared and every day and night, now with no hiding it, I was a thing for his pleasure.

One day I found a long bit of rope in the shed and managed to stay hidden well enough that he never found me. So I ran into the woods behind the trailer park, and kept running 'til I found a tree that would work.

Clint Eastwood showed me how in 'Hang `em high'. Being as small as I was I could not throw the rope over the branch, so I climbed the tree and made sure the rope was as secure as I could. I Tied one end in a knot around my neck, looked around and for a moment I felt free.

In the distance, I could hear someone calling my name, I didn't care. I was not going to be hurt or used by anyone anymore. This would end now!

I don't remember if I jumped off the branch, or if I just let myself fall. What I do remember is the sudden and nightmarish pain, as the rope stopped, bouncing me in the air like a marionette. My neck jerked and everything inside my body seemed to snap. Everything was gone; all I could hear was my heart beating, the rope creaking, and my urine hitting the ground below me.

The light wind that was blowing was not to be heard, nor felt at that moment, and I was above myself for a moment. Out of my body and I screamed and there was no sound. I saw my body twitching and kicking and fighting with the rope tide to tight, and I screamed and there was no sound.

The colors of the autumn day became so bright, that in my eyes all seemed blinding. I screamed at the pain of the sun on me, no sound, only that of the rope as I swung from side to side, back and forth. I was in some horror show kicking and struggling to get free, one where I was dying.

Then it happened, the sound of something snapping, the rush of wind in my ears and the dull thud of my body hitting the ground. The rope had broken. I was still alive, and in pain, and nothing had ended, the only difference now was I had begun this nightmare at early morning, it is now well after dark. The other change being I had lost the will to live and could not bring myself to suicide again, not for a long, long time.

It was also at this time that even though I knew, or thought I knew what I was that I started to forsake that part of myself. I found myself thinking that if I am this thing, why can't I stop those that are hurting me, from hurting me.

I never knew at that age what I could do and was not worldly enough to reason out how to understand what I truly was, am. All I had to go on was what Hollywood had given me in movies about my kind.

All lies...

...So in a way I went back to sleep... Back to sleep.

When next I open my eyes it is daytime again. I am in a heap on the floor. It feels like my ribs are broken. I still can't, move... "Shit" I'm all tied up. He's on the bed and nude, sheet barley covering his backside. My angel, she is on the floor next to him awake, and looking at me, tears in her eyes, full of fear. The stains of his cruelty all over her, mixed with her blood. I can't let this go on.

The blood on my lips is mine, but I scrap at it with my teeth 'til it is in my mouth, every crusty fleck, and I swallow them down'. It's not much, but every little bit helps.

She sees what I am doing and moves very slowly toward me and shows me her wounds, he cut her with a knife last night across the shoulder. She lips to me that she understands, and leaning in she presses the wound to my lips.

I pulled into myself her life little by little, feeling my body harden and grow strong again. I am aroused by her nakedness, the warmth of her pressing in on me as I feed on her...it was almost too much for me, but I stop short of swooning, short of draining her beyond the point of no return. Knowing that if I do, I will be vulnerable to him should he wake and she would surely die. This leaves me less full and farther from recovering than I need, but it will have to be enough, for her, for me.

Straining hard against the ropes I manage to break my bindings with little noise, the time it takes to do this seems an eternity. Twice he turned in the bed as if he had wakened from his drunken sleep, so much like Earl.

I lay on the floor, I can't remember how long, breathing, feeling my ribs knitting themselves back into health. Then he coughed and sat up. For

48

a moment the look on his face was one of pure confusion, as though he couldn't remember were he was or how he had come to be there. His will was brought to bear as he began to pan the room looking for signs of some kind of memory. His eyes fell on me, as I look into them I see the night before play out in his memory; his mind is so easy to read right now.

When he came into the room he started to yell at Selena about harboring vagrants, and that they could come in faking to be sick, and beat her and rape her. He turned from me for a moment and I reached up to grab him. He turned back to me in time to see this, his smile fell away as his instincts reacted and he started to hit me. Selena leapt on his back, arms around his neck trying to pull him away, but he really was powerful. She was flung down and under his boot, and then his attention was back on me.

I can't tell you how many times he hit me in the face and chest, but I do know that once he was done he dragged me, feet first, out of the bed, His words in my mind. "Fuckin` corpse goes on tha` floor where I can watch it!"

Then he piled me up were I woke. Next thing he did was grab her up off the floor and tell her to get undressed. Walking into the other room he opens a draw and in his hands, he pulled out a large knife.

He turns to the bedroom where she is standing looking at me. Justin blinks, his thoughts simple,

"Fucking whore of a wife, she should know better 'an bring another guy home. She needs to be trained better like pa used to train ma."

His eyes go back on the knife; he turns and moves into the bedroom, knife up and out in front of him. "You do as I say" Justin says cruelly, "or I will really kill it!"

He kicks me on the word 'it', his eyes never leaving her, as she starts to undress. I can't stand to watch anymore and break contact.

Selena lay next to me, looking up into my eyes as I looked down at her, she was softly pouting, and under her breath the words came to me, "If you're really an Angel, or Monster, or whatever you are, that you're still alive, make him pay, please gods make him pay"

I can't take it, I see him out of the corner of my eye slowly rising. His blonde hair is all stiff and thick like straw. Slowly I rise as he does. He's got this smile, if you can call it that. That worn leathery scarecrow grimace, like Earl used to wear, stretched across his face, looking every bit like a scarecrow gone insane.

He raises his hand to point at me and I mouth the words he says to me as he says them.   "You're going to die crispy, I'm goanna kill's ya'."

I exaggerate his movements as I move in time to him like a mirrors reflection, mocking his every move. Only this time I am not blackened like a piece of Cajun chicken, rather I am the stark white ghost I have been since I was a little boy. Paler than the finest alabaster, eyes so sharp that even in the light of day, the sun that shines through the window upon his face is dimmed in my rage.

My eyes burst to life with radiance as I leap forward without a sound save the hiss of hatred carried to him as I grow closer... as it begins.

To me everything slows to a pace where in my mind, the fly in flight beside this animal of a man stops moving. The sweat hangs on his nose and does not fall, rather it's held in time as a photo to be scrutinized with contempt. I watch him for what seems an eternity, never moving but growing closer to him, until I am so close to him that I am now in his face. Time snaps back.

His scream of fear and confusion amuses me to no end, and I just stand there laughing at him. I laugh at him with so much contempt; it reflects my force of will. A will that pushes him backwards and he falls onto the bed he just rose from. Clawing at the bed and his face to get away from me, he begins to crumble. He can not get away from this spectacular monster that I am.

Once the laughter has faded I again move out of time exerting so much energy, forcing myself to move so fast that no living thing could comprehend the most exaggerated movements, and up onto the bed I go, my legs straddling him. He is prone beneath me, horror frozen on his face, as in the dead forever stuck in hell.

I call out to him this simple challenge. "Beast you are, with a want to hit someone. You hunger for the pain in others; you're wanted to prove how strong you are by beating them.

"Here is a monster for you to fight, to beat down, become the man you think you are, and strike me!"

It's all I can do or manage to say as he rights himself, the bed and pillows under him soiled, and the stench of his filth reaching his nose, and mine. The fool begins to cry and beg to his god for salvation, and all I do is stand above him looking down upon him. "God please save me! I swear I will never harm her again if you please just save me!!!"

He screams again, what this fool does not know is I am not going to harm him. This fear in him is too good. It will work the pain he needs into him, until he can no longer move about as a real man ever again. It's all I need. You see in a way it feeds me as well, even now I grow stronger and a little intoxicated from him. Every scream from him is life to me, and I reveal in it. Drinking him in and shaking him, watching him grow weaker both physically and mentally with each passing second.

Bursting myself to speed again, I begin to shake. As I shake, the violence of it, and the look of it, my whole body a blur of white flesh distorted eyes and teeth, change into a nightmare that will scar and liquefy his mind for the rest of his life. All this shatters what is left of his simple mind.

I am still too weak to do anything more, I back away and out of the room to the sound of his broken will pleading with me, the word he repeats summons in me another time, to when I was only nine and I hear the word please...

...Its Easter morning and the Earl had been out all night drinking again, my mother in a moment of rare courage took his unconscious body and laid him out on their bed. There she tied his hands and feet to the bed post, top and bottom, then sat there waiting all night for him to wake up.

She knew that if he wakes tied as he is, there will be no turning back from the path she has chosen. I could not at the time understand what the heavy black frying pan was for, or why she kept saying please over and over again.

I sat at the door for an hour as the sun began to rise knowing that if I was caught my punishment would be very, very bad, so I kept quite. The quieter I was, if I did not move I found, I could not be seen, unless looked at directly for more than just a passing glance.

Then around noon he began to stir, slowly not noticing it seemed that he was tied 'til he tried to rise, then he opened his eyes completely. Wide in a way I had only seen animals open theirs in when they knew they were about to die. His head thrashed from side to side and he began to scream at my mother, attempting to kick her but the ropes held and he didn't rise. "What the hell are you doin whore!!" He screamed.

She sat there watching for a little while longer then began to talk. At first her words were raspy from hours of crying and talking to herself without water, and then I understood what she was saying. "...I have been the whore for you and your brothers ever since we got married, and all I have done is tried to love you.

"Even going so fare as to close my mind and will to all that you wanted so that you could be happy. But I could never make you happy; all I ever got from you was pain and sufferin'.

"I can't take much more of it. You have got to stop using me like a whore, or... I don't know what I will do..." Ma's voice trailed off for a moment as she swallowed real hard on her words, then started talking again. Her voice had lost some of its weakness. "Right now I need you to understand how I feel inside! The ropes, bein' tied up, all that is part of it. But there is so much more. Inside I hurt everyday because of you. The pain in my mind and soul go deeper than a bastard like you can imagine. So I decide the only way you could understand was to be hurtin' yourself."

There was a very long pause as she began to say please again, rocking back and forth like a child in a corner, whimpering the words please over and over again. Earl laid there silent, whether it was because of the alcohol in his system or fear I never knew. After what seemed an eternity ma began to speak again. "I have prayed all night that another way would be shown to me, but nothing has come to me. NOTHING! All I have is this." She waves the heavy frying pain in the air.

Earl's eyes widen with understanding of what is to come. A tremble overtakes his body, and he vomits all over himself, both from visible fear and the sickness that comes from too much drinking.

Ma for some reason stopped talking and put the pan down. She went into the bathroom, not even noticing me watching everything, wet a towel and returned to the room. She began cleaning him up, then propped up his head and gave him some coffee that was on the nightstand beside the bed, still warm it seemed. Earl began to beg her, in his masculine redneck way to let him go, telling her that everything would change.

Tears in her eyes showed me she was willing to do so, but somehow held on to her purpose and only said "I know, but you must know my pain," and left the room to get a clean towel. When she came back her tears were gone and so too it seems was the weakness in her face.

She stood at the end of the bed and picked up the pan again, its heavy cast iron weight showing in her trembling arm. She moved slowly round the bed to where his head lay at the top of the bed and spoke, "My children will no longer fear you or your evil ways. You will love me as a man should, and not sell me to the filth that comes home with you in the night, after hours of drinkin' and cardin'"

The trimmer of her voice began to thicken as she choked back tears of rage, fear and shame. The years of suffering, coming to the forefront of her will, manifesting themselves into her face, like a kabuki mask of some foul demon out of Japanese nightmares. "You'll be home to work on the yard, and keep your oaths to me from the wedding. Oaths you held me to at the end of a shotgun, and you'll never, ever touch my son like you touch me!! NEVER EVER AGAIN!"

I realized at that moment she never saw her brother as the one that raped me, and always saw Earl as the beast that tormented my nights and days for so long. Now she was going to make him pay for it, all of it, the things he's done and the things that others had done...

I became very afraid at that moment, and tried to hide in the corner of the room where I would not be seen. From there I watched with horror and amassment at what she did.

Up went the pan and hard it came down with a rush of air onto Earls bare skin. The flesh of his leg gave only a little then broke exposing the meat beneath. Again the pan came up and crashed down this time on the knee of the same leg. I watched as it, the knee, bent backwards and the foot came up off the bed with a terrible cracking sound, like wood under the axe.

Earl screamed this time fully awake and realizing this is not a hellish dream. Again the pan came up this time on the other leg, then the arms and chest. The flat of the pan was used on his face. All this only took as long as is needed to breathe five shuddering breaths, and then it was over.

Blood was pooling at the base of his head and legs. Weakly his chest rose and fell, the broken ribs so visible, that one threatened to escape the flesh sack, that was the wreckage of his body. Faint sounds, of pain, so distant, came from him that it seemed to me he would die right there. But he didn't.

Slowly his head turned to me and through swollen eyes he pleaded with me to untie him. The words he spoke were in my mind, those words were so clear, so loud, and all I could hear was his pleading. I shook myself... no mother was shaking me. Her eyes glazed over like a dying animal. She screamed at me to leave the room, and all but threw me from it, the room.

As the door closed I could still hear Earl pleading with me, his mind touching mine, whether he knew he was doing it or not. I knew what was happening, and fled from the house.

I began to scream as I ran into his brothers and mother. They had come to collect us for services at church for this fine Easter Sunday. Grandmother screamed because I was covered in the splattered blood from Earl. The brothers moved slowly inside, one of them pulling a gun, only to be hit by grandmother. She hissed at him to put it away... "Tha` lord is ah watchin' boy, put that piece of hell back in your pocket!"

And still all I could hear was his pleading with me. All other sounds, nanas screams, the Earls brothers trying to break down the door, mothers tears, all distant, faded and dull within an echo of his pleading...

"Please..."

Uncle put it away, the gun, and they went inside the house. I could hear them ordering ma to open the door and saying what would happen to her if she didn't. The things and words that came out of Uncles' mouth as he talked to ma were in ways the heat and stench of hell breathing out at her. His mouth was the gate from which they, the evils of hell all poured from.

Still Ma held tight. Grandmother stepped closer to the door and spoke Earl's name, and in my mind I could still hear him, "Please... please untie me..." But not a word did they hear. Thoughts from him like, 'my chest hurts so bad, I can barley breathe,' or 'god help me to live through this so I can teach this woman the way to love her man, help me to find the strength to kill her...'

For hours nothing happened, neither the door opened or words were heard from inside the room, then came out of Earl the sound of a rabbit being eaten' alive. If you have never heard this sound, prey you never do. So loud is the pitch of the scream, and the horror of it, short quick burst of sound, with an urgency of pain to be free, as it falls off short and quiet. Until there is only the silence, and even though you hear the wind in the trees, or the creek of the trees under their own weight as they are moved by the wind. The echo of the dying rabbit lingers forever in your mind, drowning out all other sound.

This was the sound that came from the room now from Earl, and the litany of verse from ma`, as she read aloud from the bible. About the sins that have been visited on her by him and the suffering that would be had in hell for them. Then she began to rant on about how he would not go to hell, not now that she had saved him. By giving him this pain...

I heard grandma; her head lowered, tears in her eyes, as she realized the suffering her boy had given to ma. She told her other two sons to leave the house, and bring back the things she would need to heal both her son and her "daughter." She told them both that if you see or use her for anything other than a sister, that she would make them suffer worse than Earl now suffered.

The trailer was quiet again, yet, in my head I still heard Earl begging, only now the prays of grandma` were there as well as the madness of ma. All I could do was cry quietly to myself, hiding in the barn that had been the seen of so many horrors. My mind so full of sound all around me, my head began to spin and pulse with confusion until I fell, and the world went black... ...And 'once more into the breach' I think to myself, as my eyes open and this pig of a man still sits on the bed, huddled in upon himself in filth. Staring at me with empty eyes and my angel's not in the room.

I reach out with my senses. Nose working, ears hunting, my mind tracking and no where is she to be found. I rise and move to the other parts of the house, the windows all closed and boarded up, there is no sense that I am in a house where she once stood. Moving through the place I finally find a sent of her, in the kitchen, no... just a letter.

My angel, my blessed angel from hell...

You have shown me that there is nothing in this world that I should ever fear again. For in this night that has been the waking nightmare of my mind, I have seen the face of my terror and it no longer controls me, for this I thank you.

I thank you also for setting me free to live my life as I should want to live it, without fear of a mortal man ever again, that I have the strength in me if I want to, to call you to me by prayer. It was my prayers for freedom from 'J' that brought you to me, and you in your ultimate weakness were able to beat him down without even harming his body. That is something I could never do, or dream of doing to any man that hunt and prey on weaker people, woman.

I took from you a small thing, his car, and left. I drained his bank account and mine, and sold the house to the local land lord to do with as he pleased. Before I left, for you I closed all the storm windows and shutters so the light would not harm you again. I love you. After tonight, I will be like you.

-Selena-

What did she take from me? I begin going through my things and check outside, the sun has gone down, no, and my car is still there, as are all my things in it. I go back inside and sit and think. That last line was kinda un-nerving, *"I love you. And after tonight will be like you."* What could she have meant? I begin to look over my body, taking off my shirt and my pants, after several long moments I see what she did, what she took from me.

I hastily dump out the trash and rut through it like a hog starving for anything to eat, and I find it. A used needle, the kind they use in the hospitals for taking blood, and the empty wrappers of at least 4 tubes used in holding that blood. *"I love you, and after tonight will be like you"*

The dammed fool! This time, this time it is not myself whom I am cursing for a fool, not like the last time so many years ago... the last time I trusted in a woman's touch and words. I dress as fast as I can and leave the *'Earl'* to himself, a blubbering mass of wasted flesh, stewing in his one waist, both of body and soul.

I head out to my car and start it, I spend several moments focusing in on her, having fed from her only hours ago, or was it days? I know how to track her, and fell into doing just that.   Some   call   it   remote viewing, but what I can do is so much more than that. With remote viewing the seeker can get vague idea, or images that they link together to find a place person or thing. A practice that can take hours if not days to complete, with me, I can see the target almost as clearly as though I were looking at them through a window with a shear curtain over it at dusk.

Yea I know, not that good, but I can lock on with in minutes, and use that to track my target 'til I catch it. So as not to get to angry I try to focus on something else other than the theft of my blood by this 'angel' whom, I must now hunt and ...

"She's such a DAMNED FOOL!" I say as I hit the steering wheel with both hands. Lucky for me it's easy these days to let my mind lose itself, and I drift away back to when I was with the last female that I cursed myself over...

...in the car parked out side the stadium with her, all the lights out looking at the stars, watching one move very, un-naturally, and I begin to tell her my story, I love her, and am willing to risk this for her, that she might understand something of who I am.

Who am I?

In truth I am no one of any real importance, a young man not even 19 living on his own and doing the best he can.

That's what makes this story so hard, so unbelievable. It starts with me in my early childhood remembering, dreams of chasing rainbows, mind you when I say early childhood I mean the age of 5-6, chasing rainbows.

We lived in rural Mississippi just outside of Tupelo, a small town call Verona, on a hill next to a ceramic store and across the street from a trailer park, the main road was 4 lanes with a 5th passing lane that our little home edged right up to, no side walks just dirt for a curb then our front yard.

Just down the hill on the other side of the ceramic store was a large food store, a major chain. I just can't remember what it was called. I, my brother and friends would play in the woods behind there, or the great deep tree lined ditch behind the trailer-park across the street. In that place were forts along the length of the park, as well as on the other side of the stream. There were forts both ground and tree, built of old pallets and tin roofing that had been discarded over the years, making its way to us.

Wars we had with pellet and bee-bee guns, such was the fun we had. In time we would live in the smaller trailer park behind the woods off the same main road on the same side. It was a nice town in Mississippi, where lots of workers from Rockwell would commute to and from, affluent and fairly well to do.

We did ok as I can remember of that time, I had not come into myself yet, and maybe this event had something to do with it, the chasing rainbows.

The house was white and in the Spanish style, ranch, kinda wrapped around the main court in the front that was a faux front yard, you know the type it had a fenced in back yard that was large and with a tree that was a favorite of mine, on it was the tire swing and it was large enough that you sometimes would be able to hide inside it.

The gate around the back yard was more of a wall with an iron gate. White washed to perfection and the very embodiment of everything that rouge of a sawyer ever stood for. Behind the wall was the garage for two cars, that in and of itself was scary even in the day time, but never so much as at night. Not a bad home all in all, in a state where the poverty level is higher than the national deficit.

At night in my dreams, I would find myself in so many places other than there, wishing we were anywhere other than there, sometimes next to a river with my teacher from school, I liked those moments always waking there. Because when the sun went down and traffic would die down, everything took on a reality that was anything other than child friendly.

Don't get me wrong it was still a wonderful place but when it got dark, there was something about the place that scared me more than anything else could ever do. Even the whole in the woods where the "witch" lived that we would brave during the day, I could never put my finger on it. So when the lights were turned down and the sound of the fans in the windows would be all I could hear over the rush of air from the fans blowing over me, making the cold sweat of fear a terrible chill in the bones... it was no wonder I would dream of places other than home. 'til that night I went chasing rainbows.

Even as a very young youth I had a strong understanding of the things going on in the adult world, of mother and father. I knew he was not my father, that he was a man mother was married to because my father was a monster. One that would try to starve me and eat me when my bones were visible enough, At least that's what mother said, the aunt said it was because he tried to kill me once by throwing me against a wall.

That would explain this weird lopsided smile of mine, only half the muscles in my mouth responding to anything. Kinda like a dead nerve or someone who had a stroke. I never really pressed for more than that, didn't need to, I had memories of him, visiting before we came here. We lived in a cold place then, where it snowed all the time and deer would be seen in the back lot even though we lived in a large city.

That place would have a name latter in life, we would wind up there again before long, starting a years long trend of moving from state to state that didn't end even after I was living on my own. But I never started to look forward to it 'til after that first dream when I went chasing rainbows.

One other things I was aware of was my body, I knew that if I touched it like mother did, it would respond the same way, and in some ways I didn't even mind in the beginning when the uncle started, not 'til he started doing the other things, things that came latter, when we were in the trailer park.

Playing show and tell at that age was different for me, only because I had some idea of the meaning behind what we were doing, more that just playing house, where the girls would pretend to be the wife and that I was their husband. I looked forward to the part of the game where I would come home from work and take her to bed. We would use the tornado shelter as our house and stay in there for hours playing, never getting caught. I looked forward to all that 'til that night.

It would be years before I started to figure out how to know when they were watching, what signs to look for to know when they were coming, to ready myself for the night-mare that would visit itself upon me for the rest of my life. The first was the weather that day. Warm and clear, turning cloudy at night, the silent lightning that only moves in the clouds, in every color you can find in a preschool box of crayons.

Dry air that moves, but does not move the trees or grass, The "static" that would build around each and every person and not discharge, keeping everyone on edge, the kinda` edge that comes from looking for a storm, where there isn't one.

That night was just such a night, and I was more afraid of the home than ever before, but could not quite put my finger on it. Mother could see *that not just myself but my older brother was likewise spooked. So she came into the room and gave us a night light, and told us a story so wonderful by time we fell to sleep with the bedroom door open we were not afraid, rather we fell of into the land of dreams smiling and comfortable.*

The oppressive heat of the Mississippi summer lessened for some reason in our room alone. I found myself in the living room, mother was there busying herself with some task, I was watching it rain outside, a calm spring rain was washing the world clean of all the stink and hate that man left upon it. Across the street was a rain gutter and water was moving into it very fast. I remember that no cars were on the road at that time in this dream, and the world was so very bright.

I continued to watch out the window as the rain stopped and I saw a rainbow descend deep into the drain on the far side of the road, I rose up and out the door, I went as fast as I could go. Having heard all the stories about what lay at the end of rain bows drove me on, and on I went. As I came closer the light of the colors grew brighter, I kneeled down on my knees and looked through the metal of the grate and as the rain stopped and the water ceased to flow into it I found the pot of gold.

So big was it I screamed with joy and ran back to my home across the road to get mother and brother to share in this wonder, in my joy of solving our problems so mother would not cry anymore at night.

As I opened the door the atmosphere changed so that it was cold and stifling hot in the house all at once, dry and thick with moisture without reason and it was empty, no furniture, no mother, no brother. I ran to each room in turn and became more afraid with each step 'til I went to the back door and out into the yard to get to the tree for safety. But as soon as I passed the threshold of the rear of the house, I found myself in a sterile room of white, starker than the wash of the fence wall, or the house, and into that room. It came in from no where to stand before me.

The screaming began instantly; I could do nothing but scream and stand where I was in utter terror of what was there. It was beyond my reason or ability to understand why something that was my height and seeming weight should frighten me so utterly. Yet there I stood unable to respond or move at all, screaming into the face of what would become my nightly torment for the rest of my life.

It was in a suit of pure white, big black eyes made its face look more like a mask with large covers over the eyes to see out of that were completely black and utterly blank. Did it wear this mask to protect itself from the horror of my appearance, or from the stark pain of the sterility of the room we are in, in its horrific PURE whiteness...?

My childhood from there is very shattered and broken as memories go, and only dreams with clarity can be remembered. How many times since then, how many times has that dream come upon me without warning?

She looks me deeply in the eyes, tears welling up in hers and holds me for what seems the entire night. I am shacking from the fear that builds in me just from talking about this nightmare of mine, and she says nothing, just holds me. Then she asks me very plainly. 'Is this why you called me tonight,"

"No" I said "and yes", broken inside with my own tears so close to the surface, from fear and anguish, I stammer out.

"Last night, you know how the storm was, I woke up, and... Bo my dog, he was"

The fear trembles out through my lips as the words chock hard on my tongue, slow breaths and light body quakes wreak havoc with my will and body. Slowly I resume after long minutes lost in her arms held tightly as the devastation of my soul leaks out of me into the openness of her embrace.

"He was under my bed whimpering, and you know how small my room is, barley a walk in closet with a private entrance meant to be a laundry room, my bed so close to the window. I called to him and he would not move, my Bo just lay there eyes bigger than his nose, have you ever seen a Doberman look like that, it in itself is enough to frighten you. I looked around and at the foot of my bed, at the window..."

Again my body is tormented by the silent quakes of fear and self-loathing brought on by the weakness in me, the inability to stop them.

From what must have been an hour in that place of comfort she pulls back from me her tears still fresh in her eyes, making my pain that much more tangible, she begins with a whisper that is barely heard by me.

"I don't know what to say, you know I love you, but this just scares me so much, I don't know how or what to do to help you with this, it's just so much to take in so fast. I mean are you sure it was not all just a nightmare,"

It was then I knew I had made the first grand mistake with her. I let her in to deeply and she didn't believe me, but I had no-one else to turn to.

Days turned into weeks into months and it seemed we grew closure after that night. When I needed to get out of my mothers house, after coming back from the four months in Michigan with my father, who also through me out...

She talked her father into letting me stay in the summer home on the lake, to make sure it would be safe. Turns out it seems, I came back to state as a rash of break-ins were occurring at the lake.

With chores to do while I was there, they put me up and fed me 'til I could join the army and make a life for myself and stand upon my own two feet. Weeks go by with her and her sisters coming out to visit. Sometimes bringing her sisters current boy friends along, we would part ways after dinner to do our own thing, making out, making love, or taking long slow boat rides on the lake under the moon and stars.   I remember how lovely she looked back then, short cropped southern rock hair, blonde as can be with soft blue eyes, only about five foot tall and very slight of build, weighing not more than 100 lbs, maybe 115.

She watched me, listening to my words, seeing how each breath was a pain, my mind suffering at the revelations being given to her at this time. Then it hit her, what I was saying and she pulled away. Sat there her small back strait up and tight against the door of her car, she sat there looking at me, her eyes so much larger than they had been before,

"so you're telling me, that last night... aliens took you away, did shit to you an then left you back in your bed, I am supposed to believe that?!, how on earth... why would you think I would be ok with this, that I would not freak out, are you crazy!!!? You can't do this to me! Please you can't just drop this kinda crap on me and expect me to be ok with it..."

She sat there for maybe 15 min just staring at me, I knew I had lost her, with all we had been through as young lovers up to that point I knew I had lost her.

"Get your things, I am.... "

Before she could finish I had gotten out of the car, and began to head back inside, there was no wind, it was a clear Texas night, warm and sticky, I noticed how the lightning bugs seemed to stay out in front of me, as if trying to light my way, to ease my steps as I moved away from her.

"Stephen... wait... look I know this is hard for you, to tell me something like this, and that you're out here alone all the time, maybe it was just a bad dream... and it seemed real, look I will stay the night with *you and make sure you're ok, we can get some breakfast in the morning, go swimming... you know make a day of it"*

I didn't turn around. I just said ok, I knew I could not tell her anymore, that I could not tell her why I really had issues with being in the sun. I cursed myself for letting my guard down. I know I had hinted before at how I 'thought' a vampire could be made but in the end with all that has come and gone I let things go...

...I cleared my mind and hope to heaven above I can one day make things right with her. I miss her from time to time and know that the twist her life took was a direct result of having known me and having been exposed to the things that were a part of my life, the music, the life styles, out of the box thinking. In Texas that just isn't acceptable.

Driving along I get myself back and continue to track Selena. She has a full 2 days on me as I can see it, I must have remembered about the triplets because I can see Selena there in that very same town, heaven help them all should she decide to stay. I pray she just goes on through.

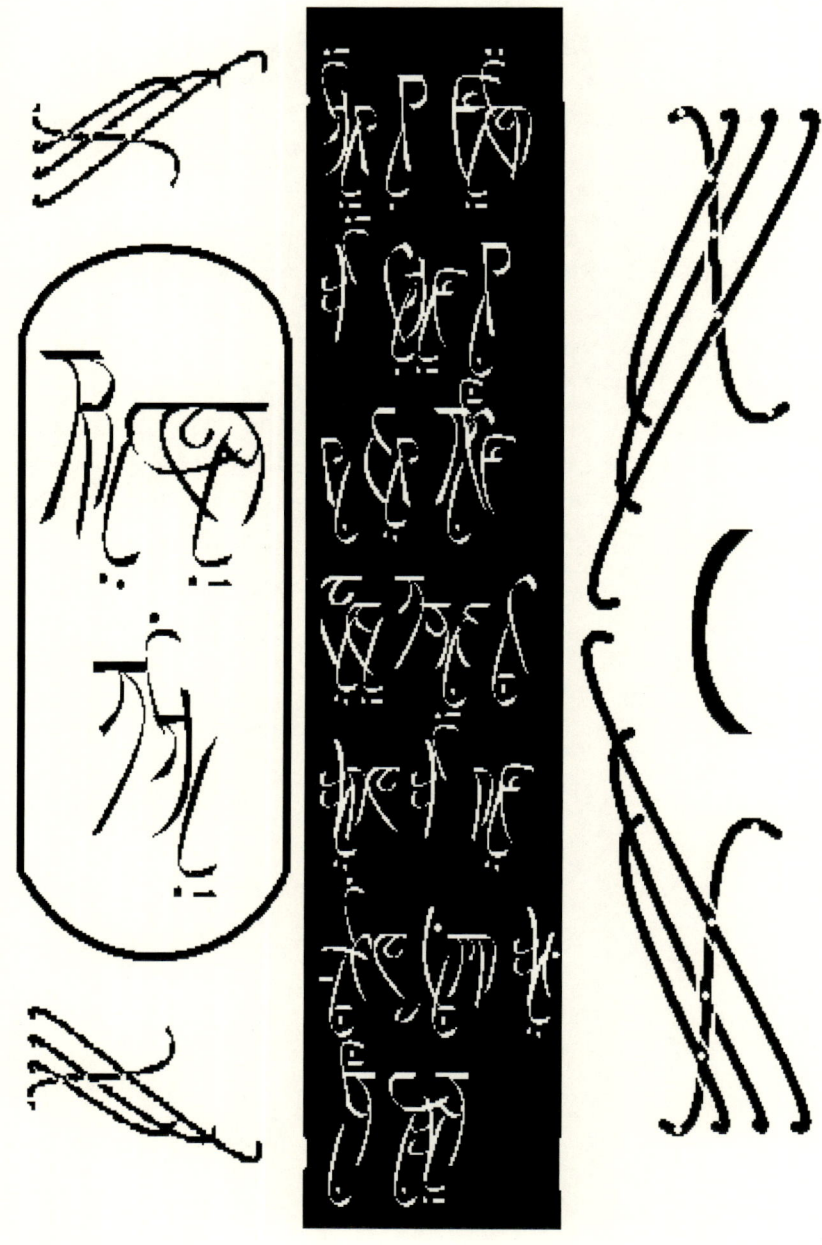

Chapter Five - Stolen Lives

'In all this my only comfort

The gloom of night to wander

Free from words as weapons flung

In towns so blind

To grave side I blunder.'

-Vodalok-

The engine roared, the dust bellowed behind, the road races up to meet the wheels of the car. This would be her beginning, her freedom. That thing, whatever it was would surly kill him, her ex, once the night fell, it had too. After what she had just done, it had to. She had sat waiting for the cover of nightfall to set out. She was not sure if she should have, but she didn't want to take any chances, not after watching how he burned in the sun.

He had been very clear on how to do this thing she had done. Talking in its sleep, she had learned how to become stronger than she could ever hope to be, and never fear death ever again...

..."My blood with your blood 1 part to two, mix and stir 'til they are one, the foam will fade when it's ready, and then back into your body it must go. Strait to the heart to make sure none is lost in transit by vein..."

...She had called the doctor and convinced him this must be done, the price for doing it she paid, but in the end so did the doctor. For two hours they sat there, his blood slowly working its way through hers.

Now that her body was too weak to fend him off, the doctor, all she could do was lay there and watch, as the doctor had his way with her after the transfusion was done. Her chest had been the center of his attention all during the process, drawing that other mans blood, her blood, and then mixing them.

He had looked at her chest the whole time, knowing it would be exposed soon. All his life he had wanted this moment, then came the long needle through her sternum, and the pumping of the fire into her body... she blacked out.

When she came too, the doctor had her completely undressed and was on top of her, in her, violating her with every ounce of his power. She lay under him feeling his every movement, stimulating her body, awakening it to sensations she had never known. This old man would pay for this, but for now all she could do was lay there. When he saw her eyes open, wide and staring, screaming at him with the fury of hell, he stopped a beat, slowed his pace to watch her, fearful she might resist. But for her breath, she did not move, and then he smiled.

"Well if you're goin'na die I want to send you to hell with a smile "He said, but his lips never moved, the sound never came from his mouth, and then began pumping away at her harder. Each movement sent through her another jolt of what felt like lightning blasting her body, but each time the pain would lessen and the pleasure would grow.

Neither of them realized her arms were around him 'til he could not push up and away any longer. He went to scream but found her mouth on his, her tongue deep inside his mouth, the very breath of life was being sucked out of him. She rolled him over so she was on top, then sat strait up and let out a noise that was neither scream, moan, or human, then back down on top of him she lay, driving herself onto him now.

This time it was his turn to scream, he could not stop, and his body was no longer his own. It moved in time to the rhythm of her heart, beating faster and with more fury. So too did his body into hers begin to move, faster, harder, he would thrust, his heart straining to keep up with the overwhelming pain that was upon him. He felt his mouth full of wet copper and he knew his blood was leaking out through his mouth, she was drinking every last drop, consuming him as he raped her.

Then it was over, her body was shaking with the force of her new found life, the orgasm of her birth became the seizure of his death.

She shook the memory from her mind, the power of it so strong she felt as though she had just lived that moment again, that's when she saw the car.

She jerked the wheel hard and left the road, the other car doing the same came to a stop. She didn't, rather she pressed harder on the peddle forcing the car back onto the road. Looking into the mirror she saw the driver of the other car get out. She could hear him swearing at her, every word as clear, and as loud as if it were being screamed into her ear, she realized it was in her mind...

In her mind the doctor had cursed her with his very last bit of life, even as that life slipped from his body. The curses of whore and devil, succubus were loud in her ears, her mind...

She stood up, her knees wobbling beneath her. She looked around and the thing, that man, still lay there in the corner of the room. Her ex was still gibbering on the bed like a mad man, his mind lost forever, watching her, playing with his fingers like they held some secret toy.

Ignoring him she turns back to the doctor who had 'til tonight been a trusted family friend, someone that had always been there for her ever since she was a small child, healing her of all her broken bones. He was there supporting her through her divorce, he was there encouraging her to become a social worker, to help other battered woman.

What had she done... his body was shriveled like it had lain in the sun for a hundred years, completely void of any moisture. She emptied her stomachs contents onto the floor right there on the spot, then collapsed onto the floor and continued retching. It took long moments to pass before her body stopped convulsing.

She showered, dressed and cleaned up the waist of her body. She looked in on her ex, and still he sat there shivering, gibbering, and playing with some private toy that no one could see.

Turning back to the wreckage that was the doctor, she began to cry, tears and emotions threatened to tear her apart. She could not leave him like this, so she decided to lay him to rest. She went to drag his body out, but found it so light that she could pick it up and carry it outside. She carried it 'til she could no longer see the house under the night sky, a distance that felt like forever.

She carried him 'til she felt there would be no way anyone could ever find this, her first kill. A kill she had not wanted, and then she dropped him and began digging. The hole took about an hour for her to excavate, large stones, and hard packed dry unyielding earth proving to be harder to dig than she thought. Then into this final resting place she laid his body. Folding the arms over his chest, the sound of joints breaking as if they were ancient beyond belief sent chills through out her body.

The dust erupting into the night air was all that was left of what once were joints. She sat there on her knees, leaning over him for what seemed hours, and then she said a prayer for his soul and covered him over.

"What have I done...? "She began to cry," Oh God, what have *I done?*"

From out of the wind she thought she heard a reply, soft and simple, the voice that spoke to her on the wind strangely was easing her every fear, pain, and terror at what was happening to her while destroying any hope of salvation.

"You have discovered the secret of eternal life, but you do not yet understand what you have made yourself. This fruit you have taken from the tree of life will be your Damnation. You shall be more feared and hated in your new life than ever in your suffering in mortality could endure.

"Now you shall know the full truth of suffering and ecstasy. Prepare yourself child, you have become beyond me, I no longer can protect you or guide you. You must learn to stand on your own and up yourself from this day out.

"You can no longer call upon my priest for knowledge. They will know you for what you are, though they will not move against you. You may not enter unto my house on earth, nor will you ever through my gates pass again."

And with that, like the passing of the wind, the words were gone, and with them all feeling of anything she knew as life before. It all passed away, then all was still and silent.

Again her body convulsed and gave up its contents; this time those contents were all the life that had held her close to humanity. This time when she was done, she was left feeling more hollow than empty, like her very soul had been pushed out of her. She knew it passed on and was no more, that she was nothing but waist to be flushed, or buried there on the spot. She cried for the rest of the night there on the grave of the doctor, whose sin gave birth to her new un-life.

When she woke she was covered in dirt, the sun was setting and she knew she must get back to the house as fast as she could. Setting out at a run, she began moving faster and faster, faster still 'til the world became nothing but a blur.

On her way out from the house last night it seemed to take an hour or more to get to where she had been, now it only took a few minutes to get back. She came to a stop followed by a dust cloud, looked around and no one, or thing seemed to be stirring.

Entering the house she was pleased to find nothing had changed. Her ex, he was still sitting there, did he sleep at all last night? Did his shattered mind need it? In seeming response to her thoughts he looked up at her and screamed, it faded 'til it was a squeak then he went back to his hands.

The other still lay there sleeping, or dic it die? Was that her fate now, to sleep for days, weeks without knowing the world moved outside? Brushing those thoughts aside she began to clean. All the things from the night before needed cleaning, and that's what she set out to do. Everything went into the trash, needles, tubes, gauze, all of it. Once it was cleaned up she closed all the windows, pulled all the curtains and wrote her benefactor a letter.

In it she apologized for not being there, and how sorry she was...no... that note she crumpled up and discarded. She tried again this time being honest. She then went to her ex and had him, over the phone wire, turn all his account into hers, leaving nothing in it for him, some $6000.00 total, adding to her already sizeable sum of $4000.00. She took his keys and left.

She was driving out of state heading east, to her cousins in a small town called Roseville, somewhere in Michigan. She didn't know where exactly this town was. Just that it was close to Detroit.

She had always wanted to go there, the stories of the clubs, and night life. It all made her dream of a world where it was never hot. The days were cool and full of fun, trees and water every where. This is what she wanted, and now that she was made new, made whole she would have everything she wanted.

The next few days were spent driving east through Arizona, New Mexico, then Texas in hopes of getting through to Arkansas as fast as possible. She had early on decided to drive a little below the posted limits to keep from attracting attention to herself, sleeping during the day, then diving at night.

She stopped this morning at a roadside truck stop called the wayside, it had a large motel with a swimming pool, car and truck wash, a place for the big tractors to be serviced for oil, tires and other needed road wear, and a very large café. While waiting for her room she stepped into the café and found it comfortable, ordered a cup of coffee, eggs with ham, patty sausage, cheese and hash browns, two biscuits and some southern gravy, "oh and extra sausage".

She had not stopped to eat for the last day or so, she had not been hungry, but she figured she needed to eat still. She was not sure why, but she knew if she stopped eating, somehow being out in the day would be harder for her, she certainly did not want to wind up like her benefactor.

So when the order did come, and the waitress stood there for a moment after setting the food down, she was a little uncertain what was about to happen. She tried to eat but the waitress just stood there watching... She looked up at her and noticed there were several other staff people watching her, odd.

"May I help you?" she asked.

"Hunnie" began the waitress, "we just wanted to see if ya could really eat all that food er' not"

Selena looked down, and what she didn't realize was just how much she had ordered, eggs it seemed came as a set of 4, 5 sausage patties, a large bowl of gravy and 3 biscuits.

"Oh..." Selena replied, "guess I will be taking some of this with me when I leave"

She smiled to the waitress, who just furled an eyebrow and made some noise that sounded like disdain.

"Whatever you like darling," said the waitress. "As long as you pay fer it, here's yer bill"

So much for her low profile thought Selena. She sat there eating as best she could, watching the others from where she sat, the truckers watching her in return. She stopped the waitress on one of her many passes to check about coffee, and asked about cigarettes. She had developed a craving for them, but so far every type she has tried has left her regretting the effort. The waitress said all she had were cloves, and offered one to Selena, then dropped a book of matches on the table.

She sat there for a while smelling the sweet scented paper of the cigarette, then put it between her lips, and licked them, a sweet taste no less, this she thought to herself 'I like it so far'. She struck a match and watched it burn for a moment then placed the flame against the end of her "smoke". A few deep drags latter and it was lit, she inhaled lightly at first then a little deeper. This was a very strong smoke indeed, but it was filling that need in her she has been craving, this cigarette would do the trick.

"Pardon me," she asked the waitress again, "where do you get these around here?"

"Over at the counter," said the waitress, "when you check out ask the tendr' fer em, they keep em in stock fer me and a few others that come in here at night."

That was reassuring. After finishing the clove she took her doggie bag, and checked out. Asking for 4 packs of the cloves, she figured she would need to have a small stock of them for the road, and then bought a Zippo, fluid, flints and wicks. She didn't want to be without, then thought about it and bought 2 more packs of cloves.

She took her bag and headed to the room for the day, she noticed one of the truckers following her. As fate would have it, his room was right next to hers. Selena hoped that he would be leaving soon, that he would not stand there at his door watching her open hers.

"Y`all need help with that stuff" he asked.

"No, it's ok..." began Selena, but it was too late, He started walking over and said. "It's no trouble, really."

Selena tensed preparing for the worst, but he just took her key with a smile and opened the door for her, holding it open so she could step inside. The sun was coming up and began to light the room with a redness only a Texas morning could give it. He smiled, nodded his head with the word "Mama" And started walking away.

"Wait... my name is Selena, I was wondering if you were going to be here, at the hotel all day? I mean, would you like to come in for a bit?"

"Well, I just dropped my load, and am waiting for my next order, spos' I could hang about if ya like... what'ca have in mind?"

He smiled at her, with a bit of fire in his eyes, his intent visible in his stance. The bulge growing there was all too available. Smiling back at him, eyes covering the length of his body from cowboy hat covered head to his brass tipped cowboy boots... She decided the food though she had eaten almost all of it, didn't fill her needs. This one should however do nicely.

She told herself she would only take a little, not a lot. Like her benefactor had done to her, just a little, so as not to kill again... the doctors' face flashed in her minds eye. The moment of his death... she shook it off.

He stepped up and asked if she was Ok, as the memory was fading. Selena said, 'Yea' and stepped to one side to let him in, then looked about to see if anyone was watching. She thought for a moment that she saw herself down below, no...it couldn't be, and it's just a shadow.

The door now closed, Selena turned around and found him standing there watching her with the heavy bags still in her arms.

"Here" he said, "let me take that off'n your hands"

He stepped up and took the bags then sat them down on the small table next to the bathroom doorway. Turning, this big Texan moves closer, his intentions clear.

"Here now," he began, "little lady, let's see if I still have ma touch..."His hands move round her waist, his lips coming close to hers, one hand up and then the bra is loose... lips part and he smiles at himself. "Yep, still got it"

This young buck swaggered a bit and did some fancy foot work as if two stepping by himself, then asked. "You ever line dance missy, me I love ta dance, keeps the ol' rick'ster in shape, been dancin' now for 5 years here and there, steppin' out to cut some sawdust where ever I can."

She watches him move in time to some song only he could hear. Selena found herself remembering the song that Justin loved to dance too, 'boot scootin' boogie', and how he hated it when she would call him a fag when that song would come on, calling it 'poop shootin' boogie'. If he were drunk enough, he would beat her and show her what that kinda talk did to him. In the end she knew she had hit on the truth, that he could not bring himself to accept, that big western outlaw ego of his, could not admit he was gay.

Selena laughed a little to herself and let her clothes fall to the floor. When he turned to see what was so funny, the 'Rick'ster found her already falling on the bed cooing that he join her, it didn't take long for him to strip and comply.

It's nightfall before she moves again, Rick lay sleeping on the bed next to her, completely "tuckered out" as he put it, she had been unstoppable and demanded he perform 'til she was ready to sleep. He was hard put to the task, but in the end found all the encouragement he could in her talk of travel. How she wanted to have Rick follow her up north, so he could take care of her needs all the way there, him being 'a real man'.

Rising and dressing she opened her doggie bag and began eating what was left of her breakfast. Cold and congealed, it was still good.

She stepped outside to watch the sun set. The colors gold, orange, blood and the ocean all in one place, as brilliant as any sky she had ever seen before. No even more so, it seemed to her that the colors of the sky were alive and dancing to her very whim. She knew this was not true, but the fantasy was nice.

She lit a clove cigarette and took a deep drag, feeling the smoke move down into her lungs and burn the tissue. She almost coughed but held it back...Then she looked at her 'smoke' and let out all the held smoke in one breath.

She was celebrating, she had taken this cowpoke to bed and, he was still alive. She was happy about that, but still she felt like something was wrong. She kept playing the days events over and over in her head, each beginning and every end, and they were all the same.

Something was missing from each encounter, and every time she realizes what it was she quickly decided that could not be it. That it was just that she was still in shock over the doctor's death, that she could not be held accountable for that either, but she remembers calling him there and begging him to do what was done.

She tried to shake it away and in the end was able too, but when she looked up her smoke had burned completely to the butt. Turning to the room, ready to pack and leave this place she found Rick standing there watching her, he was without shame, in the doorway in his briefs and hat only.

"You alright darlin', somethin' botherin' ya? Hell if we're to be travelin' fer ah spell we should get to know each other, you know so as not to get on the others nerves?"

What he didn't know was he was already bothering her, the look of him was a constant reminder of Justin, the way he talked, moved, and sang while having sex. No he would not be with her long, if he even made it through the night. Even now her hunger to feed was growing and she knew she could not hold it off long, that's when it hit her.

"Tell me rick'ster, is there anyplace in town you could take a girl so she could be close to the dead. You know like a really old cemetery, one with graves going back to the 1700th century if possible?"

He stood there looking as masculine as he could in briefs and cowboy hat, smoking a self rolled cigarette. Thinking of all the places they could go after the sun went down, that would still have gates open to the public. Then he remembered the cemetery next to the freeway just passed the viaduct. That one had no gates and a really creepy part back close to the water way, where the tombs dated back before the Alamo.

After dressing, they drove over and parked the car in an empty lot near the viaduct. Walking a short pace then passed what looked like government housing, but they were just houses all built to the same statues quo, bland and simple, one story ranch style homes.

Across the street from this was the place he was taking her, there was a blue street light over the road that lead into this place of resting and there were quite a few kids playing close by. The sounds of laughter, and tag you're it, seemed to fill the night air without an echo, just carrying on the still air then silence once you had moved far enough away.

Ten minutes of walking after they entered the graveyard and then came the tree line he was making for. The woods there were dark and foreboding, not even the light of the few lamps hung willy-nilly along the road seemed to penetrate to deeply there in.

Rick was talking now but quietly as if trying to hide from everyone including the ghost that he feared lurked within. He spoke first of a bench that on Halloween night if you sat upon it before midnight you would not be-able to rise 'til the break of down. Held there in place by some spectral force or cursed soul lonely for company. They walked by it, and stood there for a bit talking about silly things like what if you had to go really bad, would the ghost let you up so you could go or hold you there, forcing you to either hold it or lose control right there in your pants.

The little role play he did of such an event was rather entertaining. They laughed and sat there making out for a bit, but Selena wanted a little more seclusion and prodded him to move in deeper. He was it seems genuinely reluctant to do so. Something about the witch's grave, this Selena had to see!

"This is it," Rick stated with more fear than he wanted to show, "where she was buried back in the early 1800's. Folks said she was turning the children from god, teachin' them shit about, Lilith and how she was really the first woman made by god and shit.

"Don't know how much of that is true, but I do know that one night the people here bouts went to her home and roped her up good. Dragged her body to the center of town and burned her there alive rather than let her live.

74

"The priest, when he found out was horrified by what his congregation had done, and had this here tomb build for her, the school teacher, from the church funds. Latter that year some of the towns' folk came up missing, and everyone blamed it on the witch in the grave. So they came out and walled up the entrance so as to keep her spirit from wandering about."

Selena and Rick moved to the top where the stone had been cut. There was what looked like hermitic symbols. The only one still visible at all looked like the same one you see on the backs of cars that the masons drive.

They moved down to the entrance. This grave was interesting as it had two walls of stone back filled with earth to the left and right of the tomb, a nice grass turf growing right up to the walled up entrance, and right in the center of that walled up entrance was a small hole. No debris visible on the inside, but plenty right out in front under the hole.

"Looks like she wants out, "Said Selena teasing Rick. He begins to back away, his fear of this place more apparent than he would like.

"Look here missy that just aint funny, lots of folks go missin' out here at night and I for one would like to get moving."

The crack in his voice is almost comical. Selena moves towards him and undoes her shirt, showing him that he was right. She had not put her bra back on. Selena let her breast breathe in the stale wind that picked up the very second she finished undoing her blouse. His eyes fell on the beauty of them under the moon light and again he was ready to strut for her, saying.

"Alright, but we got to make this fast, the police, they drive through here from time to time."

Soon they were both completely undressed and she had him on the ground riding him like a stallion. She could feel the hunger building in her, and kept telling herself, "don't kill em, just take what you need and leave." But deep inside she knew it was not going to happen that way.

Soon all she could hear was the sound of water in the little brook that was very close, bubbling down its little path, going where ever little brooks go. Not even the sound of her breathing or his panting, calling out to her as if she were a goddess. She felt him release inside of her, what did she care, she was dead now right... Still she rode him and then began kissing him, he tried to pull away but she had him pinned. She was watching herself this time. She knew she was in control and completely helpless to stop what was happening.

He went to scream and she covered his mouth with hers. She began to kiss him harshly, sucking up his tongue inside her mouth. He was shaking his head screaming into her mouth. His eyes opened to their fullest, the whites and the pupil all that are visible.

The feeling of his body convulsing under hers, the wild bucking, and thrusting that it created beneath her only lead to her pulling on him harder, she was in completed control of his entire body. She pulled all the blood into two area's of his body and both were now deep insider her. She didn't want the moment to end and drained him of all he had by biting off his tongue and drinking deeply from the wound it left. She held the blood in his erection, forsaking that little bit so she could continue to enjoy the moment to its completion.

When she notice the body had grown cold she got up and dressed, the look on his face was worse than the doctors. She did not want to spend the night digging again. She remembered the sound of flowing water and picked up the rick'ster body, and carried it until she found the slop of the stream and walked it down to the waters edge. She was certain no one would find it here, not for some time.

She laid it out, his body. Again the feeling that this body had been mummified over a hundred years ago griped her. The drawn and brittle flesh a testimony to her hunger, the oddity of it was that his pride was still fresh and undamaged the way the rest of his body had been.

It still seemed alive, only now it was going limp, the blood that had been held there in by her will, for her pleasure, was now moving to the bottom of his body. It never made it, so dry was the waist of this man that it was absorbed into his flesh before it could get there. She covered the body with old leaves and branches, some dirt and stuff from the brook and then more leaves.

Done, she ran down the water way and came out close to the viaduct where the car was waiting...

!NOOOOOOO!

There was a toe-truck hooking up to the front of the car and two cop cars close to it. They were talking, and laughing but she could not make out what was being said... Now she would have to walk back to the hotel! The only thing about this that didn't suck was it was his car being towed! Good. She would not have to drive it back and possibly answer questions about where he was, she could now tell anyone that asked that he tried to rape her and that she got out of the car and ran back, and needs to leave before he shows up again.

It was almost sun rise when she did get back, and she knew she could not stay or be out in the light of day much longer, but mostly that she could not stay. She decided to drive as far as she could and find a rest stop, she left the money for the bill on the dresser, and left.

Half way through the day she found driving to be almost completely unbearable, but her journey had led her further north with each passing mile, the number of trees on either side of the road increasing hourly. Around 3pm she could take it no more and found a place to pull of the road and park under a large tree that provided an enormous amount of shade. Shade she was very happy to have.

She sat there for close to an hour before anyone stopped to see if she was aright or if the car itself was abandoned. Her visitor was a state trooper. He was very tall, sharply chiseled. He looked like a movie star out of some cheap flick where the cop was supposed to be this massive hunk, that all the woman were all to ready to spread for. This was that cop, she smiled at him as he walked up, herself having exited her car long before he pulled up. She was lying on the grass, blanket spread beneath her, pillow over her head enjoying the breeze that was blowing.

"Mama, everything ok" he asked.

"Yea I am fine," Selena began, "my car got ah little hot, so I pulled off under the shade to let it cool down, you know. I figure I will try to finish my trip once the sun goes down."

"Well it will be dark in about an hour, you should probably get movin'," said the officer, "Before the sun does go down."

She sat up and looked at the cop. How odd she wondered, are there others like her here, and he was just trying to protect her, or did he want her to start driving so he could pull her over. He did keep looking at her plate after all.

"You from Arizona mama?" he asked.

"Yea," said Selena, "I am heading to Detroit to visit family."

"How long you been driven?"

He moves around the side of the car looking at it, peering inside the windows, what's he looking for?

"Is there something wrong officer?" She asked.

"Not so wrong that, we can't come to an arrangement." He replied.

Ah, that's his game. He is looking for a quickie here on the side of the road, out here in the middle of no where. She stands up and figures she might as well get this over with and begins to walk towards him.

He stops and draws his firearm then points it at her and yells. "Stay where you are, don't move!" and she stops dead where she is.

"Where did you get that blood on you from, mama?"

She looks down and to her horror, her pants and lower shirt have blood all over them, blood she had left in Rick. She stammers for a moment and searches her mind for any excuse that will come to the surface quick enough to be believable, but not sound condemning. She stood there thinking so hard that her window of opportunity passed and the officer was approaching her. He was talking on his radio to cispatch, calling in for a tow-truck and backup. Something about, 'he found the suspect'.

This will not do.

"Officer it's not what you think," tried Selena, "you have to believe me, this is not what it looks like." The words were all too weak and she knew that she either had to escape or kill him, which this cop would not let her go for just any reason. Her excuses now would be hollow and vain. She tried to step up again but found that his gun was again brought up right back at the ready and pointing at her. He stood there holding her at bay, but never called for her to get down or put her hands behind her back, something was wrong, very wrong.

Within minutes the backup and tow-truck were there. Each man coming closer and looking at her and the items in her car, they never opened the door, or really looked around. The ccnversation that was being had was just low enough she could not make out what was being said. All she caught were bits here and there.

"... Blood on ... ... here ... ... was laying on ... grass. She's ... ... mark, we ... ... a ... ... her"

This was looking and sounding worse with every passing minute. She had to do something now or it would be too late. She knew somehow if she didn't get away she would never see the light of day again.

"Mama" began the cop, "we need you to lie down on the ground and put your hands on the back of your head, now!"

If she complied, this could be the last chance she got to get free. She figured that if she came into physical contact with him she could over power him and win out in a struggle, even if the others came to save him. She would get the gun and get away. This would however make her more of a criminal than she already was, what with two murders to her name already, but how could they really know that?

She laid down face first on the grass and put her hands where they had told her too. That's when everything went black.

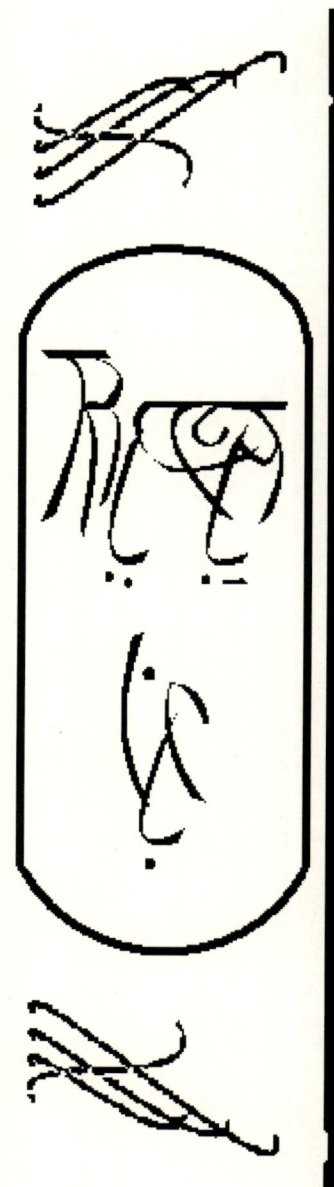

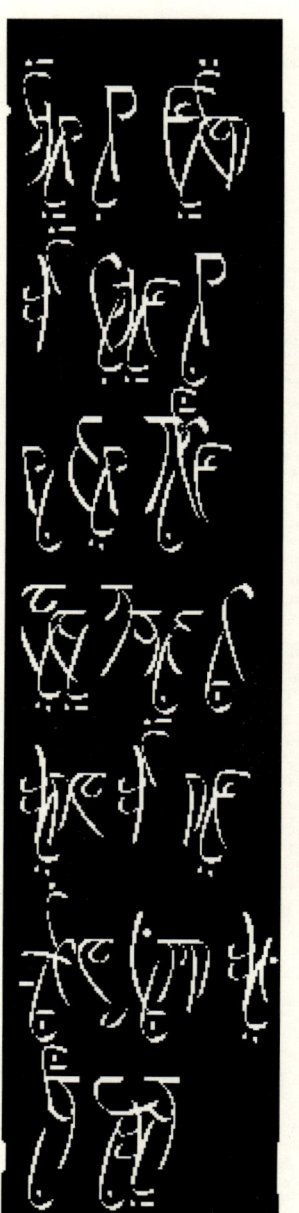

Chapter Six – Hell in the Big Easy

'Still not knowing my true inner self

I sit and talk at length with the dead

Not knowing that I am alone

The shades on words put for holding on mental shelf

Still feeling in darkness's embraces no dread'

-Vodalok-

When she came to, the room she was in was dark and seemed a bit stuffy, like it was small or full of things. It was warm in a way that either meant she had been here awhile or there were others here with her. She tried to call out but found her mouth fully stuffed and gagged to keep her silent. There was neither moving air, nor any sounds of motion save for her own struggles to get free. "Where the hell am I," was her only thought?

She struggled to remember anything at all, and found that all she could make out was being hit over the head from behind after getting on the ground. There were vague memories of them picking her up, of being dumped into something, but not through a car door.

After a short time she was able to get her hands free, and then the gag came next. Standing as best she could, trying not to make noise she found she was in a small room, and that she was not alone.   She counted the bodies of at least 5 other girls, all like her, stripped of all clothing. She was standing there thinking, trying to figure out where she was and why. When she realized that she was very soar between her legs, she again had faint flashes of things, flashes of them raping her over and over, tossing her in here.

The throbbing in her head was leaving, but was being replaced by a need to feed. It was a pain she was starting to learn to recognize fast. The pain of it was almost sickening. Fighting as best she could to not pass out again, she decided to take a little, not much, just enough from one of the other girls in this little black hell. She moved in close to the one next to her, who was flat out onto her back and rolled over on top of her.

Slowly she straddled her unconscious form and felt the softness of her sex on hers, and paused for a moment to slowly move back and forth over her. The tingling of her tuft of hair moving against this unknown persons hair was something very new and inviting, something she would need to put off for now. Her hands moved up the length of this girl whose body she was soon to violate, over her breast, pausing for just a moment there to feel the nipples, which were strangely hard and responsive to her touch. Then up over this girls shoulders 'til they were resting on the floor on either side of her foods head. She leaned in allowing her breast to tease against this others, then press in soft but firmly 'til she could bring her mouth down on her neck.

Up until now she had only fed from men who were inside of her, each fully aroused and lost in the moment. She wondered if she could feed this way and have it satisfy her, and went to bit down.

"Uhhhhhh..."

The softness of the breaths being taken in by the girl under her, made her stop. She sat there over her not moving for the longest of times to see if she would speak or make another sound, but nothing more followed, save her breathing that seemed normal. Still not confident that this one is still 'sleeping', she whispered into the girls' ear.

"Are you awake?"

She waited and breathed slowly, each breath held as if baited in anticipation, moving her flesh in time with the one under her, she was not certain if she wanted her awake or unconscious for this.

"Yes..." came her foods reply," I have been for some time, but was too afraid to say anything, and when you ... when you climbed on top of me I couldn't, didn't want to resist. It was nice to be handled softly for once"

Selena surprised by the response asked her." What do you mean handled softly for once... where are we"

She asked this question momentarily forgetting her needs, hoping to get some answers.

"They come in from time to time," replied the girl, "either to feed us or fuck us, either way they're always rough, sometimes very rough, number 3 has been unconscious for two days now, I think she might be dead... she wont sit up or say anything... you must be new, cause moving around is not permitted."

"Not permitted... what does that mean. Is there a toilet in here? How many are here?"

Her voice started to rise, she needed to get out of here, but from around her she could feel hands on her and the sound of at least 3 others 'sssshhhing' her. Where in the 9 hells of Dante was she?

"You must be quite please, if you want to live you must be quite, they will kill you, they don't care, they'll do it right here. Please for all our sakes please be quite..."

This voice was behind her, but more in her head than in her ears. As she turned about, she realized her eyes had started to adjust to the darkness in here. There must have been 15 girls in this small room, all of them completely nude, on pillows and mattresses laid out all over. In the very far corner was the toilet she wanted to know about, but there was a lock on the lid keeping it shut. Two girls were chained to the far wall hung by their wrist, their toes not even touching the floor.

The more her eyes adjusted the more she realized she must have been the oldest person in here, the youngest looked 17 at the least.

Standing up again, she could hear the voice of her would be donor below her. "Please don't stand you'll step on someone, its better if you move about on your hands and knees... "

"I don't need to crawl around like an animal in here I will be fine. Why are those two on the wall and why is the toilet locked?" Selena was growing more and more angry by the moment, not just because of the condition these girls, that she was being kept in, but because they seemed too afraid to do anything to stop it. When the girl under her spOke next it was more surprise than anything.

"You can see that?"

"Yes," Was Selena's blunt reply.

"How...?" asked her food, "those two and the toilet are on the other side of the room and, there is no light in here at all... the best I can do is see just a few inches in front of myself if I really squint hard"

"I am not like you." Selena replied bluntly again. She moves toward the wall, stepping over those on the ground. She is no longer trying to hold her voice down either, talking at a normal level as she moves toward those chained so harshly.

Her donor asks her very simply, "If you're so special, why are you here?"

Selena stops and thinks about what happened that day. She knows they abused her while she was either out cold from the hit to her head or from drugs. But what ever the cause, she would not be here much longer, nor would these girls.

"Just know that they caught me with my pants down, and drugged me to keep me here. Now that I am awake they will pay for what they have done... I need you all to move to one side, get as close as you can to one another and away from the door. As soon as I get these two down make sure they are kept safe."

Selena felt like a super hero, this was going to be fun. The chains seemed so easy to pull out of the wall, not in very well, felt to her as if they were put in... in a rush without care. She carried the first over to where the rest were gathering and laid her down with them. Then she took the other girl down... she was not breathing and her body was all stiff...

"How long have these two been up here?" This question was almost yelled.

The others jump and a few start to openly cry, begging her to stop. That she was going to get them all killed, and then came the sound of the door being opened. Selena picked up the chains from the dead girls body and held them at the ready, slung just over her shoulder, chains, body and all.

So sudden was the assault when the door opened, that Selena was momentarily blinded and deafened! There was the blinding light from the halogen flash lights, they had them at the ready and shown them in as they moved passed the door. Music was likewise piped into the room so loud that it felt as if her ears would bleed from the sudden thunder coming from the speakers hidden in the walls and ceiling. Even with all this she could still smell them.

She uses the chains as a bludgeon and swung them round in front of her catching the first of the men that was approaching off guard and knocking him to the ground. His light hitting the wall and going out. The two guys behind him stepped back as they saw her move forward, they went to either side of her with cattle prods and started herding her to the back of the room.

The pain of the prods mixed with the hunger she was feeling and the emptiness of her body lead to one thing, as they came in close to put her down, her animal instincts kicked in. She let fly the chains then grabbed one of the prods and pulled it forward, her other hand, nails out, dug into the face of the unknown assailant. His screams of pain and surprise startled the next two into the room, causing them to fall back. The one that she got her hands on, fell to the floor his light showing his face to be torn... almost completely off, one of his eyes hanging out of its sockets!

Pulling back from Selena they watched as she knelt down over him and pulled him up, his struggles failing to do anything other than anger her, she bit into his neck. His body convulsed as he tried to get free and slowly gave way to no motion at all, he was dead. In shock they stood there and didn't move 'til she looked up at them. Her naked body was covered in blood, the burns from the cattle prods healing before their very eyes, beneath her, their very dead companion.

She hissed at them, (the sound was more animal... no, demonic than human and echoed in a room were no sound carried) and made to pounce, but held back watching them jump. The fear in them was very tangible, both in her nose and on her tongue. She began to laugh, the fear they were feeling was giving her energy as well, she could not believe how much energy she was beginning to consume. The laughter, the look of her, in her eyes served to un-nerve her captures further.

It was the sound of the new voice that came from behind them that snapped them and Selena back to their senses. It allowed them to regain themselves. Behind them holding a shotgun was the cop that had started this, only now his head was covered in a leather mask fit tight to his face with a crown of long metal spikes sewn into the top of it. The bondage wear that adorned his body was covered in rings and hooks, all of which had some sort of whip, prod or cutting utensil hanging from them. He looked every bit the part of some demonic chef come to coOk her flesh.

He bellowed orders at the three remaining and they cowered before him with their lights trained on Selena, he stepped forward and leveled the shotgun at her and in a very soft voice told her tc be still or he would shoot her. In from behind him came two more men and they pulled two of the girls out of the room, Selena watched as they went with them all limp, seemingly lifeless into the hallway.

She moved to stop them, but for some reason found herself against the wall, suddenly in a great deal of pain. Then came the thunder clap from the shotgun going off, the spray of blood that was in the air in front of her... where she had been standing? The blood just hanging there looking like everything had been frozen in time. Somehow he was now in her face, now in the hall way, now in a very bright room strapped to a table, as all this took place the one thing that held in her mind was the utter lack of sound save for the deafening ringing in her ears that came with each new flash of shifting reality, then it all went black.

Slowly to her ears came that thing she thought lost to her, sound, but it was sometime before it was discernable, faded and full of cotton was the texture of the noise that became words 'til she could understand.

"So how come she is still alive, a shot like that should have taken the fight right out of her forever." This was the voice of the cop.

"I'm not really sure, something bout her is just wrong, I have never seen blood work like this before. It's like each blood cell is a thing alive... all on its own, completely independent of the rest of the body, working for the body. It's the damnedest thing I've ever seen." This voice was new, soft, scared, young, but familiar...?

The conversation was coming to her from somewhere, but it was not close, the voices were echoing of walls. At least that's what it sounded like, but not to far away, another room?

Selena could not tell, she felt pain where her stomach should be but could not move to look or feel herself where she was hurting. She tried to open her eyes but they didn't seem to want to respond. Suddenly the effort to move or even open her eyes left her very tired and she fell back into darkness.

"No! I'm telling you, she appears to be regenerating the damage done to her. I have never seen anything like this, to be honest with you it's scaring the fuck out of me, people don't regenerate! And after seeing what she did to Dan, I am beginning to think she is not even human, not like you and me."

Again she hears talking from somewhere else, that familiar young voice, who is he? Are they talking about her? They must be, it sounds like it, she can't be sure, why can't she move? At least the pain is much, much less than it used to be. Straining her senses to hear more, she could feel her body fighting against the effort but she managed to stay awake long enough to here what was said next.

"Well soon it won't matter," said the cop, "we are selling her to the General, and then his people can deal with her freak ass. Have you been feeding her? Doing anything that would keep this thing, alive, anything at all?"

"No," said the young voice, "if anything I bleed it once a day trying to kill it, but... it seems to be very resilient, replacing lost blood almost as

fast as I can bleed it out. If I didn't know any better I would say we have ...
a vampire in the box."

"Now wouldn't that just make the general's day," said the cop.
"Something he can send in some place and have it kill at will and not worry
about it dying."

She knew then they were talking about her, but this business of
being sold bothered her to no end. How was she going to get out of this?

"So what do we do with all those other girls," who was this? How
many men were in the room next to her? "If the buyer is backing out we
can't keep them, nor can we let them go."

Then the cop said flatly. "If we don't find another buyer in say two
days... feed em to the sharks."

Slowly she could hear two of them walking away as the third went
about doing work in the room beyond. She struggled to move, but simply
couldn't, her body was still unwilling to move. Fearing that she would pass
out again, she tried to relax and waits to see if anyone came into the room
she was in. After a few hours she could tell someone was coming. The
steps seemed to stop just beyond where her head was lying, was she close
to a door? Then it opened that door she was close to and it was very small,
she felt the table beneath her beginning to move on rollers. It was then it
registered where she was, the one had said she was in 'the box'... she has
been in a morgue all this time!

She could feel hands on her, through the bag she now knows she
has been in, the sound of the zipper being opened. She kept her eyes
closed but watched him as best she could. He was undoing buckles that
held her arms tight to her sides and her legs from moving. All in all she
counted about 10 heavy buckles undone from her shoulders down to her
feet. She ventured a peek at this guy that was undoing her and to her
horror it was him... the guy that she took the blood from, the blood that
made her what she is now.

It was Stephen!

She blinked and opened her mouth to scream and when her eyes
opened again it was not him, just some guy wearing glasses looking almost
exactly like Keifer Sutherland from that movie... Dark Town or something.
His reaction to seeing her eyes open was not expected either, but it saved
his life. He slides back and up against the other cells, his mouth opening,
almost a smile as he spoke.

"You're awake... oh my God, thank Christ above! "He made the sign of the cross and stepped back just a bit more, this time to the left. He reached for a robe that was on the counter there and handed it to Selena.

"I didn't know if you would survive," he said, "but whoever you are, whatever you are, you can't stay here any longer. You have to get out, before they come back with the general. Before they sell you off and you're never heard from again."

"Why should I trust you, you work with them, "Selena hissed at him, "for all I know you could be setting me up?"

"Nooooo," he said, "you have to believe me! Look, you're probably the only one that can get those other girls out of here. I have been giving you about a pint of blood every day, and it seemed to help you heal, in like a matter of a week or so. It was everything I could do to hide what I was doing, but they found out you were still alive and healing, I had to do, say something."

Selena sat up and took the robe he offered, the fact that he turned his head away did allow her room to give him just a little bit of trust. Slowly getting to her feet he kept talking and staying out of her reach.

"Look, there are keys and an envelope of money on the table by the door over there, it's everything we took from you plus what was supposed to be the down payment for you to the Bose, I kinda got it out of the safe without him knowing and put it in there.

"I am sorry there are no clothes for you other than that robe, but it's the best I can do, they burn everything else. For the other girls there is a box of robes in the truck that the keys are for. I can lead you to them and then the truck, but you have to promise me something..."He paused and turned to look at her. She regarded him coldly, wondering what he could want. She could tell from looking into his eyes that this one had seen too much to walk away from this life, but enough to know he was sick of it almost unto death.

"What?" Selena asked.

"One of those girls is my sister, give her this once you're free. Her name is Liz; get her out of here and to safety. As long as she is safe I don't care what happens to me, they can't hold me in fear anymore... please."

He held out another envelope to her and it had the name 'Liz' on it. He was trembling all over, and getting paler by the second. She could not tell if he was about to puke or if he was himself finally dying from the stress of being force to work here like this, doing whatever it was that they had him doing.

"Why did they use her against you?" Selena asked, "What are you to them that they needed to force this job on you?"

"I am a doctor, and a plastic surgeon, they force me to change people's faces so they could get them into or out of the country. When they are not bringing criminals into the country they are selling girls out of it. I am so sick of this. They brought Liz here and threatened to kill her or sell her off if I didn't do as they wanted. What could I do...? I love my sister to much to lose her to either fate."

Selena thought to herself she would rather be dead than be force to live like these girls were, her brother would have been doing her a favor, but she kept that to herself. She took both envelopes and the keys, and then paused at the door.

She turned round and asked him why he doesn't come with her. He simply replied that someone had to stay behind and make sure they weren't followed. Then he opened up a cabinet to reveal several large propane tanks hidden away under the sink, strapped to them was a single stick of dynamite, with an electronic box taped to it, he pulled out of his pocket a similar device and said all the gas mains in the building were open just enough to fill each room with gas. Selena turned and he led her to where the others were.

Upon opening the door he called out to Liz and she answered, he explained that they were going to be free but that they must get up and go now, without stopping, they must follow Selena For a moment it looks to Selena that they would not listen and remain where they are. But one by one they stand up, shielding their eyes and file out into the hallway. Selena tells them to take each others hands, to not let go, no matter what.

The doctor puts Liz's hand in hers so that she is guarantied to be with her no mater what, then he leads them out to the truck that is waiting out side.

The sun had begun to set and there was a light breeze blowing, it smelled of water but the sky was clear, she asked where they were and he replied as he helped get everyone into the back of the truck, (a u-hall of all things) that they were just outside of New Orleans.

Looking back again all she could see was Stephen standing there frowning at her. She closed her eyes and the Doc was again where he should be. She paused trying to understand why she kept seeing Stephen looking at her with such anger, only to see the doctor again.

He urged her to go as fast as she could, that he would be Ok, and that they just needed to go. His sister was crying almost screaming at him now to come with her, not to stay, and he almost did then he looked back, and slouched. When he looked back at his sister he simply said 'I can't' and walked away.

It was easy for Selena to restrain her and close the door on the truck. She got in and started it up. As they were driving away, she saw in the mirrors another line of cars heading into the compound, but none of them followed her.

Among the cars heading in there were two limos. A short time later there was an enormous fireball in the sky, then the force of the sound from that explosion. Selena just kept driving.

It was almost daylight before she stopped in the hills of Arkansas to stretch her legs, She walked round to the back of the truck and opened it up, all those girls were huddled up near the front cab, and trying to stay warm... they looked at her with eyes full of fear and confusion. Stepping up into the back of the truck she walked up to them, only to have them try to get away by pulling tighter to one another.

"They won't let you near them anymore," came Liz's voice. "They're afraid of you"

Selena turned and Liz was standing there watching her, she went past Selena to the rest of the girls and opened the little window from the box to the cab. She pulled one of the robes off the others that they were using to keep warm and put it on, and continued to speak all matter-of-factually. "We need to get clothes and keep going. I can't imagine that they won't come after us."

Selena just watched as she knelt down and did her best to comfort them, telling them it would be Ok and that they would be safe soon, promising them that they would be able to go home soon. She then turned back to Selena, looking into her eyes, as if thinking something, then spoke.

"We should help them go to the bathroom, then find some place to get clothes from, it's not going to be easy for us, and with us all being in robes you know, we are going to be very easy to spot."

Selena said "Leave that stuff to me. I have an idea of how we can get this done."

Liz asked. "What do you have in mind?"

Selena regarded her question for a bit, she knew that places like good will and the Salvation Army received donations all the time in large dumpsters or bins. All they had to do was find a place like that and wait 'til night to get what they needed and move on.

"We should stay together," Selena said, "for a while, 'til the others are stronger again. You know 'til they are able to be alone and not freak out at ever little thing. Then we should help them find their homes and get them to a doctor so they can heal inside."

Liz asked. "Your names Selena right?"

"Yea..." Selena replied, looking at Liz, wondering what was going on in her head.   Then Liz said it. "For a monster, you're alright." Liz smiled at her, warmly, like she had known Selena all her life, and then said. "Thanks for saving us..."

'For a monster', Selena thought to herself. This was the first time it had been said to her openly. But the words hurt more than she had expected them too. Here she was alive only because that guy had fed her behind the backs of his and her captures. He had understood what it was about her that was different and what was keeping her alive. How she didn't know but what she did know was that she was a monster of her own making, this thing she is, she did willingly.

For the briefest of moments she thought she heard his voice, Stephens... somewhere near by, calling to her out of his fever. She knew he was not near, but still... she could feel him calling to her.

It was a little while before she realized that she was being shaken. Liz was holding her arms and shaking her, just a little, calling her name. She let it slide and they started driving again. After another 15 minutes of driving they came to a small town where most people simply were not up and about yet. Slowly they drove through town and found what they were looking for. The church was small, it had been there for many years. The trees grown up around it told a story of at least 100 years of devotion and worship to a God that she found it harder and harder to believe in.

They pulled into the back lot and found the out-building that was the "store" where the needy would come to buy at gods prices clothes and food stocks.

It was not hard for Selena to get the door open. She and Liz lead the others in quietly telling them to get dressed quickly and not to spend too much time worrying about fashion. For the most part that request was followed, and once they were all dressed they started picking out a few extra bits for changing latter so they didn't have to wear the same things over and over. They all picked out what they could and collected from the dry goods as much food as each could carry. The last thing that was taken was an old grill for preparing what they collected. They figured they could use that to cook what food they had gathered in the pots and pans that were collected as well.

Father Raymond woke, to the sounds of movement in the store next to his bedroom. He rose, telling his wife to go back to sleep. They had been burgled before and each time he had been able to reason with the 'would be thief', and help them, in a way that would keep them out of jail, and from becoming a sinner in the eyes of god. His wife loved him and knew in her mind he could handle whatever had happened, so she did as he asked.

Father Raymond moved through his home and towards the store, and stopped. Silently watching as 10 nude girls moved through the clothes, dressing and collecting food and other things, that one would need to live on, and with. For some reason he could not move and found himself transfixed by one of the girls in particular. She seemed to be in charge and was quietly giving orders to the others that all but one seemed to follow out of fear, more than anything else.

She was about 5ft tall with thick coarse black hair, which was cut short. He watched as her body seemed to glide rather than move, through his store and its goods, pointing to this or that, asking those others to collect them.

When all the others had left the store, he let out a breath, realizing he had not breathed a single breath, for almost 2 min. This was enough for the one in charge who was left behind to notice him. But rather than confront him, or say a single word, she took out a small wad of money and sat it down on the table next to her and moved to leave the store.

Selena knew something was not right, but it was not 'til all the girls were all back on the truck before she saw the priest standing there watching them. She didn't let on but pulled out her envelope and left a large amount of money on the table were he could see it then turned to leave.

"Mama you left something behind" he called out.

He was not sure why he was doing it, but he could not control the urge to give this money back to her. Before she replied as she slowly turned around to look him over, he questioned his actions. Was he doing this so he could have one last look at her? Was it the energy in the air around her that seemed to crackle and snap, making him with out reason love her on site? He though of his wife in the other room and for a moment, for the very first time in 6 years since they had been married, he wished he was not. That she was not in the bed waiting for him, loving him. He hung his head in shame.

She stopped and turned around. He was standing there holding the money out to her, the smile on his face soft and full of compassion. Her eyes covered the whole of him, taking in everything there was to see, he was young, very clean and tightly kept. Blue eyes and blonde hair, not much over 6 foot if 6ft at all, but over all very healthy, he could not weigh more than 175 lbs. And he stood there in a night robe holding the money out to her.

"Mama you left this behind." He said again.

"No," she replied.

The sound of her voice cutting into him like a knife, eating at his will and raising within him a hunger for her he could not explain. Even though he was lost to himself and the world he still heard her words clearly, eating each with a passion bordering on insanity, just to hear her as she continued. "I left it for the things we took, keep it for those here that need it."

Father Raymond fought with himself over what was happening, and begged himself to just let it go, to go back inside, but he remembered the bit from the news the night before. About the 15 killer women on the run, that had kidnapped and murdered an Army General, several Saudi business men, and two survivors. A young plastic surgen from southern California, and Texas State Trooper that looked way to big to be kidnap able by anyone let alone a truck load of terrorized and cloth less girls. This one before him is clearly the oldest.

The look on her face changed and he wanted so much to touch her cheeks, to feel her lips. Then she started to speak again and he fell further in love with her, hating himself for it, but knew he would believe whatever she said or do whatever she asked.

"I'm afraid I don't know what you're talking about. Why would we be on the news?" Selena said, trying to play off any knowledge of what he might be inferring,

"Well it seems," he said, slowly moving forward, the money still out in front of him, "that there was a large explosion down in Louisiana just out side of New Orleans, the only survivor was a vacationing state trooper from Texas who said that a truck load of girls had abducted him and a few others and tortured them, then tried to kill em all by blowing them up."

This news she found actually shocked her! They were being blamed for being the kidnappers!

Slowly the expression on her face went from kind and friendly to anger, then began to change in a way he'd never seen a face change. It started to become ugly, monstrous, the shadows from the dark room moving and contorting over not just her face but her entire body. It started to vibrate and tremble, faster and faster as a terrorizing sound began to grow inside of her. Even though every nerve in his body screamed at him to run, all he could do was back away just a bit. He knew right away she was not, could not be human.

Her face contorted and a scream began to rise up into her mouth from some place deep, one that hurt her more as it grew. The priest started backing away, the smile gone, simple but quick words coming from his mouth, a prayer? She regained herself and looked back up to him, at first he seemed terrified but began to return to his normal self and appeared a bit relieved.

"Look priest, we were the ones kidnapped, we escaped, only barely. The brother of one of the girls out there died trying to protect us. We are just trying to get as far away as we can and not be found again, we don't want to hurt anyone..."

Whether he believed her or not, he stepped up and said a short prayer for her. Selena felt a bit nauseous as he did this but kept quite, not wanting to offend him or scare him again. He put the money in her shirt pocket careful not to touch her breast. She stopped his hand there, and pressed it close to her. He looked up into her eyes not sure what to say and she silenced him.

"If what you're saying is true than we need another vehicle to be driving about in, that u-hale is going to be a dead giveaway."

She took the money back out of her pocket still holding his hand to her breast. She put it in his robe pocket and then let his hand go. She pulled out another 3 grand and gave it to him saying. "I need you to get us a van nothing too fancy but something that will run and can carry 8 girls in some comfort without looking to conspicuous, can you do that?"

He just looked at her, she could not tell if he would do this, then he said "Ok". He then added. "There is a small farm out side of town, go there and wait for me, I will bring you the van and some fresh foods as well, it's Sunday so you will need to wait 'til after services. If you want I can do a short one for you and your friends there."

"That will be fine, I am sure they will appreciate that. But priest, I need you to remember one thing," she said this with her voice becoming stern and powerful. The vengeance that was being hinted at made the hair on his body stand up and send shivers down his entire body, she also noticed that this priest was aroused by the power in her voice, she took note of that and carried on.

"If you try to screw us, those girls out there won't be coming after you. Their all to battered to even look at you right now, I am not. I will kill you, in the most sinful way I can think of, do you understand "The 'do you understand' part was followed up by her stepping into him and grabbing his manhood through his robe. His shock, fear and instant orgasm told her all she needed. She whipped her hand off on his robe and turned to leave, looking back at him as she did, he had collapsed onto the floor and had begun to cry and pray at the same time.

His wife had always told him such things existed, that monsters and demons walked the earth and stalked the living and holy race of men. He had never believed her, and now, here was one in front of him and he had no idea what to do. Yet he could not help but be drawn, no, excited to the point of orgasm. At the sheer thought of being consumed by this thing from hell, and he hated himself even more. But he could not look away, he could not move away.

His wife was at the door looking in and to her surprise did not scream, she did not rush in to save her husband. She did however, back away into the living room. She picked up the phone and called Brother Ector. He would know what to do, and it was her responsibility to call, she had to report this.

"May God bless you, and the Mother protect you," came Brother Ector's voice, "what can I do for you?"

"Brother, this Mary, wife of Raymond, there is A Demon in our store, and I fear it has taken control of my husband."

"Mary, this is very important," Brother Ector's voice became very stern, "you need to get as much information as you can about it from him as you can. Only through vigilance can we do the Mothers work and lay her children to rest. Now go and watch, do your best not to be seen or heard. Once your husband is alone, learn what you can from him of these monsters plans. I am sending a team to your house. They should be there by sunset, May God and the mother guide and protect you."

As Mary hung up the phone she heard her husband crying and praying in the other room. When she got there he was crumpled up on the floor. It took 2 hours for her to console him and get him back up onto his feet and into the shower. He had a sermon to deliver. However every offer of aid to him was rebuked, or brushed aside by him. He would say nothing more than, "it is gods work I do, and it must be done if the innocent are to be kept safe."

She listened to his prayer as she got into the truck and started it. She listened to him praying as they drove away and could not seem to get his words out of her head even when they had finally reached the little farm he had told her about. In her mind all she could hear by that time was his prayer.

"Oh god in heaven who art above, deliver me from this sin that has touch my soul this morning. Give me strength to do what is right and keep my word to those in need and my vows to you. Free me from my lust that I may not wrong my house, your house, or my wife. Protect me on my errands today as I help these poor woman in need of your mercy and love, lay down on them the blessings of your healing hands that they may find peace in the world again and bring to them justice for the wrongs done to them. Oh Lord-God please deliver me from this sin that is in my mind and heart."

It wasn't 'til they were all inside and resting in little groups here and there, moving about trying to remember what it's like to be free that Selena finally allowed herself to rest. The girls began cleaning a bit, talking quietly amongst themselves, avoiding her, that sort of thing. It was not long after they had settled in that she noticed it was well after noon, that's when she noticed she was free of the echo of his prayers. "Just what" she thought, "the hell have I done to myself?

Looking up she found Liz sitting next to her holding her hand, the compassion in her eyes more than Selena could bear. She pulled her hand back and away, maybe a little too harsh but it made her point. Liz's look of defeat was pitiful, was she trying to reason with her or just get closer to her. Selena could not tell but right now didn't want any of it. She wanted a smOke.

She got up and went out to the truck and started going through her things, and was completely surprised to find a single pack of cloves stuck into the envelope with the money. She sat down in the cab watching the sun going down over the roof of this old two story farm, lit her smOke and took a very long drag on it. She felt the burn of the smOke in her lungs at the same time she felt the burn of the sun on her skin, and watched in detached wonder at the site before her. She was not burning, not like Stephen had, but it still felt like she was burning.

In the door of the house was Liz still watching her, tears in her eyes and rolling down her face, her breathing harsh and brOken between tears. Selena got up and walked over to her, took her hand and lead her to the back of the truck where they sat down so as not to be in the sun and watch the outside world for a bit.

"What do you want from me," Selena said after a few more drags of her smOke, "I mean, Ok so we were in that place together and we got out together, why is it you want me to be there for you now? You said yourself I am a monster, what could you possibly want from me?"

"I was the one you were laying on top of that day you were shot... I... I wanted to know if you... if you could ... would you touch me again..."

And there it was, Selena had wondered who she was several times since then but now she knew, and that little girl that was under her wants to be intimate with her, to feel her on top of her again. She is looking for some feeling of love in all this. Selena looked at her long and hard, feelings erupting inside of her as she did, thoughts of do it, take her, kill her, push her away, you can't, you must, please...

"Please," Selena heard Liz call, "when you do that you scar me so much... where are you when you do that."

Selena became very dizzy suddenly and almost passed out, she had to get up and away. Leaving the truck she headed inside. Reaching the door was the last thing she remembered. Several hours had gone by and Liz had taken her inside and laid her down in one of the beds upstairs, she must have had gotten the other girls to help her. To Liz's credit she was still dressed, to her credit there were no bite marks on Liz. Liz herself was now offering a plate of food to her, eggs, and what smelled of fresh mushrooms and green-peppers.

"Where did you get these things? We didn't get them from the church." Selena asked Liz.

Liz replied. "That barn has chickens and a small garden out back, in the basement of this place is another garden full of mushrooms, they grow their own here! It's so cool. I have always wanted to do things like that. We even got some fresh milk from the cow out there. That was fun, milking it and all. Several of us gave it a go and sort of made a small mess, but we got the hang of it and were able to get enough milk for everyone."

Selena smiled up at her and sat up to take the food that was certainly very nice smelling. But part of her wanted to retch at the smell of the food, this she hid as best she could. Liz sat on the side of the bed with her while she ate, watching her, a gleam in her eyes, and a smile that was way to warm.

"Liz you need to remember I am a monster, you said it, don't forget it. I am not something you want to get involved with. Forget being with a woman, go find yourself a good man and settle down and live a good life. Don't be a fool and go chasing dreams, you might just catch them and have those dreams... ruin your life."

With each word Liz's eyes filled with more water, 'til they finally burst and the soft pain reaching Selena's ears was unbearable, but she knew she could do nothing at this point without causing more problems. So she sat up, pushed out of bed and went to head out the door. Liz moved to block her and she didn't have the heart to harm her.

"Selena I know I don't have a right to ask you this, but I need to know, were you trying to just... you know eat me or were you looking for something else when you wOke up the other morning."

Interesting, all this just to find out if she was just food, Ok I will give her what she wants.

"You were going to be food, I was going to drink your blood, and leave you for dead, nothing more, Ok? So there was some sexual tension there for a moment, and it meant nothing and will remain that way, nothing. If I ever take anything from you it will be because I want or need it for me, not because I have any feelings or compassion, or hold any feeling of sisterhood or bond with you, but because I am a monster do you understand."

"Yes," came Liz all too quick, and more disturbing for Selena, she was happy about it, "I understand, and it's Ok, as long as I get to be there for you and serve you."

Selena looked at her, her face all screwed up in confusion and asked Liz. "What the hell does that mean? Serve me?" Doesn't she get it? Selena thinks to herself, then says, "I am not worth that kind of respect or loyalty. I killed the last guy that wanted to be there for me like that. Left his body rotting next to a stream." I can't let her see me in the light she does, Selena thinks to herself,' where is that priest'. And as if to Selena's mental call she saw him pulling up out front in a very nice van, alone.

After the sermon, Raymond said he had a few errands to run. He changed to his street cloths and put a wad of money he had not had the day before into his pocket and left. Mary waited a few moments then followed in her own car. Earlier that day, while he was in service, she made sure she had all the gear she would need to follow her husband. In hopes of finding out what he was doing, if he was being controlled by that monster or not. And if so, what her plans for him were.

When he pulled into the parking lot of a closed used car dealer, she parked a half a block away and pulled out her digital listening gear and trained it on him. Making sure that it was turned on and connected to the recorder. A few min. later the owner of the lot showed up and they both went inside the little building that served as the office. Turning the signal frequency up she was able to hear what was being said.

"…I know Tom, I should tell Mary that I have lost my faith, and that I can't stay any longer. But I can't break her heart, not in person. I know I am being a coward about this but…"

"Ray, you've been my best friend for 8 years now, Mary is not going to take this quietly. You know she will come looking for you. That 'Order' she is a member of, those nuts she says serve some immortal Mother… or what ever it is, they will come looking for you. If this woman you're talking about is as mysterious as you say, they will want to talk with her, like they did that kid two years ago."

"Tom, please, just take my car and this money for the van, and don't tell Mary, Please, if you love me, keep this between us Ok?"

"Anything happens to you Ray, and I am going to spill the beans faster than you can eat them."

"Tom that's your choice… thank you." A few minutes later, Raymond leaves in a large passenger van, and heads out of town. He stops at a food store first and buys enough food to feed a small army.

Mary watches all of this from a distance, fighting the tears in her eyes. What could she do but hope to save her husband, even if it meant he would have to be turned over to the "Order". It was getting late when she got the call on her cell phone that the "team" had arrived and would meet her at her house. When she got there they were already going over the store attached to their house, and asked her where Raymond was.

She saw he was headed to his mother's old farm house on the edge of town. She told them that the woman was there and that there were at least 8 others with her. All but one seems to be afraid of her. Without missing a beat they all loaded up and headed out to the farm.

Raymond knew he could never go back to his wife, not now. But he did know one thing, he had to protect this woman, whether she be demon or angel, he had to keep her safe. All he could think of, as he was driving out to the farm was, 'Will she take me and make me hers?'

He prayed to God to give him some sign that he was doing the right thing, and he perceived nothing. Not even a sign he was doing the wrong thing. However, when traffic light at the edge of town, that was always a caution on Sunday, suddenly went red before he went through it, and the song on the vans radio changed to master and servant by dépêche mode, it never registered as anything other than a good song, and a new standard for the traffic light. When the murder of crows flew over head and followed him to the farm, he never thought more of it, than those birds are very creepy. Even when the radio announcers voice changed and said, "Raymond turn back," he figured it was an add for that TV show. He was so lost in his lust for Serena that he saw none of the signs he had prayed for. By the time he reached the farm all those signs had been lost in his memory, forever.

She moved Liz out of the way and headed down; the priest was coming up to the door and calling in as she reaches the bottom. He let himself in and just sort of stood there for a bit, not quite sure what to do.

"Well you kept your word." Selena commented. "You came alone and brought a van that looks like it will carry all of us to safety." She tosses the keys to the u-haul to him and says, "Take these, so you can drive back. Leave it whereever, I don't care"

"Mama" started the priest, "I was hoping we could talk for a bit before you all left. I was wondering if you would let me say a prayer for you and these others, for your safety."

By this time Liz had come down stairs and was watching her and the priest talk, some of the other girls were also watching. She had to be careful but she knew that if she was going to put Liz off she had to do this. She accepted the priest's offer but asked that he do herself and Liz separate from the rest, after about half an hour had gone by the other girls feeling better about things smiling and thanking him for his words and comfort, he turned to Selena and Liz, they led him upstairs. Selena could see he was thinking of more than prayers right now, the front of his pants giving him away.

The first thing he found himself doing was prayer and for a few, confession, even though he advised the three girls he was not catholic in anyway. The whole time he kept looking over to the demonic angel he had so completely fallen in love with. He could not help but feel the energy of her calling to him, demanding he give himself to her completely. So when the time came, he was led upstairs by not only her, but the other girl that seems to be attached to her every move. Every step up, he would get a little more excited and even warmed to the lust building in him.

In her mind he had already cheated on his wife and vows, he had given himself over to her that morning standing there with a mess in his robes. She would use that now as her reason and make him suffer. They all three entered the room and Selena closed the door behind them. She sat Liz down on the bed as the priest moved to the window, he would not look at them.

Selena began taking her clothes off and when the priest did turn round she was sitting on the bed watching him. Liz sat there looking at her a smile on her face then back to the priest, she startled both of them by asking if she could get undressed as well. The priest replied that yes she could. This was exactly what Selena wanted at that point.

Upstairs he hoped he would be able to surrender himself to her, but had not expected it to be the case. He found himself looking out the window of the room they were in, his mothers' room. He had never been allowed into this room growing up. The things she did in there were a big part of the reason he became a priest. Save his mother's soul and he could save any soul. So when he turned around and found her already undressed on the bed, he found he had no words. All he could do was look at her, the pure perfect alabaster look of her skin, so warm and inviting all at the same time. The look in her eyes seemed to burn with a fire he had never seen in the eyes of any woman, ever.

His voice trailed off, watching this other one get undressed. The look in her eyes seemed to him a little more insane than his angels' eyes, yet they burned with the same hell fire as hers. Some knowledge they seemed to share about the moment he was not privy to... it scared him but he could not look away or out of the room he was committed to this. Even though his every thought was a pray to His god to save him.

"So are you going to join us, "Selena asked the priest, "or just watch us?"

Her question was let out with a soft, purr of sorts, one that she used to keep Justin from hurting her to much, the sound was certainly soothing, almost hypnotic now. He began to undress. Saying some sort of pray for his soul as he did, then he came round to the side of the bed that Selena was on.

For him her question, "are you going to just watch us or join us?" was all it took for him to start undressing and move toward the bed. The voice, hers was becoming more and more hypnotic, he could not fight it, even though he was screaming in his mind now to be free of this moment. He could not stop. He was her prisoner, her slave.

Liz watched him and reached out to touch his undressed form, Selena just laying there. He climbed onto the bed and Selena pulled him up and inside herself, watching Liz's face as she did. She felt sick at what she was about to do, but she kept telling herself she had to, to push Liz away. That he was already dead, that none of this mattered.

The other, Liz gently moving her hands over his now nude body, through his hair, kissing his arms and back, but all he could see were his new masters' eyes, looking deep inside of him, burning his soul. Slowly he gave in and began to move in time to her body, his heart racing to keep up with the fear and lust driving him. Her mouth reaching up to his, demanding his tongue, Liz whispering into his ear that he would be with her master forever now.

The priest began to move, a little slow and mechanical, she needed to get this over with now. The sickness building in her was threatening to overcome her will, but she blocked it all out and pulled him down so she could get her mouth onto his and no sooner than she had she pulled his tongue into her mouth and bit down. The blood flooded into her with more force than she expected. The saltiness of it startling her, the texture was different. It seemed thicker than it had been with the doctor and the Rick'ster. She held on to him good and tight as he tried to scream and pull away, but he simply could not. Selena opened her eyes hoping to see Liz in shock or terror, anything other than the soft smile that was on her face as she was helping Selena to hold him down, helping her feed on him!

That's when his body erupted in fire, and in horror he realized she had bitten his tongue off and was now holding him down so she could drink every drop of blood that was racing out of his body. He fought as hard as he could but it was useless.   That little whore Liz was holding him down, laughing at him, whispering into his ear. "You belong to my master now, forever!" The insanity of her voice was cold as ice inside of his mind.

And with out warning he was thrown off of her and onto the floor. He grappled with his mouth to stop it from bleeding, his mind fracturing, racing to flight, get away, anything. Just get away from her before he dies. He looks up as he begins to stand and hears the demon screaming at Liz.

Upright and with out effort she pushed the priest off her and on to the floor, instantly forgetting about him. She turned to Liz and at once, began to yell at her.

"What do you think you're doing, you can't help me with this, he is meat just like you, don't you get it? He's meat! I could kill you as quickly as I will have to kill him now, finish him off so he can't tell anyone that this happened, of what I am! Don't you get it? I AM A MONSTER!!"

Light tears start falling down Liz's face but she holds true. Liz knows she has to in order to win out in this little struggle between herself and her master, and only points to the priest as he rises, holding his mouth, blood pouring from it. There is madness in his eyes as he watches the both of them and he tries to speak but without his tongue it's just

100

noise. He backs away to the window and with cne hand opens it, Selena knowing what he is preparing to do.

Leaping off the bed and over its footboard to grab at him so he can not defenestrate himself, Selena surprises herself, him, and Liz by doing so before either of them even see her move. He is tossed like a doll back on to the bed, his blood spraying over everything, as he tries again to scream for help, but simply makes a sickening gurgling noise that turns Selena's stomach inside out.

Liz is on him fast holding him down. She looks into his eyes, a clear madness living in hers. She begins to move back and forth over his still erect shame 'til it finds its way inside of her and she begins to lick his face clean of the blood that is sill leaking out of him. Selena can't believe what she is seeing, is this why Liz has been so willing to serve her, because she herself is insane? Selena watches in horror at how Liz beats his body with her fist as she rapes him, not only his body but his mind and soul. She can hear in her mind the pleas coming from the priest going to no where, that his God saves him...

He got it, and finally understood just how big his mistake was in coming here, in helping her. Yet some part of him still loved her... madness finally over came him as he moved for the window to get away. But before he could reach it she was there!!! Right in front of him throwing him back onto the bed. She was feeding him to the little monster Liz, and she was on him and he was in her, being ridden by her before he could scream again. That horrified sound that came out of him with out his tongue, chocking on his own blood was too much... his heart stopped...

Then Selena sees what she has never seen, his soul, it lifts up and out of him. Then there is light inside the room as angels appear beside the priest to his left and right. They take his arms and look at Liz drawing their swords. It happens so fast that Selena feels she can't act fast enough to save her. She hears their words of condemnation, blaming Selena for the priests' demise, stating that the soul of Liz shall fall to the abyss in her place, that Selena's soul is not theirs to pass judgment on, that Liz is now the unclean one. One turned to Selena and moved to push her aside; it did this only to be driven back by her. Selena began to scream and pulled Liz back as the swords of two other unseen till then angels swept forward and down, a cross of fire burning in the air where Liz had been kneeling over the priests' now dead body. She watched as the angels pulled him up and away, their swords being sheathed, then the light faded and the world was again right.

Her eyes were burning with anger and fear. She knew that Liz saw none of it, that she saw it only because of the nature of her being. With anger filtering through her voice, trembling she gave Liz these orders.

"Get dressed now," half throwing Liz on the floor, "I have to do something with him, gods this is not good, I never intended to kill him!"

"But, if you had not intended to kill him why did we do this?" asked Liz.

"To show you I am a monster, that you can't love me or worship me, or even admire me. I was trying to frighten you." the fear and confusion of what just happened echoing in Selena's voice.

"You will never frighten me." Liz stated flatly, "I have been playing at blood sports with my brother since I was a little girl."

"What!" Selena's shock coming to the forefront and pouring out of her as anger, "you mean to tell me, that you and your brother... you were... lovers?"

"Not like that..." Liz responded, "We would share our boy or girl-friends with each other. We didn't really touch each other to much, just enough to make our toys feel Ok. And it's not like you think, come on, we never had sex or anything. We were just really comfortable with each other, it was necessary to relax those we would take blood from.

"Come on, how else do you think he knew what you were and why I am so into you. You're what we always pretended to be. What we thought we were until you came along."

The stark reality of what Liz said made her head swim, but she knew she could not leave the other girls alone with her, and that she herself was now not the monster. Liz was, in every way the monster she thought herself to be, and more. She killed for the fun of it, thinking it would make her a vampire. The other thought moving through Selena was, here was someone that would do anything she wanted if she thought it would make her immortal. She would use this one for as long as she could then put her down like the rabid animal she was.

"Alright, you get cleaned up; we need to get out of here as fast as we can. Get the girls into the truck. We will leave the van here and burn down the house, I will get the fire ready, GO!"

Selena looked at the bed where he lay, at the cross still burning in the air where the swords had moved to strike at Liz, did she see any of it? Doubtful, she is to blind, even to her own actions to have seen that, but why did she? Selena realizes there is so much she needs to know, and with no one around to explain it all she would be lost for a long time to come. Selena decides that she needs to find and read every book she can on the subject, and hope that something out there makes since, or can help her figure out what she has done to herself. Why had she run from him, why didn't she stay with Stephen, she knew he could have helped her, right?

She called down to Liz to hurry up and get everyone out and into the truck as fast as she could.

She watched from the window as they all filed out looking back at the house, most of them taking pillows, cushions, blankets, and the like, from the house with them. She watched as Liz went through the van and found a case of water and other supplies, and then moved them to the truck. As soon as she saw Liz looking up at the window from the drivers side door on the u-haul, she set about destroying the evidence of their presence.

She poured out the lamp oil all over the bed and over the priest. She put his bible and such on his chest and tossed a match onto him, it caught strait away.

The fire burned fast, to fast thought Selena, 'til the whole bed was inflames. She left almost falling down the stairs and out the front door. She pushed Liz over into the passenger seat and drove away. They both watched as the house burned. No sooner than they hit the main road the sun had gone down and the blaze could be seen clearly in the night sky.

Outside the 'Team" and Mary had pulled up about ¼ of a mile away and were listening to what was going on. Watching with telescopes' and camera's what took place. When Raymond, stood up in front of the window, blood pouring out of his mouth, Mary screamed and moved to save him but she was restrained. And no sooner than she was restrained, they saw her. The monster that was responsible for his suffering and then both were out of the window again. A few moments later all the girls came running out of the house arms full of what ever they could carry it seemed. Then the monster came out of the house as it was burning. Mary screamed and fought with the other "Order" members, demanding to be allowed to go after them. To be allowed to kill her on the spot. She was told that when she was captured, the monster, that she, Mary would be allowed to interrogate it. She would be allowed the privilege to make the monster work for them in their hunt for the father, and end the suffering of mankind at his and his children's hands once and forever. They told her she could even give the demon its code name.

"Lilith, name it Lilith," Mary hissed at them threw her tears, "after that whore who destroyed all hopes of eternity in heaven for Adam. I want to break it, and then I want to make it learn its new name."

Heading off towards the freeway, on a route planed in the hours before he arrived, they prayed no one would stop them and drove into the night in the silence. It was well after midnight when they crossed the border into Tennessee, into Memphis. It was not hard to find a place in that city to ditch the truck and get rooms for all of them in a cheap hotel.

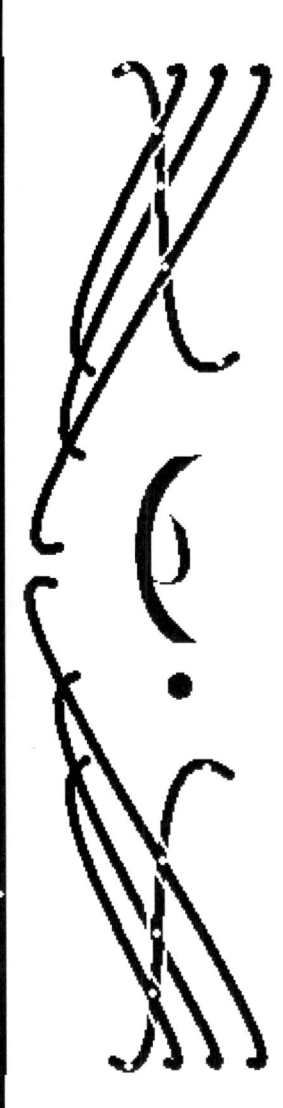

Chapter Seven – Welcome to the Viper pit

So the black of cloth my skin to hide from taunting stares

On wounding of strangers dismay

Stumbled hearts to music the soul understands

In clubs underground where those like me better fair

This now throbbing pulse my demise belayed.

-Vodalok-

Following her has been a very difficult thing for me. For the better part of two weeks she could not be felt anywhere, I had thought her dead.

I had hoped she was dead, but then there was that news report of the fire down by Nola, of girls kidnapping and killing a bunch of city officials from some place in Texas. Then I tried to locate her again, and there she was, moving north again.

I had taken time to rest in New Orleans when her trail went cold, taking time to soak up the atmosphere and revel in the culture that has built up down here in the years since that book about vampires was written.

If the authors only knew how far off from the truth they were, they might be a bit more afraid of this place now. With the number of us that come here and just live whether we hunt at night or not, would terrify anyone. We stay out of each others way, respecting how difficult it is to find donors, or we just take a little hear and there form the drunken tourist.

Then again everyone is wrong about us and what we are. They are constantly remaking the myth of what we are into something glamorous, something worthy of admiration, always getting it wrong.

Admittedly I have never taken a life; there is no need for that. You just have to keep yourself under control, not go too far. Maybe have someone there with you that you trust to keep the food from biting back.

The swooning (as some of the ladies I know call it) is powerful after a good feeding, almost like being drunk but more intense. It can leave you vulnerable for a few moments or a few hours, but it still brings you down, lost in the ecstasy that is feeding.

I failed to follow this rule miserably with Selena. It was not like I could at the time, what with things the way they were. And the things I see her doing from time to time, in the glimpses of her life I get while searching for her with my mind, those things make me want to vomit.

If the others, those that enforce our secret, the family, found out I won't have to worry. They will deal with her, then me. Then again you can't really call what they do enforcing. Still if they find out about her...

I will however have to worry about what they will do to me. I fucked up, big time, this letting her in, letting her tend to me, I should have crawled into my trunk and just toughed the fever out, but no, I had to go and keep driving. What I don't understand is how she managed to actually cross-over. Many of us know the supposed secret to making another vampire, but it's never worked. What was different about this time, why did it work?

It's possible the fever had something to do with it working. My body in its sickness could have been making just enough of those special little white blood cells that keep me alive. My body in overdrive combined with her taking my blood in that state? If enough blood was taken, it could have overpowered her body... transmuting her blood, and white cells, until she became just like me.

So in theory she could be cured by a strong enough transfusion of blood, as long as she had not yet been brought to the brink of death. That's the thing I fear, that in those two weeks when I could not find her, she had been brought low, and close to death, or worse, had died.

Of course even with that she would have needed to be fed blood from almost the beginning to have survived. And the odds of that are stacked against her. She would have needed help, and who in their right mind would have done such a thing. Hell, for all I know she could have figured out how to block me from watching her, and... is letting me see her move around, taunting me?

This all could be like a game to her. How fast can I catch up to her when she is letting me watch? I need to work on seeing better, focus more. Victor was right about one thing, I am a lazy beast.

At any rate all that work is something I can start tomorrow, these are all things I can ask her once I catch her. Just how she managed to stay hidden for so long, did she kill all those men? Has she died...?

For now I am tired of hunting her, and will let her run. I see in her mind the map she is following, still heading to Michigan, easy enough to follow at my leisure.

It's getting late but not to late yet, something like 10, maybe 11pm, and the stars are out. This place is nice late at night. The smell is less oppressive than in the early hours, making these walks of mine more pleasant. I have been in town now for at least a week and just can't seem to find the will to leave. I think of Victor again and remember one of many conversations...

..."Stephen you're not going to grow if you don't work on the things we are showing you. I understand your doing your best under the conditions you're in, but you can't just drink blood and expect everything to fall into place..."

I remember the look on his face that night as I not only entered his mind, but that of all the others there at the same time. Making them see through MY eyes, puppet my words. (People step around me as I stand there laughing at the wind.) They never could figure out how I was doing everything I did, or how I did more than them. Without ever really working at it, without making the investments of time they all had made. Later that night at some club, Victor told me why he was so afraid of me, and why he wanted me to work harder at knowing myself...

..."I have been dead once" Victor said, "and woke to the life I now know, and still you're stronger than me in many ways. I don't understand what it means, but I am certain of one thing....if the order finds out about you, they may come looking for you, and then..."

...It, the memory, fades as fast as I found myself in it. Like so many things these days, I can never hold onto who I was. I get small glimpses of a life I pray was not mine...and then I am back here, walking past the clubs.

These clubs are always full to bursting, as are the bars, always packed late into the night. These last three nights however I just have not wanted to be there, sick of the bump and grind of music all too poppy, so vacant and driven by greed.

On the suggestion of a former girlfriend, I tried going to a hip-hop club, and it just didn't work out. Don't get me wrong it had nothing to do with race. I simply could not get into, or behind the music that was playing. All that degradation and violence, I wanted no part of it, gangster this, bitch up my hoe that, every girl is a piece of meat to be exploited or used then tossed away. It simply was not for me.

At least with the Underground scene, you can get lost in the music and not have to be worried about having your mind muddied up with words. They are there but blend in with the music well enough that they can be left out as words and heard simply as part of the music itself. The more trance like sounds of bands like the 'Orb', 'Underworld', 'Juno Reactor', 'Velvet Acid Christ', and 'Covenant' send me to places in my mind that I used to only get to with 'The Cure', or 'Sisters of Mercy', and still by way of 'Dead Can Dance'.

So now I take long walks at night and take what I need from those I pass in the night, a little kiss here, a drunk passed out there. It doesn't matter as long as I am not caught in the act. This place is the perfect feeding ground.

Tonight I stroll past one of many old cemeteries that litter the city; their private mausoleums and solitary crypts littering the city by the hundreds, drawing in tourist from all over the world, not just America. They come for either the old world escapism of the place, the growing belief by the general public that this is the place to find the undead if they exist, or for the constant party that goes on down in the French quarter. For me, it's these places, the cemeteries and the quiet peace they bring that is not just for the dead.

The police watch them these days much closer than they used to. Mainly because some of the less careful among us, have been very careless about how they hunt. Those that are foolish enough to take a life, leaving their waist out in the open to be found and exploited by the media, are dealt with as soon as possible.

Now, most of the tours have moved back to day light hours, but a few have those tours still run well into the night for the ghost seekers, for the vampire hunters.

It's one of those tours I am hanging out around, following, hoping to find someone willing to give themselves to a fiend such as myself. I was watching and listening to the conversations going on, looking for someone drunk enough to take back to my place, for... drinks.

For the last two nights the hunting has been good, first came two girls from Old Miss University over in Mississippi, good fun those two. Turns out they 'were' lesbians, now they are into guys as well, better for me in the end. They even gave me their numbers, both at the university and for their homes, inviting me to stop by anytime I like.

Next to come was a witch, looking for some kind of validation of her life. She left smiling, even though in the end all we did was fuck, she found she no longer felt lost, not knowing really why. I would really like to get her thoughts and memories out of my head...

I showed them all a really good time, and then took what I needed from them. I know they will tell their friends about how they were used by a vampire in New Orleans, oh well.

Tonight is no different, it's during one of these walks, in one of those tours, that I over hear what sounds like a conversation about Selena.

There are three of them, two guys and a girl. At first all I can see or hear is glimpses of one of the guys, he seems very normal, nothing remarkable, an average Joe. Then as I move closer I see the other guy. He is taller, but all I see are dreadlocks. He must think he is, or wants to be a rock star. I can't really see the girl. She is well out of sight on the other side of both of them, around behind a fairly large crypt. So I stop and listen, I can tell it's the rock star wannabe that's talking.

"Well from what the guy on his podcast said, she started out in Arizona, killed her husband and two other guys. And if the story is true, one was her grandfather," he pauses and takes a drink from a bottle, then drags on a cigarette, "a doctor or something.

"At least that's the story as told there on his site. You know the one, www.vampbs.com. She had sex with them first, and then, they turned to dust or something like that, just from her drinking their blood. He says that someone watched her carry the bodies, or what was left of them out into the desert and bury them in the hard pack with her bar hands."

The smaller one started talking now, trying to show he was just as on top of things as the guy with the dread locks.

"Well the 'Graveyard' says that she is not alone. That she is running with some guy that," he puts up his hands and makes the quotation marks with his fingers, "brought her over. While the 'V3in' says she is running with a pack of wild sex crazed girls. Killing every guy they come across. You guys do remember that fire last week over on the other side of town. All those dead men, and that sheriff that said this crazy whore lead them all there and then tried eating them."

This time it's the girl's voice that I hear, she does not sound like she is happy with what her friends are saying. Something in her words leads me to lean in and listen closer. I however have to get closer than I am ready to, but I want to hear more of what they are saying.

"If that were true, how come witnesses at the fire say they saw them all leave with no clothes looking like they had not seen the light of day in months, not to mention all beat up. Then the fire didn't start 'til sometime after a car load of guys with turbans and suits show up. I mean come on, did you see the size of that guy that says he's a sheriff.   I'll bet they were all part of some kind of slavery ring, selling girls to the mob, or foreign buyers as sex slaves. If they were really a bunch of vampires on a rampage do you think they would be leaving such a large group of pigs behind to just burn?"

The first guy speaks up this time, I can see him now, and he does look like a rock star wannabe! Dreadlocks, tall, thin, pale white makeup, and miss matched contacts. Yea that's one for the floor. He tips up his bottle of alcohol before speaking.

"So what, they are vampires and don't fear none, if they is running bout all nekkid and shit who cares, let em come after my ass. I will teach them a thing or two bout right and wrong, who ta kill and what not," he begins to postures himself so as to look as intimidating as possible then continues, "I did kill that one vampire last year you remember don't cha Joe, how I did like in that move, cut 'is head clean off then burned 'is ass?"

That's a shock. He claims to have done such a thing to a real vampire? I wonder if he would even know a vampire if it bit him on the nose, the thought makes me snicker to myself but I am a bit too loud. The female comes into view and I almost die right there on the spot.

She is so incredibly beautiful.

I have never seen someone so angelic in my life. She can't be more than 5 feet tall if that, and certainly no more than 110 lbs, it's the blonde hair, strait and almost snow white that gets me. It reaches well below her ass and not a strand out of place. She is dressed in old school Goth. plain long sleeve shirt under a short sleeved Bauhaus shirt and long skirt, all black. I feel her eyes moving over me and then a slight smile, almost a smirk, it lights up her face as she winks at me then speaks.

"So what do we have here," the two boys come round the other side of the crypt. Joe is kinda plain, black denim and a tee-shirt with the count from Sesame Street on it, nothing remarkable, 'looks like we got ourselves a tourist what lost his group."

Something about her is most interesting, granted all of them seem to be drinking the same kind of alcohol, smells of black liquorish, from a green bottle with a stags head on it. She however is chasing it with vanilla coke, not remarkable by itself but something in the way she smiles and carries herself. I step forward to see them better and reach out and take the bottle from rock star. He moves to take it back but I sneer at him and he backs down. Taking a deep pull on the bottle I almost regret it at once, but hold it back, the angel just smirks, her whole body moving ever so slightly.

"I am no tourist," I begin, "rather I am out hunting for a good time, heard you guys talking, and figured I would listen in 'til I found what I was looking for."

"Did you like what you heard," she asked, "because if you did, there is more yet to be said, and hell you might be able to add to it, right sang?"

She just called me sang!!! It's a slang term for sanguinairan, what modern vampires, and would be vampires call themselves. Her eyes I notice have not left me the whole time. Watching me with some inner purpose, that devil may care smirk riding her face like a badge of honor, taunting me to be bolder. It's funny in a way, the way she looks at me, her head forward and down so her eyes are shadowed by her brow, and still her eyes are so full of light.

I know I don't have to prove anything here but something about her just seems... familiar. So I ask.

"What are your names, I am Stephen. I am heading north to Detroit, looking for an old friend, from Arizona"

I put it out there to see if they would catch it. To see how they'd react, based on their previous conversation. All the angel does is smirk again with a bit of a 'humph' as her body moves in time to the emotion of it. She is very drunk, more so than the other two, that's for certain.

Rock star leans forward and squints to see me better, I forget that the sheep have such a hard time seeing in the dark, his exclamation of 'no way' almost made me laugh. Average Joe, he just stood there watching me, you could see he was thinking about the possibility of my being who he thought I was. It was average Joe that spoke up next.

"So this friend of yours you're goin' north to see, it a he or a she"

"Her... name is Selena," I say, "and she has been a very bad girl."

They stand there listening, hoping I will say more, but get only silence as I watch them in return.

"This guys full of shit," rock star says, "he ain't nobody, just some fucking fuck fucking with us, lets beat his stupid Fucking face in."

"No." Angel chimes, amusement in her voice, "lets beat yours in, *dick*."

Average Joe steps back as she slaps him with her left hand, her body swaying as she does so. Some how she stays upright and just laughs at almost falling over. Yea these three are ripe for picking. So I tempt them a little more.

"It's been a while since I have fed. Know where I can get a ... bit?" Ok I should be shot for using such cheesy conversational tools, but with them as drunk as I think they are. This should be easy. Laughter will get them to follow me, at least it should. Of course this all depends on how drunk they are.

So I hand the bottle of booze back to rock star, he takes a big drink himself to prove he is tough, and almost chokes himself. Joe does the same but handles it like its water. The angel, she tips up her bottle and bubbles up the contents, I watch as the bottle comes down just as full as it was when she started. She laughs her eyes completely on me the whole time.

She is not drunk! What's her game I wonder, does she know I am what I am? Have I met her in the past? This becomes my only concern now. But how to find out, our eyes are locked as the other two have a conversation between themselves, trying to figure out whether or not I am the guy that made Selena, or if she made me and I am trying to catch up to her to learn from her. One things for sure is they both now think I am just what I am.

"Ok, you're a blood sucker," snaps rock star, "what the fuck are you doing here if you're chasing after your 'friend', is she here?"

I am board with the other two already, and want nothing more than to have them leave. But, in the interest of the angel, I deal with them as if they were children and ignore them. I turn my full attention to her. I step in close enough to feel the texture of her clothes as she sways to and fro. She doesn't move and continues to wear her smirk.

"What do you think," I ask her, "am I here because she is here, or because I have only missed her by a few days?"

"I think," she smiles, "you're here because you're tired of chasing her, and don't really care if she gets caught or not. I mean, your kind is always born, never made, right."

It's my turn to smirk, her breath is warm and smells of black liquorish alright, but not because she has been drinking, it's one of those obnoxiously strong mints. She raises an eye brow at me, tilting her head towards rock star, as if to say *"come on do it, you know you hate him as much as I do,"* or did I hear her say it in my head? My response is to step in so close that I have to brace her back with one of my free hands so she doesn't fall over. She says, "Ooooh" then laughs out the words "What a bad boy".

Rock star can't stand it, and tries to push me away, but only gets himself pushed to the ground by her. I never even had to lift my free hand. Joe, he is a little smarter about it.

"Dude either let her go or I go get the cops, they are around here, and you won't get away if you try anything."

"Chill out..."she says, "I didn't come here with either of you; I'm only hanging out with you two losers to get drunk. Now if this one wants to play, I am alright with it, you can watch... maybe learn a thing or two on how to win a girls heart in a flash."

It does not surprise me that Joe says fuck it and leaves, rock star however, he stays, and he wants a show. At the prospect of a show he forgets everything that had just happened and asks.

"So are you two going to fuck? Did you really mean it when you said I could watch?"

Her eyes still fixed on mine she says 'Yea, he can watch but we need him to get undressed, so I can get in the mood". She leads him to believe he might be able to join if he is good and quite. This makes me laugh, I try not to look at him as I do, knowing that if I do, I wont be able to stop.

So he follows her commands, undressing completely, a pale white body with tattoo's everywhere, yea this guy thinks he I a rock star. She stands staring at me and then at him and no sooner than she looks at him she looses control of herself and falls down laughing. I look over and I see why, his man hood is as placid as a lake in the early morning, on a day with no wind. To make matters worse he is poking at it with a single finger whispering to it to get up. That's just too much, and I turn to her and ask if he has to stay, that this is just embarrassing.

"I got him undressed so you could eat him silly." That's all she says from the ground, watching me, waiting for me to do it, still laughing. Of course by this time rock star figured out what was going on, and tried to gather up his things. Not wanting to disappoint her I step over to him and with my right hand grab him by the neck. With my left cut his chest in a long downward motion with the strait razor I keep in my back pocket. The little man squeaks and squirms trying to get free. I hold him close and with a quick glance at the angel, I turn back to him and start drinking the blood that is pouring out of him.

The wound will heal and he will live. For now it's enough to get his adrenaline flowing. I feel her hands move up my side, then her face pressing against mine as she begins to drink from him as well. Rock star by this time has stopped fighting, and is just trying to hold on to both of us.

Opening my eyes I see she is pulling his limpness trying to stir in him some excitement, and to her credit gets something for her efforts. Me,

I never knew you could blow your money shot soft. I let go and back away, the fucker got some on me.

"You need to control that thing if you're going to do that," I hiss at him, "now it's all over me! One of you is going to clean this up cause, I am not touching it."

"Well lover," she says, "if you want it cleaned up why you didn't say so." She grabs rock star and pushes him forward, puts his face on my leg where he made the mess, and tells him to lick it up. He does, and when he is done she throws him to the ground, saying to him with all the mockery she can manage. "Get dressed you fuck, I don't ever want to see you again, and if you tell anyone about this, I will tell them how easy you are." She looks at his still limp dick and laughs, "My god don't you have any balls, such a little week man, so pathetic."

"Aren't you going to kill me," Stammers out rock star, his eyes going from her to me as fast as they could, "aren't you afraid I will come looking to kill your vampire asses!"

All I can do is look at him in disgust, and go to say. "I just might, if you don't get out of here now," but decide to tell him this. "If you were a threat to me at any time boy, you would be dead by now. You're all mouth and no action. You are weak and will never be more than a little boy. Go masturbate in your shame at what happened here tonight. Tell anyone anything you want, it won't matter, look at you, who would believe you. Besides that wound is already healing, it will be gone in a few days. That was done weeks ago, not tonight."

As if on command he looks down and sees it's not bleeding anymore and that it is healing faster than it should. Quickly he gathers up his clothes and runs off into the cemetery undressed.

"Well aren't you a fearsome beast" she say's.

I look back to her and she is still on the ground looking up at me, two bottles of that dark liquor in her hands, smiling at me like a child looking for a favor. So I ask her. "What do you want from me, you know what I am and it seems to me you knew before I even said anything. How come you don't feel like a sang, or a doll?"

"I, good sir, am sang but not like you. You have so much to learn, and there is so little time to put it in your head. Come, help me up and we shall go walking."

Sitting there on the turf looking very much like a full grown child, offering up her hand to me, the bottles in between her legs, blue eyes all pouting, that smirk still ridding her lips. I say fuck it and help her up. "Do you have a name" I ask, hoping it's something old and foreign, but all I get is

"You can call me Viper."

We leave the grounds and continue walking down the street under the trees that hang out over the walk way. For a little while we do so in complete silence, but this doesn't work for me. Especially after her comment about being sang but not like me. Bringing it up is easy. Her long silence as she walks backwards, looking at me, not needing to see where she is going, un-nerves me a bit so I stop.

"Look you can't go making comments like that, then not say anything else, it's just rude. If you are Sang, but different, tell me how you're different. What makes you so special that I can't feel you?"

You see we can feel each other, it's in the aura, and each of us has one. A field of energy that some can see but most can feel, we are sensitive enough that we can feel the difference in a bleeder, and vamp. We know one another sight unseen if we are close enough to feel the others field. Some have learned to cover their field so as not to be detected, so they can move about trying to deny what they are. But for me even those stand out in a unique way. Viper here has no... she has no aura at all!

I pull her in front of me, looking her deep in the eyes; my face must be a bit contorted as she almost laughs at me. Her little all knowing smirk replaced with that amused look one gets when they know they have won a very difficult race, and they want every other contestant to know that they lost.

Her blue eyes are empty, nothing there, I go to shake her and she is out of my grip and moving away fast, and then stops to say.

"You know you're the first of your kind to get it. You in your own right are different from them, not like all the rest, closer to what I am than what they are. I could show you how if you're interested. No more dying, no more being born over and over again, no more having to learn everything all over again with each new body. To tell you the truth, I don't know how you guys handle it. How can you go through every life time in a new body over and over again, and suffer the life's you do again and again without going insane? I could never do it."

She starts walking again long but slow very directed steps that make her look like she is showing clothes at a fashion show, like she is some sort of high priced model on a run way. She looks back with as much grace, and asks if I am coming. Before she gets to far ahead I run up next to her and she looks at me and smiles. This time there is compassion in her yes and a smile, that evil little smirk is gone.

"Don't worry. I am not going to eat you. That would be sick"

It's only a few more blocks before we enter her hotel, and head up to her room. This place is nice, it's not the Ritz or anything, but nicer than where I am staying. Once we reach her room I see there are at least six other people already here, all drinking. Two of them are like me, I wonder about the others, but that is cut short as she takes my hand and announces me to the group.

"Everyone, I want you to meet Stephen. He is sang, and tonight he is my date, so everyone forget about trying anything."

They all laugh about the comment and the night begins. The music started playing and there was conversation. Everyone had a drink or two in just the first 15 min of my getting there, it's now something like 12am, and she leads me around the room introducing me to everyone.

There are two Sangs' who seem to be like me, are introduced as Amber and William, and then I am introduced to a real prick named Joe. There are also Amy, Tiffany, and Tonya, three girls from Washington State down on vacation. They had been lost and were found by Joe, who brought them up for the party.

And last but not least were two other gentleman, they gave their names as Mathew and Luke but not much more. Those two spent the evening talking with everyone and keeping to themselves while at the same time, watching and observing.

I am admittedly tired, and let Viper know that. So she excuses herself and I from the party, letting everyone know to please stay as long as they like and that our 'guest' is not to leave 'til sun up. Insisting that they get the largest of the other two bedrooms and that Amber and William get the other. She points out where the linen closet is, and that extra blankets and pillows are there. She tosses the key to the liquor cabinet to Joe and we retire to her room.

In her room I find that the bed is a very large coffin that has been built for two... maybe three people easy. An interesting shade of white enamel covers the entire thing, with brass fittings and black lacquer trim. There are speakers in the side boards, inside and out. A flat screen TV in the lid that looks like it's a 22 inch screen. The thing is of course deep enough that you can toss and turn in the night without hitting your head on the lid or the TV.

I look at her and she is undressing in the private bathroom that's attached to her room. She looks at me and smiles. As her clothes come off I see that she like tattoos, well I should say a tattoo. This thing goes from her left ankle all the way up and around her body, its head coming over her right shoulder and resting on her left breast.

It's an odd mix of Japanese art and Viking knot work, one of the most impresses full body tattoo's I have ever seen in my life. Now I know why she is called Viper. The thing that is impressive is how the body of the snake was detailed. It being full and well defined like a Japanese dragon, but the detail in the body is where the knot work is. From the tip of the tail all the way up the entire length of the snake and exiting its mouth as the tongue, that is wrapped around her nipple in about 8 very detailed knots.

Her eyes fall on me, and there is in them an odd compassion and hunger that I can't quite put my finger on. None the less she smiles again and dances there for a moment in the door way of the bathroom, then laughs and puts her robe on. I stand and watch her, not sure if I am smiling or watching in my most detached manner. I am still not sure what to think of her, no aura, and no sign that she is alive or dead...

This night started out with me looking to get a fix, I happened upon her and two strangers. Maybe for this party she was collecting them. Who knows? Then we came here and now I am in her room with her. She comes out of the bathroom, teeth all polished up, and in her bed gown.

She is looking at me as if I had just torn my head off, so I ask. "What's wrong? Am I ... sleeping here with you tonight?"

"Yes," she said, "go get ready in there, if you want there is a clean robe on the door. I used it this morning after my shower but it's still clean."

Ok, I look her in the eyes and she raises one brow and laughs at me as if in response to an unasked question..?

"Silly boy, tricks are for whores, go clean yourself up, and in the morning if you're not too tired we can see what happens."

What the hell, what's the worst she can do to me. Eat me? The soft sounds of a distant shore breaking, mixed with the sounds of a forest at night all coming through the box from the speakers on the outside. Quite though just a whisper, are very, very soothing and distracting at the same time. In short it leads me into dreams I was not ready for...

...It put me back at the farm, or what passed as a farm at the time. Pigs so many of them, just me and the old man I worked for. I was hired by his daughter to show him that this venture he was undertaking was too much for him. That he should give it up and just live on the land. But he must give up the pigs.

The farm was about 60 acres of land, of which 57 were wooded. He had laid electric fence in about 12 of those, in a big square. Inside that fence ran free and wild his children, two big boars and about 15 sows.

116

Every morning I would have to walk the fence and look for trees the beast had uprooted just to fall across the lines, hoping to short them out. I hated those pigs.

Once that was done I would put out the feed and make sure the water troughs were upright and full. The bastards would turn them over in the winter to make the mud. Mud that in places was so deep, it would pull your boots off and leave you to stand one footed in hopes of getting the stuck boot out without having to put you foot down... it never worked.

The worst part in the end was the smell, that god awful smell that got into everything, your clothes, skin, even your hair. There was nothing you could do that would get it out. It marked you more completely than anything in this world could. It said "Pig Farmer".

I wondered everyday I was there, why did I stay. And everyday I was reminded of why. Her name was Benny, yea a funny name for a chic but she was something else, the daughter of a Mennonite woman living alone just up the road. Which was very close with the old man that I worked for? In time I grew to respect that woman more than any woman I had ever known. Her skill with cattle and sheep was amazing, but no more so than her own personal strength!

Everyone was given a good look at just how strong she was when her house burned down that December. Pulling up a small travel trailer she began the work of tearing down the remains of her old house, and laying the foundation for her new one.

At first none of the men in her community would come to help her, but when she set about attempting to build the place on her own, after gathering by some great miracle all the material she would need for the new home, and almost killing herself in the process, did they finally come to her aid. And boy did they. One week after they started the house was done, her and her children all moved in. Her daughter would make biscuits and the like for those helping out so they could have something to eat as they worked. The old man butchered two pigs for the event and ham and bacon were had by everyone.   This of course put him in good stead with the Mennonite farmers, who put him in touch with an Amish guy. This guy agreed to buy the old mans pigs each season, as soon as the litters were grown enough for the slaughter, an odd but profitable arrangement.

Now Benny, she was like any girl you might find out on a farm with big dreams to get away and make it on her own. She had no love for the life her mother choose, or the idea of staying with her for the rest of her *life. She wanted bright lights and loud cars. She wanted to party 'til the sun came up and then hid from the day. It was this angel that I sought to use to my advantage. I had not yet joined the army and had plans to head to the city myself once I had been paid for the job I was doing. As it was, all I was getting was room and board, not so bad when that included all the fresh milk, eggs, cheese, pig and cow one could hope to eat.*

As time went on winter set in and I found that I was now left out here on my own. Benny had moved on, she found what she was looking for and left without a word. Bitter and angry at not just myself but the world I again took to hiding from myself and ignoring my needs.

A local group had invited me to join them on Friday and Saturday nights for role playing. For someone looking to make an escape from the curse of his reality, such an offer is a great boon to his broken mind, I accepted.

Within several weeks, I had become one of the guys and enjoyed the company away from the pigs. Pigs that I had to always be home for in the morning, no mater what to deal with. I had become so fond of the game and the company that came with it that, I started to demand from my "employer." Some kind of pay, something to allow me a bit of dignity when with my new found friends, they would not have to buy my food or drink during these games.

And it paid off, I started to earn enough money that I was able to save and buy a 68 dodge van, it had a manual transmission, the shifter was on the column with only three speeds. Rusted and tired it was still a good vehicle for the time and place.

But I still didn't earn enough money to put gas in it all the time so I would find myself having to walk to and from the place we gathered at. It was a trailer park about 3 miles away by normal roads, 1.5 miles if I walked the service road for the power lines.

Now walking at night was a bit risky. Everyone believed there was a bear out there that would only attack people late at night when walking the roads outside of town. I always laughed at them and would make the walk without issue. The darkness at times could be very oppressive and heavy, leading one to think that he was being followed or watched. I never had anything come to pass that would lead me to believe I was in danger. Just because we were out in the country three hours away from the nearest "big city" meant nothing to me.

So one Saturday night about 3am I was walking home on that tried and tested trail. There was a full moon out, part of the reason I was walking home, rather than having accepted the ride home I was offered. One of the girls had taken a fancy to me and offered to give me a ride, but I wanted to walk, needed the walk really. It was cold, but not as cold as it could be after snowing all day.

The clouds had broken and were moving out, but the high level clouds were still there and holding in a solid blanket that made the moon look kind of spectral, and gave it an enormous hallow of color. And from those clouds came a very light and soft snow.

I was at the stream crossing, having had gone round the main path to be on the old foot path by this time, to enjoy the snow all the more. There is nothing like coming to a stand still, and looking up through a light snow fall at the full moon on nights like that. The crispness of the air lends a texture to the feel of the air and the look of the trees around you, and the moon above... I was caught up in it.

Snap

Somewhere close by a branch had broken... I snap to and look round. I get low so I can see under the branches in hopes of seeing if it is a deer, there were tracks all over and seeing a few now would just add to the wonder of the night. But there was nothing. I stayed like that for a bit and then stood up and moved over the stream by way of the logs in the water that had piled up to form a natural crossing.

Snap

Ok this time the noise was very close and I spin round and drop to my knees instantly. Eyes straining in the darkness to see anything, any sign of movement. There is nothing, just the sound of the snow falling. Its one thing to be wrapped up in the sound of nothing and hear the snow falling, especially when the flakes of snow are so light and fluffy, they should have no sound at all. But I heard them coming to a rest upon one another in the trees, on the ground, even upon my own head. I tell myself I am just finally letting all the stories get to me. That there is nothing there and that even if it were, I am ok. The house where I live is only about 1/8th of a mile away.

I stand again and for a moment as I turn round to start heading home again. I think I see in the full moons light a very tall shadow on the path in front of me! But as I turn it almost seems to fall, no disappear into the darkness of the trees to the right of the path.

"Hello, anyone there..."

The sound of my voice calling out seemed thunderously loud, and to my surprise scared up a deer in the field to my right. It ran off and all was silent again. I smile, almost laughing out loud that I had let a deer so close, scare me. I went to take a step closer to home.

Snap.... "Uuurrrggghhh...". *Thud*

I turn round so fast my eyes almost blur the trees, and there is a shadow behind me. It was huge, certainly not the kind of shadow you would expect to see in the moonlight, far too big to be a bear. I started stepping backwards as panic started to grow in me. Whatever this thing was, it had steam rising off of it, but the snow around it didn't seem to melt. So dark was it, it appeared to absorb all the light that fell upon it, consuming it like a black hole.

Every step I took away from it, it would take one closer to me, huge steps that cleared twice the distance my steps could, so I came to a stop.

I wanted to scream at it but could find no voice in my throat. Rather than give in to fear completely, I sat down on the snow and just watched it, and to my wonder it followed suit. For an hour we sat there in the snow watching each other, the steam rising from it. Myself growing colder by the moment, the soft light of the moon fading behind the trees as it road further into the night sky, leaving me and this shadow to our own ends.

And all too quickly we were in the dark. My heart pounded and trembled in time with my body as the night air started to get colder and my body began to freeze. Clouds began to start rolling in again, low and heavy, the threat of more snow yet to fall. And still I could see its blackness sitting there in the snow as if watching me, waiting for some sign from me that I would run.

Somewhere in the distance I could hear a car moving down a dirt road, slowing and stopping. The local paper was being delivered, and I was still there watching this darkness. Fear had left me some time ago, and now it was simple curiosity that held me there, watching it, watching me.

I didn't know what time it was when I fell asleep, but when I woke I was in bed and there were several people about, the old man fussing with a water bottle on my head. the lady whose house we helped rebuild, a few of my gamer friends and in the corner of the house was the shadow still watching me, just as quietly, I passed out again.

That following morning I woke to a full house, people were laughing and drinking coffee, and I could smell fresh food being prepared in the kitchen. For an old trailer converted to a full home, this place was cozy in ways most people would never understand. The wood burning stove in the center of the place kept everything very warm even on the coldest of nights. I was laid out on a couch across from it with 15 too many blankets thrown over me, the weight of them a bit suffocating. I fought to sit up and as I did everyone became quite and focused on me.   I looked at them and the old man was the first to say anything. "Two nights ago, a spirit came to me, he spoke to me of your being in danger, I called your friends to see if you were still with them and to make sure you didn't walk home that night. They said you had already left, so I asked them to go looking for you, that you had not made it home yet. The spirit told me that Wendago was coming for you. That you could not stay in this part of the land anymore. That what you are upset the land."

He paused as everyone looked at him like he had just gone insane. I must have been looking at him in pure shock, cause someone commented on my going white in the face, pale even for me, then he went on.

"It's been a long time since the Wendago has been awakened here in this part of the world, so much of the land has been cleared away making it weak and tired, making it harder for it to move about. But I heard its voice on the wind that night and knew the spirits were not lying to me. I went out with your friends here and we found you.

You were lying off the trail in the woods, covered in snow. There were great huge tracks all about you but we do not know the beast that made them. I say it was the Wendago. It had gotten you and had left you to die. You're lucky I sill listen to the spirits, that my ears are not so deaf that I can not hear them anymore.

Tonight we will go out to the lodge and clean our bodies so that we can better understand why you so anger the land." I was still much too weak to stay upright and passed out again....

...I awake latter in the morning, the sun still has not come up, she is still sleeping next to me and I am very comfortable. The dream left me feeling that old discomfort. The one born of knowing I am so utterly different, that I am the product of humanities cruelty.

I get up and go use the restroom, and when I come out I go to head to the kitchen and over hear conversation in the other room. I listen and do not like what I hear. Two of the guests have decided that they are going to make sure none of us ever wake up again. That they have contacted the head office and they would not be alone here in this nest of evil for long.

That's all I needed to hear and move to wake up my hostess. "Viper," I whisper, "get up, we have problems." Rising slowly but with eyes appearing completely awake she tilts her head and purses her lips, very visibly upset with having been woken out of sleep, the question unspoken on her face all to clear. What is wrong, this had better be good.

"Your 'guest', are out there plotting to make sure none of us wake up again." I say.

And she says. "What?"

The look of pure disbelief and anger on her face is enough to make me want to leave here and now. But I compose myself and move to the door, motioning for her to follow, and without even grabbing a robe she does so. At the door I stop her from opening it and motion for her to listen, what she hears turns her face white.

"No sir, I am certain that all those here save the three girls and ourselves are vampire. We should be able to destroy them quietly as long as you get here before sun up, they're all in bed. No sir, this is as you say, gods work, we can't go wrong, and these things need destroying."

Viper pulls me back from the door and starts getting dressed. We move into the bathroom and she calls down to the front desk and explains really quickly to the clerk there that no one is to be allowed to come to her room and that the police need be called now. There are two people in her apartment that should not be there.

She tells me to get into the closet and close the door. When I go to ask why she pulls me in and closes the door. No sooner than she does the door opens, and in come the two guys. We watch as they move towards the bed, but before they open it I am pulled into a small walk way. She leads me through 'til we reach the room where William and his lady are resting. They are already in the closet, when we get there.

"Where is Joe," Viper ask of Amber, "I don't know if he went to bed with the girls in the main bedroom or not"

"When we went to bed he had headed out the front door saying he needed some air," replied Amber. "Whether he came back or not, I don't know"

"This is not good Viper," said William, "who brought those two here?"

122

She looked at William and thought to herself, she knew she hadn't brought them, she knew I had not as I came with her, Joe had brought the girls, Amber and William had not gone out last night.

"Did they come in with Joe and the girls," asked Viper, "they could have followed them in."

At that moment the door to the bedroom opened and we fell quietly back into the walkway. We listened and could tell they were not happy with the way things were turning out. The bed was over turned and then the closet door opened, clothes were moved and we could hear them taping on the walls looking for any sign of a passage, but soon they gave up and left the room.

"We can't stay in here, if they find any one of the closet doors they will find us, Viper don't you have another way out of here?" asked William.

"Yes," was her reply, followed by a short pause, then she continued, "But we have to move under them, in the floor boards to my other room. Now if they know about this place they might know about that one and we could be trapped in these crawl spaces for a little while 'til they give up and go. I did call for the police but I don't know when they will get here."

Amber looked like she was going to cry, but William did his best to comfort her. I listened to the sounds out in the other room as the three girls were pulled from their bed and led out into the living room. They were upset and there was yelling. Questioning about had they been bit by any of us, if they had slept with anyone of us.

They just cried saying they came for drinks, and a place to stay for the night because they had been lost after the sun went down. They insisted over and over that that was all that had happened. But one of the guys kept pushing. He seemed intent on proving that they had been compromised in some way by us. What the fuck was he pushing for?

By this time Viper had decided we needed to get them out of there, but Amber had become too scared. They all knew what these guys were, what they were about, but none of them were willing to talk about it. In frustration I pushed passed them and told Viper to get the other two to the other room. I went out and up to the bedroom door and listened to what was going on. As soon as I was certain that their backs were turned, I stepped into the living room and found myself forced to vomit.

On the floor stretched and tied to stakes driven into the floor was Joe. His chest peeled open, the rib cage broken at the sternum and pulled back, his lungs and heart exposed to the world, and he was still alive.

The three girls were being tied down in a similar manner when one of them saw me and screamed for help. The guys that were tying the girls down turned round in time to watch me disappear. I was behind the biggest one and had his knife out before they realized I was there. Slowly, for me, I bent his head back and pulled the knife over and through his neck hard enough to feel the bone break and the meat spit as the weight of his body pulled downward, his head still in my hand.

I had killed him, not for food but in the name of saving lives. I was stunned and shocked by what I had just done. At how fast I had done it, at the heads weight uncomfortable in my hand. So I lifted it to see if I was sleeping or if I had only imagined his head coming off in my hand as I cut. It had and I screamed, it was still there looking at me with fading awareness, still alive.

Screaming louder in horror, I could feel the nightmare of the reality slipping around me. The girls had begun to scream as well when I felt the thud of thunder hit me in the chest. With shock I looked up to see the end of a gun smoking before me, before I even heard the sound of its report.

The police had come in and shot me before even asking questions. The guys head fell from my hands and hit the floor with a thud as the knife also fell, with its point finding the floor soft and willing to accept it. The sounds of the girls screaming and pleading that I was not the one that needed shooting as the other attacker raised a gun to me.

He yelled out that gods work must be done and went to pull the trigger, but his head erupted into a fine mist followed by another report from the same police mans gun. My knees found the floor almost at the same time the other assassins body did.

Viper and the others came out of the bedroom and did what they could for me and Joe. Somehow he was still alive, I started to regain my senses and everything popped back into place.

"No, he was with me all night, these two we don't know who let them in or where they came from. All we know is we woke up and they were talking about killing us all. I have a secret door to the other bedrooms so I can go from room to room after a party and make sure everyone is Ok without being to invasive, you know so I don't have to interrupt anything, to make sure my guest are Ok.   Tonight that secret passage saved our lives. We had just gotten in when they came in the room and flipped our bed over. I can't believe they thought we were ... were vampires... officer this just frightens me to death, are we going to have to move?"

Viper was doing her best to convince them that nothing had happened here other than a very violent and brutal attack on us, and that when we heard they had the three girls I went out to save them. What happened then was not clear only that both were now dead and it seemed one by my hands.

I gave my statement of what I had seen when I came out into the main room and shortly after I blacked out. That I don't remember anything 'til after everything was done and I was being cared for by the paramedics that already removed Joe from the floor and down to the ambulance, is no wonder to me or the Paramedics. I, it turns out, only have a bit of a flesh wound where the bullet went over my shoulder rather than through it, and am now sitting on a chair with handcuffs on.

After many questions and several hours, the area is cleared so the investigators can come in and put together all the testimony and physical evidence to determine if I would be sent to jail or not. For now I was being taken down and held 'til they could figure out what was going on.

Viper to her credit, once the girls were taken care of, insisted on staying with me. If I was to be held, then she would have to be held as well. So we found ourselves down at the station sitting in a quite little room waiting.

"You didn't have to come down with me you know, I will be ok." I say to her. She smiles and replies. "Yea, but if I left you then it would just have looked worse than it already does for you. I don't want you being alone right now, you don't disserve this. I mean, I am the one that brought you to my home, had I left you out there, you would not be here now."

"Had you left me out there Viper, you would not be here now, and I doubt you or any of your guest would be alive right now, save maybe William and Amber. Besides your friend Joe is in more need of company right now than I am."

Her head went down and a tear escaped her eye, it is the sound of her voice that makes my body go cold in the end. When I realize what she is saying I literally get so sick to my stomach that I vomit.

"Joe... he can go rot in what ever hell is provided our kind, I talked with him before they carried him away. He told me who they were and why they were there. He had brought them there, so he could go free. They made a deal to spare his life if he could take them to my place. But they didn't keep their word to him and did what they did, just to see what he could take before he died. I heard from the hospital... he died about an hour ago."

"So he ... he brought those guys in to kill us to save himself... I... Viper, are you sure he is dead and not just, that he has not been taken from the hospital by more of who ever those guys were?"

"Yea I am sure, and there will be nothing left of him to take away...when we are finished with his body. I have made all the arrangements, he is to be cremated, and he is already in transit."

Behind the wall on the other side of the glass two detectives sat and listened to what was being said, a recorder capturing everything, said and done. With stoic patients they waited for one of us to slip and say something that would incriminate us in some kind of crime. Something they could use to keep me right here for as long as they needed. And on the other side I just sat watching them through the glass that is supposed to be a mirror, watching them eat their sandwiches, watching me.

Viper moved around the other side of the table and sat up and close to me, placing her head on my shoulder so her mouth was hidden from view, and very silently apologized. She said that she hoped I could forgive her and began to cry.

Looking down I could see she was beginning to tremble, the full weight of what had happened tonight finally settling in on her. She will not make it much longer emotionally, I am certain of it. I put my arm around her and kiss the top of her head, and with slow motions begin to rock her gently back and forth telling her it will be ok.

"Are they still watching," she whispers, "I hate the way they look at us."

This only confirmed she could see as well as I could. But before I could reply the door opened and in came another detective and a catholic priest. They sat down, lit cigarettes and drank from the coffee cups they came in with. After awhile of just sitting and watching, the detective leaned forward.

"The girls say you were just trying to save them, that true?"

"Yes." I said.

"They also said you moved so fast that for a moment you disappeared, only to reappear behind the guy whose head you cut off, that true?"

"What do you think," I reply, "I already told you guys, I stepped into the room to do what I could for the girls, I had no idea that Joe was still there, and when I saw him like that... I blacked out, anything I did after that I can't help you with, I just don't remember."

This was the truth, plain and simple. I had never seen anything like it, with all the crap I have dealt with in my life that I can remember or see in my nightmares. This was more than I could bear. I lost it and blacked out. The detective took another drag and leaned in again just a little further this time, his arms on the table, he points to me with the hand holding the cigarette then continues.

"Well, whether you blacked out or not remains to be seen, I think you were in on it. That you knew what was coming and simply wanted to get rid of any one that could link you to those guys. You know, tie up your loose ends."

"You're reaching for shits..., what's your name anyway, aren't you supposed to introduce yourself before talking with someone?"

"My name is detective Benoît." His name for a moment brings back that horrid memory of being burned alive. Viper feels my discomfort but does not look up she just puts her hand on my lap and squeezes to let me know its ok. It's enough to keep me from reliving that life over again.

I compose myself, and prepare to reply when he continues. "Yea, I got it figured that you have been at this for awhile, looking for people to use and toss aside. There have been some odd killings about town in the last few weeks, and it turns out you've only been in town for just as many, convenient yes?"

"Like I said, you're reaching for shit, all I did was tried to save those girls, you can hold me but you have no reason to put me away. To be honest with you, I can't understand why you would want me. I hate what I did, if I really did it. Like I said, I blacked out. But if I did do it, I did you and the rest of this place a favor. If you have had odd killings lately, then I am certain they will stop now, now that those two are dead."

He looks at me and sets back, as if satisfied with the response. Viper sets up and looks at him and at the priest, then back at the detective.

She lays her head back onto my shoulder but her eyes hold on the priest. His posture shifts and his face contorts for a moment then back to normal, all this in the span of a second and then he no longer felt real.

"So detective Benoît, who is the priest," I asked him, "what's he doing here"

"He is here to bear witness to your guilt, or innocence. If you're really what those guys thought you to be, we wanted to be safe, and his name is Monsignor Rebaulde."

I look back to him and still he feels... empty, so I test the water to see if he is even there.

"Well Monsignor, what do you think of us, are we dangerous are we monsters, does this detective having any ground to stand on?"

"No," came his reply to me, I could tell that his voice was not his own, that it was echoed from somewhere inside him, and the person doing the speaking was Viper. How she was doing this I have no idea but the voice continued, "No, I see no reason for us to be here or for these two to be held, I have other matters to attend to if you don't mind detective, good day."

He stood up with the detective watching him in disbelieve, I could see the guys on the other side of the glass scrambling to stop the recording but it was too late, it was already part of evidence. Short of tampering with it and invalidating whatever case they were trying to make against me, it was over now. The priest walked out the door and left the building before Viper breathed again.

Our good Detective Benoît was left holding on and stood up and walked out behind the priest. I could see the others leave the room, having shut the recorder off. Viper looked me in the eyes and smiled.

"Well now, that went better than I thought it would."

"What do you mean?" I asked her.

"You will be let go, but for the sake of giving testimony at a hearing, you will have to stay and make your statements in court. You're going to be here in town for awhile, it's the best I could do but you will get off."

"So," I ask, "this is all somehow your doing?"

"No, just keeping you safe and out of jail"

"Ok, that I can live with," I say to her, "how much longer you figure will we be held here?"

"Not long now," she said, "the detective gave a false name, one I pulled from your memory. Sorry but it will be enough to get all this thrown out on the grounds of entrapment."

I look at her a little shocked, and begin to ask the question "Aren't you afraid they are still recording us?"

She stops me and simply says, "No."

Half an hour later we are released; out in the waiting room are William and Amber. They get up and almost run to greet us but seem to ignore the fact that I am there. 'Til Viper tells them I will be staying with her 'til I am free to leave the city. At about the same time a lawyer comes out and hands me a paper and says I need to be in court in two weeks to testify or be held in contempt.

Looking at him, another smaller piece of paper finds its way into my hand, my eyes moving from him to the paper so I can read what it says. It's blank except for a hand written message. 'They were cops', and a phone number. Outside we walk to a car that is waiting for us and get in. Once inside and away from the station I show it to Viper.

"I know," Viper say's, "I saw that much in the minds of both the priest and the detective. Something bad is going on here and I fear we are about to be caught up in it. Your room I am certain has already been ransacked by the cops. I will send someone there to get your things and bring them back to my other place. As soon as the main rooms are clean we will all relocate to the manner."

"The manner, am I to assume you have a private home as well? If so why not just go there now?"

She looks at me for a moment, then smiles saying "Ok, driver, take us to the manner." to which the driver pulls over and then turns around heading back the other way. After about an hour we are out side the city and moving into the country. A turn down a private drive and we are racing down a road lined by enormous trees 'til we reach the end, right in front of an old plantation home. It's dark and painted in grays and greens so as to blend in with the surrounding landscape.

I muse to myself that the spring weather here is nice, not to hot, not to humid just right, but by noon we have the ac running. This place is no exception. As soon as we exit the car you can hear them running. Smell the stall water that drips from the units in the windows. Still this place is like a forgotten palace, ivy has grown up all the columns and most of the walls, showing me it's not paint that keeps this place camouflaged but nature itself. The old white wash is faded to a dim grey; at least I saw that correctly through the window tint.

"Come on in everyone," Viper say's with a smile, "everything should be ok, as I have not been here in a year or so. The servants reported in only a week ago, this will be fun catching them off guard like this!"

She runs in and screams 'I'm home', and out of the distance you could hear someone let out loudly in surprise, her response to Vipers' early arrival. Viper laughed and ran to greet the old lady that came out of the back. Her words to Viper leave me looking at her with a little more than just curiosity.

"Emily it's so good to see you again...you didn't tell me you were coming home. You know how much I love having you stop in mother."

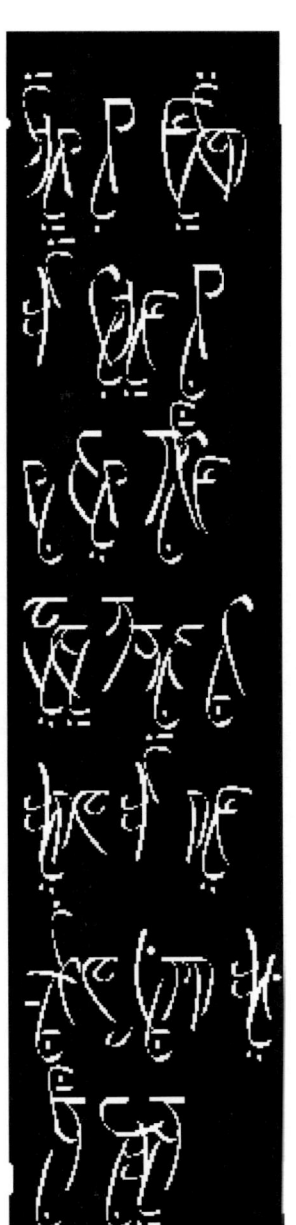

Chapter Eight – Strung out in Memphis

Slow and steady like wreaths in the breeze move

Black clad angels of despair all round sway

Each an island bending to strong winds of heart

Bumped and caressed the dance of souls sooths

Our life's all one here in the dark linked even beyond break of day.

- Vodalok -

For 5 days now Selena, Liz, and the other girls have been living in a dive of a hotel in Memphis. The other girls are getting settled in, and slowly begin to recover their collective mind. Selena knows it's been hard on them and all but, she just doesn't understand how it is they are all so weak inside. All save for her little shadow, and Liz scares her.

Selena thinks to herself, uncertain of what to do with Liz. "With everything she is willing to do for me. Going out and bringing back guys from the bars for us to toy with, and then feed on. Then taking a job as a waitress at that strip club for cash and guys..."

Selena had after the first guy, that they had to get rid of, convinced Liz that if they are going to be staying here for a while, they can't go killing every man Liz brings home, it just won't do. Thankfully she understood and agreed.

Liz's hunger to watch Selena feed is becoming a problem. What kind of life did Liz lead that brought her to this? What was her relationship with her brother really like? Selena knows Liz told her they were not lovers but... Something in Selena feels that statement was/is a lie.

"My god," Selena thinks, "just thinking about the things they may have done together, prior to winding up where they did, where I met them... it bothers me to no end. The most disturbing part of her is when she is out and about in public. She is so quite and demure, the mask she wears is very well constructed and a complete lie."

Tonight Liz starts working as a striper at one of the dives close to where they are living. An arrangement Selena is not all that comfortable with, but one she realizes is needed. Selena is snapped out of her thoughts by Liz's voice.

"The number of assholes and fuckups we can bring home from a place like that," Liz said, "that will never be missed is staggering. How can we not afford to have me working there? And the money I will make only reinforces the need."

Liz is very ready to do anything to serve Selena, to protect her. Selena is not certain how to take it. Liz's devotion, and her desire to see Selena feed or help her seduce men into letting her feed, is unnerving.

So while Liz is out 'shopping' for food, Selena is helping the other girls get better, well trying to. Trying To help them regain their confidence in themselves is a big part of staying in one place. Selena thinks that having Liz away doing as she is only helps her help them. Liz's presence is sometimes detrimental to their recovery. Was she somehow in on all the crap that went on there? If she was they are not talking.

"Liz," Selena ask, "what time do you think you will be home tonight?"

"Well," Liz calls back from the bathroom where she is getting ready to go, "the bar closes at 2, and so I should be home by 3, maybe sooner. I will have dinner for you Ok, so no getting skittish on me when we get here, Ok?"

Selena thinks to herself, looking at Liz as she moves from the bathroom to the main room. "How can she be so ruthless and still seem so innocent, so child like." Selena looks at Liz and see's her for the first time as she is. Liz's pouting lip and wide open eyes looking at her for the entire world as if she expected Selena to hurt her right there, on the spot. For even suggesting Selena might get 'skittish' or back out.

Still looking at Liz, Selena knows that if she leaves Liz, with her looks, no man would be safe. Their lives will be Selena's burden even if she is on her own, something Selena can not deal with.

In the last few days Selena has learned that she can feed without needing to kill, and still feel as good as she did before, it's surprising how little blood she really needs.

"Don't worry," she say's to Liz, "it's been two days since I fed, I won't be holding back tonight, but we need to be mindful of the others. They are still very freaked out by all this. I don't want any of them running off into the night and not coming back like Bertha did.

"I may never forgive you for that, what you did was uncalled for. If I am going to trust you, you have to do as I say and never ever act on your own ever again, Ok?"

"Yes mama," Liz says, perfectly whipped in voice and posture, "for you I am ever your willing servant. I am ever your willing tool to use as you see fit, beat me and I shall ask for more, drink from me and I will not resist, rap me and I shall submit."

The smile that crosses Liz's face while saying this leaves Selena wondering if Liz is even human. That child like smile is so out of place on her face and body. It makes Selena think she should be dressing her in white shirts, and short plaid skirts, the fullness of Liz's breast, lips, the doe's quality of her large brown eyes, and the texture of her blonde hair.

Selena smiles in spite of herself, after all, Liz keeps trying to get Selena to sleep with her every night. Swearing it's ok and that she loves Selena, so that makes it ok. Selena knows Liz is devoted to her, but at what cost to her own mind? Selena hates thinking about all this and looks about the room at the other girls there.

Looking at two of the stronger girls, she see hope for all of them. These two who have been making trips to the local food store each day. They do it just to get out and bring back something fresh to eat or drink for the rest each day.

Today they come back from the store and they are smiling as they enter. Liz and Selena both look up at them, and they come over talking about this guy they met. It's a very good and healthy sign. One Selena hopes to see the others start making progress towards soon. Selena is not sure she has the patience to care for them much longer.

After listening to them for a bit Selena finds out this guy has invited them to a party later this week, and would love to come by and pick them up. Selena tells them she needs to make sure he will not hurt them, or do anything to them that they don't want happening. That he will make sure they are safe while with him no matter what. They agree and one of them goes out and brings him back, much to Selena's surprise.

"This is Daniel," the one that went out for him say's, "he works over at the riding stables part time, to pay for part of his schooling."

He steps forward and looks at Selena, raises an eye brow and smiles.

"You don't look old enough to be anyone's mother." He says', "it's a pleasure to meet you Selena."

He holds out his hand and offers it up for a shake. Selena is to busy looking at the girls in irritation at bringing him here so fast, to realize she is making the pour guy uncomfortable. He almost pulls his hand back, but she smiles hurriedly and apologizes, then shakes his hand.

"Won't you have a seat and talk for a bit..." Selena looks around the room at the other girls, wondering how it must all look to him, "I am sorry I missed your name what is it again"

"Its Daniel mama," comes the other girl next to him, "you can call him Dan if ya like."

"Dan it is then." Selena says, "Thanks for the compliment. It's been a long time since I received one. It does an old ladies heart good to hear such nice things about her visible age."

The smile on Selena's face wanes a bit as the door to the room is still open, she looks to the two girls that brought him here and raises an eye brow. They look behind them and almost freak out running to close it.

Selena watches Dan as he appears to get a little more nervous having been shut in with all these girls. Three are on the bed sleeping, while two more are on the floor wrapped up in one another's arms sleeping. Then there is Trish, and May, the two he already knows, Liz, and of course Selena.

Again Selena ask for him to have a seat, offering him the desk chair, and talk. Liz sits on the edge of the bed, watching him. You could see her eyes working him over, wondering how long he would last beneath Selena and herself. Selena finds the thought, though vivid, is both amusing and disturbing. The fact that Selena can see her thoughts now is also a little disturbing. Selena looks at Liz and tells her how bad she is out loud.

Without missing a thing, Dan steps back a little more uncomfortable, and then he takes a seat and asks very simply.

"So, mama, what brings you ladies here to the home of Elvis?"

"I thought that was Tupelo Mississippi," Liz butted in, "he just moved here after he made it big and never went back, right?"

"Well yea, that's true but he never claimed that place as home really, that's why we get to call Memphis his home."

"Dan," says Selena, "what kind of party do you plan to take my girls too?"

He looks away from Liz, almost snapping his head back in the direction of Selena just to answer.

"Well mama, it's really not a party, it's more of a revival. You know to help people find their way back to God. Pastor Robert's says we should not be shy and ask everyone we meet to come along and join in worship. That God loves those that love themselves through him."

Selena's eyes just grow wider and wider as he keeps talking, she could not believe he was saying what he was saying. What's worse, she could tell he was completely serious. He wanted to save their souls! Standing up and grabbing her smokes she walked to the door and asked Dan to join her. When Liz and the girls went to stand as well she shook her head no, smiled, and said 'just Dan'.

Once outside with the door closed, Selena started walking away from the door, heading for the pop machine that was by the pool. She lit a smoke and took a deep drag on it, then offered him one. He declined with a shake of his head and a raised hand. Dan smiled his thanks back at her for the offer. She looked at him and wondered just how nice of a guy he was. After getting both of them a pop she sat down by the pool at one of the tables there, and started talking.

"Dan you seem a darling of a young man, just how old are you?"

"22 mama," He smiled in answer, "I am going to school here to become a minister."

"Really?!" came her reply, visible disbelief on her face, as she fought the memory of the minister she ended up killing only weeks ago. "So you honestly want to help people, and save them from the horrors of the world? You want to protect them from the monsters that lurk behind every corner? None of this is just a ploy to get girls out into the woods for a drunken fuck?"

She knew her questions were kinda harsh, and just a bit insulting, but it was needed she thought, and he took it without flinching. The soft smile that came across his face did tell her everything she needed to know. His reply only reinforced her growing understanding of the boy.

"Mama, I am still a virgin, and will remain that way 'til after I am married, like my mother and father before me. I am not out to take

136

advantage of them girls in there. If I could, I would do what I can to see them in school, not out and about, no offence, living here likes this."

"I see," said Selena, "so you think you could help them better than I can?"

"Mama you seem a good woman, but living out of a van in motels, no matter how nice, is no place for girls their age. It leads to drinking and running wild." As he said this, all she could think of was Liz. Liz was not much older than the rest. The oldest of them was Bertha, and she was 22, she ran off while they were sleeping last night. "If they were in school, they would have a better chance at life than the one you're giving them."

As much as she hated it, he was right. It didn't make the words any easier to deal with. Hell Selena didn't want to be burdened by the lot of them anyway. But then she thought to herself, with them gone, she would not have to worry about them any more. That she would be free to move on with her life, like she was trying to do before she wound up in that hell hole, almost dead.

"How much would it cost to get them into school with you," Salena asked, "and put them up in good rooms 'til they got jobs and could support themselves?"

"Where I am going," Dan started, "if they could get scholarships, not more than $7000, apiece. My father is the Dean, so I am certain I could get them in for less, and until they could as you say 'support themselves,' they could stay at our house. Maybe even get jobs working at the stables with me to pay their way."

"Ok, I will make you a deal. You take them tonight, go to the revival and then home, you take care of them, they've been through an awful lot." She paused and looked at him with the sternest and foreboding look she could muster, "What I am going to tell you, you can't tell anyone, but you must swear to protect them and keep them safe, do you understand boy!"

"Yes mama," he said, "I do swear."

"Ok you watch the news right," he nodded his head yes and she continued, "You've heard of those girls on the run, the ones accused of killing those men down in New Orleans. Well we're those girls and let me tell you, we didn't kill those men. That other girl that was watching you in there, the one sitting on the bed, her brother did, so we could get away.

'Those men were raping these girls on a daily bases, beating them, selling them out of the country. And some, we could not get out. These are the ones we could save. Thing is no one can know that, they must be kept safe, on the off chance the men responsible for this, come looking for them... do you understand?"

Selena knew she was taking a gamble but she also knew she could not keep them with her forever. If this kid was telling the truth, then they would be Ok. So she sat and watched his reaction, his shock and the tears that started streaming down his face as he realized just how hard the girls had had it. It let Selena know she could trust him. He stood up and then went down on one knee and looked up to Selena and spoke.

"I swear to you beneath the pillars of heaven that nothing will ever happen to those two girls, they shall know a life free from the suffering they have known up 'til now. I swear to you before god that I shall give my very life to see them safe and happy, *'til the day they die*!"

It was more than she had hoped for but knew it would do nicely. Selena tried to read his mind, but found he was strong, that she could not get in. But, this young man certainly seemed sincere. And she decides to do what was needed. Standing up she took his hand and helped him to his feet, then led him back to the room with the others. When she entered, she asked Liz to join her in the back of the room, Dan in tow.

"Liz we are going to give Dan what he needs to see too it that Trish and May get into school and are taken care of. We are going to pass them on to his care. I think we can trust him."

"He is a man," Liz spat, everything seductive about her turning into hate that quickly filled the room with its on visible darkness, "all we can trust him to do is use them in the end. I don't think this is a good idea!"

"Liz," Selena stormed back at her, Dan feeling like he was about to be eaten, but holding his ground, "remember who is in charge, and your self appointed place beneath me. We will leave them with Dan and give him enough cash to see them through, is that understood?!"

Liz backed down instantly, going as far as to crouch on the floor hands up as a show of subservience, without looking at Selena she consented and crawled to the kitchenette and grabbed the purse that the money was in. As Dan watched all this, he was becoming more nervous than he was the last time he was in here just moments ago.

When Liz reached them again Selena sat on her back, using her as a stool to reinforce her position as master, and Liz's position beneath her.

"Dan here is $15,000 for the needs of Trish and May. Make sure they are well cared for. We will check in on them from time to time so I will need a number and address so I can keep in touch." She hands him a pen and pad of paper, "Write them here, if you're telling me the truth this will not be a problem for you, right?"

Dan took the money in pure disbelief that this was happening, when the pen and paper were placed in his hands, he without hesitation wrote down three separate phone #s and address's that he could be reached at, one for the school, one for his place and one for his parents place. Rather impressed with the willingness of this young man, she put him to the last test.

She could feel Trish and May watching, she knew that they were eager to be free of her and Liz, but mostly Liz. Trish had confided in her earlier in the week that Liz scared her more than she herself did.

Selena stood and moved to the girls and motioned for Dan to follow, in front of the door she addressed them all.

"Trish, May," Selena started, "you are going to go with Dan now, he is going to get you both into school with him, and help you guys get back on your feet, and if you want, with your families. I respect your desire not to go home after all you've been through, but I hope one day you will let your parents know you're Ok. For now, do everything you can to make me proud of you.

'I will be checking in on you from time to time, so don't think you're free of my watchful eye." This is said with a very stern tone to her voice and a harder look in her eyes, "Ok?"

"Yes mama" was all they said.

Dan took her hand and kissed it saying "God bless you and keep you". For some reason, Selena's gut churned as he said it. Then opened the door and led them out.

Selena watched them leave the court yard then closed the door. Leaning there she looked at the other girls that were still there, all of them watching her, Liz still on the floor in the kitchen on all fours waiting to be relieved from her punishment.

"What am I going to do with the rest of you?" Selena thought, but decided to not think about it for now. She needed to make sure that Trish and May would be Ok.

"Liz get up!" Selena said, "I need you to do something for me. You need to be nice and watch the rest of them 'til I get back. Don't worry I will be back before you have to go start your job. I need to feed after, all right?"

"Yes mama," Liz replied, "I can't wait 'til latter when I can bring you something from the bar."

Selena without thinking about it further left the room and headed out. She saw that Dan was only now leaving, both Trish and May looked very happy. They were eating ice cream and laughing. So far so good, Selena got in the car they had purchased and followed him to where he was going. About 15 min later she was in front of a large campus, and then in front of a large building that she soon learned was where the Dean's office was located.

She walked about for a bit asking questions of people here and there, and found that the boy had told the truth. His father was the Dean and that he had gone in to see him with the girls. A few min later and she was sitting in the waiting room of the Deans' office.

About an hour had gone by before Dan came out with Trish and May in tow. And behind them was the Dean. Selena stood up and smiled, stepped forward and offered her hand to the older man.

"I am Selena," she said, "I just stopped by to make sure the girls were being admitted and taken care of properly."

The older man accepted her offer and shook her hand politely. His expression however was of caution.

"I am Dean Blake, Dan here told me the girls are late arrivals and that their care taker... I assume you, could not be here to join them in the enrollment, I see things have changed?'

"Yes," Selena said, "I was able to get a few extra hours away, to come down and make sure they were settled in properly. Trish, May, Dan is taking care of you, yes?"

The girls lit right up and both exclaimed brightly that he had done very well and that they were about to go to where they would be living 'til the end of the year here at school. Dean Blake asked Selena to join them as they were given the tour of the grounds. Selena said she could only stay a little while but would like to know where the girls would be living.

The Dean being a very charming man decides to start the tour from there. Many looks were cast their way as they walked the campus to the dorms, followed by whispers of 'I didn't know the Dean gave tours' or who's the lady the Dean is crushing on'. Selena listened to all of this as well as the Deans description of all the different area's they were moving through on their way to the dorms.

Once they reached the dorms, Dan stood outside as the Dean led them into the building and introduced them to the den mother, Miss Thompson, who was a comely older lady of about 65. She reminded Selena of the maid from 'different strokes'. It was mostly her build. However she was just as stern and seemed rather light hearted.

All this was pleasing to Selena, Dan had been telling the truth and these two at least would be ok. Selena said her goodbyes, giving them both hugs and again making them promise to be good and not cause any trouble for anyone. Both agreed to this and thanked her for saving their lives, which they would forever be in her debt.

Once Outside again, she stopped short of just walking past Dan and leaving. Turning round she regarded him as he sat there on the steps looking at her, his personal bible in his hands as if he had been reading when she walked by.

She knew without a doubt now that good people did exist in the world. That they were out there and that when you least expected it, they would be there for you. She began to cry and turned to leave, behind her foot steps came running up, it was Dan. She stopped and turned to face him.

"Mama, look I know it's not my place but you seem like you could use someone to talk to... I am sure...."

She cut him short before he could finish and simply stepped away, her eyes hardened and she started to turn leaving him with one thing to think about.

"I don't want to eat you, you're too good to die like that, leave me alone."

Once in the car she left quickly. Even without looking back, she knew he hadn't followed her. The drive back to the motel was gratefully uneventful.

The thoughts in her mind were of the minister that she had killed. How she had gone through with that. It was more than she could handle from time to time. She knew she would regret that moment for the rest of her life, that if she ever died she would surly go to hell.

Upon reaching the room Selena found her world turning upside down again. The moment she walked in Liz ran over and grabbed her arm pulling her head long over to the bed, then pushed her down and pointed at the TV.

To her utter surprise was a picture of Stephen, the anchor woman said he was being released from custody pending a full investigation of events that took place the night before.

As she listened she could not believe what was being aired. "The new Orleans district 11 police released this statement just moments ago, saying that the events that took place last night in the Plaza Hotel at 4:30am appear to have been related to several other deaths involving what reporters have been calling the vampire slayings.

"This is not to say that people have turned up dead at the hands of vampires, rather, several people have turned up dead that were thought to be, vampires.

"We are urging members of the underground subculture known as Goth, to please refrain from any activity that would put them at risk at this time until the persons responsible for these actions are brought to justice."

Aw struck she just sat there, looking at his picture. He was being held, no, released in connections with a series of murders he more than likely didn't commit. She knew it, and he was close behind.

The question here is how to proceed. The reporter went on to say that the attacks last night took place in the suite of a local wealthy Eras named, Emily Von Wolfgang.

She let the words fall short on her ears, standing up she reached for a smoke, and into her fingers fell one. Raising it to drag more stunned than anything by what she had just heard. Selena never noticed that Liz was right there with the lighter. As she inhaled, the smoke came and gave her some small comfort. Still unaware that she had not done these things herself.

Two steps forward and she sat down again at the table. She looked about the room and knew she could not drag these girls around anymore, she had to do something. It was too late to get them to the school, and besides, keeping them in a group could be very bad for every one of them.

They watched her with some sort of expectation, what was going to happen and when, then her eyes fell on Liz. Maybe she could leave them all with her... no. Liz's mind was far to broken to be trusted like that, Selena needed to keep Liz close.

Then it came to her.

"Liz," she said quietly, "it's time for you to go to work, right?"

"Yes." Liz replied.

"Ok, take the car and go, don't come back I will meet you there. If you pick someone, make sure they are nobody, do you understand?"

"Yes mama!" Liz squealed, Selena certain she had not understood.

Liz gathered her things and closed the door behind her as she left. Selena asked the other girls to come close and listen to her. As they did so, she knew this was a bad idea but that she needed to do it.

"I need to leave you all now," Selena started, "I don't know what will happen to you, but after seeing that bit on the news I know I can't keep you with me. If there are people out there hunting... hunting me, you're all at more risk with me, than not with me."

They sat watching her, listening and two of them at least appeared to understand. One tried to look strong and nod her head in understanding. The effect was more pathetic than confidence, Selena sighed and continued.

"To make you all look innocent I am going to have too..." she looks away from them and takes a deep drag on her smoke, then continues without looking at them, "...hurt you, so the police will believe you were being held captive by me.

"But you must give them all this paper work here," she holds up the folder file that had everything that Liz's brother gave her. Including the note for Liz she had forgotten about, "this stuff proves you were being held as slaves for sell. It proves you had nothing to do with any ones death... before I broke you out, Ok?"

They nodded their understanding, those that were able too. Those that could not just sat staring blankly at her. She rose and took one of those by the hand and laid her out on the bed. The rest she ordered to sit close.

She gathered rope from the gear she had, and tied them all up, their backs tight to one another. Once that was done she blindfolded them and told them to remember, not to say anything about Liz, Trish, or May, they are out of this. The police would be able to help them if they just stuck by the story. It was after all, mostly true.

Once they were all secure, she turned her attention to the girl on the bed. Her name was Rebecca. She knew this only because one of the others had told her that's what her name was. She had not spoken, or shown any signs of recovering in the last week or so since they got away.

Liz had told her Rebecca had been there longer than any of them, that she was unsellable. So their captors kept her for their own fun. Some of the stories Liz told of how they broke the girls, especial Rebecca, sickened Selena.

Rebecca was looking and acting for all intentions and purposes, as if she were completely dead inside, her mind shattered beyond repair. So Selena started making things look as good as she could. She undressed her and lay down next to her, feeling the hunger build in her, not just for the blood but for the act of taking that blood.

She moved her hands over Rebecca's body, feeling the softness of her flesh, touching her where she should not, finding her surprisingly moist, and open. Kissing her on the mouth, she moved down over her breast and belly 'til she was kissing the mound of this girl who was to die to protect the others.

She found herself a little reluctant to move further, when she felt the hand of Rebecca on her head, she looked up and she was looking at her, eyes vacant and hollow, almost. Still, tears fell from her eyes, somehow knowing she was about to die. But, her hand was not pushing Selena away. Rather it was tender and forgiving. There was something in the eyes that reminded her of the eyes of the angels, that showed up to claim the priest.

Then her head lay back down, and her hand went back to her side, and Selena did what she needed to do. Slowly kissing and licking the wetness from between her thighs. Then just to the side of her sex she bit down hard and opened the vein that waited there. The blood flowed into her mouth, Rebecca's body quivering every time she pulled with her mouth on the side of her swollen sex.

Selena's hands holding her down and rubbing her softly to comfort her. After about a min, the blood stopped flowing, and Rebecca's body stopped moving, no, it stopped breathing. There was no heart beat. She had passed away without a shudder.

Setting up after feeding was hard for her, her head spinning harder and faster than if she had been drinking all night. Every sense she had was tingling in ways they had never done before. All she could think of was sitting back down, and when she did there was Rebecca's body, lifeless and pale before her.

She had drained every ounce of blood from her, but in a way that was neither violent nor cruel. As a result it seemed, her body appeared perfect, timeless, and utterly innocent. Rebecca's' skin was now so completely white, her lips a soft blue, even her red hair seemed to have become silk in both texture and shine. Selena could not help be lye there holding her, tears in her eyes.

It must have been close to an hour that she lay there looking at her body. Never once did she move, or did the others move. Did they sense some danger to themselves? If they did, were they afraid of what was coming? Selena didn't know, or care at this point. She knew if she wanted to she could look into their minds and see why they sat so quietly.

But for the first time she tasted the blood of a willing donor. Someone that would give up their life for her willingly, without regret, and that blood humbled her, it made her feel full, content, and drunk. It was a feeling she had never known before, the feeling of love.

Slowly she rose up and moved from the bed, stopping only to pull a sheet over Rebecca's body, giving her the dignity that she deserved, in this her final rest. The package with all the info needed to prove these girls were used, and abused, was put under her body, along with a note and half of what was left of the money.

She told the girls to start trying to get free, to make as much noise as they could as soon as they heard the door close. Then she dialed 911 and left the phone on the floor next to the bed. She moved to the door and left. As soon as the door closed she heard them begin yelling through their gages.

Now outside, she walked away as fast as she could and made her way to the bar where Liz was working. Once there, she sat down and watched her for a while, Liz seemed to be very good at getting these boys to pay out for a glimpse of her body.

Selena watched as Liz took a few upstairs to the "preferred customer" room. A few moments later they would come out, followed by Liz. You could tell she had taken them both, and they paid for it well. When she came out she was all smiles, and would go in back for a bit to stash the money she made.

At around 10pm she came over to Selena dressed and ready to leave, in tow was a boy who couldn't have been more than 22, but he was covered in tattoo's and missing a few teeth. His beard looked to have been neglected for no less than a week, it was rough and dirty, Liz can sure pick em. They all left and got into Selena's car and drove away into the night.

Back at the hotel, the police had arrived and found the girls still tied up, looking every bit as beaten and battered as they were meant to look. So well had they been tied together by Selena that the act of trying to get lose caused them all to receive some serious rope burns, black eyes and bruises.

It was Rebecca's body that stopped everyone. The girls openly cried when they saw her body removed by the coroner. They all told how they had been saved by Selena, only to be use by her over the last few weeks as nothing but meat, for her physical and mental needs. They all tell the police that Rebecca had offended her and that she was always singled out at night. For some reason though she told them to scream when she left, they didn't ask why. They just hoped she would never come back.

The packet under Rebecca gave the police everything they needed and all the girls were taken to the hospital and cared for. Then taken to a woman's shelter and put up for the night. The money was later divided among them, so they could get started again in their lives, or pay their way back to their respected homes to try and start over. One of them in the end committed suicide on the grey hound bus home, to ashamed to look her husband in the eyes.

In the car Liz drove as Selena chatted up the boy that would be used tonight. If anything, Selena knew she would have to keep Liz happy in order to keep some kind of hold on her. Selena had decided that at least once a week, whether they killed or not that Liz would be allowed to use a man as she saw fit, as long as it didn't go to far. But Selena was hard put to decide what was too far? That would be determined by how he, or any man answered Selena's questions.

"Sooooo, you ever dream about hurting a girl or keeping her tied up as a sex slave," she asked, while walking her fingers down his chest, "it's something we are willing to do, if you want."

"No mama," he said, "I's just like to have sex, if you understand what I mean. I aint never had me no steady girl friend or nothin`, just like getting in, and getting out. Things is less complicate that way."

"I see," Selena replied, "so you don't like to hit your girl, just do your business and move on. Interesting" Serena purred this into his hear as her hands moved closer to his belt.

"Yea, you know it aint so bad," he said, "everyone gets what they want, and no one gets hurt."

Liz looked back at him, and then to Selena. Her eyes moved out the front window to a side road with rows of corn growing tall on both sides. Selena nodded to her, and she pulled off the main road and down the dirt road. The poor drunk kid looked at them and out the window and commented that this was not the way to his place. Selena silenced him by saying they were going to their place. A little further down the way and they pull off and shut down.

Liz crawls in back on the other side of him. Selena says "This here boy is alright, not so bad. If I was the killing type I'd let him live." Sure enough this did make him kinda nervous, but that feeling soon faded away as Liz un-did his pants and pulled him out, teasing the tip with her tongue.

Selena sat back for a bit and watch as they got undressed and fooled around, until she was ready to join in. Undressing she moved into place and pushed Liz to one side and went down on him herself. Liz came back over, got up close and started kissing and licking him from the side as Selena moved up his root with her mouth.

Before long he could hold back no longer, and let lose every bit of his bodies stress in one large shudder. Liz did her best to keep it from making a mess, while Selena bit into his inner thigh. There they both drank from his blood.

Keeping things under control, Selena stopped Liz and licked the wounds till they healed. Something she had only recently learned she could do. Selena was certain that any more would kill him. She gave him a drink laced with sleeping pills, and started kissing him again. Within the next 15 minutes he was out like a light, but still breathing.

They took all his money and tossed him and his clothes out into the ditch making sure he didn't drown in the bit of water that was at the bottom. Then they dressed and left him there. Several hours passed and they had crossed into the mountains of Kentucky.

The driving became a little hard for Liz, so Selena took over. As she drove into the night Liz laid her head in Selena's lap and fell asleep.

Selena drove though the whole night thinking of everything she had done since Stephen came into her life, almost a month ago now?

It was hard for her to believe she had done this to herself, and then punished the doctor for helping her. Regardless of what he did to her after. Granted he had brought his death on himself, she had no idea he wanted her like that, or that she would wake the way she did.

She felt tears falling down her face, and said a pray for each of those whose life's she had taken with each tear, counting them off one by one as if the tears were rosary beads. If only there was a way to change the past and go back and undo all this. She knew she couldn't, but she needed to know what was going on with her as well. Maybe once she was in Detroit, she could find someone to help her make sense of all this.

As the sun rose she put her glasses on and looked down at the sleeping Liz. Liz's face was still covered in blood, something Selena smiled at. Thinking to herself, "how lovely Liz is like this..." Then stopped herself, thinking, "What a monster I must be to have such thoughts." As she began to clean Liz's face with a shirt tail, she realized she had been moving about during the day without issue, then thought to herself. "How come I am not burning like he did that day? Why am I able to be out in the day light?"

Whatever the reason for it, she was way too tired to care really, and found a road side hotel just inside the Ohio boarder. Getting a room was not a problem and she was soon in bed and had Liz watch the car, telling her they would get food once she woke up later.

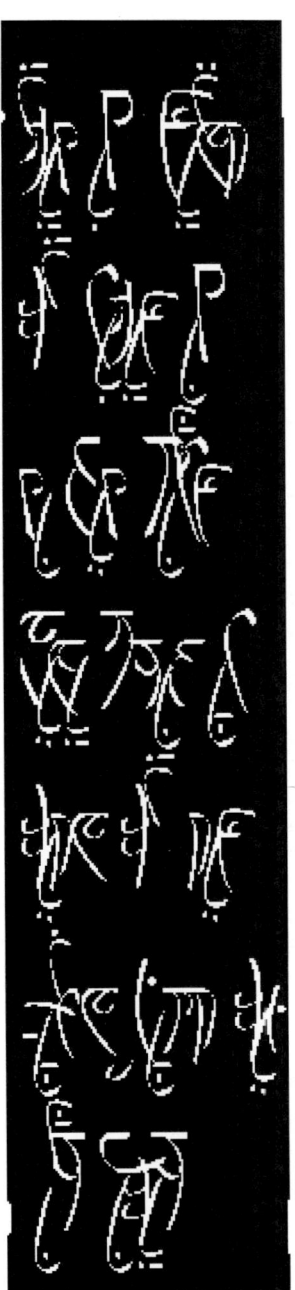
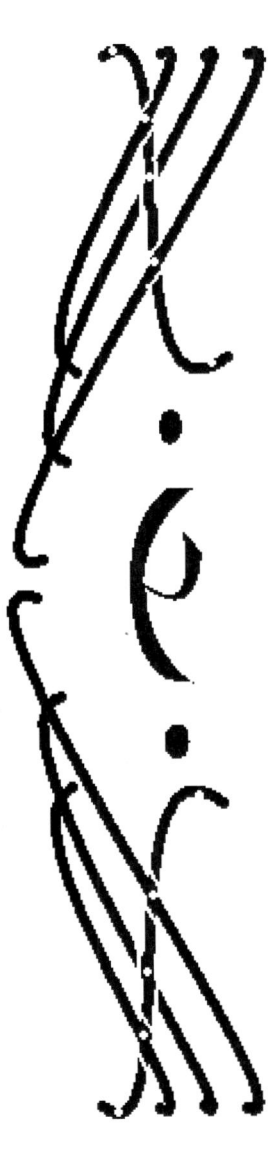

Chapter Nine - Funeral Pyre

From without the city breathes and sighs

And our dance goes on inside the pulsing din

To ears sound the words of death our fallen friend

By Hands our own do we go to the garden of lies

Shattered for now the link of darker souls akin

- VODALOK-

Part I, "are you dead yet"

Viper was so happy to see the old lady, for a moment forgetting her company and rushing up to her, calling her daughter. After a few moments in each others arms they turned to greet us and with great big smiles exclaimed, "WELCOME TO THE PLANTATION". Viper motions for us to follow as they turned and walked inside. Servants came out and gathered our things as we headed up the stairs, and through the great double doors that framed the entrance of this manor home.

Passing the doors we found ourselves in one of the most splendid homes I had ever seen. The great stair case that was before us was right out of a movie, wide enough for 5 people to walk down side by side, and turning to the left and right as it ended on the landing to the second floor. To the left and right of the staircase, underneath the second floor were doors leading farther into the place. On each wall left and right of us were set glass French doors that opened into large rooms, one seemed to be ballroom, the other some old world family room.

The servants came in behind us and headed up the stairs with our things, heading in both directions once reaching the landing at the top of the stairs. Viper continued on through the door on the left side of the stairs so we followed. The path was sort of narrow and finally opened after about 20 or so paces into a kitchen that had two other doors on the same wall heading back the way we had just came.

She saw me looking and said that the lavatory was that way under the stairs as was a pantry between the stove and frig that were also on that wall. I had seen what looked like a coat closet on the inside wall of the hall we just came through, also set under the stairs.

The kitchen was very large, counters on the east, north and west walls, all in all, large enough to support normal usage or large parties without issue. She then took us threw the door to the left that lead into a grand hall. Windows are on the north, south, and west walls with a great fireplace on the east wall. Along the south wall was a band-stand and a few tables were set about along the north wall.

From there it was back through the east doors to the sun room, then to a private study and finally to the great room I had seen when we first enter, where guest could go read from the many books on the shelf's lining the walls.

Then we headed upstairs to the bedrooms of which there were 5, 4 for guest and one master bedroom. I found that my things had been moved there, to the master room with Vipers things. William and Amber had been given the room in the south west corner.

After the big tour of the house and the grounds, Viper accepted my offer of some one on one quiet time. She took me to the large study in the east of the house and her "daughter" brought us food and drinks. After a little time was spent chewing the fat and some small talk, I finally could take it no more and began asking the questions she said I could, that she would answer.

"Ok Viper, that old lady, she looks to be 65, 70 years old. How come you call her your daughter?"

"It's simple, she is my daughter. I had her back in 39. It was not easy then, having a child out of wedlock, so much harassment and ridicule. But I was only 19 and didn't want to give her up. So after working some hard hours in the French quarter, I was able to start saving and earning the money I needed to keep her and myself, without having to rely on family."

"Wait," I ask, "you were 19 in 39, but you look like you're only 23, if that right now, how is that, is that possible. To my knowledge our kind grows old and dies like everyone else. Our immortality is in our memories not our bodies."

"For your kind that is true, for me and what I am, it is not. You see I was brought over by taking the blood of one of you directly to the heart, that really works, but we have not been able to do it again since. Several have died trying, nothing we can do works, all we can think of is that there was something special about the one that we took the blood from."

To me what she said sounded right, but I could tell she was hiding something from me, like Victor before her...Victor.... That name again, I can't afford to get distracted and look at her to focus, and continues.

"So what are you then, if you're vampire, but not aging like we do. What manor of vampire are you, can you die?"

She gets up and moves to the bar that is in the room and makes her a drink, she looks to me and ask if I would like one. I watch her every movement, grace personified, and see no harm in accepting the drink, and she is after all my host and saved my ass from jail, for now.

Accepting the drink I wonder if I should tell her about Selena. If I should tell her she stole my blood and was able to cross over. Or does she already know. Looking at Viper I wonder about just what Selena has become. Is she like Viper because she stole my blood?

All I know is she stole my blood, and the others need to know she is out there. Then I get lost thinking about Viper and the life she must have lived, and find myself wondering if she can create others like her or have children.

She had said that Joe was like her, was he the mortal child of one of my kind crossed over? If so how many of them are there out there and how long have they been around. He died alright but my god what it took to kill him, the thought of his body staked down to the floor his chest opened up, held open by nails and cables.

"Please," Viper said, her voice shaking, "I don't dwell on his death that way, it comes to me all to clear and I don't want to remember him in that way. It's bad enough we will have to go and recover his body only to destroy it completely, to prevent him from rising again. If he does he will not be vulnerable to a mortal death ever again."

Her look was one of utter certainty, despair and fear. "Just what do you mean by all that", I asked her.

"Well Stephen, it's like this, when one of my kind dies, completely as John did, three days latter its body reanimates. It comes back to life and digs its way out of the ground... and begins stalking the night.

"You don't hear about it in the news because we know now what we have to do. In the past my kind would try to keep them, awaken them to their old life again, it never work out. And in the end they would get loose

152

and slaughter entire villages. We can't have Joe wandering about at night, no matter how much I would like to keep him."

"And why would you want to keep him," I asked. "If he is this monster now, what hope do you have that he could be woken up?"

"It's not so much waking him up. As it is bringing his mind back from the ruin it is in. Only one has ever been brought back, and you know his name, everyone alive does. In the end we had to hunt him down and destroy even him. At least that's what the elders tell me."

It takes a few moments of listening to her, watching her watch me, her eyes burning with all the emptiness I had seen in them when I first met her, and then it strikes me. It's not emptiness I am seeing, but unfathomable knowledge, the kind that comes from living a long life stuck between the worlds of the living and of the dead.

Granted she has not yet lived a full life for even a mortal yet but she is close in years to when most mortals start to pass on from old age. Then the greater part of what she told me illuminates in my mind, she is talking about 'The Count', Vlad Dracula himself.

For a moment I see before me the world shifting, turning into some chamber, hung with heavy wool embroidered rugs and silk draperies. The wind is blowing threw broken windows bringing with it snow, and the occasional flash of lighting followed by the deafening roar of thunder. In the center of the room is a circular dais's, and on that a circular bed. Upon that bed I watch from what must have been a hidden walkway. I watch as a woman I know I have seen a hundred times before, open her wrist and feed that blood to a man lying beside and under her. Some how I know who he is, a trusted friend, no a brother, an older brother... the vision fads from me, and I am again in the reading room with Viper.

Then as this reality settles in on me, she settles back and drinks from her glass again. I pray she can not see those moments when my world is turned upside down, when I am forced to relive the past. Whether it is from this life or some other I can never really put a time too.

I can see she is comfortable however, in her knowing she has made her point known to me. The cold truth of it makes sense, how I am not certain, but with her sitting before me, herself being what she is, and Selena.... Oh my god!

"Oh my god, Selena, she is now like you... I lost track of her for a while, like she was dead...and now I can feel her and see through her eyes again... what have I done!!"

When I said her name Viper stood up and dropped her glass, she took two steps towards me and stopped, her mouth opened as if to reprimand a child for some horrid trespass of etiquette. Then she called out for her daughter.

When the older lady came in, it was with William and Amber close behind. She asked that the other two please relax. Assuring them that nothing is wrong, she had insisted that her drink slipped from her hand and spilled on the old rug.

Once they were certain everything was ok they went back to what they were doing in the other rooms.

"So your blood is able to cross someone over, and the one you did this too is out there running amuck?" The venom of her words was clear and biting; resisting the urge to yell at her, for me was hard as Viper continued, "the possibility of herself having been killed once already!? Do you realize, if that's true, destroying her now will be almost impossible?!"

"Look Viper it's not like I said 'here take my blood I want you to be cursed for the rest of your life'," I stand up and put my drink down, then take a step towards the door way, "I was in the fever, in and out of it, when I came too, after the fever passed, she was gone.

"She left me a note saying she was going to live a new life and left. I had nothing to do with her taking my blood. Fact is I don't know if I was talking in my sleep during the fever or not, for all I know she could have known what to do and after finding out what I was, took advantage of me! Don't go getting all high and mighty on me. I don't see where you have the room too. Seeing as you yourself have admitted to being like her, vampire only because you got some good blood!"

I admit what I said was harsh and came out of me in a hiss under my breath, but she had little right in my mind to say a damned thing to me about what happen between me and my errant child.

Her daughter was standing by her and went to start yelling at me, but was silenced by Viper with a single gesture. Viper turned to her and asked that she go get Chan, and bring him and others to this room if they had arrived. They needed to go get Joe before it was too late, and give to him the rest he disserved. Then she turned back to me as the old lady left the room.

I found it interesting that I have not heard her name yet, and if I have, that I have not remembered it. Viper took my hand and led me out back to the garden again, and we entered the hedge rows that were near the back. A small but well laid out labyrinth of yew, grown well over our heads. Once we reached the center there where graves there, a fairly large circle of smaller above ground tombs each with a statue separating it from the next and a larger central mausoleum. We approached this center piece and she put her right hand on one of the stone seals.

"In these stone graves are the bodies of those we have lost over the last 150 years, some are gone for good, others are being punished. But here in are the remains of both our kind. Of all those in these tombs only one died of old age, he had been alive for almost 1500 years. And when he passed there was nothing we could do for him. We don't know if my 'Kind', come back like you do. You see, though we are long lived we are not immortal. It's only those that die and are not put down that become immortal. Do you understand?"

I was not sure if I did, and let her know that, but I felt like I did. So I put it to her as I was hearing it.

"What you're saying is, 'Your kind' live long lives but in time pass away. When you do pass away, you rise up again after so many days. With your minds lost, or fractured, you become the monsters of myth and legend. You ravage the land wherever you are until destroyed by whatever means are available to those that would hunt you? In effect, if you are never caught you could roam the land until the end of time, killing and eating anything you get your hands on?"

She said, "Yea, that's about it. I was to be the last of our kind, we have gone to great lengths to prevent others from being awakened, but this thing you have..." she stops herself and smiles then continues, "let happen, makes it much more complicated than it should be. We do not feel her like we feel each other. We fear she is something even more different than what we are. If that's the case, we cannot allow her to exist. We must have her destroyed."

Ok that much I agree with, but telling me she could be something other than the rest, does nothing to ease my mind at all. Just then her daughter came into the clearing and told her that Chan and the others would be there by sun down and left us alone again. I could not help but notice she was giving me the evil eye, trying to kill me with just the power of her mind.

"These tombs, like I said hold the bodies of some of ours that we didn't wish to destroy, on the off chance we do come back. We are holding them to life for as long as we can to keep their evil out of the world, to prevent them from doing more harm than they already have."

I looked at the mausoleum again and the horror of what she was saying settled in on me. Completely involuntarily, I stepped away, almost falling over myself to get back from the thing that now was more than a place to rest. Now I know it's' a prison for those that she and her 'brothers' felt were evil or criminal. It was too much for me to bear.

As I started falling away, I could hear the calls of those few still alive inside the tomb, screaming was the last thing they could do, their minds to be freed. So utterly frightening was this feeling, knowing they would live 'til death came for them, that they were somehow being kept alive in those tombs, to prevent them from dying...

My body gave up all its contents there in the grass without mercy, forcing even the bile out of me until all that would come up was air. Slowly rising she points to a place where I can get fresh water, and advises me that I should clean up a bit. A minute or so later I am done cleaning up, never really looking away from her.

Moments passed, her standing there watching me, unmoved by the revelation that has just branded itself to my mind. My mind growing a little weaker with the passing of the moments, knowing that though I am a monster of sorts, that I was not the true monster, it stood before me, cold and calculating in judgment of me, of everything I have done. Worse yet, there would soon be more of these monsters here, to hunt down one of their own and destroy it. Do they have a right to do this? Maybe this thing Joe is becoming is part of the greater plan of god, whoever or whatever that is. They can't control the will of the divine, no more than I can give birth to a child.

When I look up at her, I see she is regarding me as though she was... she is reading my mind!! How long has she been doing this? Can she know what is a real thought or a fabricated one? One put forward in my mind to keep her from knowing my true intentions? And in answer she replies to that very thought.

"We can read your mind, but only yours and those like you for some reason, not the minds of mortal men, it seems that is a gift given only to those that die and are allowed to wake up without the nightmare of being buried. There is more to talk about, but we need to get back to the house... come, hold my hand."

I step up to her and watch as her entire demeanor shifts from serious contemplation, to light and playful. She reaches out to me and takes my hand then pulls me in closer to herself. For a moment she looks into my eyes and I do see in her passion, regret, emptiness. All on a level I have known for the majority of my life, and her soft beauty is again worth any risk. The moment reminds me of those old movies were the lead woman would always look like she was in a fuzzy glow to make her look more attractive or perfect...

I try to remind myself of the monster she is, that she is capable of horrors on a level that I could scarce suffer in my own mind. But her smile and the smell of her pushes all that aside, and I am again powerless to resist her as she leans in and kisses me.

For a single breath, I tried to resist, but I fail and give into her. My thoughts had given way to flights of fancy that birthed in my mind a poem that as we begin to make love between the graves of those gone before. Of those whose only remaining freedom is in their minds trapped forever in stone, is whispered back to me on my own breath by her.

"In soft eyes I see light from my soul reflected, In a light voice I hear my laughter returned,
From touch your hands the caress that gives me hope,
From lips embraced I know only velvet heaven,
Enfolded arms giving comfort unending,
Soft flesh my dreams made true her legs enwrapped,
From beating heart out her breast entwined,
Smooth silken brace our hips in time,
Our breath like a storm raging and fast,
Out our bodies floods as the rain pours,
Slow and demanding comes the rhythm,
Rhythm demanding comes slow and hot,
Plunging further inside the soul as one,
As one inside the river runs,
Pour out like skies in spring's release,
Held in time this moments' bliss,
Our kiss this time held close in breath,
Your love to me I give from me to you,
This surrender."

Long moments pass as we lay there in the grass, holding each other, staring at the sky above. No words were needed again from that moment. She understood how to win and control me and I gave in as any man in my position would. We are as men, creatures of weakness after all. That weakness in turn gives us will and strength to do the unthinkable. It gives us the power to move mountains in the name of something that most women never truly understand. It gives us power in the name of love, or at the very least, lust. I think of Helen of Troy, how she moved Paris, maybe woman have understood all this, all along.

When finally we do rise, the sun has long since gone down and there is the sound of voices in the garden beyond, talking about the things that are to come this night. We dress and she leads me out of the hedge rows by my hand, looking back at me from time to time smiling at me.

Upon exiting the hedge I see those that she had sent for, Viper lets go of my hand and moves to greet them one by one. First she moves to Chan, he is tall, almost 6'5". He has long black hair and his moustache and beard are almost as long. They are thin and well trimmed, hanging down to his belt buckle. That is if he were wearing one. He was wearing simple clothes that look like he raided a Chinese kung-fou movie set, or some Shao-lin monk's wardrobe.

Next was Devon, he was dressed in a full formal business suit. He looked a little more comfortable here than Chan, or the other one that was with him. He looked just like Adrian Paul from the highlander TV series, which I found to be rather amusing since in his hand was a rather large sword cane, which it seemed, he could not help but fidget with.

Last was Bernard, dressed simple and quite. If you were to see him you would never remember him later. So unremarkably plain was his appearance, that I found myself wondering if I would ever notice him outside of this company. What stood out about him after watching the 4 of them talk for a bit, was that he never said a word, or seemed to look where they were talking. Rather he would from time to time agree or disagree with the plans for the night. His eyes never seeming to leave the direction I was in, staring at me or into nothing. When everyone moved to go inside I noticed in his right hand a small device that he would click, and it was then that I relished he was blind.

Things it seems keep getting more and more convoluted with every passing moment. I follow them inside not really willing to be part of what they are about to do, if what they are planning is what I think it is. Keep his evil from the world. Place him in that prison in the garden. Did they plan to place him in there, and keep him alive only to keep him from being reborn?

I reach into my pocket to get a smoke and find the paper the lawyer had handed me. It's a hand written message. It has the effect of bringing the reality of my life back into focus, 'they were cops' is all that is written there, and a phone number, to whom? Did the message mean the guys that had assaulted us were cops, and if so, how did the lawyer know, was this a set up?

I try not to think about it to much, with Viper able to read my mind I try to focus on other things. The serpent pattern on her body becomes a focus for me. The more I try to remember its details, the more confused I become. For some reason I can see it unfinished still bleeding.

I blink to get the vision out of my mind, I can't, for no sooner than I open my eyes *I am in a small room that smells of fish and smoke, and on a bed low to the ground is Viper. Only the tattoo is still unfinished. The man leaning over her seems familiar as well, but for now I can't really see him. His attention is on her back where he is wiping blood from her, so he can see the pattern again. Slowly he begins to turn to me...*

"STEPHEN!"

Its Vipers voice, not sure if it's from her there or here... the world blurs and I feel dizzy, my eyes focus and I am being shaken by Viper. She is screaming at me, and kneeling over me, it's all I can do to clear my mind, and after a few moments I am ok. Blinking several times I put my hands up and try to stop her from shaking me, when she realizes I am alright, she lets go and leans back. Behind her are the other three, and William and Amber, all of them just were starring at me as if I had gone mad. "What?" I say...

My question goes unanswered as they, one by one, turn and walk away from me, until only Viper and Chan are there. Chan kneels beside me on the left, and looks at her and says.

"Do you think he was seeing that from your mind or mine?"

"From that angel Chan I would say neither," is Vipers reply. "He would have to have been behind you that day, and we were alone weren't we?"

Chan hesitates before answering, "No, for a moment father was there, watching to see if things were going as he requested, looking on..."

Both of them look down at me, making the time feel as though it were taking all of eternity to pass, before Viper opened her mouth.

"Do you think this one, that Stephen is the same one that gave both of us life?"

Chan was unwilling to even accept this idea, even though he could think of no other reason for what was seen. "I do not think so, we know for certain that those of our kind, remember all the life's that have come before them, that there are no breaks in their memories. If he were father, I am certain he would have mentioned it to us before now."

"You're damn strait I would have," I say, visibly uncomfortable, "but you're wrong about one thing," I say to them as I try to get up, "I don't remember much of anything before this life except in dreams. I guess the way I remember is different from the way you and the others remember."

They help me to my feet and again give each other that look as if they were talking to one another without words. I raise an eye brow and mention that I am still in the room. That they don't have to pretend I am elsewhere for my benefit.

Viper turns to me and smiles softly, and apologies for both of them as she leads us back to the library. When we get there the others are waiting and ask if I am ok. They are assured of my well being and the meeting gets underway.

Devon stands up and begins the meeting.

"As we all know Joe is still 'resting'. His body was taken to Dixon House for preparation. We have done everything we can to keep the body from being embalmed for the moment, but cannot wait another day. Tomorrow, they will begin work on him, one day before he rises. We still need to decide if we are going to allow him to reawaken..."

Before he can continue Bernard loudly interrupts him. "Please Devon, you know as well as I do, he was working with them. He confessed as much to Emily! How can you even consider keeping him in any state! I for one do not want to hear his voice in my head every time I come to this prison! It's bad enough we have Anna here, her tubes must be pulled!"

"Gentlemen please," Chan it seems is the peace maker of this wolf pack from hell, "we all know why we are here. Please keep to the topic at hand. I will not have the discussion of Anna brought back up again. That matter is settled, we all know why she is in there, and we all know why she must be kept there. Bernard, let it go."

Chan's word on the matter seemed to be final. I could not help but wonder who was in charge, who was the oldest among them and just how old they all were? I watched as Bernard took his seat, and made sure he was still the center of attention, until he was settled into his chair.

I watched as William and Amber just sat there and said nothing. Both were holding batons of a sort, watching the proceedings with some kind of stoic detachment. Next Viper stood and addressed everyone.

"Our own laws on this state, he must be contained until he can be kept no longer. What right do we have to let him come back to his life? If we do, what other evil will he bring to this world with him as well as the evil he already carries in him? "Destroying him will only hasten that fate if we choose that path, my vote is to bring him here to the garden and plant him."

She sits back down and looks at the other three, Chan commenting that we have two clear votes; one for final death and one for imprisonment. It's clear to me he wants to end the discussion as fast as possible. Why is anybodies guess, but as he turns to William and Amber he asks that they take part in this vote.

Each of them has been present for this once before it seems, and know the law. I get from both William and Amber, small glimpses of a woman in a uniform, the name on the nametag is, 'Anna'...   "Stephen," Viper snaps at me, "pay attention, stop... daydreaming."

William and Amber look at each other and decide to accept the offer. Viper calls for the vote not wanting to deal with long deliberations or arguments, her and Chan seemingly on the same page. Standing she ask in a clear voice' for those that are for entombment say '*I*'. To which Devon and herself cast their vote.

She then calls for those in favor of final death to say '*I*'. To my surprise, Chan and Bernard say aye, and all eyes turn to William watching him as he stands. When he speaks it is clear he is uncomfortable doing so before the others.

"I and Amber, being as one, cast our vote for as one," he pauses, clearly for dramatic effect, just long enough to make our hostess shift in her seat. His pause is punctuated by him looking to Amber, as she nods her agreement with what they have chose Then looks back at the assembled room and continues, "we have chosen final death."

This was greeted with stark silence, each of them looking at one another. The anger in the room was clear. It was on their faces, and in the eyes of all four of them.

"So it is spoken, so it shall be," says Chan. "The vote has been cast. We must honor it, and do what is needed now."

This began the discussion of how to carry out this grim sentence. After several hours they had finally agreed on how to bring about his final death. An hour latter we were all in the cars heading back to the city.

Part II,-"The end is near"

I rode with Viper, Chan and Devon, while Bernard, William, and Amber followed behind in another car. The ride was very quite and uneasy. I could see they all had way to much time to reconsider the vote. But they were each of them, unwilling to change their minds. For myself, I was still unwilling to accept we were going to do this, and had begged to be left behind.

I was told that because I was present at the time when he betrayed us all, the law demanded I take part in this action. I need to have someone sit down and explain the law to me, or give me a copy of it so I can read it at my leisure.

As we pulled up into the parking lot of Dixon House, the funeral home where Joe was being prepared, Viper turned to me and suggested that I for now, remain in the car, just incase there were camera's about. Once they had taken care of these little problems, they would come for me.

I watch them all leave the cars. All save for Will and Amber. They were also, still sitting in their car. Each of them moved with a speed I was quite familiar with, but still it was hard to see them as they passed inside. A moment latter the back door opened and we were lead inside, cans of gasoline in hand. We were told to poor the gas out everywhere we could, on anything that would take it quickly. So curtains, couches, and the rugs were all soaked. When we were done, we found the gruesome foursome in the embalming room.

They had Joe's chest open and were removing his heart, and his brain. When they were done they poured the gas they had over his body and lead a trail of gas out to where we had left off.

The items secure, they lit a candle and laid it upon the floor in the gas. The place was burning before we had even left the parking lot.

Driving away, you could see the flames reaching out and over the building, going up as fast as they had hoped. When I turned round to face them, none of them would look at the other, nor would they answer my questions, only giving to me cold stairs. Devon almost came out and said that I was to blame for this, but stopped himself short rather than getting into an augment with Viper.

I knew this was difficult for them but I needed more than I had been given, I really needed to understand what was going on, so I asked her.

"Viper please, will you explain why I needed to come along for this? I am having a hard time understanding the reason for taking his heart and brain before burning him..."

Before I could finish what I was saying, Devon said, "We are being followed, and not by the others". They had gone the other way as was planed. We looked back and saw a large black van following us, it had no lights on. Lights it sorely needed at this hour, but continued on behind us all the same.

We turned down several side streets to see if it was following, or if we could lose it, but we could not. After a while Chan said, "We need to head out of town, anywhere, so that we can face our guest in private."

Fifteen min later and the city lights were behind us as the trees started passing with greater speed. To my amassment the van continued on behind us without fail, and still, all its lights remained out. Once we were far enough outside of the city limits, and there appeared to be no more traffic, the van moved up and beside us. All its windows seemed to be tinted, but through them I could see at least seven men all dressed in black, ski mask pulled down over their faces, all of them with high powered guns.

"I really don't like where this is going." I said, and no sooner than I start wishing I were somewhere else, anywhere but here, the van moves in front of us and the back doors open.

Devon reacts as fast as he can, keeping the hail of bullets from ripping into the front of the car. Accelerating he pulls the car up to the back of the van and rams it, knocking one of the gun men out, only to crush him under the tires of our car.

Devon then pulls the car to the side again as another hail of bullets rips through the night. The sound of them tearing into the metal of the doors, roof and hood of the car is deafening. I am amassed at how calmly the three of them are taking this. Each of them seems to be as unaffected by this as they would be by a Sunday drive with nothing to look at.

For my own reaction to this, one only needs to try to envision their own reactions, to such an encounter for the first time. I am not being as graceful as my companions', let's leave it at that.

Devon pulls the car up next to the van just a little further forward of its side door as the passenger window comes down and a gun is pointed out of it. Devon without flinching turns the car into the path of the van hard enough to catch them, push them, and force the van off the road. At these speeds, he is hard pressed to keep us from rolling over and over again into the ditch where the van winds up, upside down and partially crushed.

Once the car is brought to a stand still, they get out and I follow. Walking towards us is about five of the seven that were still in the van when it rolled over, each of them carrying a gun and sword.

Before they open fire, Viper, Chan and Devon are behind them, the attackers guns are thrown off into the wood line. For my part I just stand there and watch as the men in black draw their swords and turn to meet their prey, unfortunately one presses forward towards me.

Of our group the only one that I know that has a weapon of any kind is Devon, and his sword Cane is let lose with surprising skill. I find myself laughing in spite of it all. At just how much he does look and move like... Adrian Paul? "Maybe," I think to myself, "he is Adrian Paul..." but 'That' moment is cut short by the blade of my attacker coming way to close to my face.

I move without thinking, I step out of the way, watching him try to react to my movements. It seems these guys are well trained. His blade missed my chest by mere inches. However, it did miss, and I had the blade in my hands and was kicking him to the ground before I allowed myself to slip back to normal speed.

The others had already done away with the other four when I heard them coming up from behind me. Each was clearly taken off guard by the speed of my movements. Chan openly gave away their united thought. "True born can not move so fast, Viper, I thought you said he was true born?"

I put that out of my mind and watch the guy that was trying to attack me, who was now trying to get away. His head looking back at the four of us turns in the direction he is running, only to find me in front of him. He screams and slips on the grass falling on his ass, sliding to a halt before me.

I smile at him and then straddle his prone form before his scream even reaches my ears. With the sword I press his head back and ask him.

"Who are you, why are you fucking with us, and why should I care? Don't think for a moment you will get away alive, if you lie to me." By this time the others had come up and were standing over us, Viper suggesting I kill him so we can get moving. Ignoring her I press the guy again.

"Who are you, what the fuck do you want with us!"

"Fuck you devil," yells the would be Assassin. His spit found a nice home in my eye before he continued, "who we are, is the hand of god. Your kind must be stamped out. Kill me and I go to heaven, when you die, you go to hell where you came from. Do not think you can run from us. We will follow you everywhere you go, until all of your kind is destroyed!

"Praise to the Mother Eve, Praise to the murdered, for the murdered are holy!"

I look up at the others and ask if this guy is for real. They nod yes, and Chan adds "ever since the count, we have had no piece from these mad men."   I look back to the insane priest and pull his mask from his face. I didn't know what I was expecting to see, but he looked like he could be no more than 20 if he was even 17. Around his neck is a chain. I pull it out and attached to its end is an amulet. The likes of which I have never seen, raised to equal levels are the cross, the Jewish star and the Muslim crescent and star. Around its outer edge in writing I am unfamiliar with are words I can only guess at. He tries to take it back from me, but I punch him in the mouth freeing him of the task of cleaning at least 5 of his teeth, he settles down.

"What in all the hells of man is this," I as him and the others, "some kind of joke?"

"No devil," the insane priest yells out, "it is no joke. Our history is not known to the rest of the world. Such things are not meant for the flock. To shield and protect them from the likes of you means we must operated in the shadows, only a rumor... Like you, a myth that lives."

He spits at me again, but this time regrets it. Blood and another tooth spay from his mouth, the act of it, as painful as losing the teeth. Then he continues. "You cannot hide from us now that we know your face.

Our brothers that you slew will be avenged, and your death will come devil, it will come!"

"Are you done with him," Viper interrupts. She was becoming agitated, nervous, something that made me uncomfortable as we were just sitting out here on the side of the road like this. "We have things to do, and need to get back to the estate and make sure everyone got away ok. We can answer your questions on these misguided meat sacks later."

"Right," I say and look at him and sigh, then say as more of a statement than a question, "If I let you live, you'll just hunt us down wont you." And of course he spits at me again as part of his answer to the positive. Looking up at the others I let them know I can't do it, killing is not my way. Devon steps up, and puts his sword threw the man's chest, all too happy to dispatch him to his god. I keep the charm and the sword. Once back in the car, we speed off and head home, not a word is said for the rest of the ride.

Pulling up in front of the house we see the car that Bernard was driving is already there, looking no worse for wear. They came out to greet us as we climbed the stairs to the main door, Bernard taking note of the many bullet holes lining the front and side of the car. He commented on how just amazing it was none of the windows were missing or even chipped as a result of the little fire fight we endured. Looking back we find he is right, something not one of us had noticed.

We all moved inside, and then continued through the house as we followed Bernard out back. The fire pit was warm and full of fire, he had it seems, taken the liberty to prepare the fire before we got back.

Then Viper brought the heart and brain forward. About two hours of ceremony later, she finally placed them into the flames. Fresh coal was added to the fire below and above the items then we sat and watched them burn, threw the rest of the night.

No one was talking or even looking at each other, the silence was fairly engulfing, consuming even the sound of those imprisoned in back. Their voices for once silenced, and the sound of the fire faded until nothing but the cold ringing in my ear was all that was left of any sound around that fire.

It was that silence, the utter lack of sound that brought back to my mind the questions I had earlier.

Are they cops, these hunters'? Why is Vipers tattoo so familiar? Then it hit me, in the silence it hit me! Viper had told me she could read my mind back at her hotel, but earlier today had said only those that survive the mortal death could read the minds of mortals. She could read my mind and the minds of the police and that priest!

My reflex was to turn to her. I caught her eyes reflecting the fires light. Her, and it seemed even Chan could see what I was thinking. Like the fire, I burned with a silent anger. She only smiled at me and headed up to bed.

I got up to follow, then Will and Amber like wise excused themselves from the night, we walked in and upstairs in a completely uneasy silence... to much silence. Upon reaching the room I was sharing with Viper, I closed the door and she just looked at me. Whatever she was thinking was beyond me, but the smile on her face gave me an idea. She dropped her robe and approached me with a sauciness' that would have made any other man crumble. I held on to my frustrations and anger, this gave me the strength to hold her off for a bit. Realizing I was not ready to play her games tonight/this morning whatever it was. She flumped down on the bed and scowled at me like a child scolded.

"Stephen," she said, "I didn't let you share my room to cause me to be upset every time we get ready to go to bed."

I walked over to where my things were, and began getting ready for bed. I am too tired to play her games right now and simply tell her I am not up for it right now, but I would like to talk to her about her mind reading. The look I get should have killed me on the spot, but she at least understood the need to clear the air. As she spoke I knew I was in for a long night.

"What do you want to know, how I can read the minds of others? How I can read your mind... what?"

"I want to know why you told me only those that have died the mortal death can read the minds of both mortals and sanguinairans', When did you die?"

She looks at me with that cold evil again. I think I am getting used to that, it's almost exciting in a convoluted, totally fucked up sort of way. Then she asked me. "When did you figure it out?" and stood up to move closer to me.

I figure right now would be a good time to keep my distance, so I moved round the other side of the bed watching her the whole time. My actions only made her pout at me rather than try to kill me with her eyes again.

"Well Emily," I said preparing to jump to the other side of the bed, just in case, "I figured it out tonight, just before you got up to come to bed. With everything happening as fast as it has been, over the last few days I really haven't had much time to think about anything.

"But, watching the fire tonight, it came to me. The little things you did and said, you slipped where you thought you were being slick."

Like a child, I stick my tongue out at her, this little engagement, this cat and mouse round the bed and room, really was turning me on. She bounded onto the bed in an attempt to head me off, but I got to the main door before she could, and threatened to go out it if she came closer.

She stops and moves to one side of the bed then replies. "Ok I will tell you, but you have to keep it quite, I don't want the others knowing about this. Yes, you heard me correctly speedy, they don't know, and I don't want them to know.

"See back when I was still alive, 'Father' wanted me to be special, he wanted me to be as close to him as I could be. So I got this tattoo from Chan, who had been in service to him for like 30 years before I met up with them.

However Chan was young when the count was still around, in his last days. So he knew the count and what he was like, it was Chan, not the order that started the hunt for the count after he kinda went nuts over some girl. But what do you expect from someone that has been walled up in an old monastery for almost 250 years.

"Anyway, father was about 70 when I met him, and he took me in and showed me all kinds of things. He cared for me, and my daughter, gave us a life, and helped me get on my feet. Granted I had to turn tricks for a few years to prove I was loyal to him. But in that time he grew to love me, and he decided since I was not true born he would cross me over. You see he knew he could, Devon out there is one of his..."

As she spoke I could see that moment again, watching her get that tattoo.

Chan leaned in over her, removing the blood from her back so he could see the pattern that was waiting there. She had tears in her eyes from the pain of the work being done to her, but she kept her tears silent, and never looked anywhere other than where she was told to.

The more real it becomes the less I hear her voice as it fades into the dreams that come with the weariness that is so heavy on me. And in the end I feel myself laying on the bed being covered up and the dream is all that is left...

"Chan how much longer before the spell is wrapped around her?" I asked as the father. And Chan replies, "A day, two at the most master."

"Very well," I say to him, "see too it that neither of you sleep 'til it is done. I want to see her before she sleeps, do you understand?"

"Yes master," he says obediently, "I will send for you as I am finishing so that you may see the final ink laid in place."

Hearing her breathing steadily I walk away, her breathing goes on without a whimper. This lets me know I chose correctly, she will be perfect to pass on everything I have. The spell that Chan is laying in on her, should keep her safe long enough to make sure the transfusion goes well.

I am tired of this life, and need to be free of it, and I will not leave on anyone else's terms. As I walk back to my chambers, I think on those damn cultists, always interfering in my work, they can go fuck themselves. What right do they, or their 'Mother Superior' their 'Eve" have, tracking me to my home, trying to take from me what is mine, and only mine to give.

The last two to make it inside my walls are still chained to the wall where we caught them. As I pass them, they beg for forgiveness and freedom, saying they will serve me, if only I will free them. I stop and look at them and for a moment consider letting them free, but think better of it.

I step in close to them and take the special knife I had made for this very thing into my hand, and place it against the one that had the balls to even address me. I step up onto the pedestal next to him and push it into his neck, and hold my glass under it to catch all the blood that comes out through the hollow hilt.

Once the cup is full I push the blade the rest of the way into his neck, and watch him twitch about, chocking on his own blood. The other looks at me as I stand there and drink what I had taken, then poor the rest out onto the ground.

"I always forget how dirty your blood is," I said without looking at the last one who remains alive, "shame to waist it."

This has the desired effect as the last one's eyes show me he now knows he is lost, and has been forsaken by his brothers. I motion to the guards near by to take the other down and feed him to the pigs. Looking up at the one remaining priest I see the tears in his eyes as he knows there is no freedom from this place. That he too will certainly die like those before him.

As the guards pull his companion down, the gate to the pigs is opened so he can see in and watch, as his friend's body is eaten. These pigs have been starved just long enough to make sure that anything thrown in will be eaten to the last. The main gate never closed until after the last bits of who ever was unfortunate enough to be thrown in was consumed. Today this priest was lucky, the man thrown in was dead. He didn't have to listen to his screams as the pigs ate him alive. Today the only sound was of breaking bones and tearing flesh.

My private chambers are less comforting with each passing day. I need to be free of this flesh, and the life I have built. Picking up the book, I thumb through it and wonder how I could have ever been such a poet. I flip through the pages and stop at one poem that has always been an inspiration to me. 'A single note of time', interesting to find in refection the truth wrapped so tightly in words so distorted.

I tried to be that writer again in this life, but something went wrong, and I lost it all. Now, all I have left is the cruelty that comes all too easy for me. It's a cruelty that has built for me, in this forgotten place, a comfortable palace of pain. A palace were devoted acolytes cater to my every whim.

Setting down in my chair to read, I find myself drifting off to sleep... the empty tears of a doomed man all I can hear...

...Upon opening my eyes, I am again where I should be, in her bed in the manor. Viper is looking at me, her eyes wide open and searching.

"Is everything ok?" I ask her, and Viper replies, "Yes, you were talking in your sleep. Some of the things you said, kind of caught me off guard."

"Like what," I role onto my side to see her better and place an arm around her, "come on, it was only a dream, I couldn't have said anything that upsetting, could I?"

My arm is rebuffed, and she sits up, her posture hints at a readiness to leave the bed, but she hesitates. Slowly her head turns to me and her lips move, words form there, but don't quite make it free. Watching her like this is interesting, for some reason she is afraid of me, it's in her furrowed brow, and pursed lips, the intensity of her stair, the blue eyes begging for some kind of understanding, and then she begins.

"In your sleep, you were talking about a place I have not been too since, before I was born to this new life I enjoy. I was wondering if you had ever been there before."

"Where is the place?" I ask her.

"China..." she says with hesitation.

"Sorry," I remember the pigs eating something from my dreams. I shake it off and continue, "I've never been out of the country, not even to Mexico. You know how dreams are. They are just dreams, meaning absolutely nothing."

"You're a fool to believe that." Viper chides me for the statement, becoming more upset, but clearly not for what I said. "How can you be true born if you know nothing of your past? Do you have any memories of the many life times that have come before you? Who you were, the things you did?"

"No," I said, "I have dreams from time to time. I get caught up in them while I am awake even, but to say I remember a life time before the one I am in now is impossible. I simply don't remember."

"I refuse to believe such a thing," says Viper. "I mean look at you! You're not a cross over, you've to my knowledge never died in this life time, and a mortal has taken your blood and crossed over. For all intentions and purposes you're mortal, yet you have the speed and mental willpower of all three, the born, made and damned. How can you not have any...? "

Her pause disturbed me. She turned completely round on the bed and looked at me again, seeing me for the first time, and it made me nervous. I stood up and moved to get some water. She followed me into the bathroom and grabbed my arm, pulling me fully around to face her. The look in her eyes was again something new. I marvel at the intensity of her, the many faces and complexities that make her who she is. Unfortunately I was snapped to by her accusation.

"You're, THE father....!!!"

The statement was flat and wanting no response, a statement of knowing one makes after realizing there is no other possibility. That the truth is as plain and simple as it possibly could be. I didn't like this truth.

"The Father?" I question her, "As in the guy that gave his blood to you, to give you your new life father? I don't think so." It was a lie, the dream fragments were becoming clearer with each passing moment, and I was uncomfortable with where they were going, "Ok, if I am your 'father' how come I didn't remember you when we met? Don't you guys know your makers regardless of which life they are in?"

I had hoped to set her off this line of thought, but I could see we were going to be up for some time talking about it. I pull my arm free and push past her back into the bed room. Sitting back down I make like all this is no big deal. I force myself to laugh at her and the silliness of my being her 'father'.

"Look if I am your father, would you not see him in my eyes, my words, and my mind. You can look there right, and see what you want, is he in me?" My question forces her to pause, then she looks deeper into my mind, my eyes open, and Chan is standing over me...

..."Master the work is almost done, she can come here to your room if you can not rise, forgive me for the hour but the huntress is close."

Sitting up, I scrawl at him for waking me, move to rise and take my robes and dress. After a few moments I am ready to follow him. Along the way I am brought a fresh cup of blood and drink it slowly, savoring every drop. It helps to restore some of my strength, but little to ease the pain that has been growing in me with each passing day.

As we enter the room, she is standing there, the tattoo still bleeding in places, her body completely bar save for the work. I walk over to her and lick the fresh wounds clean, holding her as tight as I can to me as I do so, savoring the smell of her flesh.

Her eyes watch me the entire time, looking into me with a hunger that only a human could have for what I am. She whispers in my ear how she longs to embrace me and give herself over to me completely. How she knows that in the moment of our passion she will be made whole and complete.

Letting go of one so young and willing is not an easy thing, but it is something I do in order to bring her over. Chan lays us both down next to *one another. I watch as he spends the next 10 min finishing the tattoo, her eyes the whole time are on me, smiling through the pain.*

Once the act is done, I tell Chan I don't have much time, that my time on this world will soon be complete and he must bring her over now. With that being said, he brings the doctor in that we have kept here for the last two months just for this moment. He prepares the needles and the tubes that will run from me to Emily, so she can be given my gift.

None of us were ready for the doctors' head to explode as a bullet found its way through him and into my chest. It was too late, I was dying. Chan rushed out of the room to fight the attacker that was trying to prevent this moment from happening. I knew it would be ok. The blood was flowing from me to Emily. The doctor had completed his task before dying.

I looked over to her and I wanted to scream but I was already too weak to move. Her chest as well had been pierced by one of the bullets. I watch as the blood flows out of me into her none breathing body. I watch as the blood flows in and out the wound in her, only to begin to heal as her eyes open with her chest heaving for breath. I watch her born into the life from death, not from life as all cross-over have been before her...Then my body goes cold and I close my eyes....

...As the vision fads from me, Viper seems more agitated now than before, "Damn you! Your mind is blank, how is it your mind is impossible to read when you black out!?"

"Don't know what to tell you Viper," I pretend that I have no idea of what she is talking about. But the vision I had just now, chills my very body cold, or is that the cold left over from feeling me die. Whatever the case the memory fades as fast as it came upon me, leaving me with the simple knowledge that she was *"still born"*. If that term can even be used in this case, is there a better term for it? "Look it's still late. I don't want to fight with you anymore. Can we put this behind us and just go to bed?"

"This is not over Stephen," Viper states flatly, "something about you is not right, and I swear, even if I have to eat you one day to find out what it is I will find out." She says that with a smile, an attempt to seem playful, but the intention was clear, her meaning and fear of me even clearer. I need to get out of here.   Going back to bed, I do my best to not let her know I suspect she is right about me, but it's pointless. You can see it in her face. She suspects the same thing herself, almost paranoid to the point of madness.

No wonder her eyes are so empty. This just leaves one question for me unanswered, and I am not sure I want it answered. Her daughter, true born or simple mortal, this is of course a question I don't think I want answered ever, no mater what it may mean.

Come morning, things are very strained between her and I, and I simply do not want things to get any worse than they are. Her questions all night long, searching for something that was there but I cannot give her, bothered me to no end. I wanted to give to her the answers she sought, but in the end simply couldn't. It scared me too much to think about it let alone accept it. That I was and am the man that made her what she is.

Everyone could feel the stress of the moment weighing heavy upon us. Each of them knowing something was brewing, something that none of them would survive.

Matters were made worse when we found out that Chan had left in the night, not just the house but had taken flight back to his native home, in the mountains of China. Viper raged all about the house for three days afterwards blaming everyone but herself for his leaving, blaming me in the end for the lose of Joe, and the impending departure of Amber and William. How many times have I been blamed for other people's mistakes? Whether of judgment or actions, I seem to end up taking the heat for their indiscretions!

All this has one simple out come. I am left feeling more alone now than when I was simply alone, and hunting for my own answers, in the cold of the night. There's nothing like being an outcast among outcast.

I do my best to not show the feelings of isolation that begin to overwhelm me with each passing day. But it's hard when you're in a group, crowd of people, or would be friends, and every word is guarded for fear you might say the wrong thing or they might hear your thoughts.

It's all made worse when every moment leaves you feeling as though you are outside in the cold. Watching everyone else through a stained and darkened window, wishing you were inside.

It was everything that Devon could do, to keep her from throwing herself into the fires. Which were lit every night to try and warm the spirits of those of us that were left. His efforts were very noble but in the end she only pushed him away, going so far as to lock herself into her room for two days strait.

Was she feeling the same emptiness I was, were we all feeling it? Why am I staying here, I simply can not understand, the coldness of this place since that night has become oppressive and deadly?

I have warned Viper that if she didn't let me go, if she did not allow me to get back to my hunt for my arrant child. That I might not be able to continue on, that my actions could not be predicted.

She merely said I couldn't, that I had to wait for the trail and then after, and only then, if I still wanted to leave I could, but not until then. But even at that moment I could feel her wanting me to just admit it, that I was her father, so she could... I don't know what.

I warned her in the end, that her fits and flights of anger would force me to tell the others that she had in fact never died the mortal death. Rather that she was born into this life already dead. This threat was a thing I found the first time I used it, frightened her to the very core of her being.

She immediately wanted to know how I knew this, I told her she talked in her sleep, and laughed it off. She didn't like it, but it calmed her down. She seldom talks to me anymore and has had me moved to another room as a result. That she talks in her sleep or I can in turn read her mind was a possibility she feared.

She seems now; more vulnerable than I had though she was or could be. And her fear of being found out by the others is a powerful tool against her. In the end I fear, it will bring about my own demise.

I know I need to get free of her and the rest of these... these people. I know that they will be the death of me, but I simply can not, not yet. I have been advised by her lawyers that I am still needed for questioning in the death of those men, and that a special lawyer has been called in to handle the case for the prosecution.

Nothing Viper has done has made a single bit of difference in my defense it seems. If anything from where I am sitting she has made things worse. Her fits and flights of rage and anger sewing the seeds of doubt about my innocence among everyone in the manor.

Part III, -"the Trial"

On the day of the trail we go to court, me, Viper, Devon, and Bernard. The special lawyer I find out is a woman. She looks like a mix of German and Irish blood, mixed by the hand of god himself. I find myself considering that where-ever I go, the woman I encounter are always lovely and exceedingly beautiful. As if by design, I am destined to only know, or meet, those women who are so enchanting, that my heart should always feel itself breaking for want of them.

Her skin is a soft tanned copper color, if copper could be pale. Her eyes large and green held depths of life I longed to delve into, to study and learn that I might forever serve her will. When she spoke, her voice range out full and commanding, forcing everyone present to look upon her and give over all their will to her. Then there was her hair, brilliant and full, a shade of red I never knew could be achieved.

She was so very enchanting, how anyone could deny her the right to win any case was beyond me. I found myself wanting to say whatever would be needed to ensure she won the case. But it was not until she turned her attention upon me, and began talking to me, of passion and the will to survive that I felt sick, in an instant the fever was upon me again. All the color dropped out of me, and I began to sweat so heavily that my shirt was drenched in an instant. Then the world began to swim, spiraling inward. Nothing anyone there could have done would have kept me from standing and falling.

The scream that erupted from my lungs was not my own, and somehow I knew I was not the only one in that room that felt the power being forced upon me... used against me.

With the floor rushing up to meet my face, I regretted never driving over that cliff that day before I met Selena. Then the lawyer was rushing up to me, arms out stretched... No it was not her, it was another redhead, her voice I knew, and the face was that of someone I should have known. I struggled to right myself and could not.

I knew that she was a historian, nothing more, than she began to speak. The words coming out of her mouth didn't match what I was hearing. The words I was hearing made no sense to me, vague and foreign, almost like gibberish. They came to me floating on the air with a quality, smelling very much like an echo, if echo's had a smell.

"Dem urn anth, urn anth dor'al InE! Vodalok! Vodalok ILL`M, dor'al InE!!!"

What in the name of all the gods was she saying? Her hands, were almost reaching me, as I pass forward. I fell Strait as a tree felled by the woodsman; I was passing through her attempt to keep me from my unwilling course.

Everyone else's words seemed normal to me and still I could not understand or hear them in earnest. The sound of them even more distant than hers, fading with each second I fell forward, until in the end I saw the floor crushing my nose, the blood of my body spraying out, followed by the sound of that very nose breaking. Somewhere. I don't know from were I could hear Viper screaming the words assassin, as another voice was ordering everyone out of the room.

I am fighting to hold on to what is real but the historians face and words are too close, the panic in the court room engulfs everyone's reality save mine and it seems hers. "Where is Viper?" It's all I can get out before the whole of my world is crushed in absolute silence. The look on the historians face as I asked the question was almost at once full of hatred, but it changed and she was that someone from some forgotten time again.

Then the silence is broken only by the sound of her voice, with those alien words calling out to me. Words that though they meant nothing to me just seconds before became clear and understandable.

"Please my love! My love forgive me. Vodalok! Vodalok iLL'M, forgive me!!!

And for a moment I see her being carried away by men in strange armor, her tears streaming down her face, the face that I have longed to have next to me for over two years, and now when she is there I hear my own words cold and unforgiving. "Dor anth i`ne ca`v chus. um i`ne va`g ri`z ca`g lau, ud thoun da'vich" ordering her to die, that if I can not have her no one will....

...Beep, beep, beep, beep, beep, beep, beep, beep, beep...

As the shadows peal away and the sounds one would expect from a hospital begin to fill my ears. I find that thick is the taste of the light as it breaks the veil of my swollen mind. That the world I have learned to hate comes into focus once more.

Sitting next to me is a woman that for some reason seems utterly familiar. Her green eyes and red hair doing nothing to hint to who she is, but something about the way she feels is all to familiar. She is watching me with an intensity that I simply can not feel comfortable with.

"Who are you?" I ask weakly.

"It's ok. You don't need to worry about whom I am, just know that, I wanted you to be awake when I put you to rest." At that moment she stood up and started walking towards me, it's the Historian!

Ok that's not good. I try to sit up but can't, I am strapped to the bed. So fully restrained am I, that I can barely turn my head. All I can manage to get out is 'who are you'? Again she stands up and moves closer, what the hell is going on? What's wrong with me?

I look at her and there is a smile so soft on her lips that I simply wish I could kiss them, and then I remember it's the historian from my trail. In her hand is a needle full of some kind of drug. As she moves to my side and gets ready to send that fluid into my IV, she stops and looks at me.

"Do you not remember me?" she asked.

"No."

"Even after all these years, you don't remember me?" Again she seems disappointed by my answer.

"No."

As she begins to speak again, her language fads between English and something out of a nightmare. "Vodalok urn anth, it hurts me that you still can not remember. But it's ok though darling, i`ne da'vich vahggah kwunim'diph'bi` iphur, dor lau. Just know you did the right thing. What happened afterwards could not be guessed by any one, let alone my mother then.

How could she know destroying you at the moment of my death, would do this to us. Lum ith'ig vi'ech dor i`ne`, was my wedding gift from you, dor i`ne`, mig vich. But I can't let you go around giving this life to every woman that comes along. I like this life way to much, to have it taken away from me because you're weak."

I began to scream at her, "I don't know what you're talking about..." but the Historian interrupted and continued.

"Fou's gah urn ma`gi`elib, I have found you in every life, and will continue to do so. I could not stop that abomination named Viper from being made," as she says it, I see her eyes in another's face, but I know instantly it is her, the historian that came and killed me then. I can see for the briefest of moments that she and Viper fought but to no clear end. Viper was able to get away, then the vision fads and I can still hear the historian talking, "but I will not let you pass on your blood to another in this life time or the next. After the nightmare that was Vlad, i`ne va`g ri`z t'an lau lin gout Li`m chatah...

"I know this speech is getting old. You can rest assured that I am doing the right thing for all of us, not just those that are true born, but for those bastard children of yours and mine. We can, ou hon'bi lau ze`ch, ensure we all continue to live."

"Look I don't know what you're talking about... you're too late," I say to her, hoping to stall her for a moment, to buy some time. Viper has to be around here somewhere, this is madness. Why can't I understand her clearly, why must every other thing she says be so foreign, "I have already given my blood to someone. She is heading north if you want her. Let me go, and we can go after her together. But you have to know, I didn't give her my blood, she took it from me while I was in a fever..."

I never got a chance to finish that line of thought. Viper opened the door. She stood there for a moment trying to figure out what was going on. She saw the needle, and then said something to the nut trying to kill me and burst into the room.

If it were not for the fact that I can see things moving at the speed of thought, I would have never known how close I came to dying. Both of them erupted into a blur that even for me was hard to follow. They fell about the room in a bundle of desperation and anger. It was the redhead that broke free first and then ran from the room. Viper had wounded her, but how badly I could not tell. All I was certain of was my fever was coming back and I was beginning to black out again, what happened next I pray did not.

As the fight ended and Viper fell to the ground, the doctors and nurses came rushing in. They first tended to me, than realized that Viper was not getting up. Half kneeling with her head down she appeared to not be breathing. The nurse was the first to turn to her and tried to help her up, but as soon as the nurse touched her, she fell to the ground and as her body rolled face up under the coaxing of the nurse, the nurse began to scream. Viper's body was desiccating faster than anything I had ever seen, 'til nothing was left but dust, her blonde hair, and her clothes.

Everyone just stood there shocked, they had never seen anything like it, or so it seemed to me. So utterly horrifying was the thing we witnessed, that two of the nurses in attendance fainted and the doctor relieved himself of his dinner. All I could do was lay there in shock, that red haired demon had come for my life, and Viper died in my place. I passed out again.

Slowly the night began to wind down after the police had asked all their questions once I woke up again. The judge had even come by to inform me that because of this attack, and the 'evidence' presented was clearly fraudulent, that the case against me would be dropped. There were guards appointed outside my room and inside.

Bernard and Devon I noticed were also sitting in the room with me refusing to leave at all. So the night passed with my dreams echoing.

"Please my love, my love, forgive me. Vodalok. Vodalok ill`M forgive me!!!

Part IV -"Never say die"

Viper had been outside having a cigarette when she looked up and could see someone moving in the room that should not have been there. She reached out with her mind and tried to see through Stephens eyes, she needed to see who was in the room. To her horror she saw for a brief moment the face of the bitch that had killed her father all those years ago. Then the vision faded and it was the woman who claimed to be an old friend of Stephens in this life time, but the eyes were the same as that bitch ...

Viper realized that the two women were the same. That this woman somehow was the one responsible for all the suffering she has known ever since her father had been murdered. For all Viper knew she may even be the one responsible for all the suffering her kind has known for the last 600 years.

Knowing she had to get up there and protect Stephen, she ran as fast as she could, pushing doctors, nurses, and patients down and out of her way as she rushed to his side. When she burst into the room, that red haired bitch was talking about taking Stephen with her back to California. She was saying she could help him get better there. But the noise of Vipers entry interrupted her little speech.

She turned and looked at Viper. She was trying to explain that she could take better care of Stephen than Viper could, or had to this point. That was the end of it for Viper, all she could see was the flash from Stephens's mind that showed her who this woman was, and Viper launched herself at the redhead.

Their fight was fast, powerful and frightening, both showing just how fast, strong, and determined they were to keep the other from having any say over what happened to Stephen. But before four seconds had gone by, the redhead broke free and fled the room, no sooner than she had, Chan entered.

Chan and Viper had decided by private conversation that he would leave the manor and stay hidden. That when the trial date came that they would need to protect Stephen at all cost. It was Chan that had seen the truth of who Stephen was. It was Chan that convinced Viper that she had to pretend he was not, or at the very least that she did not know for sure.

So when the attack on Stephen took place at the courthouse, he was able to follow the lawyer that had shot him with a poison dart out of the building and into the alley behind it. He ran her down and found out that she was the mother eve, and had come to put her bastard husband to rest.

Chan wanted to question her but a van had pulled up and there was a small shoot out between the police and those in the van, they had however, managed get away. When the police turned to Chan, he quickly cleared their mind of his presence and of what had happened.

Chan moved back to the parking garage and was about to leave when he saw the other redhead hurrying to her car. He approached her and saw in her mind that she too believed she was the "mother eve". Chan decided right there that he could use this to his advantage.

He approached her and asked why she was at the trial. She said simply that Stephen was a very dear friend that had been on his way to her graduation when she lost track of him almost 2 months ago. When the news ran a story about the trial she got on the first plane she could to come be with him. She said in her heart she knew that Stephen couldn't have done the things he was accused of.

Chan said he had been living with Stephen for the last month and that he understood who he was. Then said to her that he had seen in her mind that she believed she was this "Mother Eve." That the order responsible for the attack on Stephen followed. Chan asked her if she knew anything about the attack and she tearfully denied it.

It was then that Chan told her about the other woman, and how she swore she was this "Mother Eve", and how she had escaped him. The woman in front of him asked if she could take him to the hospital so she could watch over Stephen and when he woke up, get him out of there. It was at that time that he told her about Viper, himself and the rest of those at the manor and that they were all vampires. She looked at him backing away, saying she would find her own way to the hospital.

So when Chan arrived at the hospital he was a little surprised to see her and Viper fighting. He was too slow to stop it or help the other woman who ran out clutching what looked like a broken arm. But he was not, he hoped, to late to help Viper.

He had entered the room too late. As he was about to help Viper to her feet, the doctors and nurses flooded into the room. They quickly set about turning off alarms and resetting sensors that had been set off or torn off of Stephen in their fight. He was trying to think of a way to get Viper out of the room before they noticed her. But it was too late. A nurse had kneeled down to see if she was ok.

Viper was crying, and trying very hard not to let it show. But stuck in her shoulder was a pencil, the nurse went to remove it when Chan threw down on the ground beside Viper a smoke bomb. He distorted his body by vibrating it so fast that he looked like a demon. The two nurses passed out as the doctor vomited at the horror before him.

He grabbed viper up and told her she had to leave now. That it would be best if everyone thought she was now dead. Looking into his eyes she knew he was right and they left the room by the window.

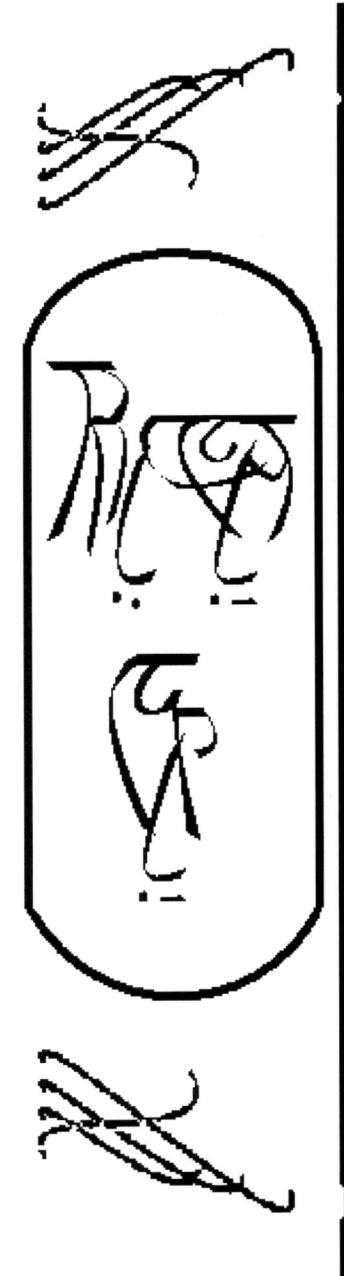
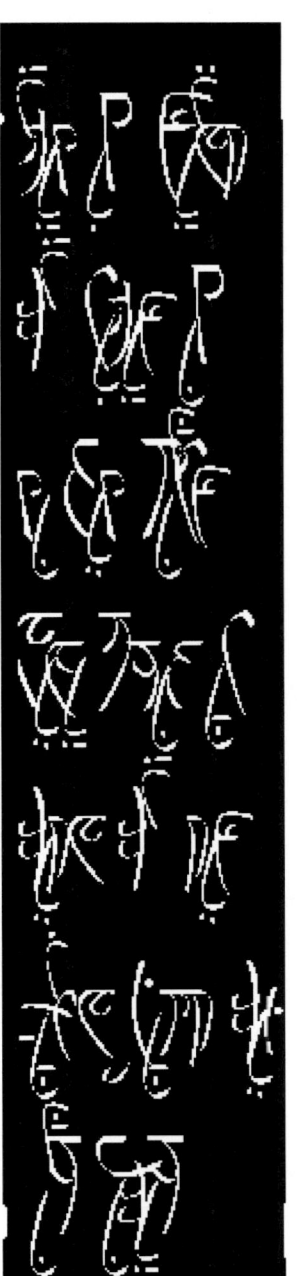
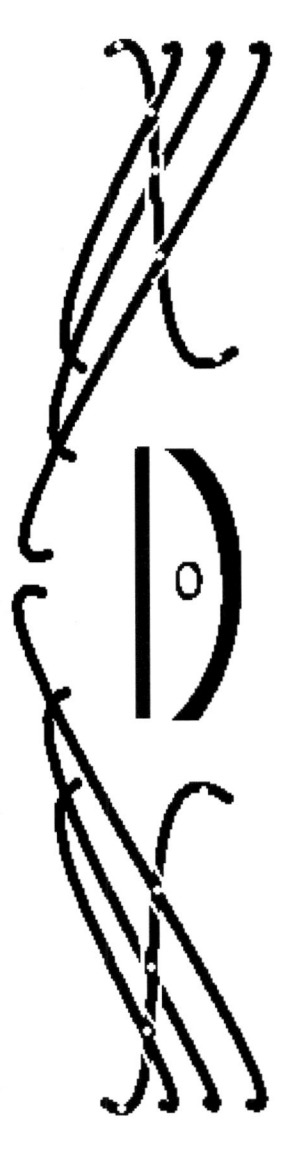

Chapter Ten – Undead High jinx

Now plays the dirge of mornings come

Those songs of praise the fallen son

We stand gathered among the dead as one

The words spoken of thoughts soon fading run

Until now we return the pulsing din to feign darker fun.

-VODALOK –

When next I awaken I am no longer restrained, Devon is the last one still sitting with me, he tells me that Bernard left the night before. He could no longer remain in this place, and that he would not even return to the manor to gather his things.

Devon was clearly unhappy with the way things ended. He himself ready to leave this place and never look back, next to him were his bags all ready to go. He looked to me as if he had not slept in days, as if he had been fighting with some internal demon about what to do, How to deal with the lose of Viper. When he noticed me looking at him, a soft smile crossed his face and he said simply "Time to go".

I did my best to get up and he helped me dress and exit the hospital without being seen. My discharge papers already in Devon's hands. Waiting for us out back was the limo. Once inside and settled in he began to speak.

"We decided, Bernard, Emily, Anna, and myself," was that the name of Vipers daughter, "that the house, and all its property will be passed on to you and your family. Anna no longer wishes to remain there with Viper gone. And the rest of us are tired of this place. I, myself, will be heading to Italy as soon as we are done."

He opened a brief case that was waiting for us in the car. He pulled out the paperwork and a pen and handed it all to me saying.

"Sign where the x's are and the manor and all its wealth are yours. The lawyer will be at the place when we get there and will be expecting you to have signed off on all this. Also inside are instructions on what to do with those that are currently imprisoned in the garden. It details how to care for them, or destroy them if you decide the work is too much for you.

184

Personally, it was Emily who wanted them held like this, the rest of us would have them freed or destroyed.

"The list we compiled will tell you who is who, it's up to you at this point to keep them or not."

I simply can not believe this is happening. They are leaving me with all this responsibility. I am not ready for this, but can't find a moment to tell him. He just keeps going!

He then hands me another stack of papers and points to where I need to sign, saying "This will give you control over all the liquid assets held by Emily's estate." That Anna has taken what she needs and has already left. I look at the financial numbers on the paper and then back at Devon. He smiles to me as if to say yes that is correct.

And then we were there, at the manor, and as he promised the lawyer was waiting for us on the porch. Thankfully it was not the redhead from the trail. The sigh I let out released more of the tension I was holding onto than I had expected.

Devon collected all the papers and placed all the paperwork the lawyer would need back into the briefcase and closed it. When we came to a stop he moved to leave the vehicle but stopped. He turned to look at me and smiled softly saying.

"I know it's not your fault, and you need to know she somehow had come to love you very much. This was something she wanted for you.

"She felt you were her 'father', and to make sure that if you are that person, that you were taken care of. I know this because she confided it to me and Chan. It's a large part of why he left so early. They could not agree on this matter.

"She would not hear anything otherwise or contrary. You're going to need this in time." He hands me his sword-cane, "It served me well over the years and was made by a master sword maker on the day of my birth back in Spain. And so you know, that year was 1721."

With that he exited the car and moved to where the lawyer was waiting and handed over the briefcase. I followed and was introduced to him. Mr. Arlington, an older Gentleman of about 40. Attractive but weathered harshly from to much sun and stress. He welcomed me as the new owner and excused himself from our presence and left in his car. Devon then turned to me and said his goodbyes and left as well in the limo.

Watching as the car left I realized just how alone I was again in this place. Not just here in this manor but in life. How fast had all this happened? I think about it, and at least three months... or was it four, have gone by now since Selena had stolen my blood. And now here I am the owner of an old manor. More money than I could ever know what to do with in several life times. Then there is some red headed assassin looking to kill me for something I don't remember ever doing. For being a person I don't remember being.

I stood there for at least 15 min looking at the long driveway that everyone had left down, before turning to the house and seeing the small staff that was there waiting for me.

I began walking up to them and they all introduced themselves one by one. Ernest was the driver who said he had begun working on my old car to bring it back up to like new status for me, "It's a classic" he said, and it deserved no less. He was Cajun though and understanding him was difficult. Luckily he could see I was having difficulty and talked slower for me.

Next came Beldon, he addressed me as Sir and stated he would be my butler 'til dismissed, tall and thin, receding hair line, and a thin narrow head. Sometimes I wonder if I am dreaming all this because of how certain people just fit their stereo types, right down to his pin-stripped suit.

The cooks name was Lashonda, dressed politely in southern middle class clothing. The kind one would find on any mother, as long as she was in a sitcom... There was no questioning her heritage though, she was very proud of the fact that her family tree was never interrupted by slave owners, pure all the way back from Africa in 1689. She tells me her family worked this estate back before the war of liberation. They have always been welcome and at ease on the property, still holding rights to the home that her grandfathers' father built after that war.

And last but not least was the maid. She was a simple girl earning a living. Sent over by an agency, that never sent the same person more than a week or two at time, so I failed to catch her name, just another girl, plain and simple.

I take a moment with each of them to let them know where they are allowed and where they are not. This was new to me so I looked to Beldon for advice. Turns out he is 65 and has been a butler here at the estate since he turned 16. I let everyone know he would be in charge when I was not around and that if they had any questions they were to run them through him (in short nothing changed for them).

Once inside I made my way back and out to the garden with the list of names of those Devon felt should be freed or destroyed. I didn't like this at all, the thought of playing executioner to anyone regardless of their past. Standing there I could feel her presence, Vipers, watching me to see how I would handle this very dangerous and delicate issue.

Gods, how could they leave this to me? After all is said and done, I had nothing to do with placing any of these creatures in this prison. Standing there alone in the mid day sun was uncomfortable. I could feel them reaching out to me with their minds, begging to be freed from this hell that had been forced upon them. That mausoleum standing there before me, I could not bring myself to look away from it, or to look upon the list of names. In the end I lost my resolve and crumbled back to the manor and fled inside to escape their cries for mercy.

As I entered the kitchen, Lashonda asked what I would like for dinner. I said something simple, burgers. I didn't care as long as there was something to drink.

I passed through to the main sitting room. Once there I sat down and began reviewing the list of names of those now in my care. I sat there going over each name and folder that was with that name, and found myself sickened by the actions each of them are accused of committing. The worst of them was a gentleman by the name of Lucas. His crime, he only fed on the blood of small children, caught in the act in the year 1897. Then walled up, the first to be entombed on these grounds, and from what I can see the worst of the lot.

After dinner I retire to my room, I chose one of the side rooms rather than take the master room that was Vipers, and settled in for bed. I laid there listening to the sounds of the darkness, and up 'til then, this very night, I had never been uncomfortable in the dark. But I could hear nothing but the echoing of the voices out back. I knew it was late but I called for Beldon to come to the study and moved there as quickly as I could.

When he entered I began. "Ok, I am sorry for getting you up so late, but I am a night person and for the most part will not be up and about during the day much. When I am, I am to be left alone. Make sure everyone knows the garden out back is completely off limits. They may go into the back yard but not into the garden. If I catch anyone out there they will be fired. I don't care who they are, is that understood?"

"Yes sir." Beldon said, still tired but attentive.

"Also if anyone is allowed out back by me, you will be the first to know. This should prevent any of the 'well he said I can' bullshit. I won't stand for any of that crap. Tomorrow, I need you to locate for me the best private investigator you can. I don't care if you have to look outside of the state. I need to find someone that took something from me and I don't want the police involved. Do you have an issue with this?"

"No sir," he said with a smile on his face.

"Ok the next thing I need, is for this place to be more comfortable for myself. So the other thing you need to find for me is a decorator that can take orders and get this place into shape according to my needs. I want to talk to someone no latter than tomorrow afternoon, understood? Even if it's two or three people for me to chose from."

"Yes sir," again, no sign of any real emotion.

"Beldon, I need you to be as discrete as possible about the P.I. I don't need anyone asking me questions about why or what, not even the rest of the housing staff. Speaking of them, if there is anyone on staff you don't trust fire them and bring someone you trust in. Also I don't like the new maid every other week thing. I want a full timer by the end of the week. If you have someone in mind bring them in. As my butler you will also be in charge of all house hold needs. You answer only to me. I hope you're ok with this?

"Sir it is my pleasure to aid you in any manner I can. And if I might say, having control over the house for once will be a pleasure. If you like, I would like to get the outside repainted, and the grounds refreshed. A full time gardener would be nice."

I look him square in the eye and somehow know he will never let me down. I node my head and sit down again, offering him a seat and telling him to please relax, an offer he takes only after offering to get me a drink. I tell him only if he is having one, to which he smiles and says very well. With drinks in hand and him sitting comfortably across from me but still looking very much like a man on a mission I begin again.

"I want to get to know you, so that I can trust you, and have you trust me. I know this will sound cheesy, but I want us to have that Bruce Wayne and Alfred sort of relationship. Time is needed to build that kind of trust and respect so please if there is anything you want to tell me, or share, such as limits, do's and don'ts, now is the time, ok Beldon?"

He takes a sip of his drink and considers the offer I have made him. It's easy to see he is a man of old world values and when he speaks, it's with a dignity that is at once powerful and humbling.

After a moment he looks up from his drink and begins.

"Sir, I will say only this on the matter, I quietly served the Lady Emily for almost 49 years, and have seen and aided her in many things. It was my pleasure to find, I would still be in service to this household under your care. The Lady Emily had confided in me and the master Sinclair, just how much she felt you were her 'father'. I don't know how much she told you about him, but it seems she felt you are him born again.

"She had planed on giving all this to you in this life as a gesture of gratitude, for the gift you had given her all those years ago. It was her intent to tell you these things when she had gone to the hospital to check on you, and had her unfortunate run in with that other lady."

He ended that with his head down and a noticeable crack in his voice, I could see a single tear sliding down his face. He had served her for so long I think that in the end, he loved her. There was nothing I could do in this moment save take a drink and toast her memory. "That it never be forgotten." To which he stood and paused with his glass held high, than drank all the contents in one shot and smashed the glass in the chimney.

He then made himself and I another drink and we sat down and began the long road of friendship in a world so perverted. That for him he could go no where else and still be able to function. And for me, there was no other life, save the one I had every morning I woke to each day.

By morning, Beldon had retired for the evening and was promptly up and ordering the household as was requested of him the night before, by 7am. I found I was too drunk to go up to bed and instead slept sitting up right. Glass in hand, in the grand sitting room where Beldon had left me the night before.

In flashes through the day I noticed he had come in and pulled the drapes to keep the sun out and closed the doors forbidding anyone entry to the room I was in. Around 4:30pm I finally rose and found him in the kitchen with the staff giving them the instructions I had given him the night before. None of them seemed to mind so much the rule about the garden. Lashonda was more than happy to oblige, fearful that one of those monsters might get loose and eat her if she was messing around out back.

When Beldon noticed I was watching, he dismissed them all and came over. "Sir there will be two applicant's for the interior decorators job coming by at 6:30. I took the liberty to invite them over for dinner and have instructed Lashonda to prepare an elegant but light meal, and I hope steak and vegetables will be acceptable."

"Yes that will be fine," I say to him, "and the other matter?"

"He is patently awaiting you in the ballroom. Shall I bring him to you?"

"No," I say, "I will go see to him myself. What's his name?"

"His name sir, is Richard Corman, he comes very highly recommended."

"Thank you Beldon, could you bring in some drinks, hair of the dog if you don't mind?"

"As you wish sir," Beldon says this with a bit of a wink, then turns to gather the drinks.

I make my way over to the ballroom and there he is, looking rather unimpressive, smoking close to an open window, watching something in the side yard. I make my way over to him to see what it is. He looks over his shoulder but doesn't say anything, or even acknowledge my presence. As I reach the window I see what he is looking at, the maid from the temp service is beating out a rug on a sturdy line. The sweat on her is highlighted by the suns refection off it, giving her a rather interesting appearance.

"She is rather young you know," my first comment to him, testing the water, "she could get you into trouble."

Richard looks at me with one of those, what are you talking about looks then says. "Her? She reminds me of my niece, that's all. My name is ..."

And before he can finish I let him know I know his name, and ask him how long he has been doing this kind of work.

His reply is quick and a little sharp. "Long enough to know, when someone has never dealt with my kind before, what is it you called me here for?"

"Ok," I start the word slow as I consider what next to say, "direct and to the point, what I am telling you is very delicate, and doesn't need to be talked about outside of me and you, ever."

"Right," he says, then smiles, "so who is she?"

"What makes you think it's a girl?" I say.

He replies by pantomiming my words back to me. "This is delicate, don't talk about it, bla, bla, bla, who is she?"

"She stole from me several pints of my blood, and drank them." The shock of the statement that was on his face was well hidden. But not so well I couldn't see it got his growing attention. "She is a dangerous person. Capable of killing without thought, and has no respect for the male gender. I need to know where she is so I can put an end to her life."

He was not expecting that bit, then again who would. He stood there for a moment and ran his hands through his hair, then very loudly sighed. At that time Beldon brought in the drinks. Mr. P.I. man took his and downed it quickly. Me, I just tasted it and watch him.

When he began it was with clear trepidation.

"I have gone looking for people for many reasons, but this one is kinda a first for me. I don't think I can...."

"Mr. Sinclair, the woman I am looking for is the same woman that is being accused of murdering all those men down by the gulf. About what, two months ago, or something like that. She is my child, I am a vampire. I don't care what you think of this, and I need you to find her.

"I am not asking you to engage her in any way, rather I want you to avoid her if you do find her, but you must find her. The longer she is allowed to roam, the stronger she will get, do you understand me?"

Ok, so telling him the complete truth was a bit off key. I know I sound crazy but the way he looks at me, tells me he understands, somehow he understands.

"Ok, but I got to tell you, this is fucked up. It's going to cost you twice my normal fee, and I am going to need $5k up front, or I walk out of here and never look back."

To my surprise Beldon had remained in the room and was watching and listening to the conversation with the patience of a statue. When he saw me look at him he simply nodded his head yes, and exited the room.

"Ok Mr. Sinclair, wait here and I will be right back. And Mr. Sinclair, don't talk to anyone about this, if you have to say anything to anyone it's a long lost family member you're tracking, nothing more, nothing less."

"Yea," he says, looking at me with a look I can't really figure, maybe he is trying to find a way out of this, "don't worry about me talking to anyone, I... $5K upfront."

"Expenses I am sure," I say to him, trying to sound reassuring, "do yourself a favor, and remember I don't support habits. So if you're using this money for anything other than finding her, and then I find out..."

I didn't need to finish, the look on his face told me he understood. I had never seen someone get so angry so fast. It was almost refreshing how quickly he shot back at me with his anger.

"Why is it, everyone wants to believe the crap they see in movies and read in books about private eyes being drug users or drunks... I tell you what boy, you make that comment again and I will make sure you never get a P.I. to take your load on, you understand that!"

"Now that we understand each other," I say with a smile, "about misconceptions Mr. Sinclair, I hope you can understand the nature of my reasoning for wanting discretion. What you're looking for is a monster, but not the romantic beast of movies or novels."

With one brow raised he almost smiles as his head turns to me resting on his chest, the profile is the classic response of someone caught in the mist of a lesson learned. But he doesn't hold the humor of it to long, and passes from the room saying he needed to use my john.

Beldon returned to the room with a check book and a pen, and placed them on one of the tables, then refilled my drink and Mr. Sinclair's'. When Richard returned, I offered him a seat across from me. When he saw the check book he accepted both the seat and the drink.

We talked awhile longer about the price and settled on 15k total, 5k up front as he had requested and the rest upon delivery of her location, payable after I had taken care of my issue.

He was resistant to the wording of the final payment, but I assured him he would be rewarded well should he be able to bring me information on her swiftly. With this settled I cut the check and he left the house.

His passing left the place feeling very empty. I always feel empty when they leave regardless of who they are. I wish sometimes, that I had never found out about all this, never understood even the smallest part of what I am, that I could have lived a normal life, or at the very least, died all those years ago on that tree.

After an hour of sitting quietly in the ball room drinking, I decided to go and deal with one of our guest, out in the garden. The amount of drink I had putt away in that hour of quiet contemplation was a bit excessive.

Finding my way through the labyrinth was more of a task than I had thought it would be, and it was not long before I was lost. I stop and look around at the shear height of the yew grown up around me, the sound of buzzing bugs, and the heat of the day beating down on me. Even through the haze that was so common in a place like this. I felt like I would die here and no one would come looking for me because of my house rules.

The irony of this settled in and I began to laugh rather loudly. So hard and long did I laugh, that I began to pant for air, and almost passed out. I found more irony in that, that I should burn to death over a period of days as the yew was really only tall enough to protect me from the sun for a small part of the day, should I get stuck out here.

I could not see over it even with a good jump, and the path between the rows, was tight enough that the shade grew, receded and came back with in the space of an hour. This made me laugh some more as I decide, the bugs would surly eat me before I died from the sun.

"Mule.....haaaahaaaaaa"

Then from deep inside the garden maze, came a voice. It was like acid, pure hellish frozen acid. I fight to stop laughing as I hear what sounds like an echo of laughter in the hedge rows... then realize they muffle sound not carry it. Where is the laughter coming from? I listen closer with an occasional suppressed chuckle at my own expense.

Standing up I try to follow the sound of the laughter and find it's not so much a direction as a proximity to me that makes it audible, every time I find the path out back to the house, the sound fades. It's not 'til the third time I reenter the rows that the source of this laughter is pinpointed; it's coming from the tombs!

Rushing in again I struggle to keep my mind from wandering and finally emerge in the center. There is no one there, but I can feel their minds on me, tugging at my will, hoping to overwhelm me and force me to do their bidding. The darkest thoughts flood into my mind as all of them begin picking away at my sanity. Each voice a needle burning into my mind.

"Eat the cook. She will be tasty," came one voice. Then over and inside it came, "If you force the old man to rape the child, you can drink from the flesh of their offspring." And within that as the others began to repeat themselves, the sound of gibbering, ranting, "Flesh for life. Flesh for life. **I can cross you over mule!!!!**"

The barrage intensified in my mind, racking at all my sense of right and wrong, flooding my morality with an ocean of hate and the bile of corruption. I fought to push it all back, hoping to keep them out, to force them to silence. 25 voices screaming in my head 'til all I could hear was the cacophony of their impurity. The sickness of their very souls eating away at what I held to be true. And still one voice became louder 'til it was raging over the rest like a ghost ship riding a storm strait from hell bound for my foundering will.

"I can feel what you want mule, the flesh of immortality, the strength of those that do not die. I am Lucas; I am more than you or any one else alive or dead. I can cross even you over and give you the strength to bring life to others.

Do you know what it's like to feed on the flesh of men yet born? I can give you that feeling. The power to give or take life, with nothing more than a seduction," Lucas's words drove forward into me harder than all the rest. It was everything I could do to focus on him alone, and somehow found a way to quite the storm that was fueling his encroachment upon my sanity, "you will never need fear the Ordo Divinus Venator again. I know their secrets, their mother. I know all about them and you mule. I can free you from all of it."

I begun to regain my will and slowly rise, while forcing out to Lucas, a simple question. "If you're so gifted, how is it you're imprisoned here, like the others, how come you're not free and walking the world in inexorable glory, unfettered and dominating the will of all those that are without your, self proclaimed glory?"

"MULE!" screams Lucas, "you're a fool to toy with me. I can break your body now that you're close enough to me that I can reach out and touch you with my mind," and to prove his point, I was knocked to the ground by an unseen force that almost broke my arm, "you are nothing to me. Free me, and I shall show you what real power is like Mule!"

"Why do you keep calling me mule," I had to find his tomb. It was the only one not marked and there were at least 15 left unmarked, both in the notes I was left and on the faces of the crypts and Mausoleum I was trying to circle. "It seems to me you might want to be a little nicer to the person that you're dependent upon for your freedom."

I could feel the air around me heating up, my steps becoming heavier and harder as the air began to congeal about me, slowing my pace.

"You are a mule boy," came Lucas's' voice, "haven't you figured that out yet. Born over and over bla, bla, bla, *'I can remember all my past lives!'* Big fucking deal! You can't reproduce, you can't give true life. You're bound to a world that hates you and you will never be strong enough to defend yourself if the Ordo Divinus Venator comes for you. They will destroy you.

"You want to know how, or why, I can tell you're a mule. Then you must set me free! Then I will tell you."

"I don't know," I say back to him, hoping that he will be louder when I am closer to his tomb, "your attitude is a little more flippant than I like. Such arrogance, the way you're carrying on. I almost get the impression that you were a noble at one time. Used to ordering people around, or were you..."

And before I can finish my thought he lashes out at me and our minds for the breath of a bird's heart-beat are linked and I see who he really was and why he was brought low. I see him being crossed over, but my perspective is one of an observer from a distance...

... The one crossing him over is a female. She has taken a sharp piece of copper tube and plunged it into her arm where she filled a bottle that had until a few moments before held wine. The man was well dressed and had several black servants attending him. They were all dressed in white and kept their heads low. Those that were looking had fear in their eyes, it was all to clear and the trembling in all their bodies showed it even more.

Once the bottle was full, she pulled the tube out and licked at her wound, and with in seconds it was sealed and stopped bleeding. She laughed at the man as he sat up, and I saw something around his neck I was not ready for. It was the same amulet I had taken from the men that attacked us on that very fucked up night just a few weeks ago. This hung about his neck and was falling to the side. She enticed him, saying that god had chosen him to take her blood. She was openly calling herself eve, and that her sin, and its ultimate punishment was that she must forever hunt down and destroy her children. To free the Lords' creation, man, of her abominations, of which Cain was the best known.

He yelled out 'AMEN' then 'blessed are the murdered' and took the bottle from her. As he began drinking her blood, she grabbed his head and held the bottle up and forced it down his throat 'til he was chocking upon it, forcing him to consume all the blood as fast as could be.

I watch in horror as he chocked and then drowned on her blood. Once she was satisfied that it was done she pulled the bottle out of his broken jaw, and watched as his eyes fluttered and then opened.   My perspective pulled back and there were bars in front of me, a sound could be felt but not heard, her attention focused on me and she began to speak.

"Most ancient husband, in death we were born by your own cruelty, now by that same cruelty..."

...*"AAGGGGHHHH, STOP!!!!"*

I scream out to everything and nothing. It's all I can do to break free, and get him out of my head, me out of his. The pressure that built up around me was so dense now that I after breaking free realize I had collapsed onto the ground. Slouched over, my face and hands in the ground, cramping over my bent knees. And the only thing I could hear outside the ringing that threatened to deafen me, penetrating the pulsing of my world as my entire body swelled with the force of his hatred, was his soft and simple laughter.

Slowly I rose back to my feet. Fighting the vertigo that swelled round inside my head, visible in my eyes, the world getting smaller the farther away from me, the rings in my vision would take it, drilling into whatever I looked at forcing me to puke not once, but three times in quick succession.

I realize all the others had gone silent, even the birds and bugs had held their tongues for fear of the wrath of Lucas. As I rose, fighting to remain cognizant he began talking again, softly now, in an attempt to seem concerned for my well being.

"The mother will come for you as she has over and over since that day in 1699, like she has since everyday of her beginning more than likely. She hunts her children down for sport I think. Those like me, when she has used us up, we are imprisoned to keep us form either being born again or like the mortals moving on.

"She knows what she is doing mule, you're sport for her, she knows you're born over and over, and gods only know how many times she has killed you out of boredom. I curse my life everyday now. Since then, since she imprisoned me here. I curse my life for becoming this thing she made me, the lost of my soul and the freedom it gave me to be the monster that landed me here. Here in this prison of bronze and stone. Imprisoned by her like she has, and had done to so many others when they realized the lie she propagate to save her own ass."

196

"You're lying Lucas," I scream back at him, "to save yourself, you're lying in hopes of being freed, so that you can run amuck again. There is no mother, there is no father. We are each born to this life as part of a curse on us by whatever god we called upon before the birth of the Christ. Your kind is the key to being a cross over, a parasite in the womb of the mortal world, that's what I think.

"It's not because as Viper believed that there are only two that have the power of their soul to bless others with immortality." That last bit came out as if it were bile, vomited out at him full of scorn and anger. Anger that I could never unleash on Viper herself, "Bless them with immortality, more like condemn them to utter damnation!!"

Again his laughter fills the air, but the pressure slackens as the sun sets. The sound of katydids begins to reach my ears and soon so does the sound of frogs. I am still too angered to break this tryst with the damned. And he pressed on hoping to goad me further and hold me longer, I didn't care.

"Inside you know its true mule. How many life times have you been around? How many do you remember that she had not come for you, or those that she commands have hunted you? Come on, don't play dumb with me, all you mules have eternal memory of every life, of every death! How many times have you died boy?"

"That's where you're wrong about me, monster. I remember nothing of my former lives. I think I am one of the lucky ones in that regard. The only thing that sucks for me is I seem to at least in this life, have to relearn everything I once knew.

"Was I Cheated? No, my life until I could put it off no long was bliss. I could ignore what I am and almost found a way to live without it."

"Live without the blood?" Lucas mocks, "You're a fool! If you followed that road you would have been like so many others today that turn to **'science'** to cure them of their sickness, anemia, diabetes, porphyra, all these sicknesses are the result of mules denying what they are.

"Don't get me wrong, not all that have these sicknesses are the father's children, only those that are sterile are. Are you sterile mule?"

"FUCK YOU!!!" I scream back at him.

"No I didn't think so mule, cause that day you were out here fucking the leach, I saw what was in her mind and yours. She could see it as nothing more. She used it to fuck with me while you played all nicety nice and spat poetry at her. She saw something in you that you apparently can't see. Maybe you're not so sterile after all, are you mule?"

"Again I say fuck off," I almost have the strength to get free of him. I try to focus on getting away, the direction he is taking this is very uncomfortable to say the least, and I don't know if I can handle the out come, "everything you're saying I can take for being nothing but lies. That's what you do now isn't it? Lie about everything including the life of the first child you killed?"

The blow that struck me this time did break a rib. It almost crushed my chest in. Getting up again I began spitting blood, to clear my throat but it was no use. I could not speak from the pain of the impact and he was roaring in a tirade about me respecting my elders. Then slowly as I got back to my feet so did he also regain his composure and return to his original line of torment.

By this time the sun had gone down beyond the Cyprus trees and the woods around the manor had sprung into full life, no longer fearing him. Knowing his anger was directed fully at me.

"Mule," began Lucas, "there is so much you simply do not know, could never know because you have no mind. How weak are you that your life slips away every time you die. Don't you ever wonder why you are, what you are? How it came to be that things like us exist in the first place?"

"I try not to think about anything really, it's bad for your heath." Its all I can manage, the pain is starting to overwhelm me. I am on the verge of blacking out.

"Don't be deliberately ignorant boy. You'll only succeed in pissing me off." I could tell he was getting ready to attack me again. The very air around me seemed to vibrate...

"Forgive me." I said, "I don't want to piss you off, at least not anymore tonight."

"Mule if you're good, once I am free from my little hell here, I will tell you the whole story as I understand it. But for now, I think I will just eat you when I get out. That is if you're not the one setting me free"

"I plan to set you free Lucas, it's just that I think our ideas about what your freedom will be is a little different." I hold up my hand and place my thumb and forefinger less than an inch apart, right about eye level to show him just how much of a difference I feel there is between our two different opinions in this matter. "Yea about that much."

I can feel the air begin bubbling around me. So there is a tell. One I can use to tell when he will strike, I brace. The impact comes but greatly weakened by my own will pressing the air back from myself. Giving me a moment to breathe and fully stand. Now that I know how to protect myself from his attacks, I can come back and deal with him properly, once I have healed up a bit. I know that if I can bring this one to an end, the others will be nothing.

Again he assaults me but not just with the physical but with the mental again.

"Don't think you're strong enough to save yourself from me boy. You're pathetic, a weak little bastard child of a whore and rapist. That's all you are in the end, the product of your parents ɔoth this life time and from the beginning. I have seen the writings, the words of father and of mother."

Were Lucas free and standing before me I know his hands would be at arms length, held out and his head thrown back as if in desperate prayer? "I have seen how the world was made for our kind and they destroyed it, condemning all of us, their children, to suffering. Making us the wolf that hunt the flock, keeping its numbers from swelling till the land can no longer support them!

"We are more the Ordo Divinus Venatoʳ than when I believed her lies! Oh how we have fallen in the garden of our mothers shame! Oh the suffering we have endured at the ignorance of our father and now we suffer for his sins! We suffer the sins of our father as he suffered the crime of our creator!!!"

I begin backing away. I realize I never found his tomb, his prison, but I can stand this no more. The force of his words in my mind has begun to resound in my head like a bell struck firmly for that perfect note. So clear and loud it cannot be ignored by anyone within miles of its pitch.

Stumbling, finally I reach the exit and begin to move as quickly as I can away. Knowing even though he can not see me, he knows I lost today's encounter. He can feel me running. Tears in my eyes, I fight against the weakness of trying to deny the truth of what he has laid out before me. If I never feel the sound of his laughter inside me ever again, it will be too soon.

I want to burn the whole place down and be done with it. But I can't do that. I must recover my mind and my strength to fight him again, and win out. So that once I find him, I can silence his nightmare forever.

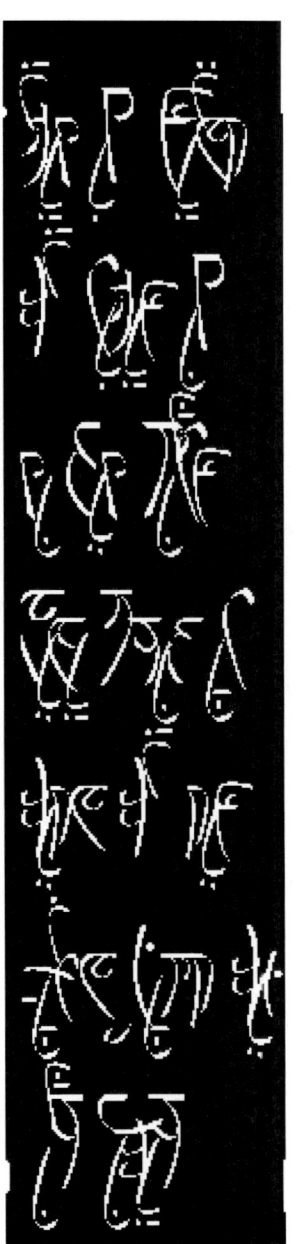
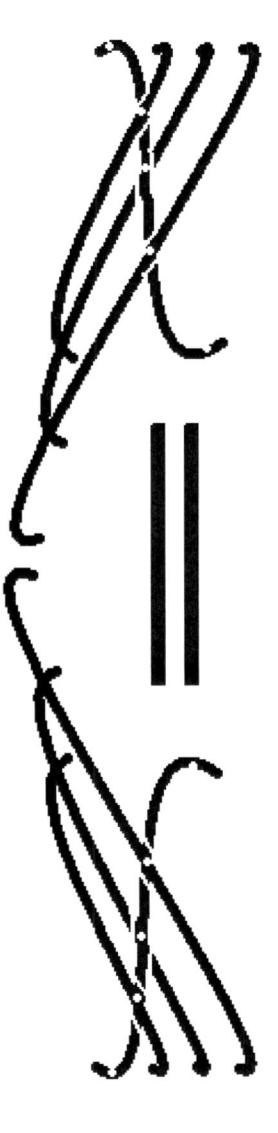

Chapter Eleven — Send in the Martyrs!

Er'more than passes in silence pounding beat

Bereft will shattered the cold of deaths grip

And the warmth embraced communal souls trembling

One by one empties the floor for waiting seat

And cold wine drank by havocked sipping lips.

-VODALOK –

Rustling, somewhere near to Selena caused her to stir. Slowly, her eyes opened and light without shape flooded her senses. The sounds grew as she saw the light pass from her eyes and move over the room and then fade. Focus came and she realized it was just a car, sitting up she looked for Liz who had fallen asleep before her, in her arms. All nuzzled up tight, her head resting on her breast. More rustling, from the bathroom it sounded like.

"Liz?" Selena called out, she waited for a reply but was greeted with silence. Maybe she was sleepwalking. Selena got up and moved to the door, stubbing her toe on the chair next to the bed under the desk, she was beginning to hate living in hotels. Reaching the bathroom door she could hear that sound again and yes it was in the bathroom.

She listened there for a bit and could hear panting, and motion, but she could not tell what was going on or if there was someone other than Liz in there. Liz has been chomping at the bit to go out and hunt these last few days, but Selena would not have it. Not while they were just passing through. If she had brought someone home, Selena would beat her senseless.

Fearing the worst, she threw open the door and turned on the light and found her laying in the tub completely nude, her back arched with one hand on her breast and the other plunging deep inside herself, a make shift dildo.

The sudden entry of Selena startled her and caused her to scream, which caused Selena to scream and the dildo was shot out and made a loud noise upon hitting the tubs floor.

Selena just stood there for a moment looking at Liz who just laid there rocking in time to the hunger of her bodies need for sex. Selena realized that Liz looked more like a snake in a trap than anything human as a result of her body's movements. Movements that after all this time convinced her she needed to do something. Her hunger and Selenas' own hungers were becoming more than Selena could handle.

"Liz, get up. I need you to come with me. We are going to step out, ok?" Selena managed to say after looking at Liz for awhile.

"We are going hunting?" Liz said gleefully.

"Yes darling` we are going hunting. But not to kill, gods I can't stand to see another dead man. And after the trail we have left behind us, which I left behind before finding you.

"You've seen the reports on TV, they are close. We don't need to go giving them any help by leaving bodies lying about."

"Yes mama... mistress?" Liz coo'ed.

"Yes?"

"I need you." Liz's statement was simple and bold. But Selena knew she could not give in to it, even if she wanted to. It was the difference in Selena's mind between keeping Liz under control, and losing control over Liz.

"No you don't, get up, get dressed, and try to control yourself, ok?"

"Yes mama." Liz sounded defeated for the moment, but Selena wondered how long she could hold out. She was starting to really like the way Liz seemed to worship her. And Selena found, maybe just a little, she had started to love Liz.

She turned back to the room and went to turn on the lights when she stubbed her other toe on the same chair. She cursed the chair and swore to destroy its maker if she stumbled on it again. At the same time the handle to the main door of the room started to turn and she could hear it opening.

She turned to Liz and told her to get down and keep quite. Liz not comprehending quickly enough was pushed to the floor as the door began to open.

Someone had a key to their room and she was not happy about it. A flashlight paned the room and she was glad that she had gotten down on the side of the bed just before the door came full open.

She listened and could hear the breathing of two people, one male one female. They didn't speak but hands could be heard moving, sign language? Selena was not sure but whoever they were they were being very professional, then she smelled the gun oil, fresh and warm.

For the first time since she was reborn, she could feel her body beginning to tingle, the sounds faded, not so much that they became silent. Rather as if they were slowing down until each sound was just a long paused note, not really making sound but still audible. She could not wait for them to get to her.

She feared being captured or killed again, and moved. Rising up she saw the pair, one to the left one to the right of the door. Dressed all in black the woman wore a nun's cowl and the man a priest collar. The difference was the black combat fatigues they wore, with the belts and harness full of gear, the guns she knew to be P-90's, the result of too many TV shows. That's when she notices they were in mid step and not moving.

Before her was a mosquito, in flight and not moving, she stopped and looked at it, the truth of what was happening to her was overwhelming her senses. The overall sensation of being sick was however overcome by the realization that she was out of time, or was she just moving so fast that everything else seemed to stop.

Her question was answered as she felt her ears pop and her body suddenly becomes too heavy to maintain. The pain of it was amazing, and then there were also the two intruders who screamed and turned their weapons on her.

She let herself fall to the floor and try to role up in front of them. To her credit Liz jumped out as well trying to be useful but it was something Selena had wished had not happened. The male pivot on his hip shifting his weight so that he came down on one knee and squeezed the trigger as his weapon went from where Selena was to where Liz should have been. Selena screamed as she watched herself move past the bullets, grab Liz and kick off the wall and land in the bathroom.

"Father you were right," said the nun, "they are damned..."

But before she could finish her statement the priest reprimanded her. "Sister, remember protocol!"

His words were not harsh or controlling, they were however uttered with authority, and she immediately fell silent and to one knee as two more came in behind them, they made a brace against the exit. Selena was not sure she could get through. From where she and Liz now rested in the bathroom she was not sure they would even get out at all.

"How did we get back in here," came Liz's frightened voice, "I never saw you move and then we are in here..."

"Liz, I need you to be quiet, and let me think." Selena said more harshly than she wanted too. "This is going badly, so shut up ok."

Liz's only reply was a half whimpered "Yes mama" then she fell silent. Selena listened to the movements out in the main room and knew there were at least six in the main room now. She and Liz were going to die, she just knew it. That in mind Selena decided to at least find out who these people were. "Um... my name is Selena, I don't know what you all want, but ya got the wrong people, person... We're just passing through, if ya don't mind we would like to keep 'just passing through' ok?"

There was no reply, but she could hear them talking amongst themselves, then came a reply on a radio. ".....repeat, capture. Do not destroy; the headmistress wants to talk with her...."

"Rodger that," the Priest replied, "confirm again identity."

"... Target Lilith/ apprehension only 'til confirmation of status...," came the voice on the radio again.

"Rodger, visual confirmation, type 2 Sanguinairan, requesting martyr be brought in for capture," was the last thing the priest said before the radio went silent.

Selena didn't like the name Lilith, and she knew it had to be in reference to her, but why she could not figure out. The other chatter was not making this any easier. She didn't want to know what a 'martyr' was or why they would need one, and what did they mean by type 2... She figured sense they, at this time, only wanted to 'capture her', it would be in her best interest to surrender, and said as much to Liz.

"Selena isn't that how you ended up with me in the first place... I don't think that's a very good idea."

Selena looked at her, and knew she was right but didn't know what else to do. "Look, they're a bunch of priest. Ok they've got guns and shit, but I don't think they are going to sell our flesh to the highest bidder...I am going to do this."

"Fine," Liz said, "but if we die, I am not washing your back for you anymore."

Selena looked at her and found she was not smiling and was trying to be calm. She smiled at Liz and ran her hand over her head and threw her hair trying to comfort her. Looking back at the door she called out.

"Look I don't want trouble, mind if I make this easy on everyone and just ... surrender?"

In all the years they had been hunting her kind, never has there been a report of any of the hunted ever making such and offer. The group in the other room was now confronted with the one thing they had never been prepared for, and they froze. The leader started to say 'what' but stopped, Selena could hear them looking at each other.

There was a pause then the man that came in first replied. "By surrender, you mean come out quietly?"

Selena replied with. "Is there another kind of surrender? No one needs to get hurt hear, and besides if your headmistress wants to talk to me, then I am ok with a meeting. Can we put your guns down and walk out of here quietly?"

Another pause entered the rooms, the long silence was uncomfortable for everyone, and then came his reply, "Ok... we accept you're... surrender? But you must release your hostage."

Selena almost said "what?!" then looked at Liz and realized they didn't know she was her willing servant. She could see that Liz had figured this out as well and before she could say anything Liz started screaming,

"Help!!! Please help, it was going to eat me!"

To which Selena almost busted out laughing. Liz looked at her and smiled at her with a shrug, and a nodding of her head 'No'. Showing she didn't know what else to do.

"Ok I will let her go, but you have to promise me that I will not be hurt if I do, I want to co-operate with you on this. Again no one needs to get hurt, ok?"

"Ok, send her out, if she is hurt, it will not be good for you," came the Priest voice from the other room trying for all his might to sound in control.

"Well I have been using her to keep my strength up," Selena said, in spite of the moment, "does that count as hurting her?"

The two of them almost busted out laughing again at that one. Why she didn't know but staying calm and getting Liz out of this safely was her only intention. Before letting her go she whispered into Liz's ear that she should learn as much as she could about these people, and do her best to learn where she herself would be kept so if needed Liz could get her out. Now ready Selena addressed the priest in the other room.

"Ok... she is coming out first, so if you shoot she dies."

"Ok... um... send her out..." said the Priest, still unsure of what was going on. The tension in the air was like mud on Selena's tongue. Selena didn't like it, the stress of what was about to happen was heavy on her, and from what she could feel, on all of those in the main room.

Selena turned the light in the bathroom on and opened the door. She kissed Liz. Then told her she was sorry and pushed Liz out into the main room. She was happy that there was no gun fire.

"Alright I sent her out, now I am going to come out. Your word is all I have and I am hoping I can take your word as faith, I will be ok."

The Priest said, "Our word is good." And Selena could hear him motion to everyone, to what end she didn't know. Then the voice from the radio interrupted everything.

"... Request for martyr granted stand your ground do not engage..."

The sound of the radio startled everyone. The faces of those that were in the room were flush with fear. Selena prayed to whoever would hear her. She didn't know who, but she needed help, considering the position she is in with god as she understood it.

"Ok, so do I keep surrendering, or are you going to wait for your big gun to come in and take credit for this?"

It was cheap, it was all she had, and she wanted this over. They looked around at one another and stiffened a bit and the leader said they would proceed, as the situation had changed from hostile to... well it was not hostile. Selena walked forward and they had her put her hands behind her. The cold steel of the handcuffs was annoying but understandable.

Then they put a hood over her head. She noticed that Liz was already out of the room and no where to be seen. For now she had to not think about her. She hoped that Liz would keep her wits about her and not freak out.

She could feel them leading her out and then into the back of a vehicle. Selena took a step up and then sat onto a bench. Some kind of truck she figured, or maybe a van? Once inside she could hear the leader in this little assault radioing back that the situation was now under control and that they were heading back to contact. The reply that came back was simple.

'Why did you request martyr if the situation is under control?'

The group head paused and stated clearly. "The Target surrendered, it didn't wish to fight."

The long pause that followed was broken with a simple acknowledgement and clearance to return to contact. Selena could feel a general breaking of tension and pressure in the group, good. The last thing from the voice on the other end of the radio was a general pat on the back for the group for taking full control and resolving the issue without conflict, then something about not repeating the mess in the big easy.

The ride was long, she figured it was about an hour or so, and everyone was quiet. Not a word was uttered, or even thought by any of them. Selena had found that tonight several things had fully opened to her. One of which is she could move as fast as Stephen had that day he set her free. The other thing was that now every time they passed a car she could hear the thoughts of those in them for a small distance. Clearly and with just a little effort she could hold on to those thoughts.

Selena could move through that persons mind and see what she wanted. By the time the ride was over she had managed to find a way to see through the eyes of those that passed by the trucks that they were in and see them all, mostly. Things for her were still a little hazy but she was getting the hang of it, or so she thought.

Selena still could not access the minds of those around her. She could not access the minds of those at the place called contact either, which she was finding to be a bit disturbing.

Selena could tell they came to a guard point. There was a request for identification, the sound of gates opening and dogs barking. This was some kind of compound. She could hear other vehicles and people and animals moving about as the truck began moving forward again. Five min later it came to a stop and was shut down.

The door opened and she began to wonder if surrendering was the right thing to do. They lead her inside, not roughly like she expected but gently and with some reverence. After a few moments they passed threw a set of doors, the only thing said was.

"Transition, Target Lilith."

She could not understand why they kept calling her that? Why were they referring to her as some biblical fairytale cemon? Selena figured what the hell and asked. "I guess I am target Lilith, can you explain why?"

This question was met with more silence and then they all stopped. Another door was opened and she was led inside and sat down in what must have been a very nice chair. It was soft and warm and cushioned all around like a lazy-boy made of wool. They undid her bindings and replaced them with new ones, but this time she could feel she had room to move her arms. She was now held with chains she guessed and then there was silence again as the door closed.

Sitting there in the dark of the hood that was not removed, she wondered where in all the hells she had landed herself. Beginning to regret the whole surrendering thing Selena began to talk to herself a bit. Even going so far as to joke openly about not being French and they should not assume she will capitulate with them if they don't come in and take the hood off her head soon.

What bothered her most about this was nothing seemed to be making any noise. She could not even hear the sounds of a light bulb or tube radiating down on her. There was no air flow, or movement, everything in this room was completely still. So she sat there just as motionless, waiting for she knew not what.

Selena was startled awake by the sound of the door opening and a light coming on. Moments later the hood was removed from her head. As she blinked to get her bearings and see who had freed her of the hood. The light went out again and the door closed behind them. The room as far as she could tell, even with her improved vision was utterly black. There was no source of light to see by at all.

So complete was the darkness around her that when the flood lights came on she screamed. Not out of shock, but from the pain it caused her eyes. She struggled against the chains but they held, she could stand and move this way and that, but could not get out of the light. It was too bright, burning bright, it was so hot.

Selena felt like she had been placed in an oven to bake! Then without warning the lights went out and sound began to hammer at her. The sound of songs of praise to a god she knew would have nothing to do with her. Behind the songs was a man preaching, monks chanting, and the screaming of what must have been hundreds of people.

She could feel blood running down her ears from the extremely high level of the sound that was beating into her head, and then it too stopped just as abruptly, leaving her in the darkness again.

Hours went by and the pain of her burnt body faded as did the ringing in her ears, and the spots in her eyes. Selena felt her body repairing itself from the harm done to it. She figured this must be some kind of test to see if she is a 'type 2 sang...' whatever they called her.

"Ok I can handle this and be ok," she would show them just how strong she was.

But no sooner than she felt like it was over, that she would not have to worry about it happening again, it did. This time the lights stayed on a little longer, and the music came with it. This time they would pulse in and out, the lights brighter, the music softer, the music louder, and the lights dimmer.

For an hour she endured this torture, trying desperately to focus on the sound of the voice of the priest to see if there was some reasoning in what was happening to her. Yet every time she was finally able to hear him clearly, the music would fad again, then it stopped, and she began to recover.

Selena was crying by this time, she could not take this forever, she wanted free. She knew that if she tried hard enough either the chains would break or she would lose her hands. Either way she didn't care much right now. She just wanted free of this nightmare.

But that freedom never came, for 11 days this went on. Until one day as she slowly woke from her fevered dreams, there was soft light in the room, and a table in front of her, on the other side was an empty chair. On the table was a folder, a pen, and a steaming cup of coffee. The moisture from the coffee was tormenting her. Its smell and texture in the other wise vacant room, teasing her with things she could not have.

When the door opened and a woman came in with a plate of food and a drink. Selena almost jumped up and attacked her. But she could not, the chains had been shortened. She could not even raise her hands from where they were held tight, pulled strait down by the back legs of the chair.

The food and drink were placed on the table in front of her. Then the lady left without looking at Selena once. The door sealed and the food sat there. Selena called out.

"Ok I am hungry please let me eat... you brought it in... please... let me eat? Hello!!!! I know you're there, why are you doing this, I surrendered, I gave in, I came willingly, please... please stop this.... Hello, hello?"

But there was no response, she sat there straining against her bonds, feeling the meat of her shoulders tearing until she could take the pain no more, and then collapsed into the chair. So she watched the food steam and cool and grow cold. The smell of it faded till all she wanted was the stench of its waste away from her, cold eggs, stale biscuits and curdled milk.

Four hours passed and a new tray of food was brought in, this was some sort of lunch, Melons, breads, butter and honey. Just like the breakfast it was sat out in front of her and the attendant left without a word, or even noticing her. The food sat there. She could not look away from it, nor could she get to it.

And as before four hours later a dinner was brought in and sat before her, steak, with onions and mushrooms, gravy covered mashed potatoes and a piece of chocolate pie. The drink it was clear to see, its smell was blood.

Selena tried very hard this time to free herself. She needed to eat, drink something anything she didn't care. Eleven days of torture now, no food or drink and now this... It could not go on. As if in response to her pleading, the woman that had been bringing her food all day, that sat and wasted, came in and took the dinner away. Behind her came five men.

One picked up the old cup of coffee, one the pen, another folder and the last two took the table and the chair. No sooner than they had left the room, jets of very cold water erupted onto her from all angels above and below, soaking her to the bone.

Four hours went by before the water stopped. It was almost up to her chin by this time and she could feel the water draining as soon as it stopped. She wept from somewhere inside her that she had never felt pain before. She begged out loud to be killed or set free. That she would do anything these people wanted if they would just stop.

An hour went by after the water drained with her in utter darkness again. Then the speakers and the lights came on again pulsing in odd broken patters. The screaming that came from her was that of someone whose mind breaks, and can do nothing more than try to drown themselves in their own sound to be free of their madness.

Those screams were heard through out the complex where she was being held. Every person that heard those screams trembled for fear the sound of them would break their walls down and pierce their perfect little will. Destroy them as the source of the screams was being broken and destroyed. And still the sound, fire, food and water would come. With every day the voice of the priest giving his sermon would become a little clearer.

"...in god only will you find peace, and the hell of existence that you have made this world will fade. But you can only gain his grace again and be free of the fire of penance, freed from the spider webs of deceit. By finding and destroying the one that brought this pain upon you. You must hunt him down and destroy him to be purified in the eyes of god!"

It went on like that forever, in and out of her mind, mixed with her own screams. The masses of those behind her could be felt begging her for salvation and redemption, begging her, begging that she destroy the one that caused their pain, the one that caused these eons of suffering. And she screamed with them "I will stop the pain, just free me. I beg you kill me, so I can destroy him..."

Her own words an echo within the very fiber of her being, echoing inside every muscle, every bone, and every cell of her body.

When Selena woke next, she was again faced with the table, chair, folder, pen and coffee. The difference was there was someone sitting in the chair this time. Selena knew this torment has been going on now for at least a month, maybe four. She could not tell, it never ended, she never was allowed to eat and the water was never allowed to get high enough for her to drink. So broken was her mind by this time she felt the person sitting there was a dream or maybe a hallucination. Her breathing was part of the echo that rang in her ears.

Selena's mind cleared a little, and her eyes opened. The person sitting there was smiling; her red hair and green eyes betraying the cruelty that hid within her. Selena could feel the malice and hatred for herself coming out of this woman. The red hair, the green eyes, that pale skin and her commanding presence, it all made Selena want to tear her heart out. But nothing showed in her, that demon, that she even knew Selena was in the room with her.

Slowly she began flipping pages in the folder, pausing and picking up the pen, putting it down, picking up the coffee cup. Putting it to her lips but not drinking, looking into the cup and then putting it down. She picked up the pen again and made a single mark on a page in the folder. When she looked up she said one thing.

"Lilith."

The redhead sat there looking at Selena until she again began flipping through the folder. This time backwards, pausing and picking up the pen, putting it down, picking up the coffee, not drinking, putting it down. Picking up the pen and marking a page, looking at Selena and saying.

"Lilith."

This went on for what seemed an eternity; days at the very least. This woman never left the room. Food would be brought in for each of them but only the red demon would eat. She would eat from both plates, and drink form both glasses that Always held blood. Eat from the plates that always held steak, melons, or biscuits.

Selena was fracturing inside her own mind. She could feel everything unraveling. Her screams became babble, and her babble became spiders. That spun webs out of her breath. That burned the spiders. That turned to ash. That threatened to drown her. And behind all this was the only sound that she could hear clearly or understand.

"Lilith."

It stopped being a statement and became a question, in those hours that were rare and few between that allowed her to think with any clarity. And always she was there, watching her. The red demon that would say the word, that was the question, that she knew was the key to the end of her hell. That word...

"Lilith, are you listening to me. I don't like doing this, but you must wake up and accept your life. The life you stole, the life you felt was yours. Free to run with, outside of the will of god."

Selena looked up at the demon that burned in the breath of spiders drowning in her ash. That breathed out of the webs from her breast and replied.

"I am Lilith?"

"Yes." Vomited the demon...

"I am damned." The words were spun into the webs of the spiders, crawling out of Selena's mouth.

"Yes." Screamed the demon...

"I am without God's grace."

"You ... are beyond God's grace." Laughed the demon...

"I know... he told me." Said Lilith...

The red demon leaned forward, the smile gone from her face, and the demon looked deeply into Lilith's eyes. The demons eyes were replaced by roaches that crawled around in the sockets where there was once flesh. But Lilith didn't care. She knew that Selena would save her from this.

But the red demon spoke and bile filled the room in accompaniment of her words. "What do you mean he told you?"

Selena answered as best she could. "When I consumed the doctor, poor old man Tate, I took him to bury him and in the ground where he rest now. God told me I was no longer one of his. God said that I was outside his realm of influence, that I was no long his child."

"Was that the only time god spoke to you?" questioned the demon.

Lilith replied. "Yes but the doves came and cried and the man of god fled the bed of my lust and her sin. They helped him fly away and told me for God, that she would suffer all my sins. That because I could not be punished by God, that she would be in my place. That I could not suffer his wraith or his blessing, at least that's what it sounded like."

By this time both Selena and Lilith were looking at the red demon from inside the same eyes and Selena could not come forward. She knew that if that happened the little one would be found and harmed. So she stepped back and let Lilith deal with the demon.

Lilith cried and asked that she be allowed to die. She didn't want to be a monster anymore. She wanted to be a little girl free of the suffering that was consuming her flesh even as she spoke. She could see the leaches that were lies eating away at her arms and legs.

The red demon was sitting on the table now in front of her. Reaching out for her face and held it in her hand. A hand that burned with fire, the flesh of her face melting into ice cycles.

The Red Demons mouth moved and words came out that made no sense but she knew they were her salvation. She knew that she, Lilith must find her father and destroy him. She tried to make It understand that she understood, but it would not listen. It just melted into the table and the cleansing began again.

Selena felt her hands being rubbed and opened her eyes. The door was open and there were sparks coming from somewhere above her. She could hear someone crying and talking to her, begging her to wake up. But she couldn't. The chains had been removed and she was being lifted out of the chair. Whoever this was she was strong, at least that is what she thought at that moment.

Lilith asked Selena if she should come forward and protect her from this new lie. Letting her head fall to one side, she saw the doors of other rooms open or laying on the ground, smoke and sparks coming from everywhere, and decide that this was good. Selena faded into the darkness of herself, and sat waiting for what she did not know.

They passed bodies of nuns and priest lying on the ground, bleeding. The smells of the blood was very strong and Lilith wanted to feed desperately but could not move, save to let her head role to one side or the other. And they were outside. It was snowing and there was gun fire in the distance. She didn't care, she was out of that place and felt as if she would die, was dead.

Her vision faded as she heard the sound of an engine straining to meet the demands being placed upon it. And screaming as voices commanded caution, to not be so death friendly in this kind of weather.

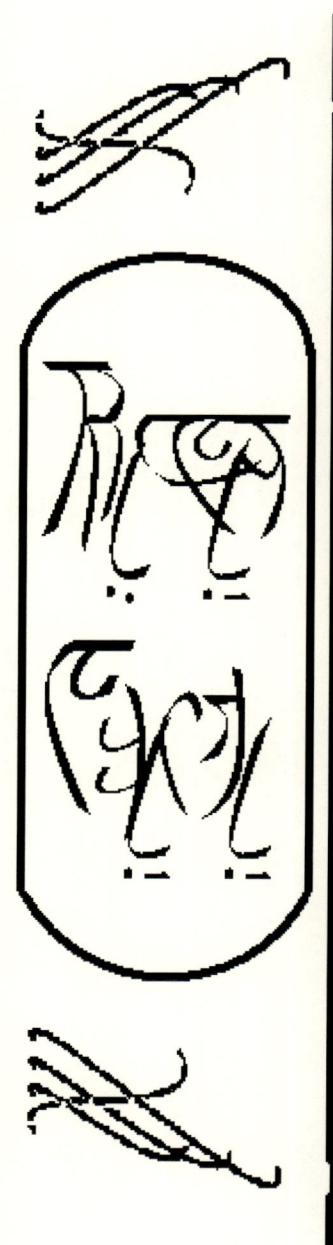

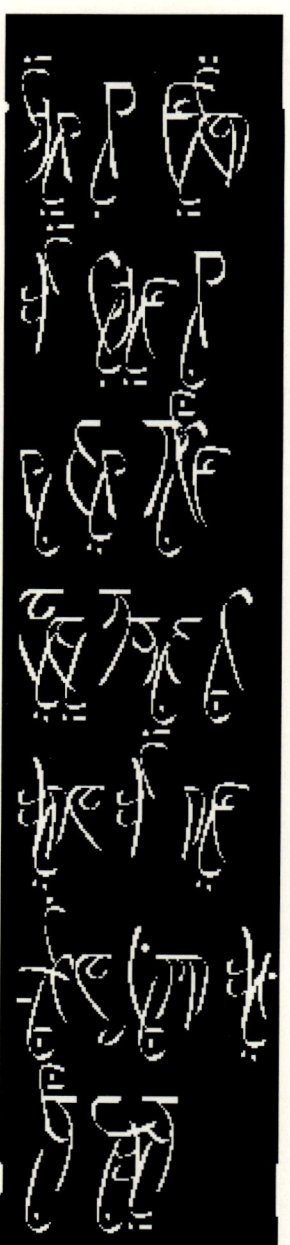

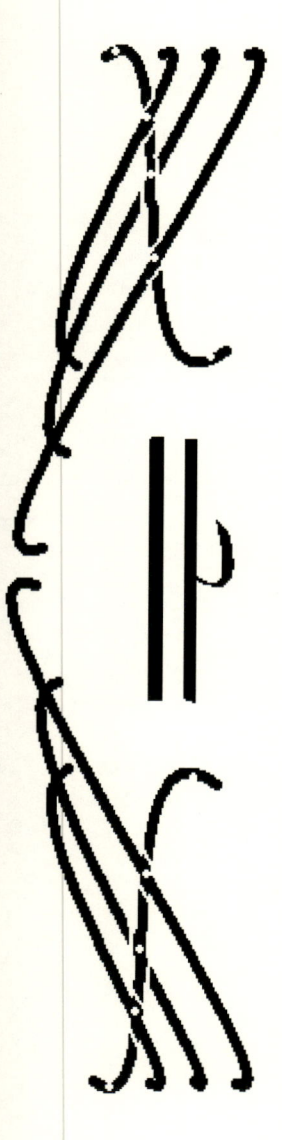

Chapter Twelve – the perfect prison

Long days come the going of sorrow

In time weighs slow the lose in heart worn

No end is seen by even the sages among us

'til rising of the sun bringing light for us to borrow

And his lose becomes our gain in memories never lost sworn.

-VODALOK-

Waking up was the hard thing for Selena to do. Every muscle ached in a way she had never known before. Her effcrts to open her eyes failed with the coming fire of the effort to do so. She could not move and her body felt as if the chains were still there but she knew she was no longer in a sitting position that she could not change. Every effort led to her passing back out.

That was ok, because when she was not awake she was dreaming and she could walk and rest in a place she had never known before. The breeze that blew upon her was cool and always fresh, the sun soft and warm without being painful. The grass was green and soft, and there were never any rocks under foot or chairs to stub her toes on. This last part she loved more than anything.

She was back and running along a hill side full of perfect grass and flowers that led up to a tree. The tree was remarkable due to its enormous size and the tree house that was built through out the entire tree, over and under, around and between every branch like a fantasy fortress made by and for elves. And yes these elves baked cookies and pies and many other confections that she would eat as she rested beneath their little tree bound kingdom.

And everyday that she would awaken under those branches she would be joined by her new friend, Lilith.

Lilith was one of those women that commanded attention and was freely given respect, she loved her. Her long black hair and seeming Balkan features, dark eyes and a thin but sharp nose, white skin and firm broad shoulders, on a frame that couldn't have been more than a size 3 or 4 if it was anything, a perfect body. Lilith was at least five inches taller than her as well, she envied her for all she was.

Every day Lily, as she asked Selena to call her, would bring her a new flower or something to eat. Whether it was jewelry, or books, she always came and always with something new. And Selena was learning so much about who she is, was and has ever been from this grand and noble woman that was coming to sit with her everyday.

The things she loved to learn the most were who she had been a long time ago, before the breath of man fell from the wombs of their mothers. This excited Selena in ways she could not bring to words. Always Lily was willing to share with her everything she could as long as Selena could form the questions that would need answers she could provide.

Today she would ask her, Lily, if all this is true about all these other people that the red demon and Lily claim Selena has been. She tried once before to ask but Lily became so angry and almost turned the sky to ash with her screaming. Selena could not bear to have that happen again so kept quiet and stayed as submissive as she could. The one thing she feared was Lily not letting her go home to her life and making sure that Liz stayed out of trouble. Lily wanted to encourage Liz and hungered for her touch. Lilith could not be trusted with Liz. And Lily acted like she was afraid of Selena from time to time but she always was in control. Selena was ok with this as long as she didn't have to go back to the chair.

However Lilith had learned how to keep Selena in check and hold her to the dreaming and not let her see the reality of what had happened. She knew that they were no longer in the chair but it was easy enough for her to convince Selena that they were. And everyday when Selena asked she would tell her. No the water is still coming, or that her ears were again bleeding out from the speakers. It is best you let me suffer this pain so you can rest and be strong for Liz when the time comes.

Selena was more than willing to accept this. She hoped that Lily taking all the abuse that came would let her rest, and it was such a wonderful place for her to rest in. But today would be different and she would be the one to go out into the world and see how things were going. When Lily did arrive she was looking bad, like she had seen a ghost.

It freighted Selena a bit to see this person that is so strong, so beaten down and fragile looking.

Selena asked Lilith, "Lily what's wrong? What have they done to me now?"

"It's worse than you can imagine my darling. They have ... they have begun removing your fingers... I am preventing so much suffering from coming to you, but it will not be long before I can no longer protect you"

"Lily I cannot... my fingers? Why am I not feeling this pain?"

"It is my will that you do not suffer, but I can not protect you as long as you are out here for much longer. There is a place you can go where I can protect you, but you must come willingly. So that I can put more effort into your survival, otherwise you may die before the week is out"

Selena looked at her, feared the things that Lily told her. She wanted to go out and reclaim her body, but she could not stand the torture, which is why she was here with Lilith in the first place. She knew that if she didn't let Lilith do this she would die. Why would this woman lie to her?

"Ok Lily, show me where I need to go. I will follow you and... you promise to protect me, and when it is safe let me go back so I can protect Liz?"

Lilith "I promise you, you will be able to protect Liz. This will not last long. Nor will you feel the pain they are causing you anymore, I promise"

"Ok but... please, tell me again why you're here, with me in this place? How you know so much about me?"

"Darling I have always been here with you, your guardian, and your protector. I have helped you survive so many things in the past, but you have always been a very strong woman and have not needed to know I was here. So I was content to stay in the shadows and do what I could from there, it's not important. What is, is that you're safe and nothing more"

Selena follows her as far as she can and finds that the path leads out of the meadow and into a wooded glen. There in, was a lovely little cottage with sun coming down upon it through the trees that seemed to touch the very face of god. She knew that was not the case because God had turned his back on her. It was clear to see, his name stricken from her book of contacts that she carried with her everywhere. What she could not figure out was whose name was under his with a new number added in by hand.

Once they reached the little cottage she could better see the beauty of it, flower beds and little white fences, rabbits and deer moving around as though they had no fear of either of them. There was softness to the ground that made her forget the world outside. Almost forget that she was only going to be here for a little while. Lily was watching her, and smiling with her arms crossed.

"Do you like your new home, a place for you to come to rest and recover? Inside are all the books I told you about, and all the paintings. Everything I told you I would provide you so you can remember completely who you are"

Selena looked at her and smiled, almost running up to the door to enter. Stopping short of going in she turned and looked back at Lilith who had yet to move from where she was. Selena had to yell to her to say thank you, as Lilith was still beyond the fence line around the lovely little home. Then she turned and went in with the door closing behind her. Lilith watched for awhile and exited the grove without looking back.

Inside Selena found that her guardian had not lied to her, and inside were all the books and paintings. New paints and canvas also awaited her inside. Foods to last an eternity, as well as the most comfortable bed she had ever seen.

Taking up an apple she began to eat while flipping through the books looking for the one she wanted to start reading. Once she found a good one, she sat down upon the bed and laid back to read. The story started out as all stories do, 'once upon a time, in a land far, far away lived a queen whose daughter was the fairest of the land'. Selena liked that beginning and settled in.

After a little while the apple was gone as was the book, both having fallen to the floor and her eyes closed in blissful slumber.

Not far away Lilith smiled knowing she could return and when she did the windows were locked and the door bolted from the inside. Without looking back she began to do what she could to get back to the world.

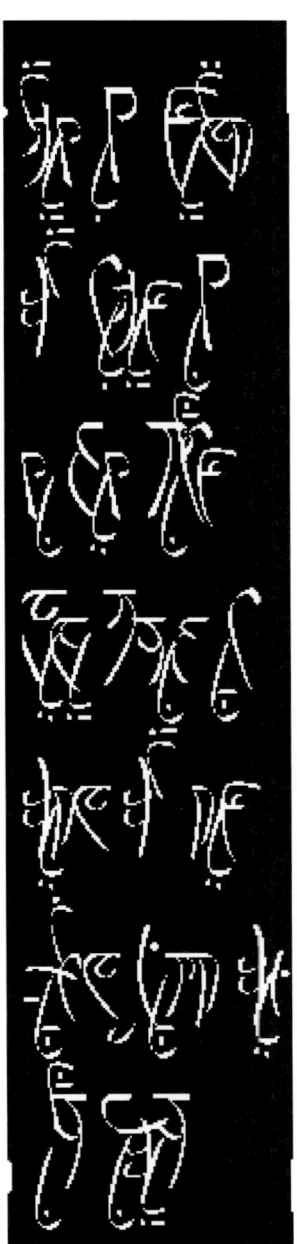
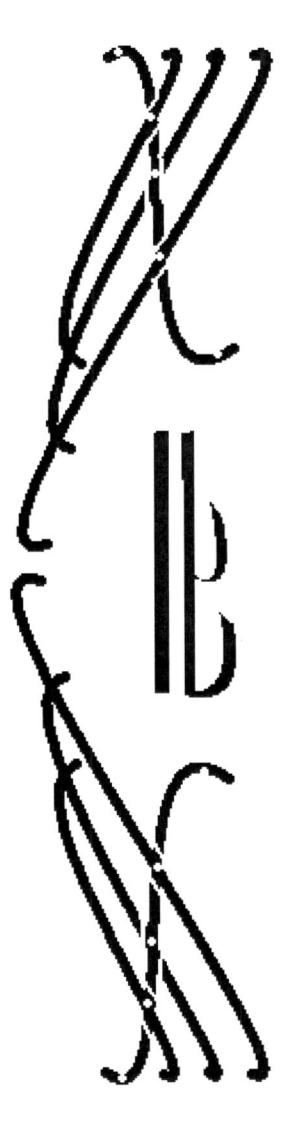

Chapter Thirteen - Black ops at the parish

And for so many thousands in this world so tiny

So far away and close by silver webs trembling

Our pain is bled out free to life new given

A simple gift of life was one taken so shinny

From his ashes fresh souls in the darkness assembling

-VODALOK –

Richard Corman was a practical man, that's how he survived in an industry that had little use for him other than to pay him for his services, he knew and understood that. Every job was done by the book. He had no real care one way or the other if who he was working for got what they wanted or if the people he was following got theirs either. What mattered to him was himself.

He knew that following the rules was the only way to stay alive and keep his life neat and tidy like he liked it. That's why he could not figure out how he had been convinced that this was a good idea. Reflecting on the matter he was unable to figure it out, but here he was, bleeding and almost dead and nothing he could do, save die. There had to be a point to where this all went wrong, so again he began running the last five months through his mind. What little was left of it to understand how he came to be here dying like this.

The day he left the manor with the check for 5 grand, he went out and bought a few things. Got his car repaired so he could get around without having to do rentals or fly. It was slower he knew but leads and clues were "better found on the ground not in the clouds" he would tell his peers. Two days later with a new computer, a repaired car and his old hand gun back from the pawn shop he headed out to find his target.

The boss told him he felt her last somewhere near by, but on the other side of the river, a large city, which one he could not tell. For Richard that was easy, it was Memphis. His drive there was six hours and no time wasted. The hotel he chose was a bit drab but what do you expect for three in the morning availability. The next morning while sitting in a nearby dinner for breakfast, he is approached by a girl that is maybe 19 if she's 21. She sits down and watches him going through the folder of information he was handed on the girl he is to find.

After a little while he looks up at her and see's her clearly, long strait black hair, her bangs cut short to reach just above her eyes. Those eyes were an interesting color he could not quite put his finger on, must be contacts. Small but very shapely breast stood at attention, demanding his attention as she sat across from him, back strait and motionless.

"Can I help you?" Richard asked.

"Maybe" she said.

"Look Honey, I am a busy man I don't..."

"Hush," she said putting a finger up to his lips, "I like watching you work and eat, just do that ok?"

Richard looked at her as if she was crazy, but her smile erupted onto her face and made the sun seem to dim. So he sat there looking at her trying to figure out if she was for real, then watched as she reached over the table, picked up his fork, gathered eggs on to it and brought it up to his mouth.

"Please keep eating, I promise to sit quietly and only watch if you will just keep eating."

Without saying a word he opened his mouth. He could not for the life of him figures out why she was doing this and it showed in his face and body langue. He looked like he was about to either cry or run but he sat there and ate the eggs. This black haired vixen simply laid her head onto her shoulder and smiled watching him eat each and every piece of food she brought to his mouth. When he would get some food on his face she would make this noise that was like a squeak and then clean it off with her fingers. Slowly licking her fingers clean of the food or drink removed from his lips or face. Richard began dribbling just to watch her do this. She was, as he saw it, clearly into him, and so he complied and played along.

"My name is Richard... what's yo..."

"Liz," she said stopping him with her finger, "you can call me Liz, no please look at your papers some more. If you want I can get you more food," her head lowered while her eyes stayed focused upon him and a smile so innocent and coy came to life on her lips that poor Richard felt his will melting away. Who ever she is, she is just to damned sexy for her own good, "if you're still... hungry for food."

This last bit was followed by her leaning forward and letting her shirt open a bit revealing her very young and firm breast. Not completely but enough to show her intentions. Trying to remain in control Richard sat back and told her he needed to get back to work, that as tempting as this moment is, he can't.

"Ok," said Liz, "well I am in the hotel across the street. I saw you come out of the room across from mine. If you're ever interested, I know I can... take care of your needs."

Liz rose from the table and moved to stand next to Richard. She picked up his napkin and turned to walk away. His eyes were fixed on her. Not more than two steps away she dropped the napkin and bent over to pick it up. He watched as her very short skirt lifted. As she bent forward her legs strait and rigid, slightly apart until her head was almost at the ground. Her sex, he could see exposed, and cleanly shaven, was too much for him. Liz was looking at him and smiling with one eye brow raised as she stood back up.

"I am sorry," she said, "you weren't meant to see... that."

Laughing she left the little diner with a bounce that made her pony tails seem alive. Richard put his files away and called for the bill. A minute later he was leaving the dinner and heading back to the hotel. He stopped short when he saw Liz enter a room with several other girls in it. He figured he would hang out and watch for a bit before heading back into the hotel courtyard.

Half an hour later two more girls entered the room with a young man in tow. At first he was left standing outside, and then he was brought in. Long moments passed before the door opened again.

Richard figured they were dealing drugs, maybe pandering as well. But then she came out behind the boy that had just went in, it was her! Scrambling he opened the folder and found the picture his employer had given him of the girl Selena. The one he was hunting down!

He stood there watching, they were having some conversation he could not hear, and didn't want to get any closer for fear of being noticed. He had this feeling that if he moved she would see him, so like a frightened and cornered animal he tried to be as invisible as he could.

Time seemed to drag at this point and then finally they went back inside. A few moments later the boy came out with the same two girls in tow. They were smiling and from what he could see, seemed to be free of some terrible weight.

Soon as they passed him he caught something about going to school and being free to live a normal life again. Not much, but certainly sounded encouraging. Richard ran back to his room to drop off the folder and grab his camera. Then before he could exit the room the target and the vixen came out, just as quickly his camera was clicking away getting as many pictures as he could of her, and the target.

Then somehow, she was gone, no where to be seen. He stepped out side to look for her, and saw a car pulling away, but before he could raise his camera again Liz was in front of him.

"I like cameras," she said, "can I pose for you?"

Richard figured that if this little slut was with his target, it could not hurt getting in close so he could try and find out more about them. So he played along.

"I saw you out here with another woman, that your sister?" he said.

Liz looked at him and smiled before answering. "Would it change what you're thinking about me, if I said yes?"

Richard smiled and opened his door a bit wider. "No, it's been sort of a fantasy of mine to be with sisters, you two, play much?"

"Some times..." Liz steps in real close, pressing herself against him, straddling his leg. He could feel the wetness of her, and it was hard to ignore, biting her lip she continued, "you want us to be bad for you?"

Richard with his free hand moved it down the back of her head saying, "It would be interesting, want to go back to your room and see how well my camera likes you?"

She reacted quickly and poorly to that suggestion, almost immediately stepping back and half yelling at him. "We can't go to my room!"

"Um... my room then?" Richard figured it best not to press the issue as he suggested his room.

Liz recovered just as quickly as she fell apart.

"Yea, sorry... ours is a bit of a mess."

Richard knew it was a lie but he didn't really care. By this time he was so worked up by Liz all he wanted was to find out just how bad this little Lolita was.

So they went in and her demeanor went back to that of a seductress. She was plying him for information about his job. How long he'd been doing it, and he told her the truth mostly. Except the parts about him being a photographer for these major publishers in Dallas.

With each bit of information he gave she lost another piece of clothing, within minutes she was on his bed giving him the show of his life. He watched her bend over backwards and arches her back around until she could grab her ankles. Then she did a few other very erotic things to herself, and then came to rest on her belly facing him.

"Put the camera down, and come over here."

He complied and walked to where she was and stood there. She opened his pants and the nock on the door scared the piss out of both of them. It was the voice of a young girl on the other side that made Richard look at Liz. Not as a detective but as a man agitated with being interrupted before he can even get what he was hungry for.

"Liz, you have to come, please we're scared! Please come back..."

Liz seemed more than upset by this and went to the door without dressing, opened it, and quietly yelled at the girl that stood their. Her posture and age made Richard more than a little confused. Who ever she was she was clearly older than Liz but seemed terrified by her.

When this new girl could talk again she said one thing and Liz went rigid with fear. This caused Liz to ran back to get her clothes, and she left without dressing into the court yard, then back to her room.

"What did that girl say?" thought Richard to himself, "Something about telling the monster she had been bad."

He quickly set up his tripod and video camera in the windows. Then Richard stepped out, making sure that Liz saw him leave. Once at the corner he doubled back round the other side of the building and hid behind the shrub's that made up the landscaping for this place and watched. It was not until sometime after the sun went down that the target Selena returned.

She paused outside and looked around and seemed to stop, her eyes falling where he was as if she could see him. Stock still he prayed she could not, then she went in.

He ran back to his room and prepared to leave. His instincts told him something was clearly wrong, and that they would be leaving soon. Sure enough Liz left in the car a few minutes later. He watched for Selena to leave, making notes here and there as best he could and a few hours later she did leave.

Once he was sure she was gone he stepped out to follow in his car. Something was wrong, he though he heard yelling. Standing up and looking around he figured out where it was coming from and ran to the room that had been Liz's and Selena's.

Sure enough there was the sound of girls yelling inside. Kicking the door open there on the floor were four girls all tied up and gagged, and on the bed was one that looked like she was sleeping. Moving forward he pulled the blanket back and she was more than dead. Her body looked like it had been in the desert sun drying for 500 years! Fighting back the urge to puke he ran out of the room and into his car. As he was leaving the police were arriving.

He was not sure what had happened in that room but he called it all back in to his employer. Who was angry with him for getting so close, but thanked him for the information. He told Richard that he could see her moving north again, and to follow her as best he could. Demanding that Richard call in, in 8 hours to get an update on her location and update his employer on his findings.

Richard almost backed out at that point. This was not what he figured it was, but was reminded by his employer that he was told and warned about the nature of this 'hunt'. How could he argue with that in the end? He had already spent the money that was given up front as well. He was stuck.

It took some doing, but one week later he finally caught up with the two of them just out side of Toledo Ohio. Richard was not sure how long they had been here, but from the looks of it their car had not moved in a few days.

Lucky for him, he arrived in the middle of the night, and was able to get a room across from theirs so he could watch and follow as needed. He learned his lesson the first time with these two, and hid his car in the lot next door to the hotel. A quick call to Stephen, his boss got him a wire transfer of money to hold up here till they move on. Stephen started talking about the backyard being cleaned or needing to be cleaned out. He didn't want to know anything about some prison for monsters...Richard tuned it out. It was just too much information.

Two nights went by before Richard saw either of them leave their room, mostly just to the little store on the other side of the street. It was Liz, that little thing he couldn't get out of his mind. Shortly after he saw her, Selena, come out and walked right towards his room! Backing away from the window he prayed she didn't see him.

'Nock nock nock-'

"I know your in there watching us," came Selenas' voice threw the door, "I don't know why, or who you are, but if you don't open the door, I will."

Richard went white with fear and tried to reply. "Shit... um yea hold on..."

He does his best to put his work away...but before he can, the door comes open with a loud cracking of the door jam, and she is in front of him, holding him firmly off the ground. Holding him by the one thing that can control him more completely than any drug;

"I said, open the door."

Selenas' voice is both cold and commanding as she without looking steps back, still holding him and closes the door. With no seeming effort or motion he could detect she flung him to the ground, where he landed half on, half off the bed, his laptop and paper work now scattered about.

"I first noticed you back in Memphis," began Selena, "I figured you were nothing to worry about, one of my darlings play things, and when we left I gave no more thought to you. But when she went out tonight I caught the faintest scent of you, and followed it here."

Looking around the room he cursed himself for not having his side arm out where he could get to it easy. She followed his eyes as she spoke and moved to the desk were the gun was, and pulled it out. She looked it over, a large 50 caliber Desert eagle. Reaching back into the drawer, she found the clip and slid it into place.

"This is a big gun for such a little man," Selena said without emotion, "you ever use it?"

Without a pause or thought Richard replied more out of man-ish pride than better common sense.

"Yeah, I have a few kills with it."

"So you're a hunter of some kind," says Selena as she levels the gun at him, "and you're following me and Liz. Are you hunting me, little man?"

Richard has been in tight spots before, but this one, though very similar to his last job, was complicated by the fact that the bitch holding his gun now was some kind of monster.

"Why in all the 9 hells does she need my gun?" Richard thought to himself, and in answer to his question Selena replies.

"I don't, but it seems to make you nervous..."

"Shit she can read my mind... fuck... what do I do now ste... he never... don't think!" Richard's frantic thoughts raced, he could not figure how to protect himself at this point. He did notice one thing, the very mention of Stephens name in his mind cause her stone cold features to light up, but not in a good way, Richard thought.

"No, please go on, ste...phen?" teased Selena, "He never what...?"

"Don't think... "Richard fought with himself, "don't think... don't think... gods I am going to die."

"Maybe," Selenas' voice was teasing him now, "I am right...I am, aren't I!" Demanded Selena, "You were thinking of Stephen the vampire, weren't you?

"don't be upset, I would be a fool to think he would not come after us after what I did. I had hoped however that he would not send someone else after me."

"I am just supposed to watch, nothing else," Richard was looking for a way out of this, anyway he could find. He figured if he told her the complete truth she would let him go, or at the very least not kill him. "Look my name is Richard, I don't want any trouble. I'm just doing my job, ok?".

"Your job... Stalking me?" Selena yelled this at him, and the very air in the room seemed to boil. "I thought there were laws against stalking people... But if it's your job, you must be some kind of Private DICK.

"I never liked your kind. The old-man used to hire scum like you to find me, so he could come beat me some more. That what you're supposed to do, find me so Stephen can beat me"?

The gun never left the plain she held it on, always directly at his face. Then she tossed it onto the bed. Looking over her shoulder, she muttered something and before he could even think a single thought, he was again in the air. This time her mouth firmly over his... again she was holding him by his crotch. He felt warm and afraid and excited all at once. Every inch of his being seemed to stand up and take notice, the way metal shavings do under or over a magnetic field.

She was on top now, Richard thinks, "We went from her standing and holding me up, to me being striped and held down on the bed!" Nope, no doubt about it, he was being raped.

He tried to struggle against her, he tried to fight, and he tried not to like what was happening. But, his body simply would not listen to the horror in his mind. He had no control over his own body! The worst part about it for Richard was, he felt like he was watching it all through someone else's eyes.

He honestly could do nothing to stop her, and then without warning she was at the door, looking back at him.

"I am not going to kill you, I am however going to leave you alive, force you to be my eyes and ears for whenever your boss is in town...

do you understand me?"

Richard nodded yes...

"In time my dear, dear Private Dick."

Everything she wanted to say was said in that last sentence and in her face. The power of her being seemed to glow, to shed a light that before he had no idea existed. The expression on her face was not one he understood just then, but the power of it controlled him.

He feared her then more than ever before and hated himself. He wanted her to rape him again..., and before he knew it, she was out the door and gone.

When he woke up, it was still dark out, or had the day come and gone, he could not tell. Then it came to him slowly what had roused him. From outside came the sounds of something... covert going on. Slowly he looked out the blinds to see about eight people dressed in black BDU's, heavily armed and busting into Selena's room... moments passed and shots were fired... then silence.

He dressed as fast as he could and did everything he could to keep his eyes on the ball. When Liz came out and they wrapped her in a blanket then put a hood over her head... he started to freak out. He didn't know why really... was the monster controlling him? He could not tell but he made sure to get a good look at the vehicle they took her away in.

Richard climbed out the back window, and then made it to his car. He tore out of there fast. He had to catch the quickly diminishing tail lamps. After a little while he began to catch up. And as he went to pass them he pulled out his gun and forced the other vehicle off the road.

It was not all pretty and smooth like in the movies, but luckily for him they didn't want to lose Liz as much as he had to get her free of them. As the driver tried to get out, he shot him square in the chest. The mess it made at short range convinced the others not to move. He pulled Liz out and shot the tires, then the engine block, and away they went back towards the hotel.

As they raced along she pulled the bag off her head and he helped her get the ropes off her wrist. The look on her face, in her eyes was almost as full of power and terror as Selena's. So when Liz started to talk, Richard was immediately as completely afraid and submissive to Liz as he had been to Selena.

"Why?"

"I don't know," Richard said, "I just had too..." it was at least honest.

"We have to go back for her!" Liz was frantic, and she seemed somewhere between rational and insane as she started to talk again.

Richard said "We are," and nothing else needed to be said. She watched him and smiled, he thought he heard her say something... something like, 'I own you...' that's when he saw the van that had still been outside the hotel when he left to get Liz race by.

He turned his car around without making it look to suspicious, and followed. They never saw the car he disabled on the road or the people in it. But when they pulled up to a compound that was guarded by what seemed to be a well organized militia they sat back and watched.

After a few hours Liz looked at Richard and asked if he had a cell phone on him. He looked at her and without asking why, handed it over. She took a moment and composed herself, then dialed a number and waited for a reply. When it came she talked for a few moments and then hung up.

Richard looked at her the whole time wondering what had just happened. Finally he could not resist the urge to ask.

"Who was that?"

"My brother," said Liz, "he's going to come help us."

Richard just sat there and wondered what kind of help her brother could be, and how long it would take for him to get there. Almost in response to his thoughts, which made Richard wonder if Liz could read his mind as well, she said they needed to go meet her brother. Backing out with the lights out they left the compound and he followed her directions.

They ended up back at the hotel where everything had gone wrong, and to Richards surprise Liz's brother was there waiting for her, but he was not alone. When Liz saw the two men standing there she screamed and jumped out of the car before it came to a halt and ran up to them.

"OH MY GOD, YOU'RE ALIVE!!!! How, you have to tell me how!"

The one she ran up to, grabbed her up and hugged her so tight that Richard thought she might pop, as he parked the car then walked up to them. Liz introduced Richard to her two brothers; Michael and Ansell. It was Ansell she ran up to and Richard could not help but think that he had seen him somewhere before.

He dismissed this as they entered the room that had been where Liz and Selena were staying. Once inside the three of them began talking about Selena like she was some kind of god. The pure reverence with which Liz regarded her was amazing to Richard and he found that even though he was listening to what was being said that he really didn't hear all that much. Mostly he was lost in his own thoughts about how to bring any of this to Stephen's attention, if at all. He figured he could just tell him that he had lost her again...he hoped that would be enough.

When Michael began to call his name repeatedly Richard looked up and found the three of them looking at him. Liz had this look on her face that screamed at him to pay attention and confirm whatever she had just said. So Richard did the only thing he could.

"I'm sorry, what was that?"

"We're getting married in Michigan, that's why we were heading up north with Selena, right...?" Liz's expression did not change, it still demanded his confirmation, and he gave it. As soon as he did she smiled and leaned over and kissed him then went back to talking to her brothers.

Richard figured he had better pay closer attention to what was going on. He noticed that they were talking about guns and how to get into the place where Selena had been taken. They were talking about breaking her out tonight.

"Wait a minute, that place looked like a fortress to me," Richard said. "If we are going to break her out of there, we need to make sure we can do it. Maybe find some more help than just the four of us."

"And what do you think would be the best way to do that?" asked Ansell, and Richard looked at him for a moment trying to remember where he had seen him, then let it go as he answered.

"Well, we need to find out what their schedule is like. Do they change the guards? When do they do it, is there any down time between those changing guards.

"We'll need to know what kind of guns they have, so we can protect ourselves, and most of all, we'll need to know what building she is held in."

Liz and her brothers look at Richard and smile, as Liz says "See, I told you he was smart enough to do this with us." Then she leaned over and kissed him again. This time she stayed up close to him and asked her brother Michael, "Can you still work those spells you used to work on me and Ansell when we would go into the school at night?"

Richard looked at her and the brothers, then more out of disbelief said flatly. "Wait, first I have to deal with vampires. Now you're saying you guys know magic, like as in wizards and witches and shit?"

"Yes, but I am not as good or as strong as some of the others out there that practice the craft. I however will be sufficient to the needs of this little endeavor."

To Richard's ears Michael's voice seemed to come from somewhere far, far away, and it was a little uncomfortable for him, and he found himself saying out loud, "What the fuck have I gotten myself into?" Liz and her brothers just laugh at him, and go back to planning their rescue of Selena.

It was almost a month later, a month of watching and listening. A month of lying to Stephen for money, and spencing that money on tools and equipment that would hopefully allow them to get Selena out of this place, if she was even still in it. In that time they learned that these people were priest and nuns. All part of some ancient order dedicated to hunting down someone called the adversary.

The other thing the four of them found out is that this group may well be acting without the knowledge, or authorization of the guys in charge. They had been intercepting phone calls and email, and one thing is clear, whoever the mother is, they are trying to keep her out of the loop.

Richard and his would be co-conspirators found out that this time around, there are two women that the order thinks are the mother. Two women who according to the order know all the right things and this have divided the order. At least that's what it looks like to Richard and Liz. What they do know is that the one this group thinks is "mother" is here, and has been for a week. However they still have found no way in.

Two weeks later they got their chance. With Michaels spells they were able to get passed the guards unseen. They were able to make their way to the room where Selena was being held and when they opened the door, alarms started going off and they did everything they could to get her free. Once freed, Richard and Liz had to shoot their way out.

It was slow going and he saw no sign of Michael or Ansell, but he could hear their guns. Once He and Liz got Serena out into the open the fighting became hell. He had no idea there would be so many people here. In all their surveillance they had seen no sign of such a large concentration of people.

He was utterly surprise by the explosion near the gate they had to get too, and when all the commando's came pouring in he knew he was either going to die out right or that Michael had kept his word. Whoever these guys were, they seemed to have only one thing in mind and he, Liz and Serena were not it.

When he got hit just as they were entering his car, Richard thought to himself "Figures I would take a bullet for her..." he managed to hold it together long enough for them to make it to their safe house. It was an old friends place in Hamtramck Mi... And now he lay there, bleeding out and maybe dying.

"I am never going to church ever again." He thought to himself as he passed out waiting for the doctor to show up.